OTHER BOOKS
BY ZACHARY SCHOMBURG

Poetry

The Book of Joshua (2014)
Fjords, vol. 1 (2012)
Scary, No Scary (2009)
The Man Suit (2007)

MAMMOTHER

by Zachary Schomburg

Mammother was written while on artist residency at Château de Monthelon in France. http://www.monthelon.org/

Published by *featherproof* Books

First edition
10 9 8 7 6 5 4 3 2 1

Library of Congress Control Number: 2017942658
ISBN 13: 978-1943888108

Edited by: Tim Kinsella
Cover Photo: Library of Congress, Prints & Photographs
    Division, FSA/OWI Collection, [LC-DIG-fsa-8a28667]
Design by: Zach Dodson
Proofread by: Sam Axelrod

Set in Hoefler

Printed in Canada

MAMMOTHER

Zachary Schomburg

a novel

*fe*atherproof BOOKS

CHARACTER LIST

Mano Medium, son of Sisi Medium, factory worker, new barber and new butcher, creator of The Death Lessons.

Pepe Let, son/apprentice of The Butcher, son of Mitzi Let.

Sisi Medium, mother of Mano Medium. Lives in her bathtub.

The Butcher, father of Pepe Let, husband of Mitzi Let.

Mitzi Let, mother of Pepe Let, wife of The Butcher.

Nana Pine, mother of Enid Pine, works in a strawberry field.

Enid Pine, daughter of Nana Pine, factory worker, works in her mother's strawberry field, suitor of Mano Medium.

Inez Roar, wife of The Barber (original), wife of The Barber (third), mother of Zuzu Roar.

Zuzu Roar, daughter of Inez Roar and The Barber (original), aka Bebé.

Father Mothers, founder of Pie Time.

Father Mothers II, son of Father Mothers, and father of Father Mothers III.

Father Mothers III, priest of Lady Blood, creator of Lady Bods, aka Father Mothers, Red Mothers.

Lil' Jorge, young assistant of Father Mothers.

The Foreman, brother of Vera Good, husband of June Good, the foreman of Pie Time beer and cigarette factory.

June Good, wife of The Foreman, lover of Vera Good, the face of Pie Time, aka Mrs. Good.

Vera Good, sister of The Foreman, lover of June Good (née Fair), founder of The Good House for Children and the Very Old, aka Ms. Good.

Father Felipe, new priest of XO-sponsored The Hole.

The Businessman, two men and one woman in charge of XO.

The Lawyer, the lawyer for XO.

The Landlord, the landlord for every home in Pie Time.

The Builder, the builder.

The Innkeeper, the innkeeper.

The Bartender, the bartender.

The Baker, father of Mary Minutes and Mimi Minutes.

Mary Minutes, childhood friend of Enid Pine, factory worker, larger sister of Mimi Minutes, formerly conjoined.

Mimi Minutes, childhood friend of Enid Pine, factory worker, smaller sister of Mary Minutes, formerly conjoined.

The Barber (original), husband of Inez Roar, father of Zuzu Roar, original owner of the Black Square.

The Barber (third), second husband of Inez Roar.

The Florist, the florist of Pie Time, friend of Mano Medium.

Roberto, childhood love of The Florist.

The Butcher (third), the butcher at XO Market, suitor of Zuzu Roar.

The Shoveler, father of Ernest and Ernesto Horn, husband of Lois Horn, inventor of the graveyard.

Ernesto Horn, son of The Shoveler and Lois Horn, older brother of Ernesto Horn, first participant in The Death Lessons.

Ernest Horn, son of The Shoveler and Lois Horn, younger brother of Ernesto Horn, first participant in The Death Lessons.

Lois Horn, wife of The Shoveler, mother of Ernesto and Ernest Horn.

Hera Horn, second wife of The Shoveler.

Leda Horn, wife of Ernesto Horn.

Lois Horn, daughter of Ernesto Horn and Leda Horn, identical triplet sister of Luis Horn and Luis Horn.

Luis Horn, son of Ernesto Horn and Leda Horn, identical triplet brother of Lois Horn and Luis Horn.

Luis Horn, son of Ernesto Horn and Leda Horn, identical triplet brother of Lois Horn and Luis Horn.

Beulah Minx, wife of The Postman (original), original owner of the black poodle.

The Postman (original), husband of Beulah Minx.

The Humanitarians, brother and sister team of XO-trained humanitarians from Nun's Hat.

The Vuillemeyers, family of The Humanitarians from Nun's Hat.

Rona Rile, wife of Lana Rile, mother of Fran Rile.

Lana Rile, wife of Rona Rile, mother of Fran Rile.

Fran Rile, daughter of Rona Rile and Lana Rile.

Irene Mire, sister of Mira Mire, oldest woman in Pie Time, lives at The Good House for Children and the Very Old.

Mira Mire, sister of Irene Mire.

Igor, boy who lives at The Good House for Children and the Very Old.

"A line? A dot? Why not a bird?"

-Yves Klein

If you felt ready to die, wanted death bad enough, and had little enough to live for, The Reckoner would grant your wish and fall on you. It would crush your skeleton deep into the ground. No one in Pie Time would hear it fall, and no one would know when it stood itself back up. But it would always stand itself back up. The blood on its bark would wash away in the rain.

In the early morning hours, after the worst day and night of his life, Mano trudged the long path through the woods toward The Reckoner from where he woke up, near the banks of The Cure. The Reckoner creaked like it was about to fall. Mano's face was in his hands. His toes moved in his shoes. He anticipated its full weight on the back of his head. His skeleton creaked inside his body waiting. He moved his hands to his sides, and lifted his head. "Please, I'm ready to die, too."

He knew though that he would have to be patient. Sometimes it could take days for The Reckoner to make its decision. He picked up a stick and chewed it like a horse. With half of his stick still unchewed, he wrote his name in the mud.

Mano Medium.

Mano was cloaked in his mother's bed sheet. Half of a black cloud hovered above him, a piece of its end missing. The poodle at his feet was like his shadow.

"Mano was a good boy." Mano tried to speak in his mother's voice. He tightened his throat and loosened his lips a little. But it didn't sound right. He couldn't remember exactly what her voice sounded like. He tried it again. "Pepe Let was a good boy." That sounded a little closer, emphasizing the *ooo* in "good." "Pepe Let was a good boy," he said again, this time hitting the "was."

Mano was not ready to go back into town. He closed his eyes, and said Pepe's name out loud again. He slowed it way down so it sounded like a creak.

PART ONE

1.

"Are you ready?"

"Ready for what?"

Sisi Medium took a drag of her cigarette, and exhaled above the bathtub into the cloud. "On your birthday, you will become a man."

"Yes, ma'am." Mano was afraid to become anything at all, much less a man.

"So, are you ready?"

"No, ma'am. I'm not ready."

She looked out the window. "What do you want?"

"What do you mean, what do I want?"

"For your birthday."

Sisi had never given her son a birthday gift before. She had no money. And she lived in her bathtub.

Mano didn't know how to answer his mother's question. He had so few things that he didn't know what things there were to want. "You mean...like a *thing*?"

"Yeah, a thing. Don't you like things?"

"I love things." Mano didn't know if he did love things, but now for the first time, he thought that he might. He was sitting on the toilet. The toilet was a thing. But did he love it? He looked at the toilet like he loved it, and then it became true. "Like this toilet, ma'am. I love this toilet."

"I'm sure you do. But you know so few toilets."

Mano counted the toilets that he knew, but could only get to four.

"Do you want another toilet for your birthday?"

"No."

"Well, what is it you want?"

Mano thought about all the things in the world and which of those things that he might want. Sisi waited, looking out the window at the top of the bare tree in the white sky. She always put her cigarette out by dipping it in her bathwater, making a quick sizzle. Then she'd pile it up like a dead body among the other butts in her glass ashtray.

It's High Time for a Pie Time.

"Grab me a beer while you think."

Mano always made sure to keep the small refrigerator in the bathroom fully stocked with cold Pie Times. Every day he brought home a twelve pack and a pack of cigarettes from the Pie Time Factory, where it was his job on some days to help brew the beer, and on other days to help roll the cigarettes.

He had his timing down just right for Sisi's two breakfast beers. He'd retrieve the first one from her refrigerator, although she could reach it just fine on her own, and crack it open for her on the lip of the bathtub. He waited until she asked for it, like a good son. If he got it for her too soon, she'd say something like, "I don't want a beer so early—are you crazy?" But when he waited for her to ask for it, she'd thank him, and then he'd go get ready for work. When he was done getting ready for work, he'd retrieve her second breakfast beer without waiting for her to ask for it. This was the key for her second beer. If he waited for her to ask for the second one, she'd say something like, "What does a lady have to do around here to get another beer?" But if he got her second one without asking, she'd say something like, "You're such a good boy. You know your mama."

Outside Sisi's bathroom window, Mano imagined a bird falling out of the tree and bouncing on the ground. Things that fly, he thought, must often die by falling. He cupped his hands like he wanted to feel the feeling of saving it.

"How about a bird?"

"You can't have a bird," Sisi said without turning her head from the window.

"Why not?"

"There are no such things as birds here."

The first thing Mano thought of to want was a thing that did not exist in Pie Time.

"But is it a *thing*?"

"I suppose it *is* a thing," his mother said more quietly to herself now, "but it is nothing here." Sisi lifted the chain of the drain with her good toe. Then she turned the hot water faucet with it. She had this way of resting her elbow on the lip of the bathtub and holding her can of beer in the air, letting it hang down between her ring finger and thumb, while she held her cigarette in the same hand between her middle finger and her index finger.

The two of them lived together, alone, in a perfectly square house on the west edge of Pie Time. It had four square rooms. Each room had two doors so you could circle through the house continuously, room to room, without having to alter course. The house's front door opened into the living room, where the furniture was green. Moving forward, like a clock, the next room was the bathroom, where his mother had been continuously soaking in the bathtub for nearly a decade. A little steam slipped out over the living room ceiling each time this door was opened. In the bathroom, the red wallpaper was buckling and dripping from the walls. It had a pattern of red ranunculuses on it. The room beyond the bathroom was the bedroom, where Mano slept alone in a bed beside a wooden chair and a brass lamp, always on call for his mother during the night, in case she woke up while soaking and called for him. Through the bedroom door was the kitchen: a white stove, a white sink in which he washed his body and face, and cold white tile floors. The only refrigerator was in the bathroom. When he walked a complete circle through the square of their house, it was like walking through the seasons of a whole year—the green spring of the living room, the hot red summer of the bathroom, the golden autumn where he slept, and the white cold winter of the kitchen. To be in a room was to be somewhere in a year. Like a clock, the only choice was to move forward, never backward, in time.

So Mano always moved forward in time through the

house. To get from his bedroom to his mother's bathtub, he took the path through the kitchen, then the living room, which had a creaky wood floor. Each step sounded like the word *eat. Eeeeeeat, eeeat, eeeeeeeeat, eeeat.* Walking through the living room made Mano feel incredibly heavy, despite how small he was. Feeling heavy made the house feel smaller, and faker, as if he was walking through the inside of a fake house.

Mano could remember very few days from before his mother got in the bathtub. Mostly, he could only remember her *in* the bathtub, smoking Pie Time cigarettes, drinking Pie Time beers, about four times a day lifting the metal chain with her good toe to drain the water, and opening the valve on the faucet with the same toe to replace the old water with new water. The bathtub was her body. The tub was red like the ranunculus of the wallpaper, the kind of red that organs are. The bathtub was his mother's lung.

There must have been a very first lowering of her body when he was very young, like an initial offering, a giving up of something hard and sugary into the hot and limpid bath water, only then to dissolve into what is now a body saturated and quaggy. His mother's skin was pulpy, bits of its flesh floating beneath the still grey surface like boiled pork. Had she known upon that first lowering how long she'd be soaking? If she did know then, he thought, then he'd feel even more abandoned, the burden of being orphaned somehow more unshakable than the burden of being left to feed and care for a sick mother. All those days that he could have had with a mother who lived on the outside of her bathtub.

One of those very few first memories of Mano's, before his mother lowered herself into the tub, was of walking along the banks of The Cure together until they came upon a launching dock for the dead. He remembered her sitting down to hang her feet into the water and telling him about his father. She talked about Mano's father uneasily, as if it was her duty.

"Your father was a hunter," she said.

"How do you know?" young Mano asked.

"He always wore a red plaid hunter's cap, even indoors, even when he slept." Sisi's answer satisfied Mano. "He never took it off."

"What did he hunt?" asked Mano.

"Mammoths," she said. "He called himself The Mammother."

Mano liked the sound of that. "But I thought you said mammoths don't exist."

"Mammoths *don't* exist, you're right."

"Like birds?"

"Yes, like birds. But birds exist somewhere. Just not here. No one here knows about birds, but that doesn't mean that birds don't exist. Mammoths, on the other hand, exist nowhere."

"Then why didn't my father just hunt birds?"

Sisi laughed at Mano's question, but really she was laughing at what she knew was his father's answer to that question. "Well, because all great hunters can find birds. But only the greatest hunter can find something that doesn't exist. Why bother spending your time looking for something that can be found? What remains once you've found it? Besides, what he wanted to find was a mammoth, not a bird." Sisi took a drag of her cigarette, holding her warming can of Pie Time in the same hand. She moved her legs around in the water off the launching dock. She tried to think of a broader way of explaining such a silly concept. "It didn't matter to your father what he *could* find, it only mattered to him what he *wanted* to find."

Mano nodded as if he understood. "There are no mammoths. But there *was* my father, The Mammother."

"Yes, indeed, there was The Mammother," repeated Sisi with a sigh.

Outside of Sisi's bathtub was her radio, which sat on the top of the back of the toilet. At the top of every hour, the news report would come on, and she would light up another Pie Time. If Mano was there, of course, like a good son, he would light it for her. She liked to time it just right, lighting it up just as the announcer would say, *It's High Time for a Pie Time*. And at that they'd both laugh. She'd crack open another can with a picture of a beautiful woman named June Good on it holding a pie that had been baked in an upside down golden crown. The radio seemed alive to Mano because the music came out of its silver speaker-mouth and silver knob-eyes. Looking out of the window above her bathtub, Sisi always remained so still, even when the music played. Mano sometimes thought about pushing the radio into the water, not because he wanted his mother to die, but because he was the only thing in his world that ever really moved.

Despite the threat of manhood drawing very near, Mano still liked to wear dresses every day to work. He liked being a girl at home, too. One of the games that he and his mother liked to play with each other was called Mother and Daughter. Mano always had long hair, and when they'd play Mother and Daughter, Sisi would braid his hair for him while he sat on the toilet. He liked to go to work in braids so that his hair wouldn't dip into the tobacco.

"How's my daughter this morning?" she'd ask some mornings. When he retrieved her beer, she'd thank him by saying, "What a good daughter you are."

"Thank you," he'd tilt his head.

"Are you excited to see your boyfriend today?"

But on other mornings, like on this day, when he asked her to play Mother and Daughter, she was too tired. She said, "What are you today?" She turned her head toward him from the window, and looked at him as if he had come to her for the late rent. The cloud of smoke was hanging low, not steam, so he knew that the news report had just ended. They both knew he would be late for work. "Look, little girl, you're going to be late for work." She cracked open another beer, a beer she had to lean over to get from the refrigerator on her own. He watched the gears in her jaw work as she drank it.

"Sorry." He apologized into the bathroom from the living room.

"It's ok. I just don't want you being late for work."

He waited for a few minutes before saying goodbye, so his apology would feel sincere enough. "Goodbye!" he yelled while stepping out of the front door into a world she knew almost nothing about.

"Wait!" she yelled.

He ran around to the back of the house. Sisi opened the window above her bathtub. Mano stuck his head in through that window.

"Have you thought about the thing you'd want?"

"Yes, ma'am."

"Well, what is it?"

"A bird."

2.

Years before he died strangely and horribly in his sleep, Father Mothers built Our Lady of the Blood with his own hands. It was a church that soon became known to everyone in Pie Time as simply Lady Blood. He built it in a field where he was met by a bear with no legs. It growled at him, fierce and loud like all bears, but of course it just stayed put. It was a bear in every way, capable of killing Father Mothers if it would have somehow been able to get his leg in its jaws. But Father Mothers didn't fear it. He just built the church right over the top of it, while it snarled and snapped and cried at night. Eventually, it stopped making noise altogether, and just watched Father Mothers build the church around it. It was a bear in a church. It got used to the first people of Pie Time. They liked to pet it and feed it, but then it died.

A bear with no legs had been an omen to Father Mothers that this would be a very special land to build his church, and to build the town of Pie Time around it. Pie Time would be particularly safe from its enemies, if the first of its most-feared natural enemies, a bear, had none of its four legs.

Lady Blood was the first structure to be built in Pie Time and he built it with only a few dozen parishioners in mind. At first, Pie Time was just a tiny village with Lady Blood at its center, built upon the banks of The Cure, the river which circled the village. The woods were to the west, on the other side of The Cure, and the valley was to the east. In the distance beyond the valley were the mountains where Father Mothers had come from.

Father Mothers was far from being an architect or a carpenter. Lady Blood was the only building he had ever built, and after a few months of construction, it became clear that the church looked like no other church anyone had ever seen before. It looked nothing like anything except a drafty and lopsided white barn. But not a barn exactly either. A little like the Pope's hat, if the Pope's hat were flat, but with a sharp ridge down its center. Or a paper airplane. It was strange to see something so new look so old. None of his early parishioners had the heart to complain.

Lady Blood was built in the days before the plague known as God's Finger penetrated the town, gripping it with anxiety and fear, and sending it down into a terrible spiral of grief and depression. The cross at Lady Blood's apex was much too modest of a cross in the face of God's Finger. It was only the size of one man.

That is why Father Mothers' son, Father Mothers II, climbed up onto its roof, toiling well into a late spring evening with a hammer and nails and two planks of wormy wood salvaged from the woods in the west hills. The new cross was much needed for these modern days riddled with sin. He planned a cross that would be twice the size of the original cross built by his late father so that more sinners could see it from further away.

Mothers II straddled Lady Blood's roof, unrolled his drafted plans, complete with the proper measurements for the new cross, and nailed the plans to the old cross, which was to stay put until the new one was constructed. While studying his plans, he was struck with the thought of hammering the new cross's horizontal plank first, nailing it to the air before erecting the cross's vertical plank. He became obsessed with this idea—convinced it was delivered to him directly by his lord. So, he considered the logistics of simply constructing the cross in reverse.

Lady Blood was the tallest structure in the valley. From where Mothers II was standing, he could see all of Pie Time, every house, and all of the fields. He could be sure that no one was watching him, except maybe some of the sheep. With the horizontal plank heavy in the grip of his large left hand, and the hammer in his right, he climbed the old cross that his father had built. With as much strength as his old-aged left arm could muster, he lifted the horizontal plank above his head, and hammered it into the air. He hammered and hammered while he held it, until the nail passed through the wood. And to his astonishment, he could feel the nail take hold in the air behind the plank. He could feel the heavy plank begin to lighten in his grip.

"It can't be true!"

The plank felt so light in his hand, he let go of it entirely, and it stayed there, on the air. "It *is* true! A miracle has happened. Oh, lord, I must tell the others."

Mothers II was in such a fever to climb down and show the others the horizontal plank of the new cross nailed on its own into the air—his heart racing at twice the normal speed—that he turned around too quickly on the old cross, and his collar caught around a bent old nail.

His feet slipped.

The sheep were baaaaing in the distance.

Little yellow flowers blossomed all over the valley.

3.

In his haste to think of a thing, a particular thing out of all things, and to leave home in time for his work at the Pie Time Factory, Mano had forgotten his glasses. His glasses were a thing, cracked along the top and the prescription outdated. Also, they were a little girl's glasses, and Mano was just beginning to feel as though he was ready for a pair of adult's glasses, whatever that meant. A serious thing to look through. The kind of glasses that he could make adult decisions through. Still, he needed something, at least for now. The world in front of him was the same as always, but the edges of all of its shapes were soft. Those soft shapes made glasses into a thing he wanted.

On most mornings, on his way to the factory, Mano would walk past the butcher shop where Pepe Let apprenticed for his father, The Butcher. They would sit on the back steps of the butcher shop for a few minutes and talk. Sometimes they would touch hands while they talked, and that was Mano's favorite part. But Pepe didn't come out of the back of the butcher shop on this morning. Mano figured he was too late, and that Pepe was already busy with his morning shop routines. The idea of missing any chance to talk with Pepe made Mano's stomach feel empty. Still, Mano waited there behind the butcher shop for a few moments, just in case. He wasn't quite ready to wade through the world with its soft shapes.

As he stood there behind the butcher shop, paralyzed for a moment by his indecision, he could see Inez Roar a few houses away across Last Street, on her front lawn, beneath a tree, holding her baby, Zuzu, in her arms. Inez was crying, but her baby wasn't. Baby Zuzu had been in the world for almost a month, but had yet to cry, not even on the day that she was born. She slipped outside of Inez's body, and blinked a few times into the light and at her father, The Barber. Sometimes,

Inez and The Barber would poke her in the leg with a pin, or scratch her on the bottom of her foot, because they wanted to hear her cry and know what her full voice sounded like. But when they did, she'd only grimace, or grunt, or even growl.

Mano squinted to be sure who it was that he was walking toward, then he walked toward them. "Are you ok?" he asked the soft green shape that was Inez.

"No, no, not at all," the soft green shape cried. "It's terrible."

"What's terrible?"

"My husband," she said. "He's dead."

Inez was twice the size of Mano. To Mano, she looked like a wedding cake. Her hair was big, curled around like frosting, and cascading down to her shoulders. Her legs were long and the size of Mano's head at the top. Her voice was smoky, and it sounded like she was always making an announcement when she spoke.

"Oh no, that *is* terrible," said Mano.

"He went...to bed..." she tried to catch up to her own smoky breath, "and didn't wake up...he had...a hole...it was..."

"He had a *hole*?" Mano clarified.

"I think it was God's Finger."

"God's Finger? What's God's Finger?"

"Mothers says God's finger is starting to come down to poke through the living who aren't living right."

Mano knew enough not to laugh. "Is that so? Do you believe him? Do you think that's what happened?"

"Well, I don't know. But I can't see how he wasn't living right." Inez looked exhausted. She wanted to say no more.

A few weeks earlier, Inez married The Barber in a private ceremony that only four people attended—themselves, Baby Zuzu, and Mothers II, who preferred that no one else was invited on account that Zuzu was born before their matrimony, which was in the wrong order for a proper wedding.

The Barber wasn't much of a talker, just a smoker. Mano

visited The Barber to deliver him a box of Pie Times each week, and to say hello, but never for a haircut. In fact, Mano had never had his hair cut. The Barber had every reason to think that Mano was a girl—he had long hair, and wore a dress. Once, The Barber suggested a bob cut, something perfect for girls. Each time, Mano refused. He didn't quite see the point of cutting it any shorter. But the real reason was, like with anything else, he was just scared of anything that he had never done before. On this last visit, The Barber, convinced that Mano would never cut his hair, resigned to tell him, "When you grow up, you'll have to at least trim your own pubic hair." This was troubling to Mano, who didn't quite yet have pubic hair, so hadn't yet thought about having to trim it. He imagined the pubic hair growing wild, and overtaking his whole body. He'd have to walk around at all times, trimming the hairs down, to be sure that he wasn't mistaken for a large mammal.

Mano squinted at the soft yellow shape that was Baby Zuzu, and then back at Inez. Mano was no good in these situations. He didn't know what to ask, or where to look, or if he should touch her. He touched her upper arm with his whole palm, and then just his fingertips, and then he let go. He thought about his long hair, and if she'd notice it, if she'd wonder why her dead husband had never cut it. But mostly he wanted to hear more about the hole left in her husband, without having to pry into the details.

"Inez, where did the hole come from?"

"I don't know," she said. Baby Zuzu smiled and clapped once. "It was just there, in his chest," she said, "like a hole. It went all the way through. I could see the bed through it."

"How big was it?"

She tucked Baby Zuzu down into her elbow to be able to touch her middle fingers together and her thumbs together to make a circle while she cried.

"Did you see anything in it?" Mano meant to ask about his

organs, his heart, that sort of thing. The top button on Inez's blouse looked like it was about to pop off. Mano wanted to see just how her body would settle out into the open air if it did.

"Oh!" She was suddenly awake to the world again. "*These* were in it." She held up a pair of men's glasses.

Mano squinted at them, and then he could see that she was holding up glasses. They were plastic and black along the top, just the kind of glasses that Mano had always wanted. "They were *in* it?"

"Yes," she said between half-breaths, readjusting Baby Zuzu in her arms.

"Inside of it?"

"Yes, inside the hole."

"Are they his?"

"The Barber doesn't even wear glasses," she said.

"How..."

"I don't..."

"Can I see?" Mano held out his hand.

Inez handed Mano the glasses, and he tried them on. She watched him try them on, and tilted her head to the side so she could see if they fit him properly. "They're for men," she said.

"I *am* a man," he said overconfidently. It sounded strange coming out of his mouth, and Inez cracked a curious smile.

The lenses in the glasses were the perfect prescription for Mano. The world's shapes had perfect yellow and green edges again. Mano looked up into Inez's red, half-smiling face. He counted all of her eyelashes from below. They were so long, he thought. He wanted to blow on them to see if they would move.

"You have a beautiful baby," he said.

4.

As soon as Mano closed the heavy iron front door of the Pie Time Factory behind him, it became apparent that it was not a good day to be so late to work. He considered, for a moment, avoiding it all, running away from the factory, and returning to Inez. If he went back to her, he could hold Zuzu while Inez washed her face. She would need to take a shower, he thought. He was a man now, he thought, someone who could be needed to stand nearby while Inez did the miserable work of preparing The Barber's dead body for its trip down The Cure. But in the factory, he still felt like a girl.

With his new glasses, The Foreman's terrible mood became visible. The Foreman was in the tobacco steaming room stretching his arms. He was a large and austere man, with a personality as dark grey as the shirt and tie that his body bulged from. His voice bellowed through the steaming machines, and into the room where Mano was hesitating, an arm halfway through a work shirt. The Foreman's voice was like a locomotive boring its own tunnel through a mountain. It was too late for Mano to turn back.

"Mano, you're late!"

"I was...someone died, I left my glasses..." Mano stammered back, knowing before he finished his sentence that he should not have started it.

The Foreman didn't hear a word of it. His voice echoed in the silence of all the other girls who had just stopped chattering. "Come here."

Mano walked through the cigarette rolling room, into the tobacco steaming room, past all the machines. About two dozen girls stood up from their tables where they had been rolling cigarettes, and formed a line to watch. It was a perk of this factory work to chain smoke, which all of them were doing, even the youngest of them, who was eight. Mary, the tallest of the bunch, walked down the line lighting the cigarettes of her co-workers that dangled from each of their lips. The Foreman waited in the corner of the room with the giant wooden spoon used to scoop the hot wet tobacco from the steaming machines. There were still bits of tobacco on the tip.

"Now." The Foreman tapped some of the tobacco from the spoon onto the factory floor.

A giant iron wall separated the rolling room from the brewery, and the girls from the boys. The Foreman's job was to supervise both rooms, and to keep the girls and boys apart. It was his belief that the wall that separated the girls from the boys was the single most important structure in the factory. The lack of any cross-gender fraternization is what kept things humming. Of course, on this particular morning, The Foreman was nowhere to be found among the copper vats of beer, and the boys could move about without supervision. The boys could sense what was about to happen on the other side of that iron wall, and they knew that The Foreman would not return anytime soon—it was too quiet on the other side. It was the kind of quiet that could only mean The Foreman was preoccupied with teaching one of the girls a lesson. For a few moments they stopped what they were doing—pouring, mixing, heating—to put their ears into the metal funnels that were used to pour large amounts of grain into the vats. They put the funnels against the wall, and listened in. There were only three funnels, so only the three oldest boys got to listen. They made gestures to the other boys to let them know what was going on on the other side, and the other boys just waited for more gestures.

"Pants down," barked The Foreman. He was loud enough that all of the boys on the other side of the wall could hear without the oldest boys having to tell them anything.

Mano unbuckled his belt, and let his trousers drop to his ankles. His briefs sat loose and grey on his skinny hips. He put his hands on the top of his head already knowing what would come next.

"Hands on top of your head," The Foreman said with a sigh, as if he was just checking things off from a list before he could get to spanking. Then he raised the spoon.

The Foreman's first spank was fierce, and delivered with more force than what was routine, as a way of proving to the line of girls that his mood was unprecedented. The girls leaned in to hear the second slap of the spoon on Mano's ass, and imagined that pain on their own asses. Some of the girls couldn't help but laugh, but not because anything was funny. Sometimes you just laugh when you don't know how else to feel, when you haven't yet learned horror, or how to behave horrified. Some of the girls who already knew horror just cried.

The oldest boys, too, leaned in, funnels to their ears, for the same reasons. They had never been spanked by The Foreman, even when they were younger and smaller. They had no fear of The Foreman, so with the sound of each slap, even though they knew it wasn't true, they were able to imagine it was Mano who was spanking The Foreman. "Split him in half, Mano," one boy said to himself.

The boys with funnels weren't the only ones imagining the spoon in other hands. This particular spanking felt different to Mano. He wasn't scared of The Foreman anymore, and he didn't anticipate each sting, or the shame, as he had on other bad days. Instead, he let a tiny rage grow. Inside his own pain, he imagined it being The Foreman's pain. He imagined splitting The Foreman's body in two with a thousand blows of the heavy spoon to his spine. Mano was half the size of The Foreman, but in his head at that moment, he was twice as big as him. And the thought made Mano laugh out loud.

The Foreman looked up after the second spank. "Enough laughing!" Then he looked to the line of girls. "Enough crying!" There was shuffling, and then only the echo of the third spank.

Usually there were only five spanks, but after the 12th, Mano's bones were sore, and his face was hot with the sting from behind him growing up his back. Still, the smile from his laugh stayed frozen there.

"How many more?" asked Mano brazenly. It was bad form to interrupt the spanking, and Mano knew it.

"Silence!" The Foreman's 13th spank was very hard.

Mano's real rage was growing very deep somewhere in his chest, but not on the outside, where his smile remained.

"How many more? I'd like to count along."

The 14th-20th spanks were the hardest that The Foreman could spank. The pain was so great, Mano's body felt hot through all of its cells. He could feel that his body was made of pain. And it felt to him like the body of a man. But in his throat, he felt cells made of love. He first thought to tell Pepe about his new cells. And he thought to tell his mother, too. And just knowing that he had the two of them to tell about this made these cells made of love multiply.

The Foreman was out of breath, and he leaned momentarily on the enormous wooden spoon like it was his cane. In that moment of silence, Mano tilted his head all the way back and yelled into the factory's ceiling. "I'm a man!" The line of girls laughed. Mano knew it was true now that he heard his own voice shout it.

The Foreman stood upright and lifted the spoon as a threat to everyone who continued laughing. Then it was his turn to laugh. "A man?" He leaned all the way over to laugh more. "You're just a little girl. Look at you."

Mano looked directly at The Foreman and repeated himself, just for The Foreman this time. "I'm a man now." He stood up straight, despite the lightning in his legs. His shoulders were small. His legs were bright with pinkness and belonged more to a child than a man or a woman. The Foreman stood in front of him to examine his red and girlish face. He tugged slightly on Mano's long black hair, while

Mano stared at him. "You're just a little girl, aren't you?"

Mano thought to spit in his face. He felt a new strength in his bones and behind his eyes. He thought about the kind of strength that his father must have felt, hunting things that didn't exist. "No," Mano answered.

The Foreman kneeled down and looked at Mano's entire body. He felt his waist through his work shirt, and then stared at his underwear. "Drop your panties. Show us."

Without hesitation, Mano lifted his hands from where they were folded on the top of his head, and pulled his briefs all the way down to his ankles. He was a man now. He knew it. Now everyone else knew it, too. He stood back up and looked at all the girls in their eyes. With his new glasses, he could see all their perfectly round pupils shrink into tiny black dots.

Mano felt unfurled, free.

The Foreman felt furious. He felt fooled. He spanked Mano more wildly than ever before.

The girls were squeezing each other's hands, poking each other in the ribs, as if to remind each other not to forget any of this, to record everything with their eyes so they could discuss it forever. They stared at Mano's bare genitals as the spanks were being wildly delivered. For the girls, they were the only genitals that most of them had ever really known in person. Mano's dick flapped there in the cold wet factory air like a shining flag of non-surrender.

The Foreman was beyond winded, and took a knee to catch his breath.

Enid Pine had seen enough. Even though Mano was a year older, she had always felt protective of him. She defended him when the other girls made fun of him, and until now she was the only girl who had ever suspected that Mano wasn't one of them, wasn't a girl. At grave risk of being punished herself, she walked over to Mano and picked up his glasses. She checked to see if they were broken, which they were not. She put the glasses back onto Mano's face.

"Thanks," he said with a smirk, as if what had just happened to him was routine. Because of the pain, Mano wasn't capable of bending all the way over to pull up his own briefs, or trousers. "Would you..."

"Yeah."

She bent down on her knee in front of him and pulled up his trousers around his calves, which were wet with blood and sweat, and around his thighs, which were even wetter. She tied his shoes, too.

The girls could not contain their excitement. Their line was becoming more of a circle. After Enid tied Mano's shoes, she returned to the circle, and the circle quickly swallowed her back up again, and spit Mano out.

5.

Enid Pine's cigarette hung from her pre-teen lips like a tiny dead mouse's tail from a cat's mouth.

"I knew he was a boy," she whispered across the table.

"Shush. You did not," Mary Minutes whispered back.

"I did."

"Then why didn't you say something?" Mimi Minutes asked. Mimi was on Mary's right, very closely, as always. They were sisters who were conjoined until they were six years old. Now separated, Mimi was half of Mary's size, and had a half arm with no hand on the end that she tucked into her sleeve. She was shaped like a tea kettle. And she rolled a cigarette with one hand better than all the other girls at the table could roll with two.

"Do you think he's cute?" asked Enid.

"No!" Mimi yell-whispered a little too loudly.

The Foreman hushed Mimi's whispered outburst. His body was stiff and stuck on one knee. He couldn't move. His eyes were half open. He seemed small and desperate to all of the girls.

Mimi looked for Mano, but he was nowhere. She wanted to look at him again to determine whether or not he was, in fact, cute, especially now that he was a boy. "Do you?" She asked.

"Well, I don't know. I mean, maybe. No?" Now that Enid knew that Mano was a boy, she was in love. She always thought that he was different than all the other girls, but still she liked him. And now she knew that this difference came from his being a boy. And she liked that. She scanned the entire factory, but couldn't find him.

"Enid! Go get Mrs. Good." The Foreman gestured with just his finger to Enid. He spoke quietly, and between breaths. "Tell her my back is out again."

Enid was giddy at the chance to play an official role in the morning's events, and she skipped up the stairs and knocked on the door to the mysterious back room. Usually, no factory worker was ever allowed entry. What happened in that room was the subject of hours of conversation each day while the girls rolled cigarettes. But no one knew the actual answer to that question except for The Foreman, Mrs. Good, and Ms. Good.

June Good (née Fair) was the opposite of her husband, The Foreman: extravagant and generous. Her loud laugh could be heard from the back room over the steaming sounds of the factory. It was June who was featured in the magazine advertisements wearing a fur coat and pearls saying *It's High Time for a Pie Time*. The fur coat and pearls were not her style as much as her costume. She had become Pie Time's mascot more or less, the image of a refined woman with a taste for sophistication. In most of the magazine advertisements, she's smoking and drinking while descending a marble staircase. No one else in Pie Time was truly refined, so the beer and cigarettes were actually for the unrefined. But the unrefined wanted the finer things. And one of those finer things, according to the magazine ads, was a bottle of Pie Time and a Pie Time cigarette, which she held in the same hand.

Most often when she was laughing, she was laughing at her husband. His rigid personality had become ridiculous to her. The only other person who could get away with poking fun at the way he dressed, and the childish ways that he managed his anger and jealousy, was his sister, Vera Good. And everyone knew that June was actually in love with Vera, and her marriage to The Foreman had nothing to do with love.

Together, June and Vera were known as The Goods. Like June, Vera had lost all affection for her brother, if she ever had any to begin with. Although she and her brother were twin siblings, they looked nothing alike. Where The Foreman had short black hair and a bushy mustache, Vera had long red hair that she most often wore in braids. Where The Foreman was squat, Vera had long legs. The one thing that they did share was that they both loved June Good with the entirety of their hearts, but only one of them got to feel what it was like to be loved by her in return.

Enid knocked on the back door, where the wood framed the frosted glass. She waited for a few seconds and knocked again, more loudly.

"Knock harder!" The Foreman yelled, easing his body into a prone position on the floor.

Enid knocked harder, but not as hard as she could. She could see two figures in the room, moving around in the light. They weren't coming closer to the door, despite her knocking. "I...they're..."

"Knock as hard as you can, Enid! On the glass part."

Enid was afraid of breaking the frosted glass. She knocked hard on it, but with some attempt at delicacy.

"Break the glass, Enid." The Foreman sounded as if he was about to cry. The girls all looked at each other. They all wanted to watch Enid break the glass, and they all wanted to see him cry.

Enid wrapped her fist with her handkerchief and punched the glass. It didn't break. The dark figures kept moving. She could hear The Goods moaning.

"I don't think..."

"Break it!" The Foreman was crying now. The girls were all snickering into their hands, except Mary, who dropped her hands to finally let her laugh go free. It flew from her body like a bird from a cage into the room above The Foreman.

Enid punched one more time and the glass exploded around her. Shards spilled over her shoulders, and down the front of her shirt. The laughter of the girls turned into a burst of cheers. The moans of The Goods grew louder and louder, both of them naked, their legs wrapped around each other, rolling on top of a long wooden table in the back room. Enid motioned for the rest of the girls to hurry up the stairs.

They crowded around the broken window and looked in. They marveled just as much about the size of the room—its shape and colors and its furniture—as they did about what the Goods were doing in it. All those years working next to a room, imagining what's inside, and then finally seeing it.

"What are you looking at? What do you see?" The Foreman's voice had changed. It was lined with hysteria. But no one could hear him.

Outside, the bells of Lady Blood rang.

6.

"Now I'm the only one who hasn't seen your dick yet?" Pepe cracked open a cold Pie Time on the back steps of the butcher shop.

Mano laughed for the first time since he had limped out of the factory. It felt good to tell Pepe the whole story. He wasn't ready to worry just yet about how he would now make the sliver of money he needed to keep the water in his mother's bathtub hot, and her beer cold. He cracked open his own Pie Time, and chugged half of it until his eyes watered. "Yup. You're the only one now."

"Maybe we'll have to fix that."

Both boys looked back into the open back door of the butcher shop.

The Butcher yelled from inside. "You got five more minutes, Pepe. These sheep won't butcher themselves."

"Yes, sir," Pepe yelled back. "Five minutes is enough time, right?"

"You could see it twice," Mano said.

Pepe laughed. "I wish." Pepe was a year older than Mano, and nearly twice his size. He was bigger than most men, taller and stronger, though he still didn't know exactly how to move in his own body. He often tripped and knocked things over. He was constantly slipping in the sheep blood on the floor, and slicing his fingertips with the sharpened knives. And unlike any other boy his age, he already shaved. He had the same stubble as his father, The Butcher, as if he had been shaving every day for a decade. He liked to touch his own face and feel it there. That morning, his father gave him his very own razor, and told him to keep it sharp. He nicked himself around his chin and lips. Mano couldn't imagine what it must feel like to shave his own face, but what he really wanted to know is what it would feel like to shave Pepe's.

Mano could see the little nicks. "I bet I can shave your

face better than you," he said.

"What are you talking about? You don't even have pubes yet."

"Will you let me?" Mano asked.

"I just shaved. I don't need one yet." Pepe felt his stubble and nicks with his cold beer hand. "Do you know how to do it?"

Mano just remembered that The Barber was dead, which meant that his barbershop would be empty. "I'm The Barber now," he said without thinking about it.

"What about The Barber? You can't be The Barber if The Barber is The Barber. "

"The Barber's dead. Died this morning."

"Yeah?"

"Yeah. Big hole in his chest. I saw Inez Roar and Baby Zuzu crying on their front lawn. It was a real mess."

"A big hole?"

"Yeah, she said Mothers has been talking about God's Finger. Maybe it was that."

"I guess so. My mom's been talking about God's Finger a lot lately, too. She stopped drinking because of it anyway. Made my dad stop, too. I don't know." Pepe kept rubbing his stubble, like he was solving a mystery. "Same thing happened to The Postman last week. A big hole in his chest. It went all the way through. Beulah's running his routes now."

"The deaf woman?"

"Yeah. I guess a little black poodle came out of his hole."

"Where did it come from?" Mano adjusted his new glasses on his face.

"No one knows." Pepe attempted his best Father Mothers II impression. "God's Finger giveth and taketh. It tooketh his life, but gaveth the world a poodle."

"Where did it go?"

"The poodle?" Pepe just shrugged.

The Butcher called his son back to work. "Time's up, boys."

"Yes, sir," Pepe responded. "Hey, think about it. Someday, you can be The Barber, and I'll be The Butcher."

The lightning pain in Mano's back and legs drained away for a few seconds at the thought. "We'll be right next to each other every day."

"We can take smoke breaks together whenever we want."

"For as long as we want."

7

Lady Blood was fuller than on any other Sunday in its twenty year history, so it was a particularly unfortunate morning for Father Mothers II to be late. Most new faces sat in pairs in the back pews, some sat alone. Some people stood on the side leaning against the wall next to a painting of Jesus Christ that the original Father Mothers painted a few years before his death. In it, Jesus looked like he was double-dribbling a basketball, but he was supposedly turning water into wine. Two of the new faces stood peeking through the doors in the narthex, half-committed to the idea of attending a mass. After more silence than a full room could bear, some chatter began.

The Baker asked his daughter, Mary Minutes, if she had fed the cat before they left. She hadn't, because she thought it was Mimi's turn. The Baker had forgotten that Mimi had a turn altogether. But Mimi hadn't fed it either. June Good leaned across The Foreman to whisper something to Vera Good, to which The Foreman cleared his throat in disapproval. The Foreman only sat between the two women each Sunday to keep up appearances. Lois Horn sat in the back talking to her two young sons, Ernesto Horn and Ernest Horn. She tied Ernesto's shoes with one hand, and Ernesto helped Ernest tuck in his shirt. Mimi wrote a note about Mano with her one hand while Mary held it in place for her, and then Mary wadded it up and threw it at Enid Pine, but it missed and fell to the floor. Nana Pine, Enid's mother, looked back at the twins disapprovingly. Inez Roar uncovered Baby Zuzu's face from under a blanket just to look at her, to be sure that she was still there. It was the first Sunday that Inez attended church without her husband, The Barber.

"Do you have any spare clocks in your workshop?" The Butcher whispered to his wife, Mitzi Let, who liked to fix broken clocks. "I may need another one for the shop."

"I do. I have one with a cow on it."

"Perfect." They held hands. Pepe usually sat between them, but that morning he claimed he was too sick to even stand up straight, so he stayed home.

Beulah Minx sat in the far back pew by herself for the first time without her husband, The Postman. It made little difference to her that Mothers II had yet to arrive. She lived in a world of silence, and it felt even more silent without The Postman's hand on her leg.

It wasn't at all like Mothers II to be late. He regularly preached about the virtues of punctuality. Sometimes he liked to walk in from the back of the church, where everyone else entered, as a way to amplify the pomp, and then he'd make a point about how we all enter and exit the same doors, or something to that effect. But they had waited long enough that everyone's heads were turning and looking at all the possible entrances that Mothers II could make.

"Is everything ok?" asked Nana Pine toward Red Mothers, who sat in a giant chair on the side of the chancel at the front of the sanctuary. Red was the only child of Mothers II. Everyone called him Red on account of his coloring. He always had bright red hair and red eyes. Even his skin, in the glass light of the church, had a tint of red upon it, like a terrible and constant sunburn. His father, Mothers II, on the other hand, looked like a yellow and brown donkey, with gigantic brown eyebrows and big yellow ears. No one, including his father, could remember what Red's actual name was. Like his father before him, and his father before him, he was chaste.

Red Mothers was too old to be anyone's son. Many people even hypothesized that he was older than his own father, who was now unacceptably late to mass.

Nana Pine's question led to more questions from everyone else. Red kept his head down, as if he was praying.

"Is Mothers asleep? Should someone go and wake him?" asked The Builder.

"Mothers wouldn't oversleep on a Sunday," said The Baker.

June Good stood up and asked, "How much longer do we wait?"

"Sit down, June." The Foreman grabbed the back of her dress and pulled her back.

"Don't tell her to sit down," said Vera Good. She leaned over The Foreman and asked June if she was ok.

The Foreman put his head in his hands.

Inez stood up, still rocking Baby Zuzu in her arms, and yelled, "Why is my husband dead? Why does he have a hole in his chest?"

Red looked behind some curtains. It was important that he at least seem as though he was searching for his father. He didn't know how to field this barrage of questions, which were increasing in intensity.

After Inez's question, there was a gasp, then everyone agreed.

"Yes, why are we dying?" said The Banker.

"The Postman, and now The Barber..."

"Why do they have holes?"

"It's God's Finger!" yelled The Butcher. "We have to..."

"I think God's touching us! But he's just touching too hard!" yelled The Baker. "He loves us too much."

"Yes! He's just trying to bless us, but he doesn't know his own strength," added The Foreman to the frenzy.

Red rose from his seat and walked up to his father's pulpit to reluctantly address the gathering. He didn't know where his father was, and he didn't know what to say. Ever since he was a small boy, he had dreamed of standing at the pulpit and delivering homilies, but he had spent his long life only watching, never doing. When he imagined it, he imagined himself yelling and gesturing wildly, saying things like *you are all bad and you have to be good*. Even though he had never spoken in front of the church before, especially on this Sunday that was more crowded than any other Sunday, he knew enough to know that now was no time for harsh lectures.

The first words of Father Mothers III's reign were rather sheepish. "I don't know where my father is," he said. "I'm sorry." He threw up his hands to shrug, and he knocked over a candle. In a panic, he stomped the flame out with his snakeskin shoes. "It's out, it's out," he announced. And his second of many announcements became, "Be calm. The church is not going to burn down."

The crowd sighed collectively, and some of them began to put on their jackets to leave.

Mary and Mimi were two of the first to exit. They walked around to the back of the church to smoke a couple stolen Pie Time cigarettes away from the dispersing crowd. As Mary lit Mimi's cigarette, a routine they had practiced many times, she heard the sound of Mothers II's sermon floating in the distance. The flames on their cigarettes died.

"Is it coming from the trees?"

"No. It's on the roof."

They dropped their cigarettes, and Mary helped Mimi onto her back. Mimi's arm wrapped around Mary's neck, they climbed the ladder that was left leaning against the back wall of the church. Together, they climbed like a snail.

More and more people were leaving the church now, confused.

Once Mary and Mimi were at the top of the ladder, they peeked up above the roofline to find Mothers II hanging on his cross, the bright morning sun framing his limp body, and the sound of his sermon louder than before. Without speaking to each other, Mary climbed onto the roof and straddled its apex, while Mimi situated herself on the top rung of the ladder. Mary scooted closer to the dead body while Mimi held her breath.

Mary scooted her body so close to his body that her shoulder knocked his foot. Mothers II swung. When she looked up, she saw his dead and purple face. His eyes were open, and he had a half smile as if here were still alive. His clothes were wet from the previous day's rain. She could hear now that the sermon she was listening to was not coming from Mothers II, did not belong to him, but was the sermon of some other priest, maybe in some other town.

"What is it?!" Mimi asked from the ladder.

"It's Mothers."

"Is he alive?"

"No! Does it look like he's alive? He's swinging from the cross."

"Well, I don't know! I can't see from here." Mimi was losing her grip on the rung, and she adjusted her legs so she could sit more comfortably on the rung below. But from there she had an even more obstructed view. "Why is he talking?"

"It's not him."

"What do you mean it's not him? Who is it?"

"I mean, it's him, but it's not him talking. It's a radio or something."

"I don't see a radio."

Mary looked around the body, and saw nothing on the flat part of the strangely constructed roof except two heavy planks of wormy wood, a hammer, and some scattered nails. From the roof, she could see people walking away from the church in different directions. "Yeah, me neither."

Very carefully, Mary balanced on the roof, and pulled herself up the cross with her hands. She felt Mothers' body for the source of the sermon's sound. She felt his legs, which just felt like hard legs. Then she stood up further and felt his thighs, which just felt like hard thighs. Then she felt his stomach, which also felt hard.

"Why are you touching him like that?" cried Mimi. "We should tell somebody."

"No, don't! Just hold on." Mary felt Mothers' chest. It felt hollow beneath his shirt. She looked into his swollen and bulging eyes, and silently, with only her mouth, she apologized to him. Then, with her left hand, she slowly unbuttoned his shirt. There was a big hole in his chest that went all the way through, and a little red radio inside of it.

"Your hearts are too small," said the voice inside the radio inside the hole.

8.

With his new glasses, Mano could see all the smallest things through the window. He saw the dust of hair on the aprons, which hung on a rack in the back of the room. Combs were floating in a jar of bright blue liquid on the counter in front of the mirror, and the scissors were hanging in their place along the wall. He saw the razors, too. Then he thought he saw a man standing in the shadows in the back, but it was his own reflection in another mirror as he peered through the window. The emptiness of the barbershop, to Inez, surely looked much different than it now looked to Mano. For her, empty rooms meant the world was ending, but for Mano empty rooms like this one made the world feel like it was on its first page. Mano knew love now. It was just hope made visible. Now, the world seemed a touch bigger in the best ways, big enough to walk all the way in. The barbershop looked ready for a customer.

Suddenly, a little black poodle licked Mano's ankles where there was still some dried blood from the punishment doled out earlier by The Foreman. The poodle's cold wet tongue startled him.

"It's ok, you don't have to do that." Mano stood still, even though it tickled. The poodle wanted to clean him, and Mano wanted to let it. He pet the poodle's fluffy black hair, then he picked it up to say thank you into its eyes.

"Are you the poodle that came out of the hole in The Postman?" The poodle wiggled in Mano's grip. It didn't have any tags. It didn't even have a collar. "What's your name?" It didn't have a name.

Soon after setting the poodle back down on the ground, it knocked over the trashcan to sniff and lick whatever was inside of it. "Hey, how did you get inside?" Mano asked the poodle.

The door that Mano assumed was locked was now ajar. Mano walked inside, and turned the lamp on. He turned over the *Closed* sign on the front door to the *Open* sign. He set the trashcan upright, then picked up a few of the papers the spilled out and put them back in. With his long hair tucked into his collar, Mano sat in the barber's chair and waited for his first customer. He waited and waited and no one came. No one even walked by the front window. He found yesterday's newspaper on the newspaper stand by the door. He had watched The Barber read the newspaper in the chair while waiting for a customer, so he thought to keep up the tradition. It seemed right. It was the least he could do.

The newspaper had officially christened Pie Time's plague, God's Finger. According to the article, three people from Pie Time were dead. They each had holes in their chests, and each had something come out of their holes upon their death. No one knew where the holes were coming from, or why. Some suggested they were caused by a contagious nightmare, since each death occurred while its victim slept. Most suggested that it was God poking his finger very hard into the chests of sinners to punish them for their sins. Others suggested it was God trying to bless the living with his finger for doing good things, but blessing them too hard. What Pepe had said about The Postman was true. It was right there in the paper. Beulah Minx was interviewed. "A poodle came out," is all she said.

"How did you get inside The Postman?" Mano asked the poodle, who was now sitting in the sun in the window. That didn't seem like the right question. "How did you come from The Postman?" No question was the right question, and it was clear that the poodle didn't understand where it had come from. "What is happening with the world?" As Mano said that, he felt more like The Barber. That would be something a barber would say. "What is wrong with the world today?"

"Up, up," Mano said to the poodle as he patted the back of the barber's chair with his hand. "C'mon." Mano decided he would need to practice with the apron, the scissors, the combs, the razors, and the shampoos, before his customers arrived. This time was precious.

The poodle stared at him.

"You're my guinea pig."

With his new glasses on, Mano could see perfectly the contours of the poodle's body, how the tiniest hairs jutted out of the crooks, and he could see the moles in the folds enough not to shave them off. He cut and shaved, lathered and preened. The poodle looked smaller, like an entirely new kind of animal, maybe something in the Family Rodentia. But it smelled clean. You could see its eyes now, and they shined in the sunlight. For never having cut hair before, Mano's first haircut was remarkable.

If Mano was going to be The Barber, he'd need his second haircut ever to be his own. No one would want their hair cut by a barber with long hair. He sat himself in the chair, and faced the mirror. He tightened the white paper collar around his neck before wrapping the apron around his shoulders.

"You look like a priest," he said to himself. "You look like Mothers with long hair." This made him laugh. "Ok, this is going to hurt." He made himself laugh again, then he held his long hair above his head and cut it with the scissors. His short hair fell to his ears while his long hair remained in his fist above his head like a bouquet of flowers. He stayed like that for a moment, staring as his face. He looked like a stranger, and for the first time his body was not his own. He felt like he was inside the body of a beautiful young man. He felt the sting that remained in the back of his legs, and that sting felt like someone else's, too. Nothing was his. Only the poodle which was now on his lap. Only the glasses. Those things felt like his because he held these things. And because he held these things, he was becoming larger.

"Hello?" he said into the mirror. He got up to look more closely into his own eyes. Standing there, he cut his hair even shorter, more madly now, wildly, like cutting the hedges, until he could see his scalp. He had never seen his scalp before. He could see the shape of his skull, and he could see what he would look like as a skeleton. "Hello, skeleton." With the razor, he shaved the sides of his head, and with the comb he parted what little was left on the top of his head.

He leaned even further over the counter into the mirror until his breath fogged up the man's face in the reflection. "What's your name," he whispered. "Tell me your name." His open mouth pressed against the breath on the mirror, and it moved in the hot fog against his reflection's mouth. His tongue slipped out along the edges, and it licked his own tongue.

The barbershop was tiny with only enough room for one barber's chair, but there was a door in the back of the shop that led to two even tinier rooms. The room on the left was the bathroom, and the room on the right was something else entirely. The walls were white and there were no windows. The only thing in the room was a black square. It was like nothing else—not like darkness or light, or joy or sadness, or air or a lack of air. It was something, but it was also nothing. It felt like a thing, of course, but it felt like a thing that was missing. If it was like anything, maybe it was like the past. The air in the room felt incredibly personal, like it could only exist for one person. And when Mano stood in the center of the room, he felt like he was the exact specific person that the room was for.

Mano took a few steps into the room so he could touch the black square. He thought he would know what it was if he touched it. Instead of touching anything, he watched his finger go into it, and then back out. It went in so far, almost all the way to the knuckle. Then he put his whole hand inside of it, and felt a pull—not like another hand pulling him, but like sideways gravity. He reached all the way in to his elbow. It felt so good to be *inside* of the black square like that.

"Tell me if someone comes in, ok?"

The poodle looked like a mouse in the doorway of the back room.

Mano hesitated a few times, but then couldn't help but give in to the black square's pull on his whole body. When the air was at its most quiet in the back room, and he could be sure no one was coming, Mano stepped up into the black square. He put his entire body inside it.

Once inside the black square, Mano could see he was underwater, sitting in cold mud at the bottom of a murky pond. Above him, on the surface, two people were treading water with their clothes on. They were not thrashing the water in a panic, but just floating there, moving their legs slowly, like they were just walking about. Their legs were lit up in the watery light. The long skirt of the woman was slowly swooshing up and down like a jellyfish, and as her skirt floated upward, he could see her legs, and the top of her garters. The man was wearing pants, and wingtip shoes, his black socks peeking out in the light. Mano was turned on from looking at the space between the end of the man's pants and the rims on the top of his shoes, where the thin socks slid down, and the space between the hemmed lining of the woman's skirt, and the top rim of her shoes, how the skin squeezed in impossibly. Both the man's and the woman's legs were moving like frogs' legs.

The man fell a little beneath the surface to unbuckle his belt, and the woman fell just beneath the surface to pull off her skirt. Mano had never seen so much skin before, like streaks in the watery silence, blurry and spinning, smearing into the movements they were making, or the ones they had just made. The pants and the skirt, and both pairs of shoes, a belt and some socks floated slowly down from the surface.

From beneath the pair in the cold mud, Mano searched for his mother. As he called for her, the word rose above his lips to the surface and made a shadow on his face there:

Ma'am? Mother? The words were everything anyone could ever want in words. Three beautiful syllables: *ma'am,* and *moth,* and *errr,* pushed together in the light until they lit up in the light, making one brightly lit word on his face. Mano's mouth was moving on its own now, *Ma'am, Mother,* in front of him, and he followed it. But he realized for the first time that what he was looking for was not a sound, but the *feeling* of a sound. And then it came, as easily from the darkness, or from the woman or the man, as from the leafy murk that *felt* like it was swaying directly across from him in the dark airlessness of the pond bottom. This sound of swaying he heard was coming from the now naked swimmers above him. It was the blood pumping inside his own heart.

The swimmers now looked as if they were dividing into parts, their arms and legs separating from their bodies and floating along the surface of the pond. To Mano, it looked like the bottoms of many boats. More and more shapes were floating on the surface, and they started to block out the light that was cutting down through the water. Eventually, the pair of swimmers could no longer be seen at all, and instead there were so many shapes floating above Mano, that Mano was left completely in the dark.

Pepe's face was clear and bright as it emerged from the middle of the darkness, and quickly toward Mano. Something felt like it was about to begin, or had just ended. And then there was no murk. And then there was no pond.

9.

"What happened to your hair?" asked Sisi.

Mano leaned forward on the toilet. He had forgotten about his hair. He touched the back of his neck, and felt all the air there. Very quietly, polka played on the radio.

"I'm The Barber now."

"Is that right?" Sisi acted impressed. "You're The Barber now? Does The Foreman mind that you're The Barber now? I doubt you can be too productive rolling cigarettes when you're cutting and sweeping in your barbershop all day."

Mano gritted his teeth. "I don't work at the factory anymore." He worried that his mother was going to ask why. He started thinking of reasons for leaving the factory that weren't as humiliating as the truth.

"Well, the factory would certainly not be the right place for The Barber to work, I'd say." Sisi smiled to her son knowingly.

Mano exhaled and let a smile grow on his own face, too. "I suppose you're right." Something felt different between them, and that made Mano feel a little older and braver. "So, do you like it?" Mano asked. He didn't usually ask his mother too many questions.

"Like what?"

"My haircut?"

Sisi looked back across her soapy shoulder to get the best view of Mano's haircut. Mano stood up from the toilet and turned all the way around for her. "No," she said.

They both laughed.

"Why not?"

"It makes you look like a man."

The polka stopped. The radio said, "It's High Time for a Pie Time."

"Tell me, how is The Barber going to steal his mother a pack of Pie Time cigarettes every day, and a cold twelve pack, if all he does is cut hair and sweep it up, cut hair, sweep it up, cut, sweep, cut, sweep, cutsweep, cutsweepcutsweepcutsweep?"

Mano panicked as his mother kept making the sounds of cutting and sweeping. He put his hands in his pockets, and felt that he had no coins there, and his mother's only spare pack of Pie Times sat alone on the shelf above the tub. "I'll buy your beer and cigarettes."

"That's a lot of money, Mano. You don't have any customers yet."

"I'll get customers."

"I bet you'll get free cuts of meat from The Butcher, too, huh?"

Mano could feel his mother fishing. "Yes, ma'am. I suppose I will." Mano asked his mother what she knew with his eyes.

"A mother knows," she smiled.

Mano had no idea how his mother knew anything that happened outside of her bathtub. He suspected that she could smell the truth on him. "Is it ok?"

"Pepe's too big for you. You're too small. He looks like a big man and you look like a tiny girl with a bad haircut."

"We're the same age." Mano knew that was only near the truth. "I'm getting bigger and bigger every day."

"Just don't fall in love with a hunter."

"Pepe's not a hunter, ma'am. He's a butcher."

"There are many kinds of hunters."

10.

The Baker sat down in the barber's chair, and Mano spun him around to face the mirror. "My Mary tells me you're all done with the factory. You're The Barber now."

"You heard right." It hadn't occurred to Mano that anything he did was of any interest to Mary or Mimi.

"My Mary tells me that Enid Pine sure misses you at the factory." His wink caught Mano off guard. Enid was one of the few girls that Mano liked. Like Mano, she only had a mother in her family, and no one else, and she sometimes helped him steal cigarettes from the factory. And, of course, she was incredibly kind to him on his last day.

Mano leaned The Baker all the way back in the chair, and rubbed the warm oil onto his face. He soaked a towel in hot water. In his first week of being The Barber, he had learned not to ask what the customer wants, but to always just begin.

"How is young Enid?" asked Mano.

"Oh, fine. Fine. She comes by the house now and then to play with Mary. Oh, and Mimi, too. Enid's mother is a different story, of course."

"Nana? Oh, how so?"

"You know how the world is these days, with God's Finger going around. She's very protective of Enid. She always needs to be home at a certain time, that sort of thing."

"Oh yeah? That's too bad. What good is living if..."

The Baker interrupted with a sigh loud enough to startle Mano. "Nana is afraid of just about everything. She's afraid of God's Finger, like the rest of us..."

Mano tried interrupting in order to point out that he was not, in fact, afraid of God's Finger. But The Baker kept talking, increasing the volume of his voice.

"...and she's afraid Enid will fall in love, just as she did. Love leaves a kind of hole, too. You know?"

"Yes, yes. I suppose I do know." Mano wasn't so sure he

knew what The Baker was trying to say. He wrung the hot towel, and twisted it into an oval on top of The Baker's face.

"Ask your mother about that." The Baker's words were muffled beneath the hot wet towel. Instead, Mano heard The Baker saying something like, "Ask Mothers about that."

"I don't go to church," confessed Mano.

The Baker was confused at Mano's response for a moment. "That's a real shame. I'd be scared for you. I'd be scared you're next. God's Finger can take anyone. Even the priest."

"Is that your take on it?" asked Mano.

"It's as good a take as any. So, you didn't hear about Mothers?" The Baker removed the towel from his face, and tossed it onto the counter. "God's Finger took one of God's own. Who knows what Mothers was up to. It poked him right there as he was standing on the cross on top of Lady Blood. It poked him while he was building a bigger cross! How much holier can you get than that?"

"On the cross?" Mano asked, though he needed no clarification.

"On the cross! God got him right in the chest, knocked him off the cross dead, and ended up hanging there from a nail on his own collar. He had the hole and everything. Nothing was found inside this one though."

"A real shame."

"If God's Finger comes to our family, it won't take Mary. I know that much. Or Mimi. It'll take me. And I can handle that."

"Still, it's a scary world." Mano felt for the straight razor in the breast pocket of his apron.

For a week the barbershop was steadily regaining a healthy business. As customers came in, they would either ask Mano to give their condolences to Inez and Baby Zuzu, or they'd have no idea that the old Barber was dead. Regardless, it became Mano's job to lighten the inevitably dark mood as he met each of his new customers. He gave everyone the same shave, and the same haircut that he gave himself a week earlier—short and parted on the side, and slicked down with oil. They all seemed satisfied without even really looking at themselves too closely in the mirror.

He made enough money each day to buy a pack of Pie Time cigarettes and a twelve pack of Pie Time beer for his mother on his way home. And at the close of each work day, Pepe would come by after his long day as The Butcher's apprentice. He would sit in the chair and spin around. Together, they would laugh at the stories of everyone in town.

"Keep it, son." The Baker flipped Mano an extra quarter, and Mano slipped it into his apron pocket. "And please don't tell Enid I was here. She'll be jealous, and she won't stop talking about it all night."

Mano didn't understand. He couldn't think of when he'd ever talk to Enid again. Still, he smiled at The Baker and thanked him.

A few minutes later, as Mano dunked his razor and scissors into a jar of hot antiseptic and swept The Baker's hair into a neat nest on one of the white square tiles, Pepe walked in. Mano's throat tightened, and he felt his legs go hollow. It was the feeling of his blood rushing into and out of all of his parts all at once. Mano wiped his glasses clean with a white cloth, which was something he did about every half hour.

"Hey, Mano, I thought of something your barbershop needs." Pepe bent down and pet the black poodle.

"Is that so?" Mano stood close enough to Pepe that he could smell the blood on his apron. Looking at this big young man in the doorway of the barbershop was like looking at a reflection of exactly how Mano wanted to appear in the world. He blurred his eyes and saw Pepe's shiniest parts—his hair and his shoes—and then unblurred his eyes to see the way Pepe's mouth stopped moving after it said a sentence.

"Yeah, look." Pepe pulled a red box from behind his back

and handed it to Mano.

"What is it?"

"What do you mean 'what is it'? It's a radio. Your barbershop needs one, don't you think?"

Mano didn't even know that he needed a radio. He never thought about the possibility of a radio existing outside the one on the back of the toilet in his mother's bathroom, but now that he was holding a radio of his very own in his hands, he could feel his own need for it. He looked around the barbershop for a place to put it. He tried to hug Pepe to thank him, but he was still holding the radio so he just leaned on him.

Pepe shooed his thank yous away modestly. "Go on, set it down. You won't believe it. I found it in the garbage behind Lady Blood. Now, who would throw out a perfectly good radio like this one?"

"You *found* it?" asked Mano.

"Yeah, and that's the thing. I found it because I heard church music coming from beneath a pile of trash. It wasn't even plugged in!"

"What do you mean it wasn't plugged in?" Mano found the perfect spot for it on the counter behind the spare combs.

"That's what I mean. Turn it on. I'll show you."

Mano turned the knob. A priest was saying things. He turned the dial to a different frequency, and another priest was saying similar things. The boys watched the needle moving down the line like a pig looking for the right chute. Another priest, saying other things.

"How does it do that?"

"Who knows? But it's doing it. That's the most important thing."

Mano picked it up and looked at the back of it. He couldn't even find a cord coming out of it. It was the best present Mano had ever received. He felt like holding it. It made him feel like he took up more space in the room.

"Thank you, Pepe."

"Yeah. Just keep playing with it. You'll find some polka on there, I bet." Pepe sat down in the chair, and Mano leaned him all the way back.

"You're into polka, huh?" asked Mano.

"Yeah, have you heard it?"

"Yeah, I've heard it. My mom listens to it sometimes."

"I'm going to start my own polka band someday, and play in other towns."

Mano turned off the knob on the radio, and grabbed a clean razor from the counter. He slid the razor carefully along Pepe's bare throat.

"How was the butcher shop today, Pepe?"

Pepe laughed. "That tickles."

Mano laughed and told Pepe to relax. "You have to hold still, or else I'll cut your throat."

"Don't kill me! I'm not ready to die!" Pepe joked. He breathed in through his nose and tried to relax. "Ok, try again."

"How was the shop today, Mr. Let?" Mano lowered his voice to be funny, and he started shaving Pepe's jaw with the razor.

Pepe used a weird voice. "I took things in and out of the freezer. I ground things in the grinder. I took the money. I sharpened the knives. I drained the blood."

Mano could smell blood in Pepe's hair. He moved his comb through it. He swept the hair from his forehead with the comb. He made a clean part. He straightened his collar. He swept more hair from Pepe's forehead with his fingers.

"We are dying."

Father Mothers III anxiously cleared his throat in front of what had become his congregation, and started over. "We are dying, one after the other, in pools of our own tainted blood, each morning, because in God's eyes we're behaving no differently than mice. We are the mice of the earth. And like mice, we scurry around beneath the feet of our enemies because we are begging to be stepped on. And then, because we have begged for it, all of our days, we are stepped on. We only serve ourselves. We take take take, and we make make make what we touch filthy. Are you a filthy mouse?" The gaze of Mothers fell upon Enid Pine, who happened to be sitting in the front row next to Nana Pine. Enid wasn't sure if she should answer his question. When she didn't, Mothers doubled the volume of his voice. "Are you a filthy little mouse?!"

"No?" Enid said, barely audibly.

Mothers' red eyes got bigger, and then he asked the same question again to the whole congregation. No one answered. He asked the question a fourth time, about whether or not you're a filthy mouse, while looking at The Butcher. "Do you want to *die* like a filthy mouse? Do you want to die beneath the vengeful and justified foot of the Lord?"

The Butcher stood up to give his answer. "It's God's Finger, Mothers, not his foot!"

"We're being poked, not stepped on," added The Baker.

"Oh, yes, of course!" Mothers apologized. "Do you want to be poked in the chest like a filthy mouse?" Mothers had been rehearsing his first homily all week in a mirror, but now his mouse metaphor was rapidly falling apart in front of him. He developed a style of speaking through his oversized teeth, with lots of crackles and pops, to hide his subtle lisp. He had a voice that sizzled as it got louder. He cut his hair very short, so it looked like a red velvet sheet cake. His priest's robe belonged to his father, so it didn't fit him quite right. It pulled and tugged at his chest and hips as he walked.

Most of Pie Time's believers were impressed with the confidence and tenacity of the new Father Mothers. Getting a few things incorrect in the first homily had been expected. They had expected to see the new priest stumble through the entire service. What the people of Pie Time admired most is that, despite his advanced age, Mothers had the energy of a young priest. They were panicked by all the deaths at the hands of God's Finger, and they needed a priest's heightened homilies to match their growing anxiety.

The questions about whether or not anyone was a filthy mouse, or if they wanted to die like one, lingered in the air while Mothers struggled to roll back his tight sleeves.

"Didn't your father die from God's Finger just last week?" shouted The Baker. "My Mary found him on the..."

Mothers interrupted him. "Ok! And now on to the baptismal ceremonies."

Mothers gestured to his new assistant, Lil' Jorge, just as they had rehearsed. Lil' Jorge was a very big boy who looked like a teenager on account of all of his fat, but was in fact likely no older than eight. No one really knew Lil' Jorge's age under all of his chubbiness, but it was true that he couldn't count past the number eight, so it was very unlikely that anyone wouldn't be capable of at least counting up to their own age. So, everyone just assumed that he was eight years old. His arms and legs were big like tree trunks, but they were also short. Lil' Jorge dragged a plastic pool of milky holy water onto the stage. He waddled as he dragged it.

Inez Roar, who was wearing a white cotton robe, and holding naked Baby Zuzu, followed Lil' Jorge and the tub out to the front of the sanctuary. She lowered her lower half into the water, clutching her baby to her chest like a piglet. She was afraid that the slippery baby would squirm from her tight wet grip as Mothers, who was standing just outside the pool, held Inez above the blue plastic rim. The pool was decorated with images of about twenty yellow mermaids swimming around.

"Mermaids don't exist," whispered Lil' Jorge earnestly to Mothers.

"Thank you, Lil' Jorge," said Mothers as he politely pushed Lil' Jorge to the side of the ceremony so that everyone could see around his chubbiness. Mothers bent at the knees next to the pool.

That's when everyone in the church heard Mano's horrible scream. It came from somewhere outside the church. Some heads turned to try to stare through the windows that transformed the bright white sky into a blocky color puzzle of Jesus Christ on his knees cleaning someone's feet, and another blocky color puzzle of a figure that looked like maybe Jesus Christ with a shepherd's crook. In actuality, it looked more like someone walking on three stilts.

"What was that?" shouted a concerned June Good.

"Maybe an injured animal?" asked The Banker.

"No. No animal can make a noise like that," said Vera Good.

"It was a person!" shouted Nana Pine.

"Who could it have been?"

Everyone but Pepe looked through the windows in an attempt to deduce whose scream it could have been, but Pepe knew exactly whose scream it was.

"Let us carry on with the baptism," pleaded Mothers.

Everyone shuffled back into their seats and tried to concentrate, but even Mothers was distracted. He looked out of the windows as he lowered Inez backwards into the pool. As he considered the scream, he held Inez underwater longer than what was routine, long enough that she got scared and scuffled with his grip on her shoulders. She came up coughing for a breath, and in the scuffle, she let Baby Zuzu slip. The baby drifted down below the cloudy holy water, down between her kicking legs.

"My baby!"

Mothers reached all the way into the water from his knees, his head and shoulders beneath the surface as if he was bobbing for apples.

"My poor baby's down there!" she screamed.

His hands were fumbling between Inez's legs. Everyone forgot about Mano's scream in that moment, and they focused instead on Inez's. They stood up to get a better look into the pool. Inez's arms were high in the air as if she'd somehow find her drowning baby above her.

The upper torso of the soaked priest finally emerged from the murk, a baby in his clutches, his eyes like a crazed eagle's. He stood up, gloriously, and held the rescued baby high above his head.

Remarkably, as is the legend of Baby Zuzu, she was not crying.

The whole church sighed, and then *awwwed*. The ones who had yet to stand up, stood up. All of them applauded.

"I present to you, Zuzu Roar, now a child of God!" Mothers was out of breath. It was his first triumph as the new priest. Inez was still on her knees, crying and holding tight to Mothers' left leg. She was looking upward, her soaked cotton dress like a thin pink skin hugging her whole body. The congregation clapped wildly, hooted and cheered. They stared at the deepest pink parts of Inez's body between the backs of her wet thighs. They stared at the dark and fertile valley there, and they stared at her hard brown nipples.

They kept clapping and cheering.

Only Pepe wasn't clapping or cheering. He escaped underneath all of the clapping and cheering.

"Where are you going?" yelled The Butcher. He broke his gaze on Inez's wet body, but was still clapping. Pepe was already out of sight.

Before the last few claps fizzled out, Mothers made his

final announcement for the day. Near Lady Blood's front door, in an open coffin, was the shirtless dead body of his father, Father Mothers II, with a hammer still in his clutches.

"Thank you, thank you. Please, sit down. Have a seat." Mothers was relishing his moment. "As many of you may know, my father passed last week. He was taken too soon." Mothers lowered his head and paused for dramatic effect, hoping his silence wouldn't be broken with shouts of "God's Finger" from the congregation. But everyone else followed suit and lowered their own heads.

Then Mothers raised his head with a burst, and continued. "We are trying to raise enough money to build a bigger cross for the top of Lady Blood. It was my father's dying wish. As you know, there can be no cross built without enough money with which to build it upon. On your way out, as my father lay there in front of you, please be so kind as to put any coins you can spare into my father's death hole. Our goal is to fill it all the way up to his nipples."

And fill it all the way up they did.

12.

On the last morning Mano would ever deliver a cold beer to his mother, he was in bed when his bed began to float. He didn't notice right away because he was thinking too many thoughts. He was thinking about love, and then money, cutting hair, and love again. His thoughts would pile up so high inside of his head that a new thought became how he could climb them, like stairs, up and back down. A lamp shade floated into his bed. The black poodle was paddling.

"Ma'am?"

Sisi Medium died in the bathtub before the sun came up, sometime between turning the faucet on and turning it back off. Mano got up from his bed, and walked through the water into the kitchen with the lamp shade in his hand. *Splish, splish.* He set the lamp shade on the counter there. He rescued the poodle onto his shoulder. "Mom!" he called with urgency, thinking that if he just yelled loud enough she'd be sure to yell something back.

He splished across the kitchen into the living room. A floating lamp without its shade, and a floating chair. The green couch was floating around like a toy boat. The photograph of his mother holding him as a newborn baby now hung on the wall centered above nothing. He thought to move it to safety, but he didn't. The water was high enough to make walking difficult, but not quite high enough for him to lower his body in and swim. He pushed the couch back to its place on the wall.

Mano leaned his forehead against the closed bathroom door. "Do you need another cigarette? Are you out? If you're out, I can go get more." Mano heard the faucet still splashing on the other side of the door. "Just tell me you're ok." He knew his life would change if he opened the door, and he didn't want his life to change.

"You need to turn the water off." Mano waited a few seconds for a response. "Ok?"

Mano knocked. Nothing. Then he took a breath and turned the knob. The knob was white and felt like the moon in his hands. He pushed the door against the weight of the water that held it closed.

Sisi Medium's body was floating just below the tub's lip. Her head was leaning back, long black hair matted across the red porcelain. One of her arms floated like a log stuck in the brush in a flood. The bathwater nearest her body was more pinkish.

"Mom." This time when Mano said it, it wasn't a question. It wasn't even a word. It felt like more of a punch to his throat than a word.

Instead of wading over to the tub to turn off the water, Mano turned his head and made a tiny sound that he didn't recognize. A new kind of mammal was trying to yell inside him. He pushed his face into the bathroom's red wallpaper, just like he did earlier with the black square. He pushed his face all the way inside it, inside the field of the red ranunculus. Mano was gigantic in the field, crushing all the flowers, pushing over the trees. His face was the whole sky in that field.

Sisi's faucet was trying to say something, and Mano left the field to re-enter the bathroom begrudgingly to hear it. The curtains in the bathroom window were drawn open, and the cold white light cast shadows of the empty trees onto the walls and the back of Mano's head. Everything was incredibly red. How did everything get so red? Was his mother's bathroom this red before? Was it ever red at all? Maybe it was yellow. For some reason, now he remembered her bathroom being yellow. Or blue. Light blue. But the towels, the tiles, all red. The red ranunculus. He felt the sudden need to count every red flower on the wallpaper, and he gave in to it. This counting became his new duty. It would have to be done. He counted the ranunculus closest to the base of the doorway, and moved upward. When he got to halfway up the wall, he had already counted to 14, which he then remembered was his new age on that very day. He hadn't remembered that it was his birthday. A son's birthday, he thought, was a mother's job. After doing some quick math, he imagined there must be 500 red flowers in the bathroom. It seemed unimaginable to Mano that his mother could have ever bathed all those years in the center of 500 red flowers. Was it all that red that crushed her, or was it all that red that held her together as she slowly dissolved?

He counted his way around the room, toward the tub, making certain that he didn't miss any of the flowers, until he counted his way to his mother. 109. His eyes hurt, and they rested on her clean black hair. He couldn't look directly at her eyes, but he could see that they were open, and that they were looking back at him. He couldn't look at her naked body, but he could stare at her hair. From the corner of his eye, he could see the hole in her chest. He could tell it went all the way through to the bottom of the tub. His eyes still on her hair, he swept it to the side across her forehead how she liked it. He could see, just then, how lonely she must have been. "I'm sorry I wasn't in here more." He touched her hair.

Mano kneeled at the tub in front of his mother, half of his body dipped in the flood from the tub. He decided not to turn off the faucet just yet. Turning it off would bring silence, and he wasn't ready for that yet. The faucet was like a hush, and it felt good. He just listened for her to breathe, and there was a second when he thought he did hear her breathe, but he listened closer and it was just him breathing.

"What's it feel like, Mom? Does it feel good?" He picked up a cigarette and thought to light one for her, but the matches were floating. His mother's cloud of cigarette smoke and steam still hung like a giant paper lantern from the ceiling. Except now it was no longer a white cloud, but a black cloud. "Did it feel ok? Did you feel ready?"

He left her in the bathtub, softening. It was private and quiet, safe from the gawkers and the panic-mongers.

The black poodle was stranded on a chair in the living room—a little green upholstered island. The lamp out in the hallway flickered, and sparked. Then it was off. Mano didn't remember turning it on. He unplugged the refrigerator in the bathroom before the water level rose to the socket. He opened the refrigerator door and let the water rush inside. A few cold cans of Pie Time floated around inside the refrigerator. He fished one out and cracked it open for her, set it on the windowsill. He lit a Pie Time cigarette, and placed it carefully between her lips so it would stick for a few seconds. He thought he saw it puff smoke, but it didn't. When it fell into the water, it sizzled out.

He opened up all the windows, something he had heard you were supposed to do when someone died, even though he wasn't exactly sure why. He stood on the tub and screamed. He screamed as loudly, and for as long as he could. It made him feel like an animal.

Outside of the house it was a Sunday. He could hear his scream bounce off of the church. Almost everyone was inside of the church. He could see the church breathing. It looked alive. To Mano, the prayers of the people inside of it sounded like clapping.

13.

Pepe was standing at the door of Sisi Medium's bathroom. His church trousers and the black poodle he was holding were soaked.

Mano glanced at him from the toilet, then turned back to his mother's dead face. He let go of Sisi's hand. His hand was shaking in the cold water of the tub. His body was nearly frozen. Her hand dropped back down into the flood.

"Everyone in church could hear your scream! Inez dropped..."

"I screamed? I don't remember screaming."

"Yeah, you sounded like..." Pepe stopped talking when he saw a woman floating above the bathtub behind Mano. "Who's that?"

"Pepe, this is my mom, Sisi."

"It's nice to meet you, Sisi." Pepe pushed the door open a little further. A wave pushed toward Mano's slouched body.

"She's dead."

Pepe turned off the faucet. The room felt remarkably silent, like everyone in it was dead. Pepe stood next to the toilet where Mano sat. They both looked at Sisi's dead body for a while. "What happened?"

"She got a hole in her chest," Mano explained. "It was that finger thing, I guess. I don't know. She's been dead all day. She's not coming back, Pepe."

Pepe put his strong warm hand on the back of Mano's neck.

Mano picked up his mother's arm and moved it around in the air a little to show Pepe. "I don't want anyone to see her like this. Ok?"

"Ok."

"They'll talk about her hole in the newspaper. Just like they did for The Postman and The Barber. They'll say she's been bad even though they don't know the first thing about her."

"And Father Mothers, now, too," added Pepe.

"They'll want to just talk about her hole. Nothing else," said Mano. "They won't know anything else to say. It's not what she'd want. I just can't."

"It's ok, I'll help."

"Will you help me take her..."

"I'll do anything." Pepe tried to study the hole in Sisi's chest without Mano seeing him do it.

"Let's wait until it gets dark."

"Ok. But she looks too soft, like wet paper."

"She's been in the bathtub for a long time."

Pepe and Mano agreed to move her body from her bathtub to The Cure at night, to bury her in the currents of the river when everyone else in town would be asleep. Sending the dead down The Cure tied to a raft made of driftwood was a common ritual for the people of Pie Time. Typically, Father Mothers would say a few words, and then the grievers would put a few flowers on the body. One griever would untie the rope, and they'd all watch the body float away to the sea. Most people wanted their grief on display, held like a baby by the people around them. They wanted their pain to be reflected. But Mano couldn't stomach the idea of any priest saying things about his mother. No priest knew his mother. Death, Mano thought, was no time for introductions.

Mano pulled the plug of his mother's bathtub and let the water drain. Sisi's body knew its own gravity for the first time in the bottom of its empty bathtub.

"She needs a moment to herself," Mano explained. "Death is very new for her."

In the living room, where the water had already slowly drained through the cracks of the floor, Pepe helped Mano out of his wet clothes. Pepe kneeled in front of him and took off his heavy wet shoes one at a time. His soggy left sock. His soggy right sock.

"You need to take off your pants. You're freezing."

Mano unbuckled his belt slowly. He was shivering. Pepe helped him slide his cold wet trousers down his trembling legs. Once past the knees, Pepe rolled them down, like a potato sack. The marks The Foreman had left on the back of Mano's legs were a different color than Pepe expected.

"Do they still hurt?" Pepe touched the darkest and deepest mark.

"No, I forget they're there."

Pepe stood up and unbuckled his own wet trousers. He pushed them down past his thighs, and Mano helped him roll them down to his ankles. Pepe's marks were much deeper, fresher, redder.

"What's this?" Mano touched the marks as if they would speak to him.

"It's nothing."

"Why didn't you tell me?"

"It's just a few times. Just little things. You don't need to worry about me."

Mano could see that Pepe's marks led all the way up his back, too. "Let me see all the way."

Pepe loosened his tie, and unbuttoned his shirt. He was standing now only in his underwear, wet trousers balled up around his shoes. Mano was tracing the lines on his back with his fingers.

The Butcher knocked on the bedroom window. "Pepe?! Are you in there?"

Both boys quickly slid their wet trousers back up to their waists, and buckled their belts.

"Pepe?"

"Yes, sir!" Pepe yelled while buttoning his shirt. Mano held his breath.

The Butcher knocked on the kitchen window. "Pepe? What's the matter with you?"

Both boys looked at each other with wide-eyed agreement. Pepe carefully opened the front door which entered into the living room, and stuck his head out into the world. "We're in here."

"I see." The Butcher removed his hat and stepped inside. "What's going on in here? Why did you run away from church so quickly?"

Pepe looked at Mano for help. He didn't know what he could say, and what he couldn't.

"I had a little problem with the water, that's all, sir," Mano explained.

The Butcher examined the room. Everything was wet. The walls were wet. The rug was wet. The poodle shook itself violently on the chair, sprinkling water on The Butcher's hand. The lamp lay on its side without its shade. The couch was a few feet from the wall.

"I see. Was it you who screamed?"

"Yes," Pepe answered for Mano. "I ran to help." Pepe was as tall as his father, but seemed half the size in this moment.

The Butcher looked back at Mano. "Didn't you used to be a girl?"

"I got a haircut, sir. I'm a man now. Well, I've always been one. Well, not a man, but a boy, but…"

"Mano's The Barber now." Pepe saved Mano's stumbling.

"Oh, yes, of course." The Butcher's face changed to one of recognition. "It's a damn shame about The Barber."

"A real shame, yes, sir."

"Poor Inez. Poor poor Baby Zuzu."

"It's a scary world," added Mano. "We can never know who'll be next." Mano just remembered his mother was dead.

"We just have to keep going to church. Right, Pepe?" The Butcher gripped the back of Pepe's neck and shook it semi-lovingly, as Pepe's face did everything it could to disguise his fright. "I can't afford…" The Butcher stopped what he was saying to redirect his attention back to Mano. "You go to church, don't you, Mano?"

"Of course, of course. I can't afford not to."

"That's right. You can't." The Butcher seemed satisfied for a moment. "I don't see you there."

"I sit in the back. It was probably the long hair. Anyway, how's business?"

"People will always need to eat their meat." The Butcher was pleased with his answer. "You?"

"Haircuts all day long. One after the other. Hair only knows to grow. Haircuts, haircuts, haircuts."

The Butcher looked at the photograph on the wall. "Do you have a mother?"

"No, sir."

"Oh? Is she dead?"

Mano's heart became heavy. His mother was dead, and she would be dead forever. "She lives with the birds."

"Oh! What are birds?"

"I mean, she lives with nuns."

"She sounds lovely."

"I wouldn't know, because she lives with nuns."

"Is she a nun?"

"No, she just does their dishes." Mano knew his mother would want to live with nuns, but also that she would never want to be one.

Mano could see in the way The Butcher was standing, facing the bathroom door, that he now had many more questions. He was going to ask more about his mother, about the kitchen at the convent perhaps, or maybe if he had a father, and if so, he'd want to know what his father did for a living. Unfortunately, what Mano knew the least about was the very basic origins of his own existence, and about the kitchens in convents. Mano quickly changed the subject. "Do *you* have a mother, sir?"

The Butcher was so surprised by the question that it appeared he had to think about it. He looked at Pepe while he answered it. "Yes, I suppose I do. But she's dead."

"I'm sorry to hear that. When did she die?"

"Same as everyone else, I suppose. At the end." The Butcher took one last look around the room, and then put on his hat. "Pepe." Pepe knew to do the same. As they walked out together, The Butcher turned around in the doorway.

"Your clock is broken." He pointed to Sisi's bathroom clock as it rested in a new place in the center of the living room floor. "It's not midnight anymore."

"Oh, you're right. Look at that." Mano wondered if his mother died at midnight last night. "Mitzi fixes clocks." The Butcher reached out his hand. "May I?"

Mano put the clock in The Butcher's hand.

As they said their goodbyes, Pepe closed the door behind them. His eyebrows moved in such a way that they made a kind of promise.

Newly alone in the house for the first time in his life, Mano stood in the living room and looked at the bathroom door. Before today, he could always be sure where his mother was, and now he wasn't so sure. The thing that made her face move, and her mouth speak, had finally dissolved completely into the air. He was all alone in the world. He felt all alone inside his own hollow body. If he felt like anything, he felt like a ball. A ball filled with cold air. So he collapsed into the tiniest ball that he could become, to look inside his own body, which was now just a tiny empty ball. But he couldn't find anything inside of there. He couldn't find his mother there. He couldn't find himself there. All he could find was an even smaller core, the core that had once made the ball around it. And the core looked like a tiny black seed.

He tucked his face between his knees, looked at the seed, and sobbed.

14.

The black cloud still hung above Sisi's dead body when Pepe returned to Mano's house later that night. It wasn't made of steam from the hot water, or smoke from her cigarettes, as Mano had assumed, but of pure sadness. Even after Mano and Pepe wrapped what was left of Sisi's body in her old bed sheets, the black cloud still hung there. They gripped the sheets to lift her up and out of the tub, and the black cloud followed. Mano held a knot of bed sheet at her head, while Pepe held a knot of bed sheet at her feet. Mano wanted to bring her back through time, through all the rooms of the house they shared, so she could see her own home one last time before being delivered down The Cure to float out to the sea.

As they moved from room to room, Mano told Pepe and his mother things that he wanted both of them to know, like a kind of personal tour. In the bedroom Mano said, "This is where I keep my books." In the kitchen he said, "This is the pantry door where I marked how tall I was each year with a pencil." In the living room he said, "This is the stool I sat on to tie my shoes."

Once outside, the lights in the windows of the nearby houses were off. The boys talked very quietly as they walked down Last Street past the front of each house. The black poodle followed close behind. As they walked past Pepe's house, they felt relieved to notice the lights were off there, too. Mitzi and The Butcher were asleep.

"Did you get in trouble?" asked Mano.

"He said I can't see you anymore."

"Why not?"

"Church."

As the boys lumbered toward the river, the moonlight washing over the bed sheet holding Sisi's corpse, Mano knew love. He could feel love's weight in his arms and back, and he could see it in Pepe's arms and back, too, and in how his legs moved. He measured Pepe's gait with his eyes, and then he tried to walk like that, too. Once on the banks of The Cure, he would tell Pepe all about his mother before they sent her off. Mano wondered if it would be too strange to have their first kiss after that.

"It doesn't matter anyway," Pepe said. "I'd rather be punished every night than not see you."

"What if you're locked away for good?"

"There's no such thing as for good." Pepe's stubble glowed in the moonlight.

As the boys walked up a little hill, on the last few steps toward The Cure, they could hear its rush of water, but that rush of water was mixed with laughter.

Pepe stood up on his toes to look at the river, then turned around to face Mano. "Turn around. Let's go back."

"What? Why?"

Pepe saw what Mano had yet to see—Enid Pine and Mary and Mimi Minutes smoking cigarettes beneath the trees on the bank.

"Hey, look at that little cloud!" yelled Mary above the sound of the river.

No, no. Pepe and Mano both turned around and tried to shuffle away quietly into the dark.

"Now it's moving away," said Enid. "It looks so sad."

"And so bright," added Mimi.

Pepe and Mano found a line of bushes further down on the banks of The Cure. They hid themselves behind the bushes, and they set Sisi's body on the ground there. As the three girls approached the black cloud, Mano and Pepe sat on Sisi's body and tried to make themselves as small as possible.

"It stopped," said Enid.

"It's so beautiful. I want to touch it. Let's lift Mimi up and see if she can touch it," said Mary. She and Enid ran toward the bushes where Mano and Pepe were hiding. Mimi lagged behind, moving like a lowercase j.

"Mano?" Enid's voice came out as a surprise to everyone, and Mano's name was spoken with elation, in a way like he had never heard it before. Her voice was an announcement, as if he was now supposed to take a lit stage.

Mano moved around sheepishly behind the bushes without standing up. "Hi, Enid." The sound of Mano's voice was the opposite of Enid's. He kept his head down, and stayed seated secretly on top of his mother's corpse.

"Is that your cloud?" Mary asked.

"No." Mano had second thoughts about his answer. "I mean, yes. That's mine."

"It's so sad," said Enid.

"It's just a cloud," said Pepe.

"Who's that?" asked Mary.

"It's me, Pepe," said Pepe.

"What are you doing here?" asked Mary.

"Don't worry about it," answered Pepe.

"Can we touch it?" Enid asked, far more interested in Mano and his black cloud. She kneeled down to be close to Mano.

"Yeah, Enid wants to *touch* it," giggled Mary.

Mano interrupted her giggling. "You can't touch it."

"Why? What happens if we touch it?" asked Mary. Mary never liked the first answer to any question.

"It's not a thing. You can't touch it like that."

"But it's a cloud," asserted Mary.

"It's a cloud, but a cloud isn't a thing. It's nothing. You can't touch it," explained Mano.

Mimi finally caught up to the group. "We sure miss having a boy around at the factory." She made sure to emphasize the word "boy" for Mano's sake. "Nice boy haircut."

"Cut it out, Mimi. Quit trying to be tough like your sister." Mano knew just how to hit Mimi where it hurt. Pepe laughed under his breath.

Mary felt proud that Mano considered her tough. "Why

did you cut your hair?"

"I'm The Barber now," answered Mano. "The Barber has to have short hair. Everyone knows that."

"Can I?" asked Enid. She wanted to distinguish her sincerity from Mary's.

It was Mary's duty to catch Mimi up on the conversation. "Mano's The Barber now. Enid wants to touch The Barber's cloud. The Barber says it's not a thing."

"Ooh, Enid wants to *touch* it," snickered Mimi alone.

"We already made that joke," said Mary.

Mimi let her laughter trail into an embarrassed sigh.

Mano and Pepe stayed still on Sisi's body as Enid picked up Mimi and positioned her on Mary's back like a backpack. The three of them started making plans to build some sort of pyramid out of their bodies that would reach the black cloud.

"Please, stop." Mano stood up to grab a stick. "Here, you can touch a little corner of the cloud, but that's it." With his stick, he stood on his toes to knock a little corner of the black cloud off. Finally, after some maneuvering and jumping, a piece of fluffy blackness fell onto the ground in front of Mary. It bounced on the ground a few times, then rolled around. It looked alive.

Mary picked it up and played with it in her hands. "It feels so sad. It feels heavy and wet."

"Let me feel." Mimi grabbed the piece of the blackness from her sister with her only hand. "I want to eat it. I want it inside of me."

"You can't eat it!" fired Mano.

"Why not?"

"Ok, go ahead and eat it," he said resigned.

"No, here, I'll eat it first." Mary grabbed the piece from her sister's weak grip, and touched it to the tip of her tongue.

"Go on, eat it." With her one hand, Mimi pushed Mary's elbow up so that the blackness smeared on her nose.

"Fuck off!" Mary wiped the smear off on the end of her

sleeve. The end of her sleeve glowed, but only Mano and Pepe noticed. "I'm going to eat it. Just give me a second." She stretched her neck in preparation.

Mimi grew impatient and grabbed part of the blackness for herself, and put half of it in her mouth immediately.

"Hey! What are you doing? That's mine," shouted Mary.

"It's not anyone's!" Pepe reminded everyone.

"What's it taste like?" Enid asked Mimi. Both Mary and Enid leaned in for an answer.

Mimi swallowed her bite of cloud, and her mood changed entirely. The corners of her eyes softened. She looked back at the river. "It tastes like nothing."

"What do you mean it tastes like nothing?" Mimi still held a piece of her piece of blackness in her hands.

"Yeah, what does nothing taste like?" seconded Enid.

"Like nothing. I don't know. It tastes like the past."

Mano walked over to the triangle of girls. He turned them into a square of three girls and one boy. "Give it back, please." He held out his hand.

Mary mindlessly gave what she had left back to Mano, because her eyes were now on something else entirely. She quickly became much more interested in the thing wrapped in a bed sheet that Pepe was sitting on. "Wait! What is that?!" Mary asked.

"Is that a dead body!?" Mimi shouted.

Pepe stood up and yelled. "It's nothing. Get the fuck out of here!" He pointed toward the factory. "I'll tell The Foreman you've been out late at night, and all your parents, too."

Mary became a different kind of animal after Pepe's threat. "The Foreman doesn't give a fuck about anything you have to tell him." Her face twisted. "I also have a feeling that The Butcher would be pretty interested to learn that you were out of your house while he slept, walking your *boyfriend* and his stupid poodle down by the river in the middle of the night, carrying a wrapped up dead body around. That doesn't sound so good, does it? I bet he thinks you're at home asleep. Doesn't he?"

"You don't know anything about me." Pepe's voice was backing down.

"Hmm, maybe I'll go with my mother tomorrow to the butcher shop and let him know, just as he's cutting the leg from a lamb with the cleaver you sharpened." Mary looked at the dead body. "Now, tell me, Pepe, what exactly do we have here?

Mano pleaded. "Please, don't."

"Mary, let's go home. Leave him alone," said Enid, siding with Mano.

"What's everyone's problem?" Mary made her case. We're just going to have a quick look. It's a dead body! We're not going to hurt it. How could we possibly hurt it?"

Sisi's toes peeked out of the sheet and looked like white flowers in the moonlight.

"Who is this?" demanded Mary.

Mano felt faint, and fell into the bushes. He couldn't see anything but a purple blur on the edges of his vision. Pepe stumbled over to Mano and held him. He wiped sweat from Mano's face while answering Mary's demands. "It's nobody!" shouted Pepe.

"Did you kill her?" shouted Mary back.

"Yeah, did you kill her?" echoed Mimi.

Enid pulled on Mary's elbow. "Let's go home."

Mano was trying not to pass out. "Please, just go away and leave us alone."

"Oh my god, you killed someone? Who did you kill?" asked Mary.

"Let's just look," suggested Mimi.

"This isn't right, Mary." Enid put both of her arms around Mary's waist and tried to turn her around. But it was too late. Mary had lifted the sheet to see an arm, and she had become something more like a wolf than a girl. As she picked up the arm, she pulled on it so slightly just to show the others. But the entire arm fell off. Sisi's body was so sodden from a decade of soaking in the bathtub that it came apart at the slightest tug, like wet paper.

Mary held Sisi's whole arm in her arms. "Her arm fell off."

That's the last thing Mano heard before passing out.

"Get out of here! Leave her alone!" shouted Pepe as he lowered Mano's body carefully to the ground.

Enid ran over to Pepe and Mano to help.

"I have her whole leg now, too. It fell off when I touched it." Mary laughed wildly.

It all happened too fast to be stopped. Mary moved quickly to uncover the sheet near Sisi's head so that she could look at her face. To her surprise, she didn't recognize the body. She moved Sisi's head so that it would look straight up, so that she could get a better look, but Sisi's head fell off into her hands. "Her head fell off."

Pepe let Enid hold Mano. She held his head and tried to fan his face with her empty hand.

Pepe tried to kick Mary off the body, but it was like kicking a wolf off half a bloody sheep. Mary growled and scowled, and showed her fangs.

Mimi said, "Look, I have two arms now." She waved Sisi's other arm around in the air by her deformed shoulder, which looked like a squashed pumpkin with a dirty sweatshirt on.

As quickly as the scavenging began, it ended. The two girls had already scattered, like the wolves they had become, each of them with whole parts of Sisi in their arms. Mary had Sisi's head, a leg, and an arm, and Mimi on her back. In Mimi's arm was an arm.

What remained was nothing that could be recognized as a corpse. Her body looked like what's left of a smoked trout after it's been eaten. Pepe and Enid couldn't even really see the spine. It was just some other kind of deathly remainder. The death of a death. A good death that died horribly.

Enid and Pepe shared an instinct to put Sisi back together before Mano woke up, to gather her parts up in the sheet, and carry what remained to the river. But there were no good recognizable parts left. There was no center. Only fleshy smears. A thing with no center can not be held or lifted. There wasn't enough left of Sisi to be a thing.

Enid sat silently next to Mano while Pepe wadded up the bed sheet. He held the sheet in front of him like a baby.

"Go home, Enid."

"Can I...I want..." Enid wanted to help somehow, wanted to erase any involvement of her own in the previous ten minutes. She started to pick up what remained of the piece of black cloud on the ground.

"Go home!" Pepe yelled at her this time.

Enid tried not to cry.

Mano was barely awake. He thought maybe he was dreaming the two voices that were now crying and yelling on the other side of his closed eyes. He thought about that word: *Home*. His home, now, was everywhere, scattered into every dark corner.

"But what about..." Enid started to ask any question.

"Enid, please."

Enid kissed Mano on the forehead. Mano wondered if it was Pepe who kissed him, but he could tell that it wasn't Pepe's lips doing the kissing. Mano pursed his lips a little. A kiss there would solve something, he thought, but he wasn't quite sure what.

As Enid walked away, Sisi's black cloud broke into two, a kind of transference of misery. Half of it followed Enid a few feet above her head down the hill. She looked up and liked it there. It made her feel close to Mano. The other half hovered over Mano as he considered opening his eyes to see Pepe, or keeping them closed so that he wouldn't have to see what had become of his mother.

It would be dark for a few more hours. Neither boy said a

word. There was little to say or do. There was nowhere to go back to. The only thing either of them could do was to lie on their backs and close their eyes. Listen to the river. Wait for the sun to come up through the trees.

Pepe set the bed sheet next to Mano, and then lay beside him. Pepe wanted to tell Mano that he loved him, but something in the back of his throat stopped him. It wasn't the time, maybe. He thought to just be quiet, and to hold his hand. That was all there was to do. Instead, he said, "Mano, I'm sorry."

Inside of Pepe's hand, Mano's hand felt like a new heart that beats on the outside. A new heart to replace his old dead one.

"Thank you, Pepe."

Then Pepe died.

END OF PART ONE

PART TWO

15.

"Pehhh...payyy."

Mano's eyes had been closed for so long that everything looked brighter when he finally opened them again. Everything was so bright, Mano thought he was dead. The black poodle was sitting on a rock. The black cloud was gone. The Reckoner must have already stood itself back up, and his blood must have already washed away in the rain.

The top of a fern twitched and squeaked. Mano walked carefully toward the fern, ready to fight, and saw his mother's bed sheet there. He must have carried it with him into the woods in the hours before the sun came up. A sharp pain flashed behind Mano's eyeballs when he saw his mother's sheet. It was better now to be dead, Mano thought. Death is nothing, and nothing was all he could handle at the moment.

Mano carefully pushed the fern aside with his foot. Two black birds were pecking at the sheet, trying to get out. In the folds, they were preening their wings. They had pecked two perfectly round holes from the center of the sheet. He unfolded his mother's sheet to look at the birds. They were just as he had always imagined. Once free, they swooped through the air in three giant circles and then landed on the bare branches of The Reckoner. They were the most beautiful animals he had ever seen.

"How did you get in there?"

Mano removed his glasses, and slipped the sheet over his head. He lined up the pecked-out eye holes over his eyes, and placed his glasses over his eyes on the outside of the sheet. Everything lined up just perfectly. He felt at home inside his mother's bed sheet. The black birds perched on top of his ghost head. Their claws scratched at his head lovingly

"Thank you, ma'am. They're just what I wanted."

Then he floated back out through the woods the same way that he imagined he must have come in.

Back in town, in the back chamber of Lady Blood, Father Mothers III was preparing for the next weekend's fiery homily about the contract with hell that non-believers were signing. With Lil' Jorge watching from his stool in the corner, Mothers practiced gesturing wildly with his hands in front of a mirror. He pushed his finger into his fist, back and forth, to illustrate what God's Finger was doing to those who sinned. Lil' Jorge attempted the gesture with his own fingers, but it just looked like he was polishing an apple.

"No, like this." Mothers held Lil' Jorge's wrist with one hand, and pulled on his index finger with the other. "We're being killed like this because we're sinners."

Lil' Jorge nodded and smiled.

Mothers' teeth jutted outward like a beaver as he practiced a few lines about the black birds of Hell. "If you see a black bird, it's here only because it lost its way in the forests of Hell."

"What's a bird?" asked Lil' Jorge, still bumbling on his own with the God's Finger gesture.

"They're from Hell. They're bad. They swallow boys and girls who didn't go to church, and they carry their bodies in their bellies back to Hell with them. They vomit the boys' and girls' bodies back up in Hell and the boys and girls would have to live there forever, in Hell."

"Is this right?" Lil' Jorge got it just right.

Mano walked down the hill through the woods back toward The Cure. A small crowd had already gathered on the edge of the river right where he had left Pepe's body. Now that he was a ghost with two black birds on his head, Mano felt more alive than ever before. He felt good and bright, and he wanted to shine like an oracle for everyone in town. He knew this would be a perfect chance for him to announce his first revelations, he thought, to tell them a few things he had recently learned about death.

Mano thought he could save the people of Pie Time from their irrational fears of God's Finger. He thought that his new job could become making revelations, and the people of Pie Time would write about his revelations instead of writing about God's Finger. There is no Hell in death—this Mano could prove. The word would get out. Everyone would be freed from needing church, freed from their fear of death, from their fear of fear. And they would have Mano to thank for that.

During his walk toward the crowd, Mano was considering his first revelation. He decided he would start by addressing everyone as friends. "Friends, gather around. I am a new ghost. I am real and am in no way a threat to you. I am just a thing, not evil, but just a thing just like you, how you are just things. I love being dead. And you will soon love it, too," he'd start. He'd kiss dead Pepe for the first time, and everyone would watch their kiss. Mano smiled.

"Pepe!" Mitzi Let screamed. It was a sound that pierced the constant rushing water noise of The Cure from inside the gathering crowd.

Pepe's body was dead on the ground in the center of about a dozen people. Everyone there was examining Pepe's dead body, and the strange thing that had become of it. Enid Pine was crying, and she seemed to be answering everyone's questions.

"Pepe! My baby!" screamed Mitzi.

Mano, the ghost with his glasses over the eyeholes, standing inside his dead mother's bed sheet, stood still on the opposite side of The Cure, near the footbridge, watching. He was too far away to hear Mitzi's screams from the other side of the river. Still, he figured everyone would be able to hear him from where he stood. Everyone's backs were to him while he started.

"Friends! Friends!" Mano yelled, and gestured his hands to bring the crowd over the footbridge toward him. But no one could hear Mano. "Friends! Gather around!" He tried again.

Instead, Mitzi shouted at the sky.

Mano persisted. "Friends! I am dead, but..." he started.

No one turned around.

Mano looked closer at the gathering and felt his heart go hollow. He saw through a few legs and arms that someone was holding Mitzi as she leaned forward on her hands and knees.

"I don't know. I don't know." That's all Enid could seem to say.

Mano quietly spoke only to himself inside the sheet in front of his mouth. "I am just a thing," he mumbled. "I am not evil. I am just a thing—just like you...you and me are just things." His breath got shorter. "I love...I love..." He couldn't quite say it.

A few minutes earlier, Mary and Mimi Minutes had interrupted Mothers' homily practice in the back chamber of Lady Blood, with the news of the most recent death. Mothers approached the crowd, trailed by Lil' Jorge. He was adjusting his white collar, having just been summoned, and was dressing himself as he walked.

"I love Pepe," Mano continued now as he watched the crowd swallow up Mothers and Lil' Jorge from afar. He spoke almost silently, only to himself.

The chattering from the crowd grew as loud as the river until a few minutes later Mothers rose out of the middle of it on the shoulders of The Builder and The Baker. "Friends!" he yelled, "gather around!"

Mano's ghost body felt reluctant to cross the footbridge to gather around.

"...We are all in the presence of Evil..." continued Mothers.

Mano tried to interrupt as loudly as he could from the other side of the river. "No, no, that's just it, we are not!" He could no longer feel any warmth in his chest. "That's what I was trying to tell you..."

Mothers continued uninterrupted, "...We're being

punished for our sins…" He was gesturing now with his index finger and fist, taking his finger out to point at everyone. "His finger is pointing out Evil!"

"No, no, see, look at me!" shouted Mano.

But no one looked at Mano. Everyone was crossing themselves while looking at Mothers.

"What was in it?" Nana Pine whispered

The Banker answered her by pointing at a broken accordion. A few minutes earlier, The Butcher had thrown the accordion to the ground in a fit of rage that the people of Pie Time hadn't seen publicly for many years.

The Butcher screamed at Pepe. His screams became a long slow whine. "My son, the sinner." He kicked the accordion until it looked like a small bag of logs.

"What is it?" Nana asked him.

The Banker shrugged his shoulders.

No one but Mano seemed to know what an accordion was. "Your son loved polka music," said Mano underneath his sheet, but still no one heard him. And still no one noticed his ghost body standing on the other side of The Cure. Mano felt like he couldn't move. He could only watch Pepe's body from a distance as it was wrapped up in a blanket. He watched as everyone eventually left. Mano had nowhere to go.

"Pepe? Where are you? We can kiss now. We're dead together."

Once the sun went down, Mano finally crossed The Cure over the footbridge. He pushed his arms out from beneath his mother's bed sheet, and picked up the accordion. It felt heavier than he expected. He liked the weight in his arms. He smelled it, and hugged it, and as he hugged it to his chest, to his own surprise, he heard himself playing the instrument beautifully. He didn't know that he knew how to play the accordion, but he did. He discovered that he already knew how to play three dirges. So he played all three. And when he tried to play a fourth, he noticed that he was just playing the first dirge again, so he played the first dirge again, in its entirety. And then the other two again, too. All night, his arms moved in and out, in and out, and out came the dirges.

16.

For three days and nights, inside his mother's bed sheet, with his glasses over the eyeholes, two black birds perched atop his head, an accordion strapped to his back, and a black poodle following him, Mano haunted Pie Time. On that first morning, he set off from his barbershop, where he picked up the radio that Pepe found in the dumpster. He held it underneath his arm, underneath his bed sheet. If the people he loved were going to die, he thought, then he would learn to love *things*. If he was going to love things, and things only, then he would have to carry them. The only way that things can die is if you lose them. The only way you can lose things is if you set them down. He could hardly fit through the barbershop door with all of his things in tow.

Like a wagon beginning to pick up and haul things at the beginning of the day, Mano floated to the factory to haunt it. He floated in through the front doors, and then past the room where, in his younger living days, he used to clock in and change into his work clothes, and then past the steaming machines. He stood at the very spot where The Foreman liked to have him drop his trousers to get spankings in front of everyone, all of the girls at the factory, and sometimes The Goods, too. None of the girls working in the factory saw this ghost floating there. It was the first time, from that spot, where Mano didn't feel watched. Instead, he was watching them. Enid Pine tucked two cigarettes into her socks and looked around for The Foreman, who was behind her, asleep in a chair. Mary lit a cigarette for Mimi.

Mano floated past the girls, past The Foreman, and into the back room where The Goods often spent their afternoons together while The Foreman kept a poor watch over the thieving fingers of the girls. The back room was much bigger than he had imagined—much much bigger. It was nearly half the size of the factory itself. Where did all this room come from, Mano wondered, and how could it possibly fit within the walls of the factory? What he imagined to be a small room with concrete walls lined with metal shelves and folders, something that smelled like paper and metal and cigarette smoke, was more like the opposite of what he imagined. The back room looked more like a banquet hall, or the drawing room of a mansion. There were no metal shelves and no stacks of paper. There was, however, cigarette smoke, which filled the air in the room.

On the back wall, furthest away from the door where Mano entered, were three large portrait paintings. The one in the middle was a portrait of a woman wearing a hat that looked like a hot water bottle. The other two were of men, one of whom was holding trophies in his hands, and the other was cutting a giant piece of cake with a giant knife. Behind Mano was a fireplace, crackling with a new log.

In the center of the room was a long shiny table made of black wood. The Goods were sitting together in the last two seats on one side at the far end of the table. Two men and one woman were sitting opposite from them. The three of them were identical to each other. They were even all dressed exactly alike, in grey suits and grey ties. Mano wasn't able to tell the two men and one woman apart, and he didn't recognize them either. Everything about them was grey, even their hair, and their ears. In fact, the closer Mano looked, and the longer he examined them, the less sure he was that they were actually three separate people at all.

At the very end of the table was The Banker, who on account of his shortness, sat upon a booster seat made of wooden Pie Time shipping boxes. The seat was so large that he became the tallest person at the table. On its side, the box read *It's High Time for a Pie Time.*

"Go on," goaded The Banker, lowering his half-glasses.

A few feet behind him sat The Lawyer, who was mostly obscured by shadows, and who said nothing. He wrote things in his notebook with a silver pen.

"They're like exoskeletons," said The Businessman, who was actually three people. Their voice was like a cat's. The Goods and The Businessman were all smoking Pie Times. June was wearing pearls and a fur coat.

"Are they heavy?" Vera asked.

"No, not at all. They're made out of something like iron. They're light enough to wear all day long, and to sleep in, but strong enough..."

"So, they're made out of iron?" Vera asked for clarification.

"It's like iron, but lighter."

"Like iron...?"

"Right."

"So, it's not iron?"

"It's a lot like it."

June had had enough of the discussion of materiality. "But do they *look* good?" she asked.

The Businessman opened a file on the table that held several sketches. The Goods and The Banker leaned in to look at them. They shuffled a few of the sketches between each other, and then they looked at each other and smiled.

"Can they come in different colors?"

"Any color under the sun," answered The Businessman.

"What kind of price are we talking?" asked The Banker.

"They'll be expensive...at first..."

June interrupted again. She had a knack for hearing what she wanted to hear in what goes unsaid in other people's sentences. "It's no matter. They'll buy it. They'll love it." June was excited that her factory would be making something other than beer and cigarettes, something that could save people's lives.

Vera was much more skeptical. "Are they safe?"

The Lawyer shuffled in his chair in the shadows, and wrote something down with his silver pen.

"Is living under God's Finger safe?" argued The Businessman. "Yes, they're safer than living that risk."

Mano felt the room getting bigger, very slowly. The three portraits were retreating from him, and the fireplace was moving further away from behind him. But the people at the table didn't notice. They kept talking.

"What do you suggest they be called?" asked Vera.

"We're thinking about XO?" suggested The Businessman.

"Yes, perfect. XO"

"Yes, XO."

"XO Skeletons."

"No, that'll just remind them of death. How about XO Cages?"

"XO Cages..." June was trying that name on for size. "X...O...Cages..." She was looking at the ceiling.

To Mano, as the room expanded, everyone's voices began to echo in the expanse.

"Hmm...XO Cages...that feels like a trap, like you're trapped in the thing," said Vera.

"How about XO *Life* Cages?"

"Yes! Life Cages. Cages for Life."

Everyone seemed pleased enough. The room was so big now, far bigger than the factory itself, and maybe as big as half of Pie Time. Mano could barely see the portraits, and the warmth of the fire was long gone. He even felt far away now from the people at the table, whom he could see were signing papers. Some were smoking. Some were laughing. Some were shaking hands.

Then, in the blackness to his right, he could hear Enid Pine's voice, like a spider tangled in its own long web. Her voice was so clear that he could see its web glisten, and he followed it down, from the corner of a ceiling he was now floating in, into a kitchen with yellow walls. A white porcelain sink full of mounds of fresh strawberries. Nana Pine had just picked them from her patch, and was preparing them to sell at market. Black and white tile floor. From directly above them both, Mano could now see the top of Enid's head, and the top of her mother's head. A small bowl of strawberries in a bowl on the kitchen table. Nana was leaning back in a chair at the table, arms crossed.

"You have one last chance, Enid. Tell me where it came from."

"It was just *there*, in the tree, on my way home from the factory," swore Enid.

"I know you didn't find this finger in the tree." Nana stood up and held a bluish finger by the top knuckle, like holding a tiny plucked chicken by the neck. She shook it in front of Enid's face.

"I did, I did." Enid was crying.

"And why would you bring a finger into this house? A finger, Enid!"

"I wanted to keep it."

"What would you possibly *do* with a finger?"

"I think it's beautiful."

"Whose is it? Look at me and tell me the truth." Nana waited for her daughter to look up and into her eyes. "*Whose... finger*...is this?"

Enid paused, then answered by copying her mother's cadence. "*I...don't*...know."

"Did Mary put you up to this?"

"Put me up to what? We didn't do anything *wrong*." Enid was growing tired of the inquisition, so she lowered her shoulders as if to make a confession. "It's Pepe's."

"Pepe Let?"

From his place on the ceiling above them, Mano became angry. He felt protective of Pepe.

Enid started in on a story to satisfy her mother's insistence. "Pepe was dragging a body to the river, and we were out late..."

"Who?" Nana was afraid if she broke eye contact with Enid, that Enid would stop giving up information.

"Me and Mary. And Mimi, too. After you went to sleep. I'm sorry. I'm sorry! But it was just us girls. And we were smoking Pie Times at The Cure, and Pepe came with the body. He was laughing and he gave us all a piece of it. He gave me a finger, and he gave Mimi an arm, which he thought was pretty funny, and then he gave Mary the head. It was like he was just handing out slices of cake. I didn't want it, but he made me take it." Enid worked herself into a real cry, even though she wasn't telling the real truth. She couldn't bear her involvement in the real truth, for Mano's sake. She couldn't bear to confess that truth to herself. "I don't know any more than that. I shouldn't have taken it. I'm sorry, I'm..."

Nana calmed her daughter down by putting a hand on her thigh. "Enid, it's ok. It's ok. It's only important that you tell me the truth."

Like the universe, the room Mano was in didn't stop expanding. The kitchen ceiling above where Mano floated was spilling into the blackness. Enid and her mother were still barely in focus, but they were beginning to blur. "It's the truth," Enid said. Sisi's finger was on a cutting board on the table.

Mano felt so hurt by Enid's half truth, how his mother was missing from it. He remembered how he was missing her now, too. He wanted to find her somewhere in this new ever-expanding system of death, orbiting in the blackness and warmth around some new star. As Mano tumbled through the void, he heard Inez Roar's voice moaning in the distance behind him.

Mano found himself standing behind a lamp in the dark. He could feel the lamp with his hand, and he felt for the chain. He pulled down the chain, and when the lamp lit the room, Inez was in the center of her own very large bed, wearing nothing. She was on her back, resting on both elbows. Her head was back, and her chin, pointing upward as she moaned, was the highest peak of the mountain range of her body. Her square shoulders were the second highest peak. And her breasts—full, round and red from nursing Baby Zuzu—were the third. Her nipples were hard. Her knees bent toward Mano.

"I know it's you." Inez lowered herself all the way onto her back and felt the back of her own thighs with her hands.

"Me?" Mano hid behind the light of the lamp, the only light in the room.

"Mano, come."

"Can you see me?" he asked. Mano looked down at his body in the sheet, and the things he held, and questioned his death for the first time.

"Yes. Of course. And I know you can see me, too, because I gave you those glasses you're wearing."

Mano put his hand up to his glasses, which he was wearing on the outside of the sheet. He took them off for just a second, and wiped them clean with his ghost sheet. Then he put them back on. He wanted to see Inez's body, all of it, everything all at once. Other than his mother, Mano had never seen a woman's naked body before. But Inez's body was different. The sight of it—how her knees slid back and forth in her sweat waiting for him to say something—filled Mano up with an ache, an insatiable new hunger.

"What are those things on your head?"

"Oh." His own visibility was still a surprise to him. "Birds."

"What are birds?"

"They fly." Mano jerked his head so they'd fly, but the birds just stayed there. "So, you can also see them? You can see everything?"

"Mano, you're not a ghost, you know? You're not dead."

"I'm not?"

"No, you're not. And neither am I. No one's dead but the dead. Now come here and touch me wherever you want to touch me. You'll see how not dead you are."

Mano wasn't ready to re-enter the world of the living so quickly. He didn't budge. He only stared. He could see her whole body all at once. And he felt her watching him, too. The ever-expanding universe that Mano had been floating in had suddenly contracted, and became just a room. Inez's bedroom.

Mano noticed Baby Zuzu's bassinet in the shadows on the other side of the bed. "Is that Zuzu?"

"It is. She's asleep."

"Isn't she going to hear"

"Hear what?"

"Inez, please..."

"Hear what, Mano? Hear me moan? Hear you take off all your things and get into this bed with me?"

"I...she..." Mano felt tangled in this new lust.

"She's a baby, Mano. It's ok. She's never cried."

"But..."

"Mano, take off that heavy broken accordion, and give it to me." Until just then, Mano had forgotten that the accordion was on his back. He didn't want to give it up, but he couldn't bear to make Inez upset in a state like this. Inez turned onto her side, her back turned to Baby Zuzu's bassinet, and faced Mano completely. Her breasts fell to the side, and her left knee became the new highest peak. Mano imagined his hand sliding up her right thigh, up and up, where everything gets softer than it already was, warmer, wetter, and darker.

While keeping the radio pinned beneath his arm, Mano took the accordion from his back, and walked it over to Inez. Inez placed it clumsily on the bed beside her, and then moved her hand over the top of it like it was a person, like she was stroking its hair. The accordion made a sound as she touched one of its keys, but the sound didn't surprise her at all.

"That's Pepe's accordion. He wanted to be in a polka band."

"Mano...shhh."

Mano felt like he was in trouble, but it was the kind of trouble he could learn to like. "I'm sorry."

"You should be. Pepe isn't here right now. Now take off your sheet and give it to me."

"No." Mano thought of what remained of his mother in the sheet. "I can't."

"Mano, give me that sheet. You're no ghost. You can't go around wearing a sheet if you're not a ghost."

Mano wanted to explain, but he knew that Inez would only shush him again. And there was no other answer he could have given Inez other than ok.

"Ok," he pulled the sheet up and over his head. The two black birds flapped off his head, and then re-landed on his head. Their claws scratched up a cowlick between them. Mano handed the wadded sheet to Inez. He worried she'd be able to smell his mother's death inside of it. Mano wasn't a ghost anymore. He was now alive again and in the world. A man in the world. A man. A radio under his arm. The black poodle quiet near his feet. He felt his own man-weight in his shoes.

"Pretend this is you." Inez looked at Mano without ever looking away. She wrapped the broken accordion with the bed sheet, then she rolled over onto it. Her body was facing the bed now, and she was much higher in the air as she straddled the accordion.

Mano watched Inez's body move, while she watched him watch her. He watched her ass as it clinched and then relaxed like she was trying to grind the sheet-wrapped accordion deep into the center of the bed. Her grinding became stronger and stronger. The muscles in her legs flexed.

Baby Zuzu awoke in her bassinet. "Milk!"

Inez kept grinding.

"Zuzu wants milk," Mano tried to interrupt as if Inez hadn't heard Zuzu's call.

Mano could see the black hair between Inez's legs move

back and forth on his mother's sheet, like she was brushing it dirty.

"Zuzu doesn't get this milk. It's for you."

As Inez moved, she made a song with the accordion. She made the accordion pump in and out, in and out, and Mano could recognize Ba Ba Black Sheep in its melody, a song that he and his mother used to sing together when he was a very small child. In his head, he sang it while Inez fucked the accordion.

Ba ba black sheep, have you any wool? Yes, sir, yes, sir, three bags full.

Mano felt his body get harder, and sadder, as the melody of the accordion sped up. It sped up until the song became unrecognizable to him. It became just a single long pump of sound, a moan or a whine, and it mixed with the sound of Baby Zuzu in her bassinet.

"Milk!"

Mano was so hard, so sad, all alone in the world, no mother, no Pepe, watching the sheet, watching the accordion break and pump, ba ba black sheep. Inez's body suddenly deflated. It looked as broken now as the accordion.

"Milk, milk!" Zuzu screamed.

Inez refilled her lungs with air and turned her head to look at Mano. After three or four long breaths, she managed to say, "I miss my husband."

Together they pushed hard the sorrow down, and deep back inside.

17.

Mano was sore. He was resting on his back on the floor next to the black square in the back room of his barbershop. He blinked, rubbed his eyes, and zipped up his pants. All the things he loved, except his mother's sheet, were still with him, attached to parts of his body, beneath his arm, on his head, and behind him, like a shadow. The accordion, more broken than before, with a living layer of Inez Roar glazed upon it, played a long slow note of struggle as Mano rolled onto his elbow.

Mano could hear the voices of many men in his barbershop.

"It's true. I saw it with my own eyes. It was tragic, really," said The Businessman.

When Mano opened the door and stepped from the back room into the main room of the barbershop, he found nearly a half dozen men crowded together, forming a line from the front door. The Builder, The Bartender, and The Repairman were standing against the wall just inside the shop's front door, and The Lawyer, The Inn Keeper, and The Chef were sitting in the three chairs along the wall. The Businessman, who were three people in total, were squeezed into the single barber's chair in front of the mirror. The Businessman had three bushes of grey hair on their heads.

"What are those things on your head?" asked The Businessman.

"They're called birds," answered Mano.

"Birds? What do *birds* do?"

"They fly. But these just sit on my head."

The Businessman glanced at The Lawyer, who anticipated their question and shook his head no.

The Chef changed the subject. "You need a bigger barbershop. Business is good, yes?" And then he answered his own question. "Business is good."

"I suppose it is," Mano said, a little stunned from his

sudden entrance back into the living world which was full of people who needed haircuts. "One at a time. One at a time. That's all I can do," Mano smiled for The Chef through his waking haze. "Is it good for you, too?"

"Couldn't be better," answered The Chef. "All the new people in town are coming in for the cheap sheep special. It's not *baaaaa*d I tell them. Not *baaaaa*d at all. And they all laugh."

No one in the barbershop really laughed.

"I can vouch for that," said The Businessman. "It's not bad. And it's cheap."

"Business is good at the inn, too," said The Inn Keeper. He went on to explain how a few travelers heard word of God's Finger and wanted to visit Pie Time out of curiosity.

"And those that God's Finger has left behind need to drink," added the Bartender.

The attention everyone was giving Mano had run dry, and they turned their attention back to The Businessman, so they could finish their story they were in the middle of.

"Just a shave and a little off the sides please, sir, and thank you," said The Businessman to Mano. Mano sharpened the blade of his razor with a leather strap. Then The Businessman continued. "So, when we all came back into the room, there she was under the table."

"She was *under* the table?" asked The Chef.

"Yeah, how did she get under there?" asked The Inn Keeper.

"Hell, we don't know *how* she got under there, or why. We all left to tour the rest of the factory, and she wasn't in the group," said The Businessman.

The Lawyer nodded his head in agreement.

"So Ms. Good ran back to the room to get her, and she screamed. We all ran back to see what was the matter, and there she was, dead, under the table."

"It was God's Finger," concluded The Chef.

"A real shame," added The Builder.

The Lawyer opened his mouth to say something, but just wrote in his notebook instead. Mano leaned The Businessman back as they were talking, and he rubbed their grey face with oil.

The Businessman continued, nearly prone, "It was our first time seeing a death hole up close. It was just like the others, as far as we understand."

All the others sighed a single sigh, knowingly. They looked at each other in some mutual understanding while The Businessman, who had only been in Pie Time for a few days, were back in Mano's hands, looking at the water stains on the lowered ceiling of the shop.

"What was in it?" Mano asked.

The others looked disgusted by his question.

"*In* it? You mean, in the *hole*?"

"Yeah," said Mano, "...in the hole."

"Well, now that you ask, there was a hot water bottle in there."

"A hot water bottle? Huh, you don't say?" said The Builder. "I wonder why God would leave behind a hot water bottle."

"In fact, it's right here." The Businessman pointed to their briefcase. "We put it in our briefcase just to get it out of the way."

"Do you mind?" asked Mano.

The Businessman lifted their head and looked around at everyone else in the room, and then finally at The Lawyer. The Lawyer nodded his head yes. "No, we don't suppose we do."

The Lawyer rifled through The Businessman's very large briefcase and found the hot water bottle. It was red and made of rubber. It was just like the one in the portrait painting Mano saw in the back room of the factory. The Lawyer handed it to Mano, who set down his razor on the counter. Mano filled the rubber bottle with hot water and then he lifted his shirt. He readjusted the accordion on his back, and tucked the radio further up into his armpit. He pressed the water bottle against his lower back. "Ahhh, this is just what I needed," he exhaled. Mano then secured the bottle to his lower back by wrapping it around his stomach with the paper that he used to keep hair off of his customers' collars. Mano added one more thing to his body, which was now bigger because of it. He put his shirt back down around the bottle, and picked his razor back up.

"It was only taking up room in our bag. You're welcome to it for keeps."

Mano thanked The Businessman as the muscles in his back softened.

"Why are you holding all those things?" asked The Baker.

"I love them," said Mano.

The Builder put his head back against the wall, and steered the conversation back to the original main road. "What a tragedy. June Good was a good one. She kept this town humming, no doubt. Before her and The Foreman, Pie Time was just a smear on the map. Simply tragic."

Everyone nodded in solemn agreement. The Chef put his head in his hands and added, "She was the class of Pie Time. Tragic, indeed!"

"The real tragedy of it is when we had to tell The Foreman about her death," said The Businessman between their teeth. They didn't want to move their jaws while Mano shaved them with a straight edge. "He didn't take it well. Not at all."

"But how was Vera? How did *she* take it?" Mano asked.

"*Ms.* Good?" clarified The Businessman.

Mano nodded his head yes.

Everyone looked at Mano, confused.

"What do you mean, son? I'm sure Ms. Good was as sad as everyone else, but The Foreman, he lost *so* much. He lost his wife under that table. He was a real mess."

"Oh, right, yes, of course." Mano backed away from the good intentions of his question.

The Repairman had been steaming, and finally bubbled over. "This has *got* to stop! We need to put a stop to this! Before long, we'll all die, just like that. We're bound to this death now, God's Finger. We're all just biding our times until it happens to us. But, what can we do about it? That's what I say. What can we *do*. It's time we do something about it before we all have death holes in our chests, like Mothers says, like the dirty sinful little mice that we are."

The Businessman sat up in the barber chair with the same motion that corpses sit up from their coffins. Now they were facing the line of men who were all charged by The Repairman's speech. Mano stayed small behind them cutting their hair with his shears.

"Have you thought about protection?" the Businessman inquired, as if they were taking a survey.

The Lawyer looked sternly at The Businessman, and forced a cough.

The Chef started rambling, as if he was offended by The Businessman's question. "What do you mean, have we thought about protection? We're dealing with God's Finger! We're being poked all the way through, one at a time! So if you think we haven't thought of protecting ourselves, well then..."

"We're just being blessed too hard," argued The Chef, as if to remind everyone of the complexity of the situation. "We need to protect ourselves from God's blessings."

"Then why haven't you done it yet?" pressed The Businessman. "It's clear that Pie Time has a new kind of death to deal with. That's not in dispute. So why aren't you protecting yourselves from God's Finger so that you don't die like dirty mice?"

"Of course, but I don't see..."

"We just have to be better..."

The Businessman interrupted. Their eyes were lighting up. This was their chance. "No, no. Being better doesn't mean you can't also protect yourselves. Now, how much would you *pay* for it? To be protected against your future pokings?"

The Lawyer looked around at the results of the survey without moving his head.

"Anything, I suppose."

"I'd pay anything."

"Of course, anything."

The freed grey hairs of The Businessman were like confetti around their heads now. The grey hairs lit up in the rising sun through the barbershop window, and their new shorn heads looked as if they were in a bright snow globe. "That's it then! I believe you. It's coming, friends. Your new life without fear is near! Trust in *me*."

The Businessman then rose to their feet, dramatically pulling off their own barbershop cape, and undoing their own paper collars. They asked The Builder if he'd like to get a drink with him at The Bartender's bar that night. Everyone seemed to be in agreement.

There were problems. The Businessman could smell them. And these were problems to be solved by business.

18.

In a very short time, Father Mothers III's reign as priest had become the most productive reign in the brief history of Pie Time. With the money he had raised from his father's death, Mothers built a bigger and better cross on the top of Lady Blood. He used his father's plans which had been found nailed to the smaller original cross, but he doubled the size of his father's intended cross using the hired expertise of The Builder and the unusual strength of Lil' Jorge. The cross was now the size of five men, and could easily be seen from anywhere in Pie Time, and perhaps from anywhere in the entire valley.

The Builder climbed up onto the new cross to test its strength, and to nail the last nail. "As God intended," Mothers said to The Builder. "Pie Time will be safe now."

Because of Pie Time's recent fervor for attending church, Mothers had raised much more money than the money that he needed to build the cross. In addition, he built new pews for the growing congregation out of wood harvested from the trees west of Pie Time, and he built a new donation box out of the skull of his own father, Father Mothers II. It was, essentially, a pine box, but the lid of the box was the deceased priest's skull. The people could open the skull's mouth and just slide the money in. Mothers knew how much the children, especially, liked to push rolled-up cash directly through the teeth of their last priest.

However, Mothers' most talked about update was the new confession booth. The booth was built in such a way that Mothers could sit behind a screen designed to be directly in front of the confessor, and only the priest could see through the screen, and not the other way around. In this way, the priest could see the confessor in full frontal view, but the confessor could not see the priest.

Mothers had recently taken up an interest in photography,

and he liked to take photographs of the naked. He began saying things in his homilies like "A naked body is its most pure, free from sin, vulnerable to the lord." It was his idea then to photograph the naked bodies of his confessors at the very moment that they confessed, for the sake of invoking their truest confessions, for creating a condition of vulnerability and exposure in the face of new purity, for cleansing oneself of sin. And, as he saw it, people were dying rapidly at the hands of God's Finger, so his photographs were also taken for the sake of posterity. His record of sinners free from their sins were pinned to the north wall of Lady Blood for everyone to see. It quickly became clear to the believers of Pie Time exactly who had confessed, and who hadn't.

The first one to step into the new confession booth on its first morning of use was Vera Good. She was wearing a black veil and June Good's fur coat and pearls. Until she lifted the veil, Mothers thought he might be seeing the ghost of Mrs. Good.

"Good morning, Vera." Mothers took his place at the back of the confession booth behind the screen. Vera opened the door, and skeptically examined the new booth.

"What is this?" she asked, looking for a seat other than the seat that was placed directly in front of the screen.

"It's the new booth. Do you like it?"

Vera didn't answer. She set her veil on the hook on the back of the door. She saw another room to the side, behind a curtain, and took a step toward it. "There's another room? What's in there?"

"That's the changing room."

"What's it for?"

"I'm going to need you to take off your clothes before you confess, Vera. Truth can only come from the nude. There are hooks in there for you to hang up your clothes so they don't get dirty on the floor."

"But..." Vera considered objecting, but she didn't quite

know where to start.

"...and there is a mirror in there, too, and a light. Oh, and a sink. Take your time."

Distraught and bewildered, Vera entered the changing room of the confession booth as if she were entering a new room of a dream. She took off June's fur coat and pearls and hung them on a hook, and she took off June's long black dress and hung that on another hook. June's bra, June's tights, and June's panties were hung on the third hook. Vera stood naked in front of all those hanging clothes and cried.

"Vera, are you ok in there?" asked Mothers.

Vera didn't answer. She turned to look at her naked body in the mirror, but could only see June's naked body there. She could see June's long arms and June's long neck. She wanted to touch it, but there was nothing left of June to touch. She touched the cold steel faucet of the sink instead. She splashed cold water on her face. Then she pulled back the curtains and walked back into the main room of the confession booth completely naked, and faced the screen. "Forgive me, Father, for I have sinned."

"Yes, go on."

"I loved June Good. And June Good loved me." Just as Vera confessed, a bright hot flash of what seemed like lightning lit up the room. Vera fell violently backward against the door. "What was *that*?!" The wood felt cold and hard on her bare shoulders.

"Oh no, no. It was nothing," Mothers explained. "It's ok. I took your photograph just as you confessed."

"I shouldn't have come here," Vera said defeatedly, her back against the door. She retreated to the changing room, and put June's clothes back on. It felt good to put her arms and legs back inside the fabric of the person that she loved the most.

Mothers remained behind the screen. "Come back out, Vera. I have to give you your penance now."

"Just tell me." Vera put the veil back over her face, and looked at herself through it in the mirror. "I can hear you fine from in here."

"50 Our Fathers."

"50?" complained Vera.

"Yes, 50. We just can't be too careful these days. It's your love that may have killed her."

19.

There was so much hair on the floor of the barbershop later that afternoon that for a moment, Mano thought he might have lost the black poodle. He called for it, but it never barked. The poodle never made any sounds. So Mano swept all the brown, grey, black, and red hair of the men of Pie Time into a mountain range of hair, and through that valley appeared the black poodle.

"Let's go say goodbye to Pepe," Mano said to the poodle and to the birds on his head. Mano turned the open sign of the barbershop into a closed sign, and closed the door behind him. Last Street was busier than normal. There were already customers in the windows of The Bartender's bar and at The Chef's restaurant. Mano didn't recognize any of them. With his pockets full of coins from a full day's worth of haircuts, he walked to The Florist's flower shop to buy a handful of yellow ranunculus.

"One bouquet of yellow ranunculus, please."

The Florist picked a few yellow ranunculus and snipped the ends, and handed them to Mano. "One bouquet of yellow ranunculus for the man with things on his head. Where are you going to hold these?" The Florist rarely spoke, on account of his embarrassment of his thick accent.

Mano pushed up his glasses with his finger, and shuffled his accordion, radio, and hot water bottle around in order to reach out a hand.

"These things, what are they? These things, where do they come from?" asked The Florist.

Mano tucked the bouquet between the buttons of his shirt, and they stayed there. "I don't understand."

"These things..." The Florist pointed to the birds on Mano's head, and to the accordion on his back, "...are they..."

Mano finished his sentence for him, "...these things I love. These things, they are these things I love."

"So, you..."

"...they are these things, these things I love."

The Florist became frustrated and tried a different line of questioning. "Who are these beautiful flowers for? They are so beautiful. These flowers, they must be for someone beautiful."

"These flowers are for the beautiful, yes," Mano answered, trying not to pick up The Florist's accent. "And these flowers are so beautiful because these flowers are dying."

"Yes!" The Florist felt as though Mano understood him. "I am in the business of making beauty from death."

"We both are," Mano added.

The Florist agreed. "These flowers, they are for your poor Pepe?"

Mano felt relieved of what he had been hiding inside. "Yes, these flowers are for Pepe. How did..."

"I watch him come to your barbershop. I watch you two in there. He is beautiful. And he's even more beautiful now. We should not be so afraid of God's Finger." The Florist was the only person who recognized this love inside of Mano. The Florist threw up his hands. "To death!"

"Yes, to death!" Mano playfully agreed. He threw up one of his hands.

"Are you going to the river for Pepe now?"

"Yes, sir."

"Here, take another bouquet with you." The Florist snipped more ranunculus, arranged them quickly, and handed another bouquet to Mano. Without Mano reaching out his hand, The Florist poked them through the button of Mano's shirt just below the first bouquet. "Take these flowers to the river for me. And send them to their death."

"And in whose name am I sending them to their beautiful death?" Mano asked.

"Roberto."

"Roberto," Mano repeated to show The Florist that he

would be memorizing the name. "Roberto's a beautiful name."

"He made me laugh when we were boys."

"He sounds funny."

"He was, very."

The Florist and Mano said their goodbyes like new friends.

It started to rain on the footbridge of The Cure. Mano sat on the edge in the center of the bridge, readying himself to send flowers to their deaths in the name of both Roberto and Pepe. His feet dangled above the loud stream. He didn't mind getting wet. He thought about the last time he had cleaned his body. Usually, he washed himself while standing up in the large kitchen sink in the home he would never return to. But the days of that kind of cleaning were over. He wondered what it would feel like to just slide into The Cure with these flowers and finally get all the way clean, once and for all, tumbling and drowning into death. He watched the water rush from under the bridge, under his feet—it knew exactly where it was going.

"For Roberto." Mano held up the first bouquet of yellow ranunculus above his head, an offering to the rain to ready it for the river. Each blossom bloomed wide just before he dropped them between his knees into The Cure. "You were loved!" The bouquet tumbled and dipped below the surface, then came back up and got stuck on a rock. A few seconds later, it freed itself and disappeared downstream.

Mano swung the broken accordion from his back to his chest and he played its three dirges over the sound of the rushing water. The trees leaned in, and the bushes, too. The clouds opened up, and the rain stopped. Mano swung the accordion back onto his back, satisfied with the world's attention to his goodbye. He took the second bouquet from the lower button of his shirt, and held it out in front of him. He said nothing. He only closed his eyes. Behind his eyes was an image of Pepe, hair parted to the side, cutting an apple in half for the two of them to share. He held the bouquet in front of him for as long as the muscles in his arms could stand it. "For Pepe," he said. Then he dropped it between his knees into The Cure.

At the precise moment that Mano opened his eyes to watch the bouquet fall into the river, Pepe's dead body, on its back on a grave-raft made of logs, floated from beneath the footbridge. The bouquet Mano bought for him landed on top of another identical bouquet of yellow ranunculus that Pepe's hands were positioned to clutch. Pepe was wearing a suit and tie, and his hair parted just how Mano was imagining it a moment earlier. Two identical bouquets on this corpse chest.

"Oh, dear Pepe!" Mano yelled.

"Pepe!" yelled The Butcher in the distance upstream.

Mano turned around on the bridge to see The Butcher and Mitzi Let upstream behind him on the banks. He failed to see them there earlier. Their arms were moving above their heads.

"You let go too soon!" The Butcher yelled back at Mitzi.

"*You* let go, not me!" Mitzi yelled at The Butcher.

"I thought *you* were going to set the blaze?"

"You said *you* were."

"I wasn't ready! He wasn't ready!" cried The Butcher. Just then, he threw his body into the center of the stream, while yelling for his son each time his head could come up out of the rushing water for a breath. Mitzi was left alone on the banks of the river, with her hands on her head, and her face frozen in fright.

The Butcher was approaching the bridge too quickly for Mano to know what to do to save him. Mano laid on his stomach on the footbridge, and reached his hand as far below him from the bridge as he could, and spread his legs to steady himself for the weight and pull of The Butcher's potential grasp. But by the time Mano had positioned himself,

The Butcher had already floated beneath the bridge. For a moment, The Butcher's body got stuck on the same rock as Roberto's flowers, and in that moment he looked right at Mano as if he knew him. The Butcher reached his arm out for Mano just before the river freed him from the rock, and sent him tumbling downstream.

Then came Mitzi Let beneath the river. She didn't even yell. She didn't even reach. She just bounced off of every rock in her path, following her husband and son to the sea.

20.

Nana Pine had four full baskets of strawberries when she died standing up in the strawberry patch. Enid had two. It was an especially good harvest. Nana had been standing still for some time. Enid thought Nana was thinking, or maybe counting. Whatever she was doing, she was letting Enid catch up. The two of them always played the same game in the strawberry patch. Enid won the game if she picked at least half as many baskets as Nana. It was unusual for Nana to let so much time go by without picking any new strawberries. It was unusual for her to allow Enid to catch up.

"Nana, I'm starting my third basket!"

The sun was falling, and Nana's shadow was getting longer. It almost reached Enid. Nana always picked strawberries wearing the same dress, a white gunnysack with a pattern of tiny red strawberries. It waved in the late evening breeze, but her body did not.

"What basket are you on?" Enid knew the answer to this question because she could see. She threw a ripe strawberry at the back of Nana's head, and it bounced off onto a bush. "Nana? Oh no."

She pushed her way through the scratchy strawberry bushes to stand in front of Nana's body. Nana's eyes were looking directly into the sun, and she was holding a single strawberry with both hands out in front of her, as if she were offering it. More than a corpse, she looked like a statue.

"No, no, no, *no*!" Enid took the strawberry that Nana was offering, and threw it at Nana's dead face, partly to wake her up, and partly to punish her for being dead at a time like this.

Nana didn't wake up.

Enid wasn't ready to be on her own. She thought of all the days in her near future with no mother, and no father, no brothers or sisters. Only the factory, and only Mary and Mimi, whom she had recently grown to hate. She looked around at the field of strawberry patches with new eyes—no longer a game she played with her mother, but a burden of growing, picking, and selling.

Like the others, in Nana's chest was a deep hole. It was God's Finger, though Enid didn't quite believe in such a thing. In Nana's death hole was a black telephone. Enid had never seen a telephone in person before, but she knew about them. She knew how to use one instinctively.

Enid caught her breath, and she pushed Nana's arms down to her side. They were rigid. They moved like a plastic doll's arms. Enid picked up the receiver of the black telephone, and listened for a voice. She knew to do that much.

"I'm sorry for your loss," said the voice inside the shiny black receiver. Enid dropped the receiver and its spirally cord hung from Nana's torso like a spilled black intestine.

She quickly picked it up again to listen to what else the voice had to say. "We're sorry for the loss of your grandmother. We'll be there to help soon."

"She's my *mother*," clarified Enid into the phone.

"We'll be there shortly."

When The Humanitarians arrived in the strawberry field, Enid was still standing in the same position, and so, of course, was Nana. She was still holding the phone to her ear, maybe to wait for further instructions, but also because she couldn't imagine one single other thing to do. She longed for instruction so much that she would spend many of the rest of her days being quiet so that she could listen for it.

The Humanitarians were new to Pie Time. At first, they rented a room at The Innkeeper's inn. They were always together as a pair. They both wore clean light blue jumpsuits with a white oval patch on the breast pocket. In the oval patch was stitched a red XO. The Humanitarians appeared to have a very clear and kind mission. Their work was done cleanly and efficiently, and they were highly practiced in their methods. Their interactions with the grieving public were respectful and professional.

One of The Humanitarians approached Enid with two folding chairs. She unfolded one for Enid, and asked her to have a seat. "Your grandmother was very special," she said.

Enid sat down in the chair in the middle of the field of strawberry patches. "But she was my mother."

One of The Humanitarians unfolded her own chair and sat down on it. She checked her notes. "Either way, she was very special. Everyone enjoyed her strawberries. And she loved you very much, even if it seemed like she was especially strict at times."

"Who are you?" asked Enid.

"I'm a Humanitarian."

The other Humanitarian began the process of disposing of Nana's body. He tipped her stiff body backward onto one of the strawberry patches, then drug it next to a long wooden box. He tipped the box toward Nana's body, and rolled her body in. He returned the box to an upright position, then closed the lid. On the lid was a large red XO.

"What are you doing with her?" asked Enid.

"We're taking your grandmother to a beautiful meadow with other grandmothers. She'll make friends there. There'll be deer and butterflies."

"She's my mother."

"Your mother, I mean."

"And she hates deer. Deer eat the strawberries."

"There doesn't have to be deer there."

"She's dead," said Enid. "I think we should take her to the river. Maybe you can help me take her to the river?"

"You don't have to worry about her ever again. We'll take care of everything." The Humanitarian tried to give Enid a hug, and Enid obliged for The Humanitarian's sake.

A few days later, the new postman, who was also new to Pie Time, delivered a bill for services addressed to Enid

Pine with a large red XO on the envelope. In handwriting at the bottom of the bill, it read: *Sorry about the loss of your grandmother. XO, The Humanitarians.*

21

"I'll take two legs," said The Florist.

Mano was happy to see The Florist again, but very nervous about using the cleaver in front of him, about maneuvering the dead sheep's rump on the chopping block.

"Two legs. You got it."

"How did it go, with the flowers for Roberto, and for Pepe?"

Mano nervously dropped the cleaver on the floor. It was heavier than he thought it would be. He maneuvered the accordion on his back, and the radio deeper into the pit of his arm, then bent over to pick up the cleaver. He washed it off in the enormous sink, and then started cutting off a sheep's leg. "It went fine, very fine. Roberto told me to tell you he wanted daisies, not ranunculus." Mano winked.

The Florist laughed. "Well, Roberto was always very particular."

Mano gave up on cleanly cutting the first leg, and started instead on the second.

"You're doing it all wrong, son," said The Florist. "Here, let me show you." He walked behind the counter and stood next to Mano next to the chopping block. He took Mano's wrist in his grip, and showed him the proper motion of a chop.

"First off, you're holding too many things," said The Florist.

"I have my hands free," explained Mano.

"Ok, yes, well then you got to chop it right here, at the joint, hard and fast. Think of it like it's hair, or a flower stem. That's all it is. Death. It's already dead, just like everything else."

Mano thanked him, then took a whack at the second leg. The dead sheep's leg fell clean off with a single whack.

"Perfect!" The Florist picked the leg up and started to wrap it in brown butcher paper. That's how Mano figured out where The Butcher's butcher paper was.

Mano thanked The Florist, then made an appropriate excuse for himself. "First day."

"Well, tomorrow will be your second," said The Florist.

"Very true."

"...And by the third you'll know as much as The Butcher ever knew."

The Florist had both legs now wrapped in paper, and he walked back to the customer side of the counter.

Mano whacked at a few other things on the sheep, even though he wasn't quite sure what they were. He wrapped those bloody things up in brown butcher paper, too, and handed them over the counter to The Florist.

"That's too much."

"It's on me," said Mano.

In the days after all of the Lets sailed their own bodies down The Cure to the sea, Mano became Pie Time's next butcher in addition to maintaining his position as the town's barber. In many ways, this was good for Mano. He didn't want to return to the house he shared with his mother, and he wanted nothing more than to avoid idleness. Also, being a butcher made him feel like a Let, as if he were married into the family through his profession. He was The Butcher now, just like every Let man had been before him.

Despite the patience and generosity of his very first customer, The Florist, being The Butcher was very difficult for Mano at first. Chopping the arms and legs off of all the dead sheep only reminded him of the horrifying de-arming and de-legging of his mother. It was a reminder he didn't need, yet being The Butcher meant that reminder would be constant, daily.

In his first days of being both The Butcher and The Barber, Mano was very tired. He worked all night in the back of the butcher shop, cutting all the meat, cleaning and sharpening all the knives, draining all the blood, and preparing everything for sale for the next day, and then he'd lock up and walk to the barbershop, where he'd open for business until the middle of the afternoon, cutting hair, then sweeping it up into piles. He got so good at sweeping dead hair that he wouldn't even need to touch it with the broom. He could just use the broom's breezes to make a little mountain. But there was no time for sleep. After he closed up the barbershop, he would return to the butcher shop in time to sell the meat for the customers returning home from their own jobs. He kept the butcher shop open until 8PM, to be sure that everyone had their meat for dinner, and then he closed the shop in order to begin cutting the meat for the next day. It was a schedule that his customers learned quickly, and understood. They stood in lines in the hours the barbershop was open, and they stood in lines in the hours the butcher shop was open.

On the first day without sleep, Mano was incredibly tired. He rested his eyes for a few minutes in front of the black square in the back room of the barbershop. He began drifting down to the bottom of the pond again. He let his body rest there, at the bottom of the pond, the man and the woman taking their clothes off in the murky sunlight above him on the pond's surface. But then the jingle of a bell came from a customer at the front door. After a few days like that without any sleep, Mano grew more accustomed to his sleeplessness. His body adjusted. It became more capable. It grew more agile despite its extra weight. The things he held became more and more a part of his body. His hands were free as they cut hair and meat. His body grew to know its own rhythms and repetitions, and it knew them well. His body worked without him even having to think about it. Sometimes, while his arms were moving like a machine, he thought that all he was was a body. Not a person, but a body; not sleeping, but moving, cutting, holding, talking, growing and growing.

While at the butcher shop, one of his duties was to tend to the half dozen sheep that were in a pen out back.

"Come here now, Curls. It's your turn."

Mano gave names to all the sheep, but all their names were the same. *Curls*. Before he butchered them, he cut their hair with the same kind of shears he used in his barbershop, instead of the electric shearing machines that Pepe's father had used. Mano was much more comfortable with the shears, and the electric shearing machines reminded him of the steaming machines in the Pie Time Factory. Using them would feel like a step backward. At first it took Mano about an hour to cut the wool from one sheep. But after a few days of practice, it only took him about 15 minutes.

He held Curls around her waist and spoke gently to her. "I'm going to cut all of your hair off, then stun you with a hammer between your eyes so you don't feel me slit your throat while you hang upside down from your feet. All of your blood will drain out into a pan. Then I'm going to chop you up into pieces so that people can eat you." He said this to each sheep each time before he did it, and each time it made him feel like dying, too. It made him very sad. But he knew she was ready, because each time he would look her in her sheep eyes, and ask her, "Are you ready?" And he would wait until Curls looked him back in the eyes. And before he stunned her with his hammer, he asked her out loud for her forgiveness.

Mano thought that death wasn't a thing to fight, but a thing to be ready for. He thought that if we could all just be ready for it, it could be beautiful. It was important to him that everyone in Pie Time knew that. If his customers were going to eat the sheep, he wanted them to know that he had to kill the sheep first. These arms and legs they ate, the thing that was giving them life, was death. So on Monday mornings, the day that the barbershop was closed, Mano started a community education program in the sheep pen behind the butcher shop called The Death Lessons.

The Death Lessons were for children. On the first Monday morning, the first children to attend The Death Lessons were Ernesto, and his younger brother Ernest. Their mother, Lois Horn, picked weeds in people's gardens, and their father, The Shoveler, shoveled what the people needed to have shoveled. The Shoveler was willing to shovel anything, but mostly he shoveled snow. It hadn't snowed in Pie Time for a long time.

"I heard you were giving away free meat," said The Shoveler while opening the door of the butcher shop for Lois and their two sons.

"It's true, it's true," confirmed Mano. "But the children have to have their Death Lesson first."

The Shoveler picked up Ernest and held him. Ernest put his arms around his father's neck and looked back at Mano.

Lois wanted to leave at the first mention of death. "Sorry, we don't..."

"It'll be fun. Here..." Mano motioned for the family to follow him around the counter, and he led them to the pen of sheep in the back.

"Sheep!" cried Ernest. He tried to squirm out of his father's grip.

"Yes, they're such beautiful animals," encouraged Mano. "Go on, you can say hi to them."

The Shoveler lowered Ernest from his arms onto the ground, and Ernest walked over to one of the sheep to look closely at it. But he was too scared to touch it.

"All of their names are Curls," explained Mano.

"Hi Curls," said Ernesto to a different sheep than the one his younger brother was staring at. Ernesto put his hand on Curls' back and pet it slowly.

"I need your help." Mano adjusted the hot water bottle on his back, then bent his body at the knees so he could speak directly to the children. "I need you boys to pick out one of the sheep for me."

"This one!" Ernest was suddenly very excited.

"No, this one," argued Ernesto, as he continued to gently pet Curls.

"You can take your time. We'll put a saddle on them and you can ride around the pen, and..."

The Shoveler interrupted. "How much will this cost?"

"The Death Lessons are free," explained Mano. He continued to talk to Ernesto and Ernest. "You can ride them, pet them, talk to them, tell them your secrets." Mano was tightening a saddle onto the back of Curls. "And then once you pick one out, you can say your goodbyes. You can say whatever you want to say to it, and you can take as long as you'd like. And you can ask it if it is ready. And then, when *you're* ready, I'll take it inside and kill it so you and your family can eat it."

"Yay!" Ernest shouted.

And that's how it went. Lois helped Ernesto onto the saddle of his sheep, and The Shoveler helped Ernest onto his. They both rode around the pen, bouncing off the railings, and falling into the grass. Ernesto got his sheep to lie down on her side with him, and they talked while they snuggled. It was Ernesto's sheep that the family finally settled upon. Curls.

"Say your goodbyes," prompted Mano.

The entire family cried, including The Shoveler, and especially Ernesto, who wasn't quite ready. And then, after much goading and consolation, he was. Mano took Curls into the butcher shop, and a little while later met the family at the front of the shop with the entire sheep butchered into parts, a few dozen chunks wrapped in brown butcher paper. The Shoveler and his wife, Lois, were very thankful, while their sons were still rubbing their red eyes.

"Meat comes from where death goes." That's what Mano said every time after he handed the many packages of meat over to the families that participated in The Death Lessons. Meat comes from where death goes.

The Shoveler held Ernest in his arms and bounced him up

and down. "Say thank you, boys."

"Thank you," Ernest and Ernesto whined in unison.

The Death Lessons·became popular with the poorer people of Pie Time. While its popularity was a bit of a strain on Mano, who was overworked, he continued to stay true to the original values of The Death Lessons. He always refused to take money for the sheep butchered on Monday mornings. However, it did become important that he receive *something* in return.

As God's Finger continued to plague Pie Time on a nearly daily basis, and the tolls rose, Mano knew that the dead were leaving things behind in their death holes. The people of Pie Time were in a steady state of panic. Mano made a sign that hung on the walls of both the butcher shop and the barber shop.

Bring me your things of death.
Bring me things your dead have left.

Those who were grieving did not want to keep the things that were born from the holes of their newly dead. On the other hand, they didn't want to throw those things away either. They knew where they could go if they wanted the thing returned to them. In the meantime, Mano held their things, and he loved their things. Quickly, Mano became a kind of living heap of the town's grief—a walking, talking museum of loss and pain, a hard-working receptacle for the sorrow of others, hidden from their view should they choose, yet accessible, the way that kind of pain works best.

In the first full month of The Death Lessons, Mano was given many things from the poorer mourners of Pie Time to hold in exchange for complimentary cuts of sheep. He was given a black umbrella, an electric toaster, a house plant, a hatchet, a pair of crutches, a smoking pipe, a frisbee, a birthday cake with 14 lit candles, a complete set of encyclopedias, and an oscillating fan. He became a magnificent holder of things. He learned exactly how to arrange the things on his body so that they could become his body. It became a real skill, but was more like a magic trick to the others. Some of the richer mourners gifted him a death thing, not in exchange for free cuts of sheep, but just to see how and where he would hold it, how he could make it disappear into the folds and layers and shelves of the other things that he was already holding. For some mourners, this ritual became like throwing a coin in a fountain. Mano's body was becoming enormous. It was becoming mammoth. After a month of holding more and more things, on his head and legs and back, Mano was much taller than Pepe was, and much heavier than Pepe would have ever become. Mano was the mammothest person in Pie Time, and growing mammother by the day.

Early one morning, after a full night of cutting up sheep at the butcher shop, Mano maneuvered his huge body through the door to walk to the barbershop, so he could prepare the scissors and razors for a day of haircuts. It was becoming increasingly difficult for him to maneuver his body through the doors of his shops. That, too, became a kind of trick. A heavy left leg last out of the butcher shop door, a heavy right leg first into the barbershop door.

The barbershop door jingled as he squeezed his hips past the doorknob. Inez Roar was already there, waiting for him in the chair. Baby Zuzu was asleep in a basket on the counter below the razors.

She didn't say hello. "I never told you about the black square in the back room," she said.

Mano was nervous to see Inez, and he wanted to start at the beginning of the conversation instead. "Good morning, Inez."

"The black square," she insisted. "Come look at it with me." She stood up and found Mano's hand, which was at the end of an arm full of an umbrella, a pair of crutches, and a butter dish among other things. Together they walked into her dead husband's back room, and stood in the center. "It's a painting of me," explained Inez.

"That's you?" Mano couldn't see what Inez was talking about.

"Yes, look here. Look closely." She pushed her dead husband's glasses further up on the bridge of Mano's nose so that the details of the black square could be sharper for him.

"What exactly am I looking at?" Mano asked.

"Those are these." Inez's hands held her own breasts.

"I don't see them."

"No, no. Ok, look. Look here." Inez pointed to somewhere in the center of the black square. "These are my legs."

"That's the sun shining through the trees through the surface of the pond," argued Mano.

"No. It's not, here, let me show you..." Inez lifted up her black dress. "Go on," she said. "Get on your knees if you can."

Mano instinctively wanted to bury himself in the blackness beneath her dress. He moved his body clumsily onto its knees. The set of champagne glasses he was holding between his thighs clinked together. Inez helped him lower his gigantic body down to one knee, and then she slowly lifted her dress above the black birds, and the jar of buttons on his head. She climbed on top of the whole pile that was Mano's body.

Once inside the dress, Mano found Inez's legs, and then eventually he found her breasts. Now that he was just beginning to grow tired from his lack of sleep, and from holding so many things, he felt relief inside Inez's dress. It was a dark space that for a moment held *him*.

Once Mano was completely beneath Inez's dress, a sad and lonely Enid Pine walked in through the open front door of the barbershop. She stepped over the black poodle that didn't move. She peeked at Baby Zuzu sleeping soundly beneath two layers of blankets in her basket. The sun was pink and new in the window behind her. Enid was holding the black telephone that she found inside Nana's death hole. She had no more use for the telephone. She came to Mano's barbershop because she wanted to see him, and she wanted to see where he would put the telephone on his growing body. But mostly, she just wanted to see Mano. Instead, what she saw when she peeked into the back room of the barber shop was only Inez, her black dress moving beneath her body like the oiled gears of a giant combustion engine, moaning wildly like a feral cat into a black square which looked, to Enid, like a painting of an endless strawberry patch.

Enid set the telephone inside Baby Zuzu's basket before she sprinted for the door. The receiver of the telephone fell off and rested on Zuzu's forehead.

"I'm sorry for your loss," said the voice inside.

22.

Ernesto and Ernest Horn were playing cowboys when they found their mother, Lois Horn, dead in the bushes behind their house. She had been picking weeds in the morning. It was the afternoon when they found her. At first, they thought maybe she was playing a dead cowboy, but she wasn't. She died of God's Finger. Two toy guns were in her death hole, but her sons didn't want them. They gave them to Mano one Monday morning during a Death Lesson. But all of Ernesto and Ernest's training in The Death Lessons could not have prepared them for their mother's death.

The day after Lois died, her husband, The Shoveler, had a stroke of genius that would briefly transform his small poor family into a small family of means. Ernesto and Ernest would never again have to ride a sheep at The Death Lessons in order for their family to eat for free. Instead of hauling Lois' body to The Cure, building a raft out of logs, and setting fire to the body before sailing it down the river to the sea, which had always been the tradition in Pie Time, The Shoveler decided to use his one skill to dispose of his wife's body. Shoveling. This way, he saved time and he saved money. The Shoveler adamantly refused the forced good will of The Humanitarians, a refusal which took hours of effort. Instead, in the back of his modest shack on the outskirts of town, with the help of his sons, The Shoveler shoveled a hole six feet deep, six feet long, and two feet wide. The three of them lowered Lois' body with ropes into the hole. In a private ceremony, they said their goodbyes above her, and wished her well as they shoveled the hole back up with dirt. Her body turned back into the earth that it was buried inside, and before long, white ranunculus grew from that spot.

The stroke of luck and fortune, however, came from the fact that this shoveling ceremony was witnessed by a small crowd of people walking to The Innkeeper's inn past The

Shoveler's shack after church one Sunday. Most significantly, the crowd included both The Businessman and The Lawyer.

"What's that you're doing there? A new kind of gardening?" shouted The Businessman across the field so that The Shoveler could hear them.

The Shoveler walked over to the crowd, his sons trailing behind him. "Oh, no, no. The wife died. God's Finger. We're just burying her, saying our piece, and our goodbyes."

"*Burying* her! We've never heard of such a thing. What's wrong with saying your goodbyes at The Cure?" asked The Businessman.

"Nothing's wrong with The Cure, I suppose. We just want her here with us. We can say goodbye whenever we want. We know right where she is."

"Death is where life comes from." Ernesto repeated something of what he learned from The Death Lessons.

"We're going to make a garden," added Ernest.

"Is that what The Butcher's been teaching you?" The Businessman directed their question to Ernesto.

Ernesto and Ernest both nodded their heads yes.

The Businessman, The Lawyer, and a few other people in the small crowd laughed at the young boys. It was this shaming laughter that triggered the lucrative idea inside the mind of The Shoveler. Later that very afternoon, with the meager savings that he and his late wife had been stashing between the mattresses of their marital bed, he purchased a very undesirable five acre plot of land on the eastern banks of The Cure. He bought it directly from The Lumberjack, who had no need for the land now that it had been completely cleared of trees. It was nothing more than a field of tree stumps. Then with the money he had left over, The Shoveler bought a respectable black suit and tie combination from The Tailor. Within a week, with the help of his sons, he shoveled dozens of 6 x 6 x 2 holes in the land, each at the foot of a tree stump.

After The Shoveler and his sons dug the holes, Vera Good was the first in Pie Time to bury her dead in The Shoveler's new graveyard. In the month following June Good's death underneath the table at the factory, Vera hadn't quite been ready to say goodbye. Her public grieving was particularly disturbing to the productivity at the factory and to The Foreman. She wore a black dress and black veil every day for that month, and sobbed endlessly into the announcement microphone. Normally, when the girls at the factory heard the announcement microphone click on, they expected to be told it was time for a smoke break, or a lunch break, or that they were rolling their cigarettes too slowly to meet the daily quota. But after Mrs. Good's death, every time the announcement microphone clicked on, the girls only heard the deep sobs of Ms. Good.

All the while, June's body was kept in a deep freezer in the basement of the factory where the overstocked Pie Time cigarettes were typically stored. June's body just rested there for the month, frozen on top of hundreds of cigarette boxes with June's face on the front. *It's High Time for a Pie Time.* The Foreman was so annoyed by his sister's grief—grief that was supposed to be his own—that he avoided talking about it at all costs. Productivity was down, despite the fact that demand for Pie Times was up. And morale, because of his sister's mourning, was down even lower. So, The Foreman was careful never to suggest to his sister that it was time for June's body to be taken to The Cure to be sent to sea. He figured it wouldn't hurt anyone for her body to stay in the freezer until the moment Vera was ready to say goodbye to it.

So, when Vera heard about The Shoveler's graveyard, an open stump-field in which to bury the dead without having to really say goodbye to them, to let them flower up from the surface of the earth, and to be able to visit the flowers they became, her challenges of grief felt resolved.

Vera picked out the most private hole in the very back of

the new graveyard, and chose to have a very private ceremony which only included herself, the deceased, The Shoveler, and his two sons. Without The Foreman's knowledge or permission, Vera paid The Shoveler and his sons to help her remove June's body from the factory freezer, carry it in a wheelbarrow to the graveyard, and then lower it into the grave where it would thaw and flower.

"I loved June Good and June Good loved me," Vera began, hands clasped in front of her. She was wearing June's fur coat and pearls. She would wear them every day for the rest of her life.

The Shoveler and Ernesto had their heads lowered and eyes closed, but they peeked at each other as Vera began. Ernest was playing in the mound of fresh dirt.

She continued, now with her eyes open. "That's all I know. That's all I care to know."

"Very beautiful," said The Shoveler.

With his knife, The Shoveler carefully carved these words on the face of the tree stump at the head of the grave: *June Good is dead / in here*. With the writing on it, the tree stump looked like a birthday cake.

"Let's put candles in it," suggested Ernest.

It felt like the right time to start traditions, so Vera agreed.

"That's a good idea, son," said The Shoveler. "Run home and grab us some candles from the kitchen."

The Shoveler, wearing his new suit and tie, shoveled the dirt back into the hole on top of June's frozen corpse. The first shovelful of dirt filled June's death hole in the center of her chest. "May the dead be happy there," he said. He thought about his wife, Lois, when he said it.

Once the grave was filled, Ernest returned with a handful of wax birthday candles. He carved out two holes in the stump, and stuck the candles in there. Vera lit one of the candles with a match, and insisted that the other one stay unlit. That felt like a proper idea for a tradition to everyone—

leaving the other candle unlit.

Then June took out four Pie Time cigarettes from her purse, which was actually June's purse, and handed three of them out to The Shoveler, Ernesto, and Ernest. Ernesto and Ernest both looked at their father as if to ask for permission, and permission was granted. They each lit their cigarette on Mrs. Good's birthday candle.

"To June," Vera said, as she took a drag.

"To June," repeated The Shoveler, who took a drag.

"And to my mother, too," added Ernesto. He took his first drag ever of a cigarette, and coughed.

"Here, here!" The Shoveler cheered.

Vera laughed at Ernesto. "First cigarette?"

"Yes, ma'am." He kept coughing.

Ernest just chewed on his cigarette like it was a piece of gum until the fire on its tip died.

23.

Enid Pine was asleep in the changing room of Lady Blood's new confession booth when Lil' Jorge walked in. He was the booth's primary caretaker, and it was his job to sweep it and dust it for the day.

The confession booth had been well-used since it was built. Many people had made their first confession, and already, the north wall of the church had over 100 naked confession photographs on display. Over 100 people had been cleansed through their willingness to become vulnerable, and therefore pure, in the face of their own sins. Also, Mothers was quickly becoming a skilled photographer with an exceptional eye for the contours of the naked human body. He added another lamp in the booth, and arranged the lighting so that the body would be lit most complimentary. He could recognize a naked person's problem areas and shade them by adjusting the light, and he understood which parts of everyone's body should be accentuated with more light. He added a window to the confession booth, too. The window had curtains, so the natural light streaming through it could be controlled.

Each week more and more people came to church on Sundays, which was partly due to the success of the beautiful naked confession photographs. Each Sunday, some believers even had to be turned away because of a lack of capacity in the church—a sign, claimed Mothers, that a church is blessed. Despite his fiery homilies, his damning sentiment, and his finger pointing, Mothers had become the most successful of the three priests in Pie Time's history.

A sign-up sheet on the front door of the confession booth was managed by Lil' Jorge. He allowed no more than a dozen people into the booth each day. Enid's name was not on the list, and the booth wasn't to be open to the public for another ten minutes. Lil' Jorge had no way of knowing that Enid, who had snuck into the booth overnight because she couldn't bear the thought of another night alone in her home, was already inside the changing room, just now waking up.

Lil' Jorge walked behind the screen where Father Mothers sat during confessions to pat the dust out of the seat cushion.

Pat, pat, pat.

From the changing room, Enid heard the patting of the cushion, and knew it was time for her first confession in the new booth. Days earlier, Enid had overheard Mary and Mimi Minutes talking about the new booth. She had stopped talking to Mary and Mimi after they tore apart Mano's dead mother like wolves, but she couldn't escape hearing their conversations with each other all day at the factory. Mary and Mimi's favorite part to talk about was how you were supposed to take off your clothes once you entered the booth.

In Enid's ears, Mothers was taking his seat. She imagined him cracking his knuckles, and loading new film into his camera. She lifted her red blouse over her head, and lifted her knees up through her red skirt. She kicked off her red Mary Janes, and unsnapped her white bra. Her white panties had a pattern of strawberries on them. When she pulled them off of her body and placed them on top of the pile of her clothes, for a moment she thought that the pile looked like a full basket of strawberries.

When Enid entered the main room of the confession booth, she became the first naked person Lil' Jorge had ever seen in real life, outside of Mothers' photographs. The sight of her naked body shocked him, because it was living and moving, and gave off a heat that filled the booth. It was the first time he had ever thought a person was beautiful.

Enid's impulse was to become smaller when she was naked. Her shoulders fell forward to hide her chest, and her chin dropped to hide her face. Her bangs were cut far too short to hide her eyes, but the rest of her hair fell like curtains to hide what they could. Her body didn't feel like her own. It felt like some other woman's, maybe her mother's, or Mary's, or maybe even Inez's, but not hers. She didn't even really know how to move it. She tried to suck in her belly, but her knees bent instead. Her new hips felt like an empty basket that she had to carry, but she didn't know with what to fill it.

"Forgive me, Father." She braced herself for a bright flash of light as she spoke. "I am full of envy."

Lil' Jorge was paralyzed, at first by Enid's moving body, and then by her voice. He was standing on Mothers' seat, and bending down to gaze at Enid through the lens of his camera. Her body, to him, was its own bright flash of light. And he was stunned by it.

Enid continued, still bracing, "Father, also, I have had impure thoughts."

Lil' Jorge put his hands on the camera to make it look more closely at the bends of Enid's body, the parts of her body that the light held.

"Should I go on?" Enid paused. "Father?" She assumed that Mothers' silence meant that she hadn't confessed quite enough, or perhaps not specially enough. She thought maybe her confession wasn't yet worthy enough to warrant a photograph be taken. So, she continued more deeply into her confession. "Father, all I can think about since my mother died is this new feeling of emptiness. A void. A hunger to fill the void. There's a hole deep inside me that I need filled." Still, no photograph. Enid took a breath, and went even further. "I can only have it filled by a certain boy, a boy who loves a woman. I mean, a different woman. Not me. I don't think. A boy who...who, who...Father, I'm ready. I'm ready to be a woman."

The fat little hands of Lil' Jorge slipped in that exact moment, which caused the bulb on the camera to flash. Enid's photograph was finally taken. Her body burned a shadow behind it on the wall of the booth, and she stumbled backward into the door. Then she fell to her knees in the center of the booth. Her eyes were wide when the flash came, and she was briefly blinded.

At that point, thinking the knock of the door that Enid had just made with her body was some sort of signal, The Businessman, who were patiently waiting for their confession outside the booth, opened the booth's front door. Their name was the first on the list for the day. Just then, Mothers walked in through the back door into his area of the booth, and thanked Lil' Jorge for preparing the booth for the day, for his sweeping, dusting, and patting.

"You can go now, Jorge," said Mothers. Lil' Jorge leapt from the chair, and ran from the booth.

The Businessman nearly stepped over Enid, who was still on her knees on the floor. "Mothers, it appears that you have a naked girl on your floor."

Mothers peered through the screen for the first time and was shocked at what he found there. "Enid, is that you? I haven't seen you in years. What's gotten into you? You have to wait your turn. Is your name even on the list?"

The Businessman sat on the stool while Enid escaped, confused and embarrassed, into the changing room. She drew the curtains. She began the task of assembling what looked like a basket of strawberries back into the wardrobe she was wearing.

While Enid dressed, The Businessman asked her questions from the other side of the curtain. "Young girl, what do you know of death?" They opened a briefcase as they asked Enid their question. The briefcase was full of plans and propositions, contracts and sketches. They had not planned to use their time with Mothers for confession, and certainly not for disrobing. They set their briefcase down on the floor next to the stool, in order to take a notebook and pen out of their breast pocket. "Little girl, are you afraid of the finger? What is it worth to you to fight death?" The Businessman clicked the pen.

Enid was still silent in the booth. The Businessman stood from their stool to pull the curtain back a little with their fingers. "You have a body that needs protecting. No one would want to see it get poked..." said The Businessman.

Enid bit one of their fingers from her side of the curtain. The Businessman howled in pain, and fell backward onto their stool to nurse their wounds in disbelief.

"Settle down, please. This is a place of worship," pleaded Mothers.

Enid walked out of the changing room back into the main room of the confession booth. She was somehow even more naked than she was before she retreated. "I'm not a little girl," she said. "And I'm not afraid of death, motherfucker." She pointed her finger into all three faces. The Businessman didn't know where to look. They were still squeezing their throbbing finger. "I won't fight death!" shouted Enid. "And, I especially won't fight yours. May it come too soon."

"Enid, your anger!" Mothers tried to calm Enid down.

"My sin is not anger," Enid said.

24

With little apology and without approaching Mano first, The Landlord, with the help of The Lawyer, lawfully ceased ownership of the house that Mano had shared with his mother his entire life. According to Pie Time's laws, any house that goes abandoned for over 30 days can be purchased by any interested party. And the interested party was always The Landlord. The house where, every morning, Mano delivered his mother a cold Pie Time, a pack of Pie Times, and talked to her while sitting on the toilet, was now the property of someone who had never set foot inside of it. The value that the house now held for The Landlord, was a fraction of the love it once held for Mano.

"It's a lovely home, really."

"Thanks." Mano was emptily thankful for The Landlord's empty compliment. He was trimming the long hairs coming out of The Landlord's deep dark nostrils.

"You know, Mano, it's a business decision. You understand."

"I do, I do," said Mano. And he did, he did understand. In a way, Mano was happy to let it go. He hadn't been in the house since the night his mother was torn apart at the banks of The Cure, and simply owning the house was a burden. He didn't want to return to it. He didn't want to sleep in it. He didn't even want to sleep. And he didn't want to look inside the bathroom where his mother lived. Yet he didn't know what else to do but leave it sit, to let it settle in. Like a memory. The house was only there to remind him that he was born in the present, which also reminded him that he will die in the present, that the past and the future can never be places to store his love and his pain.

The Landlord sold the home to The Humanitarians, a man and a woman who had traveled to Pie Time from a neighboring town called Nun's Hat. Nun's Hat was nestled into a bend in The Cure much closer to the sea. Sitting on the banks of The Cause—which is what they called The Cure in Nun's Hat—the people of Nun's Hat would watch dead bodies float past them to the sea. They liked to count the bodies. Sometimes they would count two or three corpses in a day, each one burnt and each one with a hole in its chest. Eventually, the people of Nun's Hat built a net, and stretched the net across The Cause to catch all the charred and chest-hollowed corpses. They would make a tally mark on a giant chalkboard set up in their movie theater where, in the time when the body count was increasing most rapidly, this giant chalkboard was built to replace the screen. Everyone in Nun's Hat would come to the movie theater to see the tally marks on the giant chalkboard instead of seeing a movie on the screen. Watching the tally marks tally up became the new entertainment in Nun's Hat, which unlike Pie Time, was a town filled with artists, poets, architects, and counseling psychologists.

With the help of their best architects and artists, the people of Nun's Hat stacked the charred bodies they fished from The Cause into a giant pyramid, and they hollowed a tomb from the pyramid's center. The pyramid of dead bodies had no other purpose other than to be a monument to the dead, a concept that would have been difficult for the people of Pie Time to fully understand.

The death pyramid was a monument of great cultural significance to the people of Nun's Hat. The poets often spent their days and nights in the tomb in the center of all those charred and chest-hollowed bodies that came from nowhere anyone knew, and wrote poems. They wrote poems mostly about the origins of the mysterious dead, and about where this death came from, where it floated into Nun's Hat from, which naturally led to poetry about where their own deaths came from, and where their deaths were going.

Some of the first people of Nun's Hat to dare to answer

that question were The Humanitarians who bought Mano's house in Pie Time. Instead of helping to catch bodies in a net, or make tally marks, or stack the bodies in a pyramid, the man and woman wanted to see where the charred bodies with hollowed chests were floating in from. So, they simply walked up the banks of The Cause.

The Humanitarians eventually became so busy with the business of God's Finger in Pie Time that many of Pie Time's original residents thought they had lived there all along. At every death, which was daily, The Humanitarians were in the center of its activity. They were somehow the first people to arrive at the scene of each death. How they knew of the deaths so quickly, no one really knew. They just knew. They were tuned in; their ears were pinned. They would immediately hold the hand of whoever was grieving the most, and tell them that they were sorry. They would ask the griever what he or she needed. And they would say it was ok to cry. That was the most important thing. Grievers sometimes needed permission to cry, and they needed to hear that permission be given out loud, and they needed to be held as they cried. They needed a soft wall to cry into, something that would catch all the grief so that it didn't spill all over the earth and soak back into the soil. Grievers want to look at their grief, and they want to love it. They want to hold it like a baby when no one else is around.

It was The Humanitarians belief that *someone* must grieve over the body, that every dead body deserves grief be spilled over it, and the body wasn't concerned about who that griever was. It wasn't the *griever* that was important, but the *grief*. The Humanitarians' grief would be real. This was the most impressive thing about them. They somehow knew just how to manufacture sincerity.

The Humanitarians said nothing of what was actually becoming of Pie Time's dead bodies downriver in Nun's Hat. The death pyramid in Nun's Hat was reviving the spirit and economy of that town, and The Humanitarians wanted to avoid being the reason that the people of Pie Time stopped sending their dead down The Cure.

The Humanitarians always, respectfully, sent a bill of service to the grieving. What they provided was indeed a *service*—no one was doubting that—and all services deserved to be paid for. It was with this money that The Humanitarians purchased Mano's house from The Landlord, and it was with what remained of this money that they completely redecorated it in a way that reminded them more of what they were familiar with—white walls. All four rooms of Mano's house were repainted in white.

Mano's old house became unrecognizable to him, and it was unlike any other house in Pie Time. The Humanitarians even put abstract sculptures on the front lawn. One sculpture looked like the sun eating or giving birth to a baby. One looked like a bird with a broken wing, even though no one in Pie Time was really sure what a bird was.

Mano was just brushing the hairs off of the back of The Landlord's neck and onto the floor.

"I brought a thing for you to hold," said The Landlord.

"Thank you." Mano's voice was tired.

"You don't mind getting any bigger do you?"

"It's not really up to me," explained Mano flatly. "What is it?"

"It's a saw." The Landlord reached down into his briefcase, and pulled out a saw. "The Humanitarians found it at your house. I mean, *their* house. She saw and he saw the saw." The Landlord was pleased with both his joke and his gift.

"What was a saw doing in the house?" asked Mano.

"A lot of things were left in it, actually. It seems some squatters had been living there since you moved out. One of them died from God's Finger. A saw came out of his hole."

Mano accepted the saw reluctantly, and pushed it

somewhere into the swelling and swirling mess of the bottom half of his body. He moved things around, and they clanked as they shifted. Accepting the saw felt like a betrayal somehow. It was the first thing that he held on his gigantic and lumbering body that he wasn't so sure if he loved. It didn't even look like a saw, exactly, but a sharp triangle of metal held by a rectangular piece of wood. It was born from the body of someone living where he was supposed to still be living.

With the addition of the saw, Mano's body was becoming too big for Pie Time. In the most recent weeks he had been given a bicycle, a pitchfork, a metronome, a book of stamps, a set of golf clubs, a letter opener, a bicycle pump, a step ladder, and now a saw. Some of these things were given to him in exchange for free sheep as part of The Death Lessons, and some were given to him because he had become as known for being Pie Time's receptacle of grief as he was known for being its butcher and barber. The things Mano held and loved were settling into his flesh. All that grief. Like a sweaty putty. The things Mano held and Mano's body were now nearly indiscernible. Mano was mammother than ever before. Children began to point at him.

"Why is he so big?" some children would ask while pointing.

"Remember what I told you about Mano," their parents' would answer.

So, with that saw, Mano cut the doors in both of his businesses into double doors. The double doors of the barbershop and the butcher shop were the first ever double doors in Pie Time. Mano would no longer have to squeeze his body through the doors. He could simply push open both doors and walk in more gracefully, like everyone else, without drawing attention to his enormous body and the many things he held on it.

One afternoon, as Mano was closing the double doors of his barbershop for the day, two children Mano didn't recognize pasted a poster on the front window. In big black letters, on white paper: *WAR ON DEATH*.

And at the very bottom of the poster, in black letters: *XO*.

"Excuse me," Mano said. The two children paid no attention to him, and they kept pasting the poster. "Excuse me, but I'm sorry. You can't just paste that poster anywhere you'd like. This is *my* barbershop. This is my barbershop window."

"Then you take it down, mister. It's your shop," said one of the children.

The other one giggled as he looked at Mano. "Yeah, take it down, if you can find your own arms in all that fat." At that, they ran through the alley behind the barbershop, having already pasted their posters on every window on Last Street. And they stapled the posters on all the poles.

"It's not fat. It's things," Mano said to no one.

Mano looked down at the mess of his body, and then back up at all the white posters, all the black letters, The Humanitarians on the sidewalk across the street shaking hands with the people of Pie Time, no more death, no more death, save us from more death, and all the men in yellow construction hats building new buildings on the other end of Last Street, all their rising hammers, all their falling hammers.

Mano retreated back into his barbershop through the double doors, and locked them behind him. He walked directly into the back room.

War on Death. XO.

25.

Mitzi Let and The Butcher are each at one end of the table. Pepe is sitting across from Mano. The Butcher passes a loaf of bread to Mano.

"Do you want me to slice it?" asks The Butcher.

"No, thank you. I can slice it."

"Do you want a knife to slice it?"

"Yes, thank you. I'll need a knife for that."

Mitzi hands Mano a knife to slice the loaf. Mano slices the loaf.

"Do you want some butter?" asks Mitzi.

"Yes, please."

The Butcher passes the butter to Mano.

"Do you want me to butter it for you?"

"No, thank you. I will butter it."

"Do you want the kind of knife needed to butter it?"

"Yes, I'll need that kind of knife."

Mitzi hands Mano a knife to butter the slice. Mano butters the slice.

Mitzi uses her knife to cut her hand off.

"Would you like to eat my hand?"

"No, I would not like that. I would not like to eat your hand," says Mano.

The Butcher pushes his knife into his mouth and cuts his tongue out. With his eyes, he asks Mano if Mano would want to eat his tongue. The Butcher holds his tongue up.

"No, sir. I would not like to eat your tongue. But thank you."

Mitzi looks sad that Mano does not want to eat her hand or The Butcher's tongue. "What more can we do for you than this?" she asks.

A black cloud spills out of Mitzi's wrist, like ink underwater, and it spills out of The Butcher's mouth, too.

Pepe doesn't notice. He is looking upward instead.

"Your parents," Mano pushes a whisper to Pepe in order to get Pepe's attention.

"What are *parents*?" Pepe whispers back.

Above them are the hooves of a herd of animals. Everyone watches the animals moving. Their hooves move in big circles. Mano asks Pepe what kind of animal makes up the herd the hooves move in, but Pepe doesn't know what kind of animal makes up the herd the hooves move in.

"Are you dead?"

Inez pushed Mano's leg to be sure that he wasn't dead. He wasn't dead.

Mano had been sleeping below the black square on the floor of the back room of the barbershop for three days and three nights without waking up. His hulking pile of a body took over most of the floor. No one but Inez really understood why the barbershop and butcher shop were closed for three days, and she knew it was best for Mano to finally get his sleep. With her key to the barbershop, she visited Mano on each of the three nights, even though she was sure he wouldn't remember it. The first night, she found him inside the black square, half naked in the mud of a sheep's pen. On the second night, she entered the black square, and couldn't find him at all. On the third night of Mano's sleep, Inez was worried he'd never re-enter the world. She stayed at home, but she couldn't sleep. She was lonely, so she tried to sleep with Zuzu, curled up in the bassinet. Her neck and back ached. She used her key to the barbershop to let herself in. ·

"Am I?" Only Mano's eyelids moved. "Am I dead?"

"No, you're not dead." Inez was bouncing Baby Zuzu in her arms while standing above Mano. "He's not dead, is he Bebé?" Inez started to make a habit of calling Baby Zuzu, Bebé.

Because it had been Mano's first sleep in nearly two months, it was less of a sleep than it was a correction of time in Mano's cells. There was a point at which he remembered maybe seeing a house plant in a window, but he didn't recognize the house plant. He remembers being at the bottom of the pond again, too, but also sitting at a table with Pepe and his parents.

Inez was cleaning Mano's glasses in her hands with a cloth. She tried to imagine her husband wearing them before he died. He would've looked quite handsome, she thought. Mustache, glasses, and a balding head. A rigid jaw, and big ears. When she looked at Mano, despite his new very large size, she only saw a scared little boy. Her late husband's glasses were still too big for his face. Still, she wanted to preen Mano as he lay there on the floor. She wanted to lighten his load, and lick his wounds. It felt good to have Mano in her days.

"What happened? How...?"

"We were naked in the mud in the sheep's pen. It was raining."

"Did we?"

"No."

"You were on top of me...and we almost...but you fell asleep."

"Oh, yes, yes, the pen of sheep and the mud. I remember. That was last night?" Mano rubbed his eyes.

"No, that was a few nights before. Today is Thursday."

"Today is Thursday? Really? "

"Really." Inez was happy to see him waking, and she wanted him to remember what they did inside the black square a few nights before. "We were sinking in the mud, so I couldn't quite find your body. It took hours to get all of you in my arms. I had to take off all of your stupid things by myself."

"No, you should've..." Mano panicked.

"Mano, it was all I could do."

Mano looked down at his body to see he was still holding so many things. "My things aren't stupid."

"I'm sorry, you're right. I didn't mean it like that. Your

things aren't stupid."

Mano thought hard about all he must have missed while he slept. "But what about The Death Lessons? I missed The Death Lessons."

"The children came, and I let them ride the sheep."

"Did you kill the sheep for them?"

"No, I didn't. It's ok. The Death Lesson this week was that sometimes sheep don't die. That's what I told them. I told them that sometimes you just ride the sheep, and you go home."

Mano thought hard about that particular lesson. That seemed like a good death lesson. Some days sheep don't die. "And the barbershop...?"

"I put the closed signs up. You needed to rest."

Mano groaned.

"By the way, you're welcome," prompted Inez.

Mano didn't apologize for his tone, and just continued to groan. His body felt a little lighter. He looked down at his body again. Some things had clearly been cleaned while he slept, dusted, wiped down, maybe even licked clean. "What have you done?"

"Mano, you smelled. You needed to be cleaned. I didn't throw anything away," pleaded Inez. "I put it all back where you held it."

Mano felt around his body for the things that he remembered holding there. He felt a few of the larger things, including the accordion. He turned the radio on and then back off again. The priest on the radio was saying something about forgiveness.

"It's all here, right? So, it's all still here?" Mano asked.

"Well, no. I *did* throw away a few things. Mano, the birthday cake was rotting."

"It wasn't your cake. I wish you wouldn't have just thrown it away. I loved that cake."

"You *loved* that cake?"

"Yes, I *loved* it."

"I don't know if you know what *love* is, Mano."

"I *do* know what it is, and I loved that cake."

"Mano, it was rotten."

Mano didn't want to keep talking about the cake, so he looked around for something else that was missing. "Where is the black poodle?"

"I gave it a bath." Inez clapped her hands, and the black poodle waddled into the back room. It looked bigger to Mano, poofier.

"Ok, thank you for washing it. It looks a little like Curls now." Mano was trying to calm himself down. He told himself it was ok that she threw away the birthday cake. And maybe a few other things. He felt a little lighter, cleaner. He breathed through his nose.

But then Mano felt the top of his head. "Inez, where are the birds?" Mano started to panic again.

"The animals on top of your head?"

"Yes, *birds*."

"Birds! Oh, I tried to clean them, and you won't believe what happened. They flew through the window. They *flew*. Did you know they could fly? It was very magical! They just..."

"They flew away?! Out of the window? Where did they go?"

"I don't know where they went. They just flew away."

"And you let them?"

Inez bounced Baby Zuzu higher and harder in her arms, and Baby Zuzu started to climb up Inez's shoulder. "Mano, the way they flew, it makes me think that maybe those birds belong to the world, not to you. Do you know..."

Mano sat up and started gathering some of the cleaned things that had fallen around on the floor as he slept. He gathered them back into his arms, and between his legs, on his back, and around his neck. He grew bigger right there in front of Inez and Baby Zuzu.

"If you give some of the things to me," suggested Inez, "I can keep them for you. I can clean them. Or I can..."

"No! I can't. I can't lose them."

"I'll hold them for you."

"It doesn't work like that." Mano suddenly wanted to be anywhere but his barbershop with Inez. He wanted to leave, though he wasn't sure where he'd go. The last thing he needed to find was his leather boots, and he found them. "You wouldn't understand..."

Inez spoke at the same time, "I wouldn't understand?!"

Mano continued without any hesitation. "These things aren't yours. I *love* them. They're all I have left."

Inez stared at Mano blankly while Baby Zuzu arched her back in order to wriggle out of Inez's arms. Inez set Baby Zuzu down on the floor. She sat there silently while the two of them continued to raise their voices.

"These *things,* Mano. These things are *all* you have left?"

"Yes."

Inez let out a sarcastic *huh*. She considered every word before she said it. "My pain is invisible to you." She took a breath, and stepped closer to Mano. "But you *love* a rotten cake."

"Inez, no..."

"Mano, I found a black telephone on Bebe's face while she was sleeping in the barber shop the other night. It was on her face! Things come out of people's dead bodies, and they somehow land on my daughter's face!"

"Why didn't you give it to me? You know how..."

"Mano!" Inez searched Mano's enormous body for a few seconds to find the black telephone found in Nana Pine's death hole that Enid Pine had left behind on Baby Zuzu in the barber shop. It had become one of Baby Zuzu's favorite toys until Inez took it away from her to put on Mano's body. Once Inez located it behind Mano's right knee, she threw the black telephone phone at him. "I *did* give it to you! And you didn't even notice!"

The black telephone bounced off of Mano's head, and the receiver fell onto the ground. Mano picked it up.

"I'm sorry for your loss," said the telephone.

Mano rubbed his head where a bruise was forming in the exact spot on his head where the birds had just flown from.

Then Inez said this: "Mano, give me back my husband's glasses."

Mano could see his mistake in her face. He shrunk down to a new size. Inez picked up Baby Zuzu from the floor with one arm. Baby Zuzu did not even give the tiniest whine. Inez held out her hand for the glasses, and Mano hesitated.

"I can't see, Inez."

Inez said nothing. She couldn't look Mano in the eyes.

Mano took the glasses off of his face, and put them in Inez's palm. He slowly made his escape out the front door of the barber shop.

Inez thought to warn him about what he'd find on Last Street outside of that door. Pie Time had changed dramatically in the three days Mano had been sleeping. But she decided not to mention it. She wanted only to let go of him, like releasing a pet pig, poor eyesight and all, into the woods of snapping and snarling sounds.

26.

The sun was bright. Mano thought Pie Time looked different because he couldn't see the sharp edges of all its shapes without his glasses, but also because there were so many new unrecognizable shapes that he had never seen before. He walked up to each new shape and squinted at it until it came into focus.

While Mano slept, Pie Time had changed.

Across from Mano's barbershop was a new barbershop called XO Haircuts. It had a row of five barber's chairs, and had at least three barbers cutting hair simultaneously, like a factory of haircutting. Each XO haircut was over with very quickly, and there was very little waiting. XO Haircuts took reservations for their haircuts, and the customers were asked to show up on time. If the customers arrived early, they were offered a cup of coffee, which was always brewing in the coffeepot. And the XO barbers were trained to know more than one style of haircut. They were trained by XO Haircuts' main barber to ask the customers what kind of haircut they wanted, and then the barbers were trained to cut it just like that. Already, Mano recognized a few of his customers walking around with different kinds of haircuts that he had never before seen. Some of the younger boys, for example, started wearing what Mano called the table-top. Mano didn't really know how to cut hair into a table-top.

Lil' Jorge, for example, had a table-top. He walked past Mano with his new table-top. "Please don't eat me," screamed Lil' Jorge.

"Why would I eat you?" asked Mano calmly.

Like Mano's barbershop and butcher shop, every new XO business also had a double door. They became the only other places in Pie Time that Mano, with his enormous body, could still enter. However, all the XO double doors were much more special than Mano's double doors. They were electric. They were the first electric double doors in Pie Time. Everyone, not just the children, liked to stand in front of the electric eye of the XO double doors and move side to side so that the doors would open automatically for them. To Mano, it felt like being food, and walking into the opening and closing mouth of a giant animal. Mano stood in front of the electric double doors of XO Meats for two minutes while the blurry electric mouth opened and closed. The animal wanted to eat him, he thought. It was bigger than him. And Mano finally let the animal eat him.

XO Meats was cold inside. It had a separate room in the back where they did all the butchering so that none of the customers could see what was really happening to the animals. The meat just came out in different shapes. It was put in the glass display case for all the hungry families to point at. They'd say, "I'll take that oval shape of meat," or "I'll take this oval shape of meat," or "No, no, I want that tube shape of meat." They'd say things like that, not even knowing what kind of animal that shape came from. Those shapes came from all different kinds of animals. Sheep, of course, but also wolves, deer, cows, pigs, and horses. Inside XO Meats there was no smell of blood—no smell of death at all. It was clean and bright with white light, like a room built in a time after death was just a problem to be solved, and inside XO Meats it had been solved.

There were also two new places built on Last Street on each side of The Chef's restaurant. One was called XO Cafe, which served coffee and biscuits all day and all night long. It was always open. The other was called XO Diner, which was also always open. Across from The Innkeeper's inn was a new inn called XO Inn. In every room was a radio, and a clean bathtub. Across from The Bartender's bar was a new bar called XO Bar. Like The Bartender's Bar, XO Bar had just one beer on tap, except it wasn't Pie Time. It was XO Beer.

The Pie Time Factory was now closed and gutted of many of its machines and vats. In the last three days, construction had already begun on the new XO Factory, which was three times the size of the Pie Time Factory. The wing that was responsible solely for the manufacturing of XO Life Cages was nearly complete, and the concrete foundations for the XO cigarette wing had already been poured. The beer silos were already being built, too. The large billboard on the side of the Pie Time Factory with the words *It's High Time for a Pie Time* and a picture of June Good smoking a cigarette in her pearls and fur coat was in its first days of fading in the sun. On the enormous outside walls of the new XO Factory there was just a white sign with big black letters that read: *War on Death. XO.*

And in smaller letters below the XO, it read: *Beers for Life. Smokes for Life. Cages for Life.*

Mano looked for his lost black birds in this new world, but there were still no such thing as birds. His eyes hurt from squinting at all the new shapes. Maybe he felt like he had just walked onto the first battlefield of a war, and that his birds had been swallowed up by it.

"Birds!" Mano cupped his hands and called for the black birds as he walked down Last Street. "Birds!" He didn't know how else to call for them other than to just yell the word for what they were called. He squinted into the trees behind the new shapes, but the shapes looked birdless. So, instead, Mano bent down and put his palm toward the ground, and the black poodle walked underneath it to be petted.

People that Mano didn't quite recognize were walking past him on the sidewalk. A few were wearing large black cages around their torsos. The people wearing cages looked very large in their cages, though not quite as large as Mano, so he immediately felt comforted simply by their size, as if he was no longer alone. But when he squinted, their size and shape was see-through, whereas his was not. These people looked like lightbulbs, but not like they could light up. Bulbs, for sure, but not light bulbs. Bulbs with a head and legs and arms sticking out of them. And they weren't made out of glass like a light bulb. Mano wanted to push one of them over to see if they would break, or roll.

"What is it you're calling for?" asked a tall man with a black cage around his torso.

"Birds."

"Birds?"

"Have you seen them?"

"What are birds?"

"Nothing," Mano said, defeated. "Forget it."

On one of the bars that spanned this tall man's face was a white rectangle, and in the rectangle were black letters. Mano squinted to read them. *War on Death. XO.*

The War on Death, Mano thought, was not a war at all, but a milking. It was a way to milk death for what it was worth, instead of loving it for what it had to be. In Mano's mind, death wasn't a thing to fight *against*, but a thing to fight *for*. And in some small way, if this war on death was a war at all, he thought, it was a war on The Death Lessons.

"Do you think XO makes a cage big enough for *that* man?" asked a woman wearing a black cage standing behind the tall man in a cage. She pointed at Mano.

Mano overheard her. "I don't want your stupid fucking cage," Mano shouted over the tall man's shoulder.

The tall man turned around and tried to put his arms inside the woman's cage to protect her from Mano's surprising vitriol. The tall man used his arms to comfort her, but his arms just kept clunking around on the outside of her cage.

"I'll take the Reckoner Tree over your fucking cage."

The tall man tried a little harder to cleanly find the woman's body inside her cage. "What's the Reckoner Tree?" he asked Mano.

"Forget about it," Mano said, resigned.

"He's a monster!" she yelled. The tall man and the woman turned around and walked in the other direction away from Mano.

Mano felt especially heavy. He spotted a few more blurry people in cages. Everyone in their cages was looking at Mano as if he was a giant monster—as if he was something suddenly uncaged.

It was time for Mano to go butcher some sheep for the children.

27.

Pie Time was swelling with death tourists. XO was spreading the word of God's Finger to nearby towns, and tourists wanted to take their chances to see a resident of Pie Time show up dead with a large strange hole in the chest. No one who was not a resident of Pie Time had yet died, so the tourists felt safe. With the exception of The Humanitarians, no one from Nun's Hat had known anything of God's Finger in Pie Time until very recently.

The Humanitarians walked into Mano's butcher shop wearing XO Life Cages. The man and woman had the same kind of beauty that June Good had, the kind that belonged in cigarette ads. Their skin was so perfect, and their teeth were so white and straight, it was easy to forget that a skull hid behind them. Their bodies seemed indestructible, impervious to any kind of death. They looked sturdy and giant in their cages. They looked like something a child would want to play on.

"I think you're looking for XO Meats," said Mano. "It's across the street."

Other than all of the new XO businesses, Mano's butcher shop and barbershop, with their double doors, were the only other places that people wearing black cages were physically able to enter. These were the only doors wide enough for people with cages to enter. Soon, the people who could afford XO Life Cages for their bodies could also afford to cut larger doors into their own homes.

When The Humanitarians entered Mano's butcher shop, The Shoveler, Ernesto, and Ernest were already standing just inside the double doors. The Shoveler had been waiting for the cuts of sheep that he had purchased. His sons, Ernesto and Ernest, were behind the counter helping Mano grind the mutton. They had become very familiar with Mano's butcher shop, and they were quickly becoming experts with the equipment. Ernesto ran around the counter and jumped up on the lowest bar of the woman's black cage. He swung his feet around to the second lowest bar on the cage and then he hung upside down from his knees.

"Ernesto! Down!" commanded The Shoveler.

"It's ok. He's just having fun," said the woman. The Humanitarians had been trained well to be calm and polite in any situation.

Ernesto climbed higher until he was inside the black cage with the woman. The woman hugged Ernesto.

"It's safe in here with me, Ernesto. You see, thanks to XO, in here we're safe from God's Finger," she explained to him, but really she was explaining it to Mano and The Shoveler. Like XO, it was in The Humanitarian's best business interests that people keep dying. God's Finger created as much demand as panic, and the XO Life Cages could only be rented by the month, never owned, so that demand would never dwindle, even if God's Finger appeared cured.

The man reached into his black cage with his arm to tip his cap. "Gentleman, sorry to bother you, but we're not looking for XO Meats at all. In fact, we're just here to tell you about how you can rent your own cage."

"We already know about it, asshole. Thank you," said Mano dismissively, and with the same angry tone he used with everyone else wearing cages. "Would you like some sheep? I butchered one last night."

"Hey, I didn't mean to upset you," pleaded the man.

"Do you want some sheep? Or not?" Mano asked, holding up a bloody sheep's leg.

Ernest put down his own cut of sheep to walk over to The Humanitarians. He moved his finger along one of the woman's iron bars.

"Do you mind?" asked The Shoveler as he shook the man's cage a little.

"No, of course not. Do you have any questions about it?"

asked the man.

"What is it made out of?" Ernesto asked.

"It's like iron, but lighter," answered the woman.

"Like iron, you say, but lighter..." said The Shoveler.

"That's exactly right."

"So, is it iron?"

"It's a lot like it," said the man.

The Humanitarians tried to act natural while their cages were being studied by everyone but Mano, who was making his lack of interest very obvious. The Humanitarians acted as if what they were wearing was as common as a man wearing a cardigan with trousers or a woman wearing a sun dress.

"Look, if you're going to be in here, you'll need to buy some meat," demanded Mano. He chopped off another leg of a sheep so hard that it threw itself onto the floor. "I'm trying to run a fucking business here!" Mano picked up the leg and set it back onto the chopping block.

"We understand," said the woman. The Humanitarians fought Mano's shortness with pleasantness, grace, and etiquette, which frustrated Mano even further. "We'll take two cuts of whatever the special is."

"I don't have any specials. You want a leg?"

"Yes, please, a leg. That sounds lovely."

Mano wrapped the leg that had just fallen onto the floor in brown paper. As he wrapped it, he half-heartedly blew on it to clean it. He set the package on the counter.

"How much do we owe you?" asked the man.

"It's free," said Mano.

"Free?" asked the man, surprised. "But you said this is a business. How do you stay open?"

"It's free for people who participate in The Death Lessons. Now you're going to need a Death Lesson," insisted Mano.

"What is a Death Lesson?" asked the woman.

"I'll show you exactly what it is if you'll have one."

The man and the woman looked at each other nervously

while Ernest joined his brother climbing on the cages. Ernest had climbed all the way to the top of the woman's cage, and was preparing to leap from the woman's cage to the top of the man's cage where Ernesto was maneuvering. "I don't see why not," said the woman, struggling to stay upright so that Ernest wouldn't fall off the top of her cage.

"Sure, yes, please, give us a Death Lesson!" The man steadied his cage with the shifting weight of Ernesto above him.

"Great news!" exclaimed Mano. "Ok, first you'll have to take off those unsightly cages."

Without hesitation, the man explained that taking off the cages was the only thing that they weren't really willing to do.

"If death can't get inside your cage, then neither can a death lesson," explained Mano, suddenly proud of himself. "Now, take them off!"

The man and woman from Nun's Hat had been in Pie Time for many weeks before investing in XO Life Cages, and they hadn't yet died. It seemed reasonable to them that removing the cages for a few moments with Mano in the sheep pen would likely be ok. Besides, they knew they would have to remove the cages at various times during their lives for basic maintenance.

"Let's do it," said the man.

"If you say so," said the woman.

They took off their cages like scuba divers taking off scuba equipment. A body that was once in a cage designed to protect it seems awfully small and vulnerable once it is removed from that cage. Like a turtle. The man and the woman, although still very beautiful, looked very small and soft.

In that moment, Mano looked even bigger.

Everyone, including The Shoveler and his two boys, walked through Mano's butcher shop, past his bloody chopping block, and out of the double doors in the back. Everyone stood in a line on the edge of the pen.

"You can ride them," said Ernest.

"You ride them?" said the man in disbelief. "Don't you think I'll be too big and heavy to ride on the back of a sheep?"

"They're strong. And they *want* to carry you."

"I see."

Ernesto also added some basic information before Mano had the chance. "They're all named Curls."

"You can pick one!" shouted Ernest.

The Shoveler tried to shush Ernest who was getting very excited about his chance to co-teach a Death Lesson. The Shoveler picked his son up and held him. But Ernest squirreled out of the hold.

"Pick one for what?" the woman asked Ernest as he slipped from his father's grip.

"To die!" answered Ernesto.

Mano filled in some of The Humanitarians' unanswered questions, and then he tightened the biggest sheep saddle he had on Curls. The man, reluctantly, lowered his weight down onto Curls, who was the biggest of all the sheep in the pen. He was reluctant to let go of all his weight, fearing that he might injure the sheep, but Ernesto encouraged him.

"It's ok," he said." Just lift your feet off the ground now. They're strong."

So the man from Nun's Hat did. And so did the woman. As they rode around in the pen, they laughed harder than they had laughed in a long time. They felt free, and full of joy. They felt lighter and alive. They felt like they were a part of the world.

When the woman fell from Curls, she decided to rest in the mud instead of getting up right away. Curls walked over to her and licked her face. Curls' cold pointy tongue tried to hollow out her nostrils. It made her laugh so hard that she cried. She rolled around in the mud until her entire body was covered in it, and she kept crying. The man, seeing her roll around in the mud, fell off of Curls and rolled around in the mud with her. Together they laughed and cried while Mano, The Shoveler, Ernesto, and Ernest watched.

"Now I will need your help," Mano interrupted the rolling. The Humanitarians sat up on their elbows in the mud and listened. "I need you both to pick out a sheep."

Unlike all the children before them when Mano asked this same question, the man and the woman refused to pick a sheep. They knew Mano's intentions.

They whispered to each other, then turned to Mano. "We don't want to pick one."

"That's no good. You have to pick one," Mano insisted. "In order to complete your lesson, you must pick a sheep."

They whispered to each other again. The woman was most convincing in her whispering, and the man resigned with a sigh.

"If we must pick a sheep, then we'll pick the smallest one." It made some sense to them that if a sheep had to die, that it be the one with the least meat, the one with the least to lose from death, the one that took up the least amount of space inside of their guilt. They picked the one that was, to them, more of an afterthought of a sheep.

They pointed at the black poodle in the far corner of the pen.

"Which one?" Mano was confused as to where The Humanitarians were pointing. He tried to clarify.

"The smallest black one," said the woman. "That one right there."

"I'm sorry, that's not a sheep," said Mano.

"That's Mano's poodle," said Ernest.

"It looks like a sheep. Look how poofy it is!" said the man.

"It does look poofy like a sheep, you're right. But it's not a sheep," explained Mano.

"But that's what we picked," said the woman. "We've followed all the rules of your Death Lessons, and you asked us to pick and that's what we've picked."

And it was. It *was* what they picked.

The Death Lesson on this particular day had quickly become Mano's own. He trudged slowly and sloppily through the mud to plop down into it next to the black poodle. He pet it, and he told it he loved it. It was his first real chance to tell something that he loved it before it died. And he did love it. He didn't love it like he had loved Pepe, and he didn't love it like he had loved his mother. But it *was* love. It was the kind of love that he had for himself, a love born from understanding, because they shared a space for so long. They had for so long now walked the same steps. They survived together. "I love you," he told it. And just like that, the love was true.

"You don't have to butcher the poodle," said The Shoveler, who put his hand on the back of Mano's shoulder as he sat in the mud. He tried to lean all the way down and give Mano a hug, but his back hurt from all the grave shoveling he had been doing lately.

"I don't?"

"No, you don't."

But The Shoveler was wrong. Mano *did* have to, and he knew it. Learning to let go of the thing you love once it is picked is the whole point of The Death Lessons. Without that point at its center, The Death Lessons just becomes senseless killing. So, he picked the black poodle up, and he carried it inside. He thought for a moment about Beulah Minx, and her dead husband, The Postman. It was The Postman's death hole from where the poodle came. The black poodle's butchering would be a butchering of Beulah's grief as much as it was a butchering of Mano's own love.

The Shoveler and his two boys followed Mano inside, then they said their own goodbyes to the black poodle. They left the butcher shop because they understood that Mano needed to be alone. The man and woman stayed on their backs in the sheep's pen, resting their bodies completely in the mud.

Mano could hear them still giggling. When he looked back at them, they looked happy. They were staring at the sky. When they both closed their eyes, two black birds flew overhead.

Mano sobbed as he told the black poodle what he was going to do to it. He looked it in the eyes and explained everything. "I'm going to stun you with this hammer," was the first thing he said. He showed the poodle the hammer that would stun it. He felt the weight of the hammer in his hands. It felt so heavy. It felt like maybe it was the same weight as the poodle. The poodle looked at the hammer as if it didn't know what a hammer was for. Mano picked up the poodle and placed it on its side. He held it down with one hand so it couldn't stand back up. He held the hammer above the poodle.

Mano wasn't quite ready, so he said something else. He said, "I shouldn't have let you play in the mud today after Inez gave you a bath. Look at you. You're so muddy." Just the thought of Inez made the hammer in Mano's hand even heavier. He couldn't hold it up any longer, and he couldn't look at the poodle while the hammer came down, so he looked at the door.

That's when Mitzi Let came back from the dead to knock on the front window of the butcher shop.

28.

Mitzi Let opened the double doors of the butcher shop slowly. She had never seen double doors before. Her eyes were wide open. "Our dead bodies are not going to the sea!"

Mitzi was out of breath. She was alive, but she looked entirely dead. Her face was full of cuts and scrapes, and one gash stretched all the way across the bridge of her nose, past her cheek, and to her ear. Her clothes were torn and heavy with river water. She wasn't wearing any shoes. Her hair was matted with blood. She smelled like a rotten animal. Her left arm had been broken in many places, and it hung off her shoulder. It swung at her side when she walked. In her right hand, she was holding Sisi Medium's bathroom clock.

Mano thought he was seeing the dead. Seeing the dead walk in at the very moment that you're about to kill your poodle was just enough of an omen for Mano to spare the poodle. He set down his hammer next to it on the chopping block.

"Mitzi?" Mano had never really met Mitzi in person before, other than when her body floated beneath the bridge after her husband and Pepe. So he wasn't even so sure it was Mitzi at all. The poodle was licking Mano's ankle. The dead felt like they were now living all around him. "It's nice to meet you. I'm Mano. I'm Pepe's..."

Mitzi interrupted Mano as he searched for the right word. "There is no time to talk now. I've come to tell you something. They're catching our bodies down river in Nun's Hat. But they don't have enough. We need to send more."

"Mitzi, slow down. This is all too much. I watched you die in the river."

"...There is a pyramid there. It's made of all the dead bodies..."

"Mitzi, Mitzi..."

"They put me on it, right near the top, but I woke up."

Mano needed Mitzi to slow down. He didn't understand what she was trying to say, and her eyes were too big for him to look into.

"I yelled for three days and nights, 'Hey, I'm not dead, I'm not dead, please help me,' but no one came."

Weeks before, when Mitzi woke up from her coma near the top of the pyramid of dead bodies in Nun's Hat, everyone in that town was waiting by the nets in The Cause for more bodies. The monument was nearly complete, but the bodies stopped coming at the worst time. They needed just a few more to make a pinnacle, but the charred and chest-hollowed bodies stopped floating downriver. When the bodies from upriver stopped washing up in their nets, they had to wait for their own to die. But everyone died natural deaths at the very ends of their long lives in Nun's Hat, and everyone was young there. So the pyramid would stay incomplete for some time.

No one in Nun's Hat could hear Mitzi's call from her spot near the top of the pyramid, so she had to crawl down the monument without anyone's help. She was much too cold to wait for anyone to help. It was the middle of the night. The moon shone on the dead faces of everyone she knew from Pie Time as she used their bodies like a staircase. She saw the faces of The Postman and The Barber, and she saw the face of her son, Pepe. She took the chance to finally kiss it goodbye. She told it she loved it, and she brushed its hair. It wasn't burned like the others. She didn't see the face of her husband, The Butcher, even though she looked for it on every body she stepped on.

Mano pulled out a stool from behind the counter for Mitzi to sit on. "Mitzi, would you like a seat? Can I get you some water?"

"They want more bodies." Mitzi's eyes were still wide and unblinking.

"Ok, ok, they want more bodies. But first, drink some water."

"They want more bodies to finish the monument. They're waiting for us to send more bodies down the river."

"Mitzi, who are you talking about? Who wants more bodies? What monument?" Mano put a glass of water on the chopping block next to Mitzi.

Mitzi set down Sisi's clock, and picked up the water with her good arm. "You said you needed more clocks for the shop, so I brought you one."

"I said that?"

"It doesn't have a cow on it though. Still, it works. I fixed it." She looked around the butcher shop for a place to put it. "Did you change things around in here? Didn't the chopping block used to be further in the back?"

"Yes, it did. I wanted customers to watch me do their butchering." Mano was being patient for the right time to ask Mitzi about the bodies and the monument again. But it seemed like Mitzi was suddenly less interested in that subject, and more interested in the changes Mano had made to the butcher shop since her husband's death.

"I like it. Change is good." Mitzi stood up and dragged her broken body around the rest of the shop to see what else had changed. She picked up Sisi's clock from the chopping block and put it on a shelf next to the jars of salt. "You are so much bigger. Look at you!" Mitzi was now completely focused on Mano's body. She moved her head up and down. "You're gigantic! I mean, you're mammoth!"

"Ok, yes."

"How did you get so big? Was I really gone that long?"

"You've been gone for a month or so. You're counted among the dead." Mano sat down on the stool. He was relieved that Mitzi was alive. He felt like that would make Pepe happy, if he could know that. Mano thought about all the questions he could ask her about Pepe.

"But I'm not dead." Mitzi was standing directly behind Mano now. She threw her torso forward and to the side so that her broken arm was tossed over Mano's shoulders. "Can't you tell?"

"Yes. I know, now, of course. Here's your water. Drink, drink." Mano picked up her glass of water and was about to turn around to hand it to her.

"Do you need me to prove it to you?" With her good arm, she pulled Mano backward into her body. He felt her big breasts on his back. She smelled like an old raccoon that had been rooting in trash. Now that his body had been washed the night before by Inez, it was a smell he was acutely aware of.

"Mitzi, this isn't..."

Mitzi shushed him. She moved her arm upward in front of Mano, where Mano was holding so many things. She pressed her finger against where she thought his lips were, but she was pressing against his nose. She closed her arms and pressed her forehead against the back of his neck. She had to push some of the encyclopedias on Mano's body to the side. "It's ok. Pepe's asleep."

"Oh! I'm not..." Mano stopped his sentence to think. He suddenly understood that, in her eyes, he was her husband, The Butcher. He thought to tell her that Pepe was dead, not asleep, and that her husband was dead, too. Instead, he continued with a different strategy. "I think Pepe is waking up. Will you go check on him?"

"But I missed you. I want *this* first." She pushed her hands down past all the things that Mano was holding around his chest, and down through all the things he was holding in front of his stomach, past the paper strap that held his hot water bottle tight against his back, and past the bicycle pump. She pumped the bicycle pump a few times, then let go. Mano felt the puffs of air between his legs. Her hand kept moving past the black umbrella, which accidentally opened halfway. She pushed it closed, and her hand kept going down.

When her hand moved further down, past all of the things Mano held there, he stopped her. "You can't have this yet, Mitzi. You have to check on Pepe first."

"I do?" Her hand held as much of Mano in it as it could. It was warm and strong.

Mano grabbed Mitzi's good arm and carefully pulled it out of his pants. A few of his things fell to the floor and made a crashing sound. He turned around to face her. "Don't you hear Pepe crying?"

"Yes."

He was stern. "Go put him back to sleep, then you can have whatever you want."

"You promise?"

"Yes."

Mano gently pushed her toward the double doors at the back of the butcher shop which led out to the sheep pen. He gathered his things to his body, and stood up straight. He thought about leaving her alone in the butcher shop, a space that was familiar to her, until she gained her reality back, until she knew how to be among the living again. He started walking toward the front doors.

"Pepe!"

Mano was just slipping out of the front doors when he heard Mitzi's voice calling Pepe from the sheep's pen. Her voice sounded different than before. It sounded more like what he imagined her voice to sound like when it knew reality. Mano understood he was now supposed to be Pepe for her. "Yes, mother?"

"There are two dead people out here."

The caged man and caged woman from Nun's Hat were the first people not from Pie Time to die in the plague of God's Finger.

"They're so beautiful!" Mitzi yelled.

"Are you sure they're dead?" he yelled back, standing still in the double doors at the front of the butcher shop, now wanting to escape even more than before.

"Yes, I'm very sure. They have death holes, just like you did."

"I'm not Pepe," Mano whispered to himself.

Once outside, Mano saw the man and woman were still on their backs in the mud. Curls was still licking the woman's face. Both of their faces still looked happy. Their cages were still side by side, open on the ground outside of the pen.

"What are those?" Mitzi was pointing to the cages.

"I'm not sure."

"Hmm...*War...on...Death*," she read out loud. "It looks like these two lost that war."

Inside the death hole in the woman's chest was a red dog collar, and in the man's death hole was a set of dog tags. Mano picked up the collar and the tags. He thanked the man and the woman. He folded their arms over the holes in their chests, and he moved their hands so that they were touching. He didn't know if they loved each other while they were alive, but he thought they would at least appreciate being able to hold the hand of the one they died alongside.

"Tomorrow, I'll take you to The Shoveler's new graveyard," Mano said to the dead bodies. "You'll like it there."

Mano walked back into his shop, leaving The Humanitarians just as they were. He left Mitzi outside, too, as she was trying to figure out how to wear the smaller of the two cages. He felt overwhelmed now with death, with all of the things that he was holding on to, with the idea of being Pepe in the face of Pepe's mother, with the idea—even for a few moments—of being a son again.

Mano didn't know the black poodle's name, or if it had a name, so he couldn't etch its name into the new dog tags. Instead, with his most precise knife, he etched *I'm Sorry* into the tags, and hung it from the poodle's collar. The poodle looked happier with a collar. It looked more like a pet now than a shadow.

"I'm sorry," Mano said to the poodle. He held the tag forward in his hands. "See how easy it is to say?"

Mitzi walked back in through the back door. She was wearing the smaller of the two XO Life Cages around her body. She had been crying. The sun was going down. "We should send those bodies down The Cure so they can finish their monument."

Mano sighed with helplessness. "Mitzi, I don't know what you're talking about."

"The pyramid for the dead," she explained. "It only needs a few more."

"Mitzi," Mano put his hands into her new cage and held her shoulders to face him. With Mitzi in a cage, she was now almost half the size of Mano. "Do you know who I am?"

"Of course," she said. "A mother knows her own son."

Mano looked Mitzi directly in her eyes and asked her to go home and wait for him there. "I have to work in dad's shop tonight, but I'll be home soon."

"Ok," she agreed. Mitzi opened both double doors, this time with more awareness of how they work. "Wait...what do you think?"

"What do I think about what?"

"About my new cage?" She did a circle for Mano.

"I think it looks great," said Mano.

"Should I wear it?"

"Yes. And you should never take it off."

29

The XO House of the Lord Everlasting was the official name of Pie Time's new church, but it soon became more widely known, simply, as The Hole. The Hole was only the second church ever built in Pie Time, but most importantly, its capacity to hold believers was more than twice that of Lady Blood's. The Hole was a cathedral—something Lady Blood could never claim—and it was built with the expectation of future generations, with stone and granite and iron or something like it. It was flanked by flying buttresses, and stone carvings of all the apostles at the last supper were above the cathedral's entrance. Even the faces of Judas and Jesus were made distinguishable, which could not be said of the wood carving rendition of the last supper above the main doors of Lady Blood. Its windows were made with stained glass, and its pews, of which there were twice as many as Lady Blood, were made of wood imported from other countries, not wood cut for the sake of efficiency from the trees west of Pie Time.

The Hole was clean, strong, serious, large, and most importantly, it was new. It was exactly what Pie Time wanted, or needed, at that exact time in its history, even though it didn't know it wanted or needed it until it had been built. It made Lady Blood look more like an old round white barn, which, more or less, it was, and very few people were willing to continue attending church in an old round barn when something like The Hole existed across the street.

After the construction of The Hole was complete, which only took a week—a feat that many in town claimed was a miracle—a mass exodus from Lady Blood began. That week Father Mothers III delivered his most fiery homily of all time, though only six people were there to witness it. "Friends, we're already in purgatory. Can you feel it? Can you feel the hellfire licking its pointy rat tongue between our toes?" He looked right at Beulah Minx, who was deaf, and he waited a few seconds for her to answer his question, but no answer to his question ever came.

So, technically, only five of the six people in attendance heard it, because one was Beulah Minx. And another one of those remaining five people was Lil' Jorge, with his table-top haircut, who could barely speak, and who was eating an XO chocolate bar behind the pulpit during the homily. The remaining four people were in attendance primarily to get another chance to study the nude confessional photographs pinned on the north wall.

At The Hole, the new priest in town, Father Felipe, regaled his new attentive audience with stories and music from foreign lands. His hair was shiny and black, and his eyebrows were thick and even blacker. His lips were small and rough from cigarettes, and he got his shaves on Saturdays at XO Haircuts. So by Sundays, he had a perfect layer of stubble. When he introduced himself, he did so at length, and with a very charming accent that floated around, bouncily at the vowels, and came down softly on all the consonants, always with a Spanish guitar in his arms, which he strummed beautifully and effortlessly as his sentences flipped and twisted, and always with an XO Smoke in his mouth that gestured as if it were conducting its own tiny orchestra just outside his mouth as he spoke. That's how Father Felipe told of his travels. He was a traveling priest, and would go where there was the most need. Unbeknownst to the residents of Pie Time, the news of God's Finger was spreading widely with the help of The Businessman.

Unlike in Mothers' homily, there was no talk of God's Finger in Father Felipe's homily, and there was no sense of doom—only the kind of language that made the world seem much larger than anyone ever knew. At the eucharist, he served wine imported from the Burgundy region of France, and bread imported from a tiny town where he once served as priest in the mountains of Oaxaca. "*Bahty* of Christ, *Blaht* of Christ, *Bahty* of Christ," he'd say over and over again with his charming accent, as he poured good wine and pushed good bread into the mouths of the scared and sad.

The people of Pie Time had been scared of death, and had been saddened by the deaths of their loved ones. They knew they had to be free from sin, and being good was the only way they knew how to not die. Going to church was one of the only ways they knew how to be good. But on Sundays at The Hole, they were able to forget about God's Finger in the worldly stories and music of Father Felipe. Going to church was as much of an escape as it was a reckoning.

"Thanks be to God," he'd say.

"Thanks be to God," they'd say.

"Thanks be to XO," he'd say.

"Thanks be to XO," they'd say.

Directly behind The Hole was now Pie Time's second graveyard, XO Graves. Unlike The Shoveler's Graveyard, which originally sparked Pie Time's new craze for burials, the plots at XO Graves were less expensive, and it was open 24 hours a day for anyone who would like to visit their dead at any hour. Grief was on no reasonable schedule, and used no reasonable clock, so XO Graves would never close. At the entrance of XO Graves was a gate where the griever was to pay a very reasonable price to enter for a visit with their dead. Also, just inside the gate, was XO Flowers, a florist with fresh flowers that grievers could purchase to put directly on the graves of their dead. It was both convenient and respectful. XO Flowers also sold other items like rosaries, tiny crucifixes, tiny bibles, snow globes with the most famous scenes from both the New and Old Testament, and the same French wine and bread from Father Felipe's eucharistic rites. If you liked the worldly taste of the eucharist, then you could have it at home as well.

The one characteristic of The Hole that Mothers was never

able to accept wasn't the priest who was far more dapper than him, or his music or stories, or its graveyard. It was the one thing he was actually capable of competing with—the size of The Hole's cross. Mothers thought if he could just build a bigger cross, much bigger even than the one that he had recently built with the money collected in the name of Father Mothers II's death, then Lady Blood would be in a much better position to compete with The Hole. The new cross, according to Mothers' plans for it, would need to be the size of a dozen men, so that everyone at the last supper, theoretically, could have comfortably died upon it at the same time.

It was a project that Mothers knew he had to complete alone. The Builder, who had helped him with his most recent modifications of Lady Blood, had been seen in attendance at The Hole, and there was no one left to ask, alive or loyal. He would have to build the cross by himself, just as his own father would have, and *his* father before him. Sharing the name of Father Mothers had meant, up until then, that you were self-sufficient at the very least. And loyal. The new cross on top of Lady Blood would shine with newness, and be big enough for the Lord himself to climb down upon it from the heavens, on Easter Sunday no less, and speak about loyalty right there, in person, through the body of Mothers, for all to see. Yes, loyalty would make a fine subject for his Easter Sunday homily, Mothers thought. Where had loyalty disappeared to, he'd ask into the faces of his returning flock of believers.

By himself, on account of Lil' Jorge's shortness of stature, shortness of breath, and general ineptitude, Mothers toiled over the cross' construction for three days and nights. He hammered his own nails, tied his own ropes, and painted the entire thing gold. Upon the cross' completion, Mothers was very proud.

"Let us bless it, Lil' Jorge." Mothers and Lil' Jorge stood together outside of Lady Blood and looked up at what was, in those moments, the tallest man-made structure in Pie Time.

Mothers held Lil' Jorge's hand and then lovingly rubbed his table-top. He said a general Ash Wednesday prayer, and then he said a specific prayer about blessing the cross on account of its exceptional size.

"What do you think?" asked Mothers.

Lil' Jorge clapped his fat hands together. He wasn't looking at the cross.

"You like it? I like it, too, Lil' Jorge. We did a good job. I don't want to thank you for your help, because you didn't really help, but I do want to thank you for something far more important. Your *loyalty*. You have been loyal to me, Lil' Jorge, and you've been loyal to this church. That is unmistakable, and irreplaceable. So, thank you. You have been like a son to me. No, you're much more than *like* a son—you *are* my son. You are my son, Lil' Jorge, and I love you."

Lil' Jorge clapped some more, like a dolphin would. He watched his own hands clap. He clapped and clapped until it hurt.

30.

The deaths lessened.

Nearly half of the people of Pie Time were now living their lives entirely inside of their own XO Life Cages. The only people living outside of a cage, vulnerable to the plague of God's Finger, were those who couldn't afford one. What the caged were giving up in general comfort and freedom of movement was worth what they were getting in return: the security of not being poked or blessed too hard by God when they least expected it. The choice of cage was especially important, to get one large enough for their body so that they could complete simple tasks, like brushing their teeth at night or making sandwiches, or planting a tomato bush in the garden, or masturbating, but not too large so that their bodies would accidentally slip out of the cage's bottom latch when attempting any of these kinds of tasks. The more expensive XO Life Cages were painted gold, not black, and custom-made to fit their torsos and their lifestyles perfectly, and were worn only by The Businessman, The Banker, The Lawyer, The Landlord, and The Foreman. They wore their gold custom cages very proudly, and were sure to be seen wearing them at the XO Cafe on a daily basis.

The only person in Pie Time who could have afforded a custom life cage, but who didn't wear any cage at all, was Vera Good, despite the fact that she had helped conceive of the idea of the life cages. Vera hadn't spoken with her brother, The Foreman, since June Good's death. In fact, she hadn't spoken to anyone except for The Shoveler and his two sons, Ernesto and Ernest Horn, who also lived their lives uncaged.

"Can we have coffee and cigarettes in the cafe today?" asked Ernesto.

"No, our coffee and cigarettes are better here at home. Let's drink and smoke here again. It's better here," said Vera.

"Fran and her mothers took us to XO Cafe a few days ago

and the coffee and cigarettes there are TDF."

"They did, did they?"

"They have strawberry cigarettes for kids," added Ernest.

"What's TDF mean?" asked Vera.

"To die for," answered Ernesto.

"There's only one thing I would die for, and it's not coffee and it's not cigarettes." Vera looked at Ernest and Ernesto's disappointed faces. Their faces had quickly become her favorite two faces in Pie Time. She changed her tune. "But maybe they're just *that* good, yeah?"

"Yes, yes, please, can we?" said Ernest, already walking over to his jacket by the front door.

"I knew I shouldn't've let you spend your afternoons at Fran Rile's house."

On Mondays and Wednesdays, while The Shoveler kept up with his new grave digging business, Ernesto and Ernest were babysat by Rona Rile and Lana Rile, the mothers of Fran Rile, who was the same age as Ernesto. But on Tuesdays and Thursdays, and more recently also Fridays, Ernesto and Ernest were babysat by Vera Good. They spent most of their mornings in the music room or drawing room of Vera's very large house, drinking coffee and smoking cigarettes and talking about their dreams from the night before. Ernesto would most often dream of space and the strange people who lived there, while Ernest would most often dream of himself on a stage. He talked about wanting to wear beautiful dresses and singing country western songs.

After June Good's death, Vera had never been as happy as she was on the days that she got to spend with Ernesto and Ernest. In the afternoons, they'd often sit on the swing on Vera's wraparound porch. Vera would always wear June Good's fur coat and pearls, while Ernest would wear one of June's childhood dresses that Vera managed to salvage from The Foreman's attic before he cleaned it out completely.

Ernesto dressed like his father, with trousers and a work shirt. Together, just like that on the porch swing, they'd watch the people of Pie Time walk past them on the sidewalk wearing large black cages. The three of them liked to make fun of the cages and laugh.

But today, Ernesto and Ernest wanted something different.

"Ok, this *one* time. It can't hurt, can it?" Vera indulged the boys.

"Yay!" squealed Ernesto.

"And there will be plenty of people in cages at the cafe we can make fun of."

As soon as Vera, Ernesto, and Ernest walked through the double doors of the XO Cafe, they noticed everyone but them was wearing gigantic XO Life Cages on their bodies. In a room like that, the three of them looked incredibly small, like the seeds of some pod had spilled out into the room, and were tiny on the tile with no soil to burrow into. Because so many people were now wearing cages, those who were not looked tiny and vulnerable wherever they went.

"Look! June Good is alive!" said The Businessman, as they slurped hot coffee from their XO coffee mug. Everyone in the room laughed, and their cages shook around their torsos and rattled against the tables.

Ernesto took it upon himself to introduce Vera to the caged hecklers. "This isn't June Good. Her name is Vera."

Vera put her hand on the top of Ernesto's head to let him know that he didn't have to do any speaking on her behalf.

"We know very well who that is, son," said The Banker. Then The Banker spoke directly to Vera. "You haven't made a deposit in a while. I'm wondering when you'll be in next. I have a few ideas."

"I won't be in anytime soon," said Vera. "You can count on that."

"You can't count on a lot these days. I can't even count

on you walking out of here alive if you're not going to wear a life cage." The Banker reached his arm outside of his cage, which looked like gold monkey bars, and carefully pulled the mug of hot coffee back through the bars and to his lips. "You want a smoke?"

"No, we brought our own. Thanks."

"You buy your coffee up there," Ernest pointed to the counter for Vera. A girl Vera had never seen before stood waiting for them wearing a white scout hat with black letters on both sides. *XƟ*.

"Vera." The Businessman introduced a new, more serious tone, the same tone they used on Enid in the confession booth. "If you choose not to wear a cage, that's your own damn hard-headed stupidity. But it's just not right putting the kids out there without one. You might as well poke them straight through their chests now by yourself and get it over with."

Vera ignored The Businessman. She and the two boys walked to the counter.

"We'll take three black coffees please." Ernesto did the ordering. "And one strawberry cigarette." He remembered to order Ernest's cigarette.

The girl behind the counter looked at Vera as if to get approval for the addition of the strawberry cigarette to the order.

"Yes, one strawberry cigarette," Vera said, reluctantly.

"Did you hear what happened to The Humanitarians?" asked The Builder to Vera's back. "The big ugly monster, Mano Medium, made them take off their cages."

"He *didn't*!" interrupted Ernesto. "We were there. And Mano's not a monster."

Vera shushed Ernesto, and she escorted the boys to their own table.

"He did *indeed*," The Businessman corrected Ernesto. "They had no choice. It was one of those Death Lessons he likes to do on people."

The Businessman, The Banker, and The Builder began talking among themselves. "As soon as those poor people took off their cages, they got fingered."

"You don't say? Just like that?"

"Just like that. A monster like that has no right..." The Businessman trailed off while reaching for their coffee, but they knocked it over. The girl at the counter walked over to sop up the spill for them. They tried to help, but couldn't position themselves in their cage correctly to sop up any of the spill on their own.

"It's ok. I got it," she said, and then she retreated to pour them another cup. It was the second cup they had spilled that morning.

"Well, it sounds like they sure learned a lesson all about death."

"Hell if I learn about death like that."

"It's a damn shame." The Banker stood up to adjust the waist of his trousers, but couldn't fit his arms around the gold bars far enough to tighten his belt. Then he dropped his cigarette, but he couldn't bend down far enough in his cage to pick it back up.

"A damn shame is right," agreed The Builder while looking out the window to allow The Banker to struggle with picking up his cigarette without being stared at.

"We all have to die," interrupted Ernest.

"It's ok, Ernest..." hushed Vera.

"Is that right, son? Go on..."

Ernest kept talking. "It's not a matter of fighting death, but a matter of loving it, like anything else."

All of the men laughed. "Did that big monster Mano teach you that?"

"Yes, Mano taught me that." Ernest was proud.

"Did Mano teach you how to wear a dress, too?"

The men laughed.

"Smoke your cigarette, Ernest." Ernest puffed on his cigarette, and Vera and Ernesto puffed on the ones they had brought.

Ernesto got up from the table to help The Banker pick up his cigarette. He handed it to The Banker, but The Banker didn't thank him.

"You can't even bend over, mister," said Ernesto.

"I can, too, look." The Banker bent halfway over, but his cage knocked the corner of his table, which then tipped over onto the floor, spilling all three mugs of hot coffee onto the tiles.

"I bet you can't do *this* either." Ernest slid around on top of the coffee spill, and kicked his right leg up high. His dress flew upward and got caught on his shoulder. His exposed legs were bending into his cowboy boots, and he started singing a country song into an imaginary microphone.

The girl came from behind the counter with a mop.

"Well, I may not be able to bend over in this cage, and I sure as hell can't do whatever the hell that little girl is doing. But I'm not going to be the next person poked dead by God." The Banker was looking right at Ernesto, and pushing his finger back and forth into his own fist. "You and your little sister *are* going to be the next people poked dead by God! Or maybe it'll be your new pretend mother. Is that right, Vera? Two death-poked mothers in a row for the Horn boys. Now, that'd be a real shame wouldn't it?"

"Let's go." Vera stood up, and walked toward the door with her XO mug of coffee left untouched.

The Businessman stood up to feign politeness as Vera exited. "No one has died in a week, Vera. Not since those poor Humanitarians. And *no* one has *ever* died inside a life cage. We'd like to keep it like that."

"Would you? Is that really true?" Vera asked knowing the answer to her own question. "You of all people want to keep people from dying? Is that the best way for you to make money?"

"Of course, we don't want anyone to die," said The Businessman.

"This coffee is terrible," said Vera.

"And the cigarettes are too sweet," said Ernest.

31.

Mimi Minutes was on her sister Mary's back inside their shared XO Life Cage. Mary was standing by the table full of fruit salads, egg salads, potato salads, jello salads, crustless triangle ham sandwiches, fruit pies, and two very similar refried bean dips. Behind the dishes was a two liter bottle of XO Cola. Sharing a cage with Mary felt to Mimi like she was conjoined with her sister again.

Mary stuck her finger in the apple pie that her father, The Baker, had made specially for the pot luck, but Mimi, who was growing slowly like a large hump on her back, licked it clean before Mary got the chance. Mary stuck another finger into the apple pie, but used a finger on her other hand so that Mimi couldn't reach it with her mouth. Mary turned her head away from Mimi and licked that finger clean.

Father Felipe corrected them. "Patience is a virtue," he said. "You need to wait, Mary. We will all eat after the smile contest."

The pie looked like Sisi's Medium's torn apart body.

"Can I be in the smile contest, Father Felipe?"

"No, Mary, you're much too old. The smile contest is for children." Father Felipe poked his hand out through his cage to indicate that a child was someone who was only as tall as his knee. "But your sister! She is welcome to compete in it." Father Felipe tilted his head to the side and gave Mimi a very charitable look. "She has such a beautiful smile."

"But we're the exact same age," complained Mary, with a tongue smear of pie on her finger. "We're twins."

"Patience, Mary."

As a way to celebrate the unprecedented week-long span without a God's Finger death in Pie Time, Father Felipe announced that he would be honoring the heavenly gift of XO Life Cages, in addition to the resurrection of Jesus Christ, by hosting the first ever XO Pie Time Easter Sunday Contest Fest and Pot Luck. There would be four contests: a pretty baby contest for the newborn babies, a smile contest for the young children who had yet to set their sinful feet down the path through puberty, a beauty contest for men dressed as women, and a life cage decoration contest. There was also a row of carnival games, including a ring toss, a balloon dart game, and a weight guessing tent.

It was a particularly cold and windy Easter Sunday with no spring sun in sight. The celebration seemed terribly important for a town that had, until now, only death to celebrate.

"Today, we celebrate resurrection! We celebrate life!" With his elbows tight at his side inside his cage, Father Felipe awkwardly strummed his guitar on "resurrection," and then again on "life."

"Yes to not dying!" added the new Postman, who raised his XO Cola though the black iron bars of his cage, and into the air.

"But to more than that! To fighting death! To the fight against dying, just like Pie Time is doing today!" exclaimed Father Felipe.

"And Jesus, too!" shouted Mimi.

"To that, too!"

Everyone raised their XO Colas through their cages.

Then Father Felipe yelled, "Now bring on the pretty babies!"

Of the dozen babies entered in the pretty baby contest, only one wasn't crying. Only one wasn't inside of her own XO Baby Life Cage. The rest of the babies were propped upright by their own caged mother or father in a special chair designed to prop up babies who were in baby life cages, so they could sit up like little adults. The wind was cold on the babies' faces, and shiny snot trickled down their philtrums onto their top lips. The mothers and fathers covered their babies' faces with blankets right up until the moment Father Felipe passed by to judge them. As he judged the prettiness of each baby's face, the mother or father dropped the blanket, and their babies cried in the wind, red-faced and wet with snot.

The uncaged Baby Zuzu was the only baby who did not have her face kept warm with a blanket by her mother or father. She was the only baby not crying. She was the only baby not in a cage. She was laughing into the sharp teeth of the wind.

Inez was in a folding chair in the front row with her head down, not watching Baby Zuzu's prettiness be judged by Father Felipe. Inez was only there because she thought there could be the chance she would see Mano there, too. Every few moments, Inez lifted her head and looked around, hoping to catch sight of him. She kept her eye on the weight guessing tent in particular. Mano's glasses were in her purse.

Father Felipe had completed his judging, and he was prepared to announce the winner. "The prettiest baby in Pie Time *is*..." he looked down at his notepad to be sure he was pronouncing the name correctly. "...Zuzu Roar!"

There were a few polite claps, but the crowd of caged mothers and fathers were audibly disappointed. "My baby is prettier indoors," whined one of them.

Father Felipe then announced Baby Zuzu's prize. "And what does she win?! Nothing other than her very own XO Baby Life Cage!" There were more claps following this announcement. Even though many caged mothers and fathers wanted to see their own baby as the winner of the pretty baby contest, they had a difficult time not supporting such an appropriate prize for the one and only uncaged baby.

Father Felipe placed Baby Zuzu in her new baby life cage, and held her high above his head for the crowd to see. The crowd *ooohed*.

For the very first time in her life, Baby Zuzu cried.

When the caged Baby Zuzu was handed back to Inez, she didn't quite know how to calm her. Baby Zuzu was a new kind of baby, and it felt to Inez like she was holding a cage instead of her daughter. "Thank you, Father," she said over the strange new piercing sound of her baby's wail.

With a caged Baby Zuzu in her arms, Inez walked around the perimeter of the festival in order to calm her down. She was also looking for Mano. Her eyes scanned for people not wearing cages, but she found no one other than herself. She was cold. She put her arms inside of Baby Zuzu's new cage to warm her, and to warm her own arms.

"It's ok, it's ok, Bebé." Inez sang into Baby Zuzu's cries. "It's ok, it's ok."

Baby Zuzu kept crying.

"Do you not like it in there, Bebé? You're safe in there. You're safe now. You're not going to die."

Inez sat on a big rock on the edge of the festival, bouncing Baby Zuzu, and talking to her from outside of her baby cage. After she calmed down, Inez told Baby Zuzu all about her father, The Barber, and all about Mano, too, who was now The Barber. Every time Inez said Mano's name, she'd look up and around into the crowd of caged folk, and into the weight guessing tent.

"He's just a *boy*, Bebé. Just a *stupid* boy."

Baby Zuzu said her first word. "Boy."

"Yes! *Boy*! Good job. *Boy*. Boy."

"Boy."

"Yes, now say *Mama*. I'm your *mama*."

"Boy."

"Mama."

"Boy."

"Mama."

Baby Zuzu slowed down and tried to shape her mouth just right. "Mano."

The winners of the smile contest and the beauty contest were being announced on stage by Father Felipe. The best smile in the valley, according to the new priest, was that of

Fran Rile, who was just growing into her new adult teeth—a detail that was no doubt a key in her victory. Fran's mothers were ecstatic at this news. This family had figured out the most intimate way to make a triangle of bodies while still inside their cages, and in this triangle, they hugged for a long time.

The beauty contest winner was none other than The Foreman, who was wearing one of June Good's long and elegant sun dresses, despite the day's lack of sun. He wore June's high heels and her pantyhose. He had applied her lipstick just as she had done, and even managed to mimic her walk. He became her. It was so uncanny, this becoming of his late wife, that most people in the crowd shouted June Good's name as The Foreman took the stage. There was so much applause, in fact, that Father Felipe had no choice but to announce The Foreman as the winner.

"My sister isn't the only one who can pretend to be June," he said to The Businessman as they stood next to each other on the stage. The Foreman was posing, turning and blowing ridiculous kisses.

"You make a better June than Vera," said The Businessman out of the side of their mouth. They all laughed, though no one else knew what they were all laughing about.

Like all the other grand prizes, the winner of the beauty contest was to be presented with an XO Life Cage but, of course, The Foreman was already wearing one custom designed for his lifestyle, and he even had a few spare cages as well. So, in the spirit of Easter generosity, The Foreman commandeered the microphone from Father Felipe and made an announcement.

"I'd like to award this XO Life Cage I won to anyone here who doesn't yet have one." With one hand, he gestured to the cage which was propped on a little display stand, and he placed the other against his brow to imply a gesture of searching the crowd.

Everyone's heads twisted and turned to help him search. "Inez Roar needs a cage!" shouted The Tailor. He pointed to the back of the crowd where Inez was still sitting on the rock talking to Baby Zuzu.

"Two cages in one day for the Roar pair! That is quite the haul. Inez Roar, come up here and claim your new life cage." The crowd cheered.

Inez sat on the rock and stared at a crowd that suddenly all turned around to look at her. She heard her name, but she wasn't quite sure what she was supposed to do.

"Go up there and claim your cage," encouraged Lana Rile.

Inez didn't need Lana's encouragement to move from her seat on the rock. She only needed a town's worth of eyes on her. She had no choice, really, but to stand up and walk toward the stage. The stage was now a magnet, and she was pulled toward it. And in the center of that magnet was an even stronger magnet, with such an acute pull of gravity that she had no choice but to fall into it—an open life cage. Baby Zuzu started crying again, and her cries mixed with cheers and chants from the crowd. The crowd was chanting X-O-X-O-X-O. One leg at a time, Inez's body fell into, then became, the cage. She and her baby were like a planet and its moon being sucked into a black hole.

"May you two live very long and natural lives inside," said Father Felipe. And then to the crowd, he announced, "Now let's eat!"

As the cage clasped around Inez and Baby Zuzu, and as the crowd turned toward the long table full of homemade dishes, there was an enormous rumbling. Everyone froze, terrified they would be swallowed into the earth by an earthquake. But the sound wasn't an earthquake.

As most of Pie Time was celebrating the week of deathlessness at Father Felipe's XO Pie Time Easter Sunday Contest Fest and Pot Luck, Mothers was across the street inside Lady Blood under the largest handmade cross anyone had ever seen. He was delivering his fieriest homily yet, on the subject of loyalty, alone to Lil' Jorge, who was the one he needed the least to hear it.

"Our loyalty has disappeared. And just where has our loyalty disappeared *to*?" Mothers began quietly and slowly into the empty room. Then he screamed his homily into the fire. "Into *hell*. Your loyalty is burning in hell, backsliders! It is pulling you down into hell with it. Do you feel its weight? *Do* you? Do you *feel* it hanging like a weight from your fangs? Your fanged faces are burning in the hot steam above the boiling. That's your *loyalty*, there. That's *your* loyalty. You've made enemies with your own loyalty. Look at it! Do you see it? Where has it gone? To *hell*. And that's right where you're going, too. To follow it. And may you follow it all the way down down down, the whole way knocking your own *stupid* heads inside your own *goddamn* cages!"

And with that, came the explosion that everyone had heard. At first, Mothers, too, thought it was an earthquake, but an earthquake that was coming from above. Then, he thought perhaps it actually was the sound of the lord parting the clouds and reaching down from the heavens onto his new cross to push, with his righteous finger, all of the unloyal sinners deeper and harder down into hell. But, of course, none of that was true. The obscenely gigantic cross Mothers had built just a few days earlier on Ash Wednesday was far too heavy for the small concrete foundation that he had poured for it on the roof. It was far too tall and wide to withstand the slightest gusts of wind.

The cross came crashing down through the old roof of Lady Blood, tearing apart every piece of the unsound structure in its path. Wood beams were snapping in half. The last nail Mothers had hammered, still poking out from the intersection of the two planks of the cross, was the first point on the cross to impale Lil' Jorge in the center of his forehead, where four-day-old residue from his ashes still remained. The enormous weight of the rest of the cross flattened Lil' Jorge's body, along with everything else, completely.

In the center of the dusty rubble, stood Mothers surrounded by what remained of Lady Blood, crying into the sky, suddenly open above him.

"No, Lord! You've taken the wrong one. My son, my poor, poor son." He sobbed while he wiped the dust from his face. "You've taken the only loyal one."

"Oh, dear Mothers, what has happened?!" Father Felipe was out of breath, and the first to arrive. He was good at running even with the added new weight of his life cage around his upper body. The others were just catching up behind him. "Are you ok?"

Mothers pushed some of the rubble off of one of the pews. He sat there with his head down, silent.

"Mothers, are you ok?" Father Felipe tried again. This time, he strummed his guitar in his cage on "ok."

Mothers lifted his head to look into the new priest's eyes. "Rot in hell, Felipe." He pushed those words through his clenched teeth.

Fran Rile and some of the other children were poking around in the rubble beneath the gigantic fallen cross. Fran found the body of Lil' Jorge at the bottom. Blood was still gushing from his forehead and down over his table-top haircut. It was making a purple mud when it mixed with the dust. Fran also found a death hole in Lil' Jorge's chest the same size and shape as all the others. "God's Finger is back," she said.

Something small and colorful was inside of Lil' Jorge's hole. As Fran moved her hand above his hole, the small and colorful thing rose from the dead, resurrected right there into the palm of her hand. It felt warm.

"I found an egg!" With her award-winning smile, Fran lifted it above her head to show everyone. "I found an egg! I found an egg!"

"A painted egg!" shouted a few other children.

And that's how the tradition of hunting for Easter eggs began in Pie Time.

32.

The gigantic cross that crushed Lady Blood spared very little in its destruction. After the dust settled, and everyone went home for their Easter dinners, only Mothers and his confession booth were left standing where Lady Blood once stood.

Mothers couldn't stomach the thought of burying Lil' Jorge at all, especially in XO Graves amongst the plots of backsliders, but he also couldn't bear the thought of burning the corpse of his only son and sending it down The Cure to the sea, either. If anyone found out that he used such a passé way of disposing of his dead, then he'd lose all chance of regaining any of his deserters. So, Mothers buried Lil' Jorge himself, beneath the floor of his confession booth—the one place on the entire planet that Mothers knew that Lil' Jorge loved. Lil' Jorge loved spending time in the booth behind the screen with him, helping him set up the camera to take photographs of the nude, and also helping him develop the film.

Mothers also didn't have the heart, the energy, or the skill to rebuild the church his grandfather had built. So, he made due with the only structure left standing on the lot: the confession booth. The booth operated the same as before, only now he decided it would be open 24 hours every day to compete with XO.

Of course, Mothers did not allow life cages to be worn inside his booth, though his blindly vindictive reasoning was different than the blindly idealistic reasons why Mano didn't allow life cages to be worn during The Death Lessons. Before entering Mothers' confession booth, people were instructed to step out of their cages, and then to step out of their clothes. Then they were to tell Mothers of their sins. It became exactly the sort of thing some people in Pie Time really wanted—a place where they could feel free for a few moments, exposed and vulnerable, to move their arms and legs around in the dangerous air. His booth was a kind of station where they were lightened.

Because Mothers felt betrayed by his god who took away the only person in this world who had been loyal to him, he stopped the tradition of having people confess their sins in the name of god. Instead, Mothers had them confess their sins upon the body of Lil' Jorge, since they were, literally, confessing *upon* Lil' Jorge's dead body. "Upon the body of Lil' Jorge, tell me your sins," he would say. And they would do it. They would jump, spread their legs and flail their arms, and tell Mothers how they were bad, and then the flash bulb would go off and burn an image of their temporary moment of false freedom into the recorded history of Pie Time.

One night while wrestling with sleep, face down on the floor in the main room of the confession booth directly above Lil' Jorge's body, a vision came to Mothers. In his vision, the booth looked like a submarine with four round holes on the two longest sides of the booth. Instead of submarine sailors looking *out* of the holes, the people of Pie Time were looking *in*. It was a major shift of perspective for Mothers. Once inside the booth, he thought, there is nothing to see when we look out. There is so much to see though once we look inward.

The first thing the next morning, Mothers cut eight small round windows into the wooden walls of his confession booth, four on each side. And just like a submarine, he installed a wooden periscope with a convex lens at the very top, and a ladder at the back, so that the children could climb up on the roof and peer into the periscope to get a peek at what was happening inside, from above. Now anyone who wanted to watch the uncaged and naked confess would be able to. Above the front door, Mothers built Pie Time's first neon sign. He installed it above the front door of the booth where a cross

197

would have gone. In big electric neon letters the sign read, LADY BLOOD'S SUB.

The sign did manage to attract a few new participants to the booth, however, it was certainly not inexpensive to maintain. There was the cost of electricity, of course, and also the maintenance for all that neon. Despite Mother's falling out with the lord, he still felt it would have been very wrong to take money for confessions. People would not pay to confess, that was clear.

After the remodeling of the confession booth into the Lady Blood's Sub, Mothers struggled for many days about how to pay for the expenses that he was incurring. He prayed into the floor above Lil' Jorge's body about his mixed feelings. After much deliberation, he decided it would be acceptable— *responsible* even—to make money from this venture. The electric bills must be paid and he must be paid for his time. It was only right. So, below each circular window, and right next to the base of the periscope on the roof, Mothers installed a mechanical coin slot. These were the first mechanical coin slots ever to be installed in Pie Time, just a few days before the mechanical coin-slotted XO Cola machines were set into operation outside XO Meats. At Lady Blood's Sub, for a dime, a person could peep upon a live confession for one minute. For a quarter, a person could peep upon the entire live confession.

With that, Mothers figured he had entered into a healthy competition with The Hole, and with all of XO. It could be argued that he was in business, but he was hardly in competition.

33.

No one wanted a haircut. Mano didn't want to give anyone a haircut. He wanted only to feel his own clunky weight grow and settle into his own barber's chair, and he wanted to swivel in it, back and forth, back and forth, like the slow metronome he held somewhere on his body, in and out of the little parallelogram of sun that sat in his lap and reflected off the more metallic objects there—the saw, the radio Pepe had given him, the clock of his mother's that Mitzi had returned to him.

Outside of his window, a crowd of people had gathered in the street, but they were just more shapes. He didn't care why they were gathering, and he didn't leave his barbershop to ask. Without his glasses, he had no idea which shape belonged to which person. He had no idea that the shape of the one crawling on the ground at everyone's feet was Mitzi's. And he didn't care. Blurs in the stupid light.

As Mano swiveled in his chair, he caught a glimpse of the black square on the wall in the back room. For the first time, he could see a body in it. He couldn't see a face, but he could definitely see a body, and the body was getting bigger and bigger as he looked at it. The body was becoming bigger than the black square itself. The body was no longer even the shape of a person. It kept growing until it was bigger than the black square. It filled the entire back room and then it filled the barbershop. It grew and grew until it wasn't even a shape at all, but a feeling. The feeling took up all the space in the barbershop around Mano's body. And then the feeling became Mano's body.

Mano looked down at his own body. It was far too big. It was so big, there was hardly any space for the chair to swivel and recline. His size had become freakish, and could not be ignored by even his most loyal customers. His head and shoulders had collapsed inward toward his own center. His body was its own cage. The things he held settled into his body until they became his body. They felt nothing at all like love anymore. He held onto them only because he didn't quite know how to let them go.

Mano straightened what had become of his legs to rise from his barber's chair. He walked into the back room. He pushed his nose against the black square. "Are you in there, Pepe? Will you show me your face?"

Pepe showed his face inside of the black square.

Mano wanted to go inside the black square with Pepe, but the black square was just a black square and nothing else. "I can't come in there with you," Mano said. He couldn't hear Pepe say anything back. He couldn't hear a voice. He couldn't remember what Pepe's voice sounded like. And he couldn't remember Pepe's smell either. How is it we can lose a sound or a smell so easily once someone is gone, but their *face*—their face is always right there, floating in front of our own to haunt us, to taunt us back into a realm that doesn't really even exist, and where we aren't even welcome if it did.

Mano pushed his nose into the black square against Pepe's own nose, and breathed in like that so deeply, he almost lost his balance. He wanted to breathe in the whole world, but couldn't. There was no smell he recognized in that air other than the smell of the living.

Then Mano finally asked what he had meant to ask. "Are you in there, Mano? Will you show me your face?" Mano dug around into the mess of his own body, and found the radio Pepe had given him. He turned it on. He wanted to hear Pepe inside of it, from very deep in the future, maybe playing a polka, but instead some priest's voice inside of the radio said, "Do you feel his love?"

"No, I don't," answered Mano. "I don't feel it."

Mano could only feel the weight of the radio asking the question. It was just a radio. It was just a radio. It was just a radio. He threw it at the black square.

The black square cracked perfectly in half. A new horizon right in front of Mano's eyes split the world inside the black square into a top half and a bottom half. The top half of the black square fell onto Mano's head. It was heavy. Mano saw a sharp bright white light—a bolt of lightning behind his eyes. He kept his eyes closed to will death into taking him further into the darkness beyond the lightning bolt.

Beulah Minx was suddenly standing above him. She helped him lift the top half of the broken black square off of his head. She stood there, silently, waiting to see if Mano could still talk.

"What do you want?" Mano squinted at her.

"We're looking for Father Felipe."

Mano could barely understand Beulah. She spoke with the kind of voice that she, herself, had never before heard. "Who?"

"Father Felipe. Was he getting his haircut?" Beulah tried again.

"I can't look for anything. I don't have my glasses," Mano said. He didn't know if it was Beulah's deafness or his sore head that was causing her voice to muddy and echo in his ears. He knew only that Beulah could understand how it must feel to not only not remember a voice, but to have never even known a voice, and to have never even known your own. Mano thought she had asked him something about his father. "*What* about my father?"

Beulah stood there, perplexed, not answering his question.

"Father?" he said loudly, exaggerating his lips so they could be read. "Fah...thurrr."

Beulah was staring at his mouth.

Then she tried again. "Far...ther...Far...lee...pay," she said again, but more carefully this time.

"Who is Father Farlipe?" Mano asked.

Beulah shrugged her shoulders and turned around to walk back out into the crowd on the street. As she left, she looked down at the black poodle that was born from the death hole of her dead husband, The Postman.

"There you are! There you are!" she exclaimed in a voice that to Mano sounded like, "Dear, war! Dear, war!" Beulah picked up the poodle, tucked it under her arm, and walked back out onto Last Street.

Mano felt so alone. *Dear, war. Dear, war.* In these trenches, we can't trust even our own eyes upon the loyal.

34.

The Vuillemeyers were the father, mother, five sisters, and three brothers of The Humanitarians from Nun's Hat. The Humanitarians were siblings within the Vuillemeyer family. All twelve Vuillemeyers were of different ages, of course, but they all shared identical shaggy blonde hair, and they were all exactly the same height. When news of The Humanitarians death finally reached Nun's Hat, The Vuillemeyers were determined to find and recover the bodies of the two adored members of their family. All remaining ten Vuillemeyers traced The Humanitarians' route along the banks of The Cause. Because they were all the same height, when they walked in a single-file line they looked like a blonde caterpillar.

Pie Time was described to The Vuillemeyers only in letters from The Humanitarians. Their letters never mentioned the first thing about God's Finger. There was money to be made in assisting those who were left behind to deal with the newly dead, and The Humanitarians were to make as much of it as possible without sharing. In the very last letter received by The Vuillemeyers, The Businessman was described as "the most generous people" they had ever met. The Humanitarians also wrote that they had gotten a well-paying job from The Businessman "simply by walking around town, shopping and holding conversations, while wearing beautiful cages." None of The Vuillemeyers knew what the cages were for.

Just before The Vuillemeyers arrived in Pie Time, Mitzi Let was crawling on her knees down the center of Last Street in front of the XO Cafe like a cat that had gotten the worse half of a terrible fight, dragging her broken arm behind her along the ground. She was not wearing the cage she found in the sheep's pen behind the butcher shop.

"They need two more bodies." Mitzi's words fell from the gashes of her body, into the dirt of the street. "Two more...

bodies…for their pyramid."

The Banker stood from his favorite table inside the cafe and walked up to the window. "Is that Mitzi Let?" he said into his mug of coffee. "I think I'm seeing things. I think Mitzi is back from the dead."

"No, no, once you die, you die. That's one thing I know for sure," said The Landlord.

"Well, have a look for yourself." The Banker pointed at the woman on her hands and knees in the middle of Last Street.

"We've stopped dying, and now we're all going to come back," said The Businessman. "We'll be able to make something off the coming *and* the going!"

"Slow down, slow down."

The Businessman, The Landlord, and The Banker waddled out the front door of the cafe in their custom gold cages, and stood in a line on the sidewalk outside of the cafe.

"Mitzi?! Mitzi, is that you?" shouted The Landlord, from about 30 feet away. "Are you ok?"

"They need two more," Mitzi yelled.

"My god, that *is* Mitzi," said The Landlord to The Businessman. He yelled back to her. "What's that you say? Two more what?"

"Two more bodies. For the pyramid," Mitzi answered.

"Why aren't you still dead?" shouted The Banker.

Mitzi fell down to her elbows and stopped crawling. The crowd that once stood at a distance now collapsed closely upon her in the middle of the street. She looked as though she was in her last minute of life.

"Someone, go get Father Felipe," said The Chef. "Mitzi's about to die."

Inside the crowd, Beulah Minx could read The Chef's lips. Her need to feel helpful sent her into the nearest business to ask around for Father Felipe. The nearest business was Mano's barbershop. She returned a few minutes later with no new information and a black poodle under her arm.

"They're coming back to life now!" shouted The Businessman, as if to celebrate Mitzi's return, as she choked for air near their feet.

"Mitzi, tell us about the two bodies," asked The Landlord, more to the point. "Who needs them?"

"Nun's Hat," Mitzi choked.

"What's the Nun's Hat?"

"Nun's Hat saved me from death in the sea. Then I woke up on the pyramid."

"Mitzi, we need you to speak clearly now."

Mitzi hung her head, exhausted. "They need two more. For the pyramid."

"She's gone mad," said The Businessman to other people in the crowd. "There's nothing that can save us from death except our XO Life Cages. We all know that. Poor Mitzi, poor poor Mitzi."

"What pyramid is she talking about?" asked The Chef.

"Two more bodies for what?" asked The Landlord.

"I think she's dead," said Mary, who nudged Mitzi's shoulder with her foot.

Mitzi revived for a moment and said, "Pepe?"

"Pepe is dead," said Mary, trying to help in her own way. "Remember? You were there. Down by The Cure?" Mary pointed toward The Cure. "You were there, Mitzi."

Mitzi put her hands on the ground and tried to remember. Then she started to cry.

Just then, that blonde caterpillar, The Vuillemeyers, approached the gathering crowd on Last Street. They were tired and weary from their long journey from Nun's Hat, walking up toward town from the banks of The Cure, past Mano's barbershop.

"Who are you?" asked The Landlord.

"We're The Vuillemeyers," said all of The Vuillemeyers simultaneously.

"Can we help you?" asked the Businessman.

"We've come looking for two people," they said.

"Two people, huh? Where do you come from?" asked The Businessman.

"Oh dear, were they Humanitarians?" asked The Landlord. "And were they beautiful? A man and a woman?"

"Yes, exactly!" exclaimed all of The Vuillemeyers.

Everyone in the crowd looked at each other hoping someone else would be the bearer of the bad news, which was that The Humanitarians were freshly buried in XO Graves.

"Ask them where they're from," said Mitzi.

"Where are you from?" The Landlord asked the Vuillemeyers.

"Nun's Hat," they all said.

After some silent debating, The Businessman broke the news to The Vuillemeyers. Grief struck hard and swiftly. It reverberated loudly, like static electricity between all ten of them.

35

The sun was the first of three things to rise. A minute later, the bodies of The Humanitarians from Nun's Hat were the second and third.

"Good morning," said Father Felipe solemnly. Then he lowered his head before saying the rest. Father Felipe was presiding over Pie Time's first ever exhumation in the back of XO Graves. While the priest spoke, The Shoveler and his two sons, Ernesto and Ernest, conspicuously handed out brochures to the congregation which highlighted the differences in amenities between XO Graves and their own graveyard.

"We have gathered this morning to raise back up into the world this beautiful man, and this beautiful woman, whom we did not know well enough in life, to return them to their beautiful family, and to the very special town further down The Cure known as Nun's Hat, our new sister town, which we will know in life very soon." As Father Felipe spoke to the congregation, he held the hand of the mother Vuillemeyer, who was standing nearest to him.

"You know, Nun's Hat's been there this whole time," Father Felipe added. He was going off script for a moment to passively scold Pie Time's blindness.

"It sounds beautiful," said The Landlord.

Then Father Felipe returned to the script, sticking his arms through the bars of his cage to gesture. "Life, friends, is a boring cage. Your bodies are cages, and your cages are cages. But death! Death is *no* cage. Death is your *freedom* from a cage. But you *must* wear a cage in life, or else, from *what* would you gain your freedom?"

The crowd released a collective *ahh*, as if they had just understood the simple solution to a very complicated math problem. Ernesto tucked a brochure for The Shoveler's graveyard into a woman's purse. Ernest curtsied to a man who politely declined a brochure, and then he tucked one into the bars of the man's cage anyway. Most of the people attending the exhumation had a bouquet of flowers purchased from XO Flowers in their fists.

"They died the moment they took off their cages. Forgive them, Lord, for their carelessness, for getting lost in the momentary allure of vulnerability, and forgive Mano Medium, whose misguided lessons on the love of death brought them to you before you were ready, and before they were ready."

"That's not how it happened," interrupted Ernesto.

The Businessman shushed Ernesto. All ten Vuillemeyers simultaneously shifted their weight from all their left legs to all their right legs.

The caged Father Felipe ignored Ernesto's correction, modeling that gesture of ignorance for everyone else to follow, then picked up the guitar that was resting inside of his cage. "*These* cages, *these* cages, *these* are not *these* people's *final* cages." He strummed his guitar on each *these* and the *final*. "Their final cages belong at home with the Vuillemeyers in Nun's Hat."

With that, The Shoveler and his sons stepped aside, and the rest of the crowd lifted The Humanitarians on top of their heads. They formed a line. They looked like ants carrying two bread crumbs.

All ten grief-stricken Vuillemeyers led the way.

It was the first time the people of Pie Time had ever ventured down The Cure. The path never strayed from the banks of the river, following its side at every bend like a shy child to a parent's leg. The noise of the rushing water comforted the weary travelers along the way. They walked slightly downhill mostly, and trampled on dead grass. The exodus was, for the most part, a mass exodus. The path in front of the people was grass, and the path behind them was worn down into dirt. They were making the path visible behind them. Some people saw apple trees for the first time, and some of them saw beavers for the first time, building a dam.

Father Felipe spoke from the very front of the line. He was a knowledgeable guide for their tour. "That is a beaver, folks. See how it makes a home, just like you? It wants what we all want." He spoke loudly with a kind of eagerness that fueled their walking. "Open your eyes! See the world around you. It is full of mystery. You need not be blind to it." The people were like a train, and Father Felipe was their engine.

Mary Minutes got out of line to pick three apples from a tree despite The Baker's clear conditions regarding staying in line. She gave one apple to her sister, Mimi, and she gave another one to Mitzi Let, who was lagging behind and looked as though she needed food. Lana Rile explained the difference between the sun and the moon to her daughter, Fran. The Landlord ran out of XO Cigarettes, and forgot to bring another pack, but The Foreman gave him an extra pack from his shirt pocket. Beulah Minx had a rock in her shoe, and the new Postman waited for her while she took the time to sit down on the path to remove it. Then he helped her back up to her feet.

The Cure was meant for the dead, and in a way, this path alongside it was no different. Though, instead of placing a corpse on a raft made of sticks, logs, and brush, saying goodbyes, setting it aflame, and launching it downriver from a sad little dock, the people of Pie Time took upon themselves the difficult task of carrying the bodies of strangers, the exhumed Humanitarians, alongside the river. For the first time, the people of Pie Time were seeing the world that their dead had seen, and in doing so, they were making it a path for the living.

The Humanitarians' bodies were transported in two strong burlap sacks donated by the XO Factory. They were sacks that had once carried tobacco from the tobacco fields to Pie Time. They each had a giant XO stenciled with black paint on the side. Each of the men in the group took turns carrying the bodies above them. As their shoulders became tired, they'd let the weight of the Humanitarians' bodies rest on the tops of their life cages. They could easily keep the bodies balanced there. They'd puff on an XO Cigarette while they walked with the body resting on the top of their cage. Father Felipe lectured them when he saw the bodies resting on the cages. To him, it was disrespectful to the dead to not hold their full weight in your arms. True respect for the dead should be painful. Pain is a gift. "Hold them high! Hold them as high as *you'd* want to be carried," he shouted from the front of the line. The men's backs stiffened. Their shoulders became rocky cliffs.

Almost all of the men in town were in that line, except for Mano and Mothers, who were both instead nearly dead on the floors of their own businesses. Pie Time had been left alone to the very few.

"Pepe?"

"I'm not Pepe."

Even though Mano could not conjure the sound of Pepe's voice, it was clear that the voice of the person now entering his barbershop was not Pepe's. The voice belonged to a woman. Mano had been awoken at some point in the middle of the night by it. The room was dark. The parallelogram of sunlight that lit Mano's lap in the barbershop earlier that day, or perhaps the day before, was now a parallelogram of blue moonlight. For a moment, Mano wondered whether or not his barbershop had electric lights at all. It had been a long time since he had been inside of it during the night.

Mano could see the blurry shapes of someone's ankles in the moonlight, the back of her calves, and her shoes. She was standing on the top half of the black square. Mano tried to get up into a sitting position on the floor, but the weight of all the things on his body was too great.

"Inez?" Mano whispered at the back of her calves. "Is that you? I can't see. I'm sorry, Inez. I'm sorry. Will you ever forgive me?" Mano could hear her replacing a photograph on the wall and straightening it so it would hold there.

It was eerily quiet outside of the barbershop window. There were no voices, no sounds, not even the hum of the new electric street lights. Pie Time was empty. Mano thought maybe he had been wakened deep in the future.

Because she had moved into the moonlight, he could see now that she was wearing red Mary Janes. Mano squinted as the white gunnysack dress moved over the top of his face. He saw tiny red strawberries. She wasn't wearing underwear.

"We are ants!" Father Felipe was getting a wilder look in his eyes, as he spoke now for an entire day without taking a breath. During his tenure in Pie Time, his temperament had become more and more like Mothers'. "We are ants carrying our crumbs," shouted Father Felipe above everyone's antennae. "We are just ants. We know nothing! Can't you see how small we all are? Can't you see? We're being poked by God, not because we're bad, but because we can't be seen!"

The travelers from Pie Time arrived the next day at the base of the pyramid in Nun's Hat. The Vuillemeyers led everyone past very little of the town itself—not the nets in The Cause where the people of Nun's Hat caught the bodies, nor the theater where they tallied the bodies—only the pyramid.

It stood tall in the center of town. It stunk and it shined. No one from Pie Time could have imagined its shininess. But it shined like a diamond—hairy and decomposing, yet still a diamond. Its mathematics were flawless, clean lines and structurally sound, clearly built more by artists than by grievers of the dead. The pyramid was a beautiful and thoughtful monument—not just a pile of bodies. The moonlight glinted off of each corpse, off of each eyeball and tooth.

"Its beauty is blinding," said the new Postman.

Everyone in line from Pie Time was paralyzed by the pyramid's strange beauty.

"We should never look so directly at anything so beautiful. It's a sin to even look upon it," shouted Father Felipe over everyone's heads.

The men rested the weight of The Humanitarians' bodies on the tops of their cages and wept. Everyone was crying.

The pyramid's size, which was double or triple the size of anyone in Pie Time's wildest imaginations, was what was most overwhelming. Everyone was looking directly at their sadness, their own loss, their dead loved ones. Their grief appeared to them in the form of beauty. This is what made them all cry as they looked upon the pyramid, paralyzed. That and its smell, which was beyond unbearable. The pyramid was a pungent punch of death into their stinging eyeballs.

Enid Pine bent down to lift Mano's mammoth body from beneath his armpits, until they both collapsed. Mano's back felt broken. His forehead felt as though it had been split into two halves. He felt blinded and disoriented in the silence and the darkness. Some of his things fell off of him and rattled around on the floor next to Enid, who was now on her knees beside him. She tried to catch her breath, her mouth open, her top front teeth resting against Mano's shins. It had taken all of her strength to attempt to lift him. Mano felt heavy enough to sink into the earth, but when Enid's arms were beneath him, they felt strong there. He wanted to sink into them instead. And he wanted to sink into her voice, too.

"I want you," Enid said to Mano from her knees. She untied his shoes, and took them off.

His feet felt free, like light opening up in the darkness.

"I want you," she repeated. "But this is not yours." Enid slid her hand up Mano's leg and lifted the black umbrella he held there.

"That's mine," said Mano.

"No, it's not yours," she said. She threw the black umbrella onto the floor. "Let go of it."

"Please, don't..."

Enid interrupted by pushing her hands further up Mano's legs and spreading them apart. She put her hands on the complete set of encyclopedias he held there. "I want you, but this is not you." She lifted each encyclopedia, starting with A and ending with XYZ. She threw them each onto the floor, one at a time. "These are not your body."

Mano silently protested.

Enid pressed her own weight into what was slowly becoming Mano's lap. Her nipples carved two trails along the top of his thighs as she climbed upward.

Mano was getting harder and emptier as he became lighter and lighter.

"I want you..." Enid lifted Mano's shirt and unclasped the metal pin that held the gauze that held the hot water bottle onto his back. "But this is not yours." She unplugged the top of the rubber water bottle and poured the hot water onto her own body, all over the front of her own gunnysack dress. She poured some of the hot water onto the front of his body, too, until it pooled at the bottom of the crook of parts that they had made between their bodies. She threw the empty bottle on the floor. "This grief is not yours to hold, Mano."

"But these are my..."

"Shh..." Enid slid her hand down beneath the strap of his underwear. "I want you, but this is not you." She wrapped her hand around the bicycle pump he held there. She pressed it against his hardness and pumped it, up and down very slowly. "This is not you," she said. She threw the bicycle pump onto the floor.

"But..." Mano could feel more of his back as he leaned backward on the floor.

Enid's mouth was open above his mouth and now, instead of talking to him, she just slowly let her hot breath fall out of her body and into his mouth, down his throat. She slid her body downward letting her weight fall against the things that still remained there. As she slid, her body pushed more of the things off of him. They rattled loudly on the floor.

The bottom of Enid's wet dress caught on the receiver of the black telephone he still held on his body. It lifted up slightly as she slid down. She moved her bare hips on his things, back and forth in the dark light. "This is yours," she said. "Put your hands here."

Mano's hands were full when Enid shook them free. More things rattled on the floor. Something made of glass broke.

The black telephone born from the death of Enid's mother rang. Mano had never heard the telephone ring before.

"Don't answer it," said Enid.

"Why not? It's ringing."

"It's just going to tell you it's sorry for your loss, but it's not." The black telephone rang a second time and a third time.

Enid picked the receiver up and threw it hard through the back room door and against the front window of Mano's barbershop. The window exploded into a thousand pieces of glass. All the glass on the floor was glinting in the moonlight.

The receiver fell upright on top of a sea of glass outside on the sidewalk. It was so quiet on Last Street that both Enid and Mano could hear it say, "I'm sorry about your loss."

Mano picked up a glass jar from his body and threw it hard at the pane of glass in the front door. That glass exploded loudly into a bright flash. The jar broke into pieces into the street.

Enid pulled her dress over her head. She put Mano's actual body inside of her. She made herself naked again. There was nothing to confess.

There was nothing to say at the bottom of the pyramid, so the travelers of Pie Time said nothing. The Vuillemeyers hoisted ropes around the pyramid's stiffest and strongest corpses, the ones that had settled in to reinforce the pyramid's structure. Up these ropes the people pulled themselves. Hundreds of the grieving stepped on hundreds of their own dead like an organic staircase. Some of the bodies nearest the base of the pyramid had become half soil and mossy, red and yellow ranunculus, dandelions, and white carnations growing out of them. The XO Florist, upon his first few steps up the pyramid, picked a few carnations from an eye socket.

The XO Life Cages made climbing very difficult, but when their arms and legs became unbearably tired from the stepping, lifting, and holding, their cages could also hold their weight. So their cages made them tired, but also allowed them to rest.

Many of those who climbed the pyramid of death recognized the corpses that they stepped on. They cried and climbed, cried and climbed, stopping occasionally to say a few words and bless the dead that they had missed for so long.

Rona Rile introduced Fran Rile to the corpse of her biological father. The Lumberjack sat on the corpse of his dead wife and kissed what was left of her forehead. Even The Banker, who hadn't cried once since his mother had died, found his mother's dress and coin purse, even though he didn't recognize what was left of his mother's body. He slipped a dollar bill inside the purse.

"This one is mine," said one.

"I found my mother," said another.

"Here is mine, mine, and mine."

"This is not a pyramid of mines," said Father Felipe to the climbers. "These are not yours. These dead belong to the pyramid now. Let go of them."

Some people protested, but an orderly line slowly formed again. The pace to the top of the pyramid quickened with a new determination.

"We are not here for ourselves," continued Father Felipe. "Let us go to the top, and once and for all complete this pyramid with what it needs. Two bodies! Two Vuillemeyers! And may our own plague of death likewise be complete!"

"Here, here!" prompted The Lumberjack. "To the Vuillemeyers!"

"To the Vuillemeyers!" yelled everyone in unison.

But when they reached the pinnacle of the pyramid, as the men unloaded the exhumed corpses of The Humanitarians from the burlap sacks and began arranging them like stack-work on the pyramid, it became clear that three bodies, not two, were needed to complete the design of the pyramid.

"One, two, *three*..." counted The Businessman very slowly and carefully. They were pointing to the open spots left on the pyramid where bodies could be placed. This time they tried counting by pointing with their fingers. "One, two, and three."

"One, two...hmm...*three*, yes." The Banker checked The Businessman's work.

Mitzi Let, who had claimed only two more bodies were needed for the pyramid to be complete, and therefore, perhaps even for the plague itself to be satisfied, was only partially right. Two more bodies *were* needed when her own body was upon it. But when she had awoken from her three-day coma and walked down the pyramid, stepping on her dead husband and son along the way, she crawled her way back to Pie Time to tell everyone two more bodies were needed, failing to count the space left behind there by her own body.

Everyone looked down upon Mitzi from the pyramid's pinnacle as she was just now approaching. Mitzi looked up at Father Felipe with a smile.

"See, I told you. It is complete now? It is over?" she asked.

Father Felipe looked at The Vuillemeyers, and also into the face of every member of his congregation who had lost a loved one. He looked into the face of everyone who had been standing upon their dead, as if to ask them for some sort of silent approval. Father Felipe knew they'd need one more.

"Yes, it's over, Mitzi. It's all over," he said. "Come up here, and have a look."

Mitzi's face softened with relief. It was lit by the moon.

"Closer," he said. He guided her firmly by the elbow. "That's right, closer now."

"One, two, three..."

Mano lost his mind inside of Enid. When he opened his eyes, he saw the shapes of three black birds in what was left of the black square on the wall.

"Four, five, six, seven, eight..."

Enid blew a shushing sound lightly onto his lips as she moved on top of him. It was the first time she had ever had anyone else's body inside her.

"Nine, ten..."

"What are you counting?" Enid whispered.

Mano didn't hear her question at first. He counted black birds in the black square until his body turned itself inside out inside of Enid. He let go of everything he had ever held, and he let her hold everything in those seconds. The image of her blurry body on top of him in that moment was singed into his memory.

Mano let his head fall back again on the floor. "One, two, three..."

Moving so slowly that only she could tell that she was moving at all, Enid took Mano's empty hands and put them back on her hips. "What are you counting?"

"I'm counting black birds."

Enid looked up at what was left at the black square and could see them, too. "Oh yes, I've always loved birds."

"You know about birds, too?"

"My mother used to tell me that my father used to tell her about birds. He didn't like hunting them, but I can't remember why." Enid stopped moving her body on Mano. She held his hands on her hips while she sat still in his lap.

"Yeah, mine, too," said Mano.

"Hey, I'm sorry for that night your mother was torn apart," Enid said.

"It's ok," he said. "You didn't do anything wrong."

"I wish I could put her back together for you." Enid laid her head now on Mano's chest.

"Me, too. But it's too late."

"I'd even put you back in her arms if I could."

"That wasn't even her, Enid. She was already dead. She'd been dead for a long time." Mano thought about all those years his mother soaked in the bathtub. He wanted to change the subject. "Your mom's dead, too, isn't she?"

"Yeah," Enid answered. "She died standing up."

"The black telephone, right? That's where the telephone came from?"

"Yeah."

Mano and Enid both looked through the back room door at the broken windows. The telephone was on the sidewalk saying *I'm sorry for your loss*. They both laughed. I'm sorry for your loss was filling the silence outside.

"Now I have no one left," Enid said.

"Your father?" asked Mano.

"Nah. I never met him," said Enid. "How about you?"

"Nah. Same."

"You know, you have the same illness that my father had though," Enid said.

Mano was offended, but wasn't quite sure why yet. "I do? What illness did he have?"

"My mother always said my father only hunted things that didn't exist. You do that, too. Like with Pepe. Or with whatever's in there." Enid pointed to what was left in the black square on the wall.

Mano froze. "What was he?"

Enid thought for a second about the name for what her father was. "A mammother."

Mano felt the sudden need to vomit. "Please stop talking," pleaded Mano. He pulled his body up very quickly which sent Enid tumbling onto some of the broken glass on the floor of the main room. New blood flowed in the bright moonlight.

"What's the matter, Mano?" Enid was panicked on the floor. "Is everything ok? What did I say?"

"Nothing, nothing. I'm sorry." Mano was trying to calm himself.

"I tell you my stupid father hunted for animals that don't even exist and you..."

"He wasn't stupid!" shouted Mano. "He was the greatest hunter. Only the greatest hunter hunts for what doesn't exist."

"What do you know about my father?" asked Enid sitting in the glass.

...sorry...loss.

The voice inside of the telephone had been on a loop for so long, it was becoming a loud flap of noise. It flapped into the night, onto Last Street, and through the broken windows of the barbershop. A thousand black birds flooded in, wild, pecking, squawking, breaking what was left to be broken, the mirrors, the chairs, the magazine rack, and burying everything that Mano had ever held, burying everything Mano had ever loved, with their shit.

END OF PART TWO

PART THREE

36.

Zuzu Roar walked into the woods. She walked in even though her mother, Inez, had always forbidden it. As soon as Zuzu began walking, she was told she could walk anywhere, except she could not walk into the woods. Perhaps it was her rebellious streak, and her fierce independence, that had brought her into the woods initially, but it was the loud moans of a woman in pain that brought her upon a gigantic cabin with a gigantic front door and gigantic windows, so deep inside the center of the woods that the woods had folded over upon it. It was the kind of cabin that could only have been stumbled upon by someone who didn't know it was there. It was buried in shade, half-covered by fallen branches, and on the backside of a hill.

Despite the fact that Zuzu had never been in these woods before, the cabin looked familiar to her. It was as if when she was looking at the cabin, she was looking inside herself, at the parts of her that belonged to her, but that she had never seen with her own eyes. The cabin's roof looked like it was made entirely of birds' nests, and the door hung on one of its hinges.

Zuzu kept a safe distance. She left enough of a head start between herself and whatever it was that was making the woman writhe. Zuzu had no plans to help—only to look. And then to run. Her feet were already pointed away from the cabin, even as her eyes were squarely pointed at it.

What she saw through the cabin window first was its face. It wasn't like any face she had ever seen before. Its face was a cake of blood. The hair around its face was wild, and stiffened with more blood. It sat in a chair at the end of its dinner table which had upon it a very large meal. The large meal was the woman who had been making the horrible sounds Zuzu heard from the edge of the woods. The woman was naked, blood on one leg and on her mangled hip. One of her arms was already gone, and her ribs curved around her torso in a strange way. Zuzu watched the woman's one breast shudder as she made those sounds. It seemed as though the woman was surprised by the new pain made by each of the monster's bites. Her good leg was in the air. Her remaining arm reached outward like it was looking for something to grab.

Zuzu had never seen anyone in a kind of pain quite like this. It was a pain that she didn't understand. It wasn't a kind of pain she knew. It was softer. For the first time, as she watched the naked woman in the window writhe in this new soft pain, Zuzu felt her own rush up her thighs and spill inward into the center of her body like a heat, up her spine, and into her breasts. The same curiosity that brought Zuzu into the woods, and that led her to the woman's moans, made Zuzu want to know this kind of pain. Zuzu unbuttoned her corduroys, and held the heat hard there.

Suddenly, the monster looked up from its meal, through the window, directly at Zuzu.

"Bebé?"

Zuzu should not have been there. She knew she'd never be able to get away if it wanted to eat her, too. She stood paralyzed instead of running. Her hand was still in her pants. Her eyes were still locked on its eyes. Did it yell my name? she thought.

The monster's voice sounded human through all the glass of the gigantic window. It stood from its chair at its dinner table, and lumbered toward the window. It walked like an injured pack mule, slowly and falling to one side as if it had a nail stuck in its hoof for years. It walked like that over bloodstains on the wood planks of the cabin floor, over piles of blond, brown, and black hair. A torn blue dress with yellow flowers. A torn pink dress with green dots. A torn white dress with orange stripes. A dark green pair of trousers. A light blue pair of trousers. A white work shirt. A little square of yellow sunlight. The woman on the table rolled over onto her knees, and took the chance to tend to her own pain, the places on her body where she had been eaten alive. She collapsed onto her chest on top of the table. Her long black hair swung down and nearly brushed the floor.

Frantically, the monster tore down the red and white curtains in the window. Zuzu could see the monster much more clearly now, its huge body filling the entire frame of the uncurtained window. It rubbed its eyes and smoothed its mane of coarse and matted hair to the side to make a part, as if this would make its appearance somehow more palatable to Zuzu. She thought she heard something like her name again out of its mouth. She couldn't be quite sure. Then it said something like it again.

"Bebé." It wasn't a question this time. It was just that pet name that only her mother called her. The monster said it to itself, into its own hair.

Zuzu wanted to say something back to it, to simply just say that yes, she was Bebé and that she wasn't scared. But her legs were too scared, and they had a very different idea. Her legs wanted nothing to do with the monster, or its cabin, or being eaten alive for dinner. So her legs ran. She had no choice but to follow above them, back down the muddy path on which she should have never been on in the first place. She ran past the row of tallest trees in the woods, the birds chirping above her head madly.

"I didn't see you in the garden today, Bebé." Inez was sitting at the dinner table in front of a pork chop next to her new husband, The Barber.

A third place at the dinner table had been set and was getting cold. Zuzu was in front of the kitchen sink washing her hands. "Was today the garden?"

"You know Tuesdays are the garden."

"Is today Tuesday?"

"You know today is Tuesday."

"I thought today was with Vera at The Good House," said Zuzu.

"So, you were at Vera's?" asked Inez.

Zuzu realized she had just led herself into a trap. "You caught me. Ok. I was in the strawberry patch feeding Enid again."

"Zuzu, don't treat me like a fool." Inez stared at Zuzu, then turned to The Barber and apologized by raising her eyebrows and lowering them.

Zuzu kept washing her hands. She didn't want to turn around to find her mother's glare. She couldn't tell her mother the truth. She would be killed right there in that dingy dining room. Regardless, she wasn't even so sure she could confess the truth if she tried. She wasn't sure what the truth was.

"And what did I tell you about dressing like a boy?" Inez asked.

"Really, pork chops again?" Zuzu's complaint about the pork chops was a terrible failure in the game of distraction.

"Your trousers are dirty at the bottom, Zuzu, and your zipper is undone."

Zuzu was drying her hands now in the sink in the kitchen. She knew she now had to give up something of value, something that wasn't the truth, but was something to be hidden, something to get her mother off the correct scent.

"I was at XO Meats. I was helping The Butcher. Ok?!" Zuzu's false confession managed to break the silence. She waited for how the words would fall into the room, what they would knock over.

"Wait. You were at XO Meats? You were with The Butcher?" Inez asked, more curious than upset. Her tone was more surprised than disappointed. Her forehead moved like she was doing complicated math inside her head. "You were helping cut meat? You know they have these machines that..."

"No, not like that."

"What do you mean then?"

"I mean, I was just there. Like friends."

The Barber, who was by all accounts a remarkably boring man who could speak only of the weather or of the pain in his back, or of how the weather affected the dull pain in his back, spoke to Zuzu through Inez, which was his usual route. He had never once said a direct word to Zuzu, who he had been living with now for many years.

"Tell Zuzu that The Butcher's too old for her." The Barber cut his second bite of pork chop and spread it around in the yellow marinade. He winced with back pain as he lifted the bite from the plate with his fork.

The Barber's cat walked underneath the table and peed a little.

Inez started three responses to Zuzu, but swallowed each of them before they came to fruition. Instead, she resorted to, "Go out to the garden. Pull some radishes."

Since Inez and Zuzu moved in with The Barber, Zuzu didn't have her own room. She slept on the couch in the living room. When Inez and The Barber wanted privacy, she was sent to the garden.

"But it's dark," complained Zuzu.

"Then just go out there and sit in the dirt in the dark and think about what..."

"*You* think about what I've done," Zuzu cut her mother off. "Because *I* have no idea what I've done." Zuzu re-entered the dining room, but kept the water running in the sink in the kitchen.

"Take your pork chop."

Zuzu looked at the pork chop alone on the plate. It looked incredibly sad there, and grey. "I don't eat meat." She could only think to reject the one thing that was being offered, and to reject it permanently. She tossed her hand towel on top of the pork chop and walked out of the back door to the garden.

"What does your new friend, The Butcher down at XO Meats, think of the fact you don't eat meat?" asked Inez to her daughter's back.

Zuzu was able to escape her mother's inquisition, and she only had to give up meat for life and feign an innocent romantic interest in The Butcher to do it.

The Barber cut another bite from his pork chop and winced. With her own knife and fork, Inez cut the rest of his pork chop into a dozen bite-sized pieces for him. She cut it for him not out of love, but because his winces at each cut with his knife were becoming unbearable to her.

"Thank you," he said.

"Do you think..."

"Of course."

"Is that..."

"She's a woman now, Inez. It's time she..."

"I can't get her to wear a dress. I can't get her to grow out her hair even..."

"That's her haircut, alright. Every time, only like that. Short, a clean part, to the side, so..."

"No, no, it's not even that." Inez leaned back in her chair and slumped her shoulders. "She's always been like that. She loves only books for boys. She likes to fix broken things. She is a boy. She's been a boy her whole life. There is no woman in her. She refuses to cross her legs." Inez pushed a bite of pork chop around on her plate with her fork. "On the day we left our cages, she ran to Vera's. She was so free. She could have run anywhere, into my arms, wherever she could have imagined. But she ran straight to Vera's."

With both hands on the top of the table to steady him, The Butcher stood up and looked out the window at the dark clouds gathering above the hills west of XO City. "We're going to get some rain."

"Sometimes I think Vera would make a better mother for her. Do you know what I'm trying to say?"

"We don't need any more rain right now," said The Barber flatly. He rubbed the back of his neck with his hand. Six bites of his pork chop remained on his plate like sleeping pigs.

"Will you please just answer me?"

"She wasn't at XO Meats to cut meat with The Butcher with her zipper·undone, Inez. She's more like you than you know."

Inez cut her meat and took a bite. The bite was cold. She got a whiff of fresh cat pee.

Zuzu never really felt like doing anything she was told to do. She never worked in the garden when she was ordered to. Typically, she'd climb the tree at the far back of the garden, and work on the rudimentary tree house that she had started building there. It was just a handful of planks nailed into the crook of the tree, with one wall built up the side. Her next step in the construction of her tree house was to cut a window into the wall, but suddenly, since walking out of the woods, she felt much too old to be building a house.

Otherwise, when ordered to the garden, Zuzu would instead run around the streets of XO City on her own, completely free. She rarely walked, only ran. Running made her feel freer than walking. She didn't really remember the caged days, as people now called them, but she'd been told a lot about those days. She wondered if living the very first part of her life in a cage was what made her want to run now. Zuzu liked to run from house to house looking in people's windows. She liked to watch people move around inside their houses.

Zuzu's favorite windows to look inside were the windows of The Good House for Children, The Old, and The Very Sick, which was Vera Good's house, despite the fact that Zuzu spent every Wednesday and Friday inside that house babysitting everyone's children. She changed diapers, led games, sat with the older ones on the swing on the porch, those sorts of things.

But the nights inside that house, when Zuzu wasn't working, were different from the days. At night, there were no children of anyone else's to watch. The house was still so full and warm with family. The Shoveler lived inside the house with his new wife, Hera Horn, and so did Ernesto, who lived inside of the house with his wife, Leda Horn, and their identical triplets, Luis, Luis, and Lois Horn. Ernesto and Leda's daughter, Lois, was named after their grandmother, Lois Horn, The Shoveler's first wife, who died by God's Finger when Ernesto and Ernest were just young boys. Ernest also lived inside Vera's house with his cats. And, of course, there was Vera, who rarely left the house to be in the world, and who was, in that way, a pure specimen of a human to Zuzu. Zuzu lay awake some nights on the couch at home just concentrating on what she remembered of how Vera walked, and how Vera smelled. Zuzu wanted to be a woman exactly like that woman.

What was most remarkable about The Good House to Zuzu was that it was big enough for everyone, and everyone had their very own rooms. They always sat together at the table, even Ernest's cats would eat their food in the same room and at the same time as the humans, but they never peed on the carpet like The Barber's cat.

The Good House was in the same neighborhood as The Barber's house, which got smaller and colder in Zuzu's mind after each day she'd return home from The Good House. Running to The Good House to stare into the windows was always a risk. Zuzu had to be sure to get back to the garden in time to sit in the dirt before her mother called for her to come back in.

On this night however, when Zuzu was ordered to the garden, she didn't go to the tree, or run to The Good House to watch that family glow through the window. The sun had just gone down, and a black cloud was gathering over the part of the woods where she had earlier found the monster, and the woman it was eating alive, and the gigantic cabin. Most people would have wanted to hide from a black cloud like this one, but for Zuzu, a cloud like this one was a beacon. She would have never been able to sleep that night knowing the monster was still where she left it. Zuzu just stood there in the garden looking at the cloud, thinking about the monster. She wondered if it was thinking about her, too. She needed to know what it wanted from her. She needed to know how it knew her name. But, mostly, she needed to know something more of that new pain. It was growing in her own body and it needed a way out.

The feeling that made Zuzu feel as though she were too old to keep building her tree house was an awareness that she didn't care if her mother called her back in from the garden and she was nowhere to be found. She didn't care anymore. The blind impulse to obey her mother, or to please her, had disappeared. It was replaced by the need only to please herself.

While her mother and The Barber were inside discussing Zuzu's stupid lie about visiting The Butcher at XO Meats that she had fed them at dinner, Zuzu walked back into the woods, breaking her mother's most important rule, twice in a single day.

37

"I want to show you something," says Pepe. His head bobs up and down, above the surface of the pond. His strong bare shoulders move forward and backward, as if he is rowing a boat to stay afloat.

"Can you just show me from here, from above the water?"

"You can't see it from up here. Don't be so scared all the time."

"I'm not scared." Mano's shoulders are up around his ears. He is struggling to keep his mouth above the surface.

"You are, too. I can see it in your face, Mano. Don't you trust me?"

"Of course, I do."

"Ok, then all you have to do is hold your breath and follow me down. Stay close behind me or else you'll get lost. It's dark down there."

Pepe's eyes get big. "Ok, ready? One, two..."

"Wait, wait." Mano swims a little closer to Pepe. "What are you going to show me."

"I can't tell you that."

"Why not?"

"Because if I just tell you, you won't believe me. And you won't even go down there. You'll see."

"Pepe." Mano finds Pepe's hand under the surface. He pulls himself even closer. Their faces are almost touching. "Ok," Mano says. "I'm ready."

"Ok, one, two..." Pepe smiles knowingly for Mano as he counts. "Three."

Mano follows Pepe under the water keeping his face as close to Pepe's hips as he can. The water is cold and murky, but a little bit of sunlight cuts down through the water like a blade, over the top of Pepe's body. Mano wants to open his mouth and drink it all in. He stares at the muscles in Pepe's legs, how they tighten and roll as his knees bend upward toward his chest. Pepe's legs move like a frog's legs to propel him further down, deeper toward the bottom of the pond. Mano wants to propel himself, just like Pepe, but his legs work differently. Mano looks back at his own legs, which move nothing like Pepe's, but at least he can see that they are free.

When they reach the bottom of the pond, Pepe looks back over his shoulder at Mano and points to a black square. The black square is on the side of the pond and is framed with stones. Pepe puts his head inside the square, and then his shoulders. Then Pepe puts his body completely inside the square and disappears. Mano's lungs are filled with fire. He wants to retreat to the pond's surface for a breath. But he decides instead that if he dies, he'll die with only trust left in his lungs following the beautiful boy into that black square. Pepe's hand pokes itself back outside the black square and grabs Mano's hand by the wrist and pulls him in.

Inside the square, Mano feels his lungs ease. His lungs pump air. In front of him is a long hallway. Mano looks back at the black square that he came in from. It isn't there anymore. Nothing is there.

"Don't look back," says Pepe. "Let's go this way."

The hallway is incredibly long, and a long red rug leads to a very large and bright window. It is framed with red and white checkered curtains, and the curtains are on fire.

Somehow, Mano can see Pepe already on the other side of the window.

"How did you get outside?" Mano whispers only to himself.

Mano is unable to run fast enough to bridge the gap between them. The window stays the same distance away. Pepe is framed in the curtain of flames. His hands are in his pants.

Mano watches Pepe touch himself. He wants to climb through the giant window to be with him, but the fire from the curtains is too hot. Mano rips the flaming curtains down and stomps on them, his bare feet burning, the flame licking the hair on his legs, until it is out, and he can breathe again.

The fire inside of his dream finally woke Mano. He was no longer in a long hallway, standing in front of a window, but in his own cabin that he had built for himself from the wood of The Reckoner. Many years ago, Mano chopped The Reckoner down with the axe and the saw that he had been holding, and built a cabin that he could fit inside. There was no place for him in XO City. He was too big to fit inside the newly built houses, and he lost far too many customers to XO Meats and XO Haircuts. After many years, Mano's long hair grew over the things he held without any good way to cut it. He weighed roughly eight tons now, and was as tall as three tall men.

Mano's mind was tearing itself in half, somewhere between dream and reality. Mimi Minutes was still on his kitchen table—that much he knew was real. But strangely enough, Pepe still seemed to be standing outside of his window. Pepe looked very real and very alive. His real hand was in his real pants.

Through the window, Mano could see that Pepe's hair was parted to the side, like he always liked it. Mano suddenly remembered his own overwhelming growth of hair, and he wanted to tame it. He used his long fingernails to make a part to match Pepe's. "Pepe?"

Pepe said nothing. He touched his chest with his other hand.

"Pepe," Mano tried again. This time it wasn't a question.

When Mano left his window to walk to his door, Pepe had already run away. "Pepe! Where are you going?"

Mano trusted his reality more than his dream, but there was Pepe's back, running back down the well-worn path through the woods toward XO City. Mano could see him so clearly. Pepe's clothes, Pepe's hair.

But reality was still inside the cabin. Mimi Minutes was now sitting up on Mano's gigantic table, blood stains all over the mid-section of her naked body, her bloody panties dangling like a dead soldier from her best big toe. Mimi was crooked—leaning at a 45-degree angle toward the gigantic kitchen sink made from three normal-sized kitchen sinks.

"Who was that?" asked Mimi.

"I don't know. Maybe Pepe? No, no, it couldn't have been. It was just some boy. Some boy who looked a lot like Pepe."

"It wasn't Pepe." Mimi tapped an XO from the pack and lit it.

"So you saw? You saw him, too?!"

"I didn't see nothing, but I watched you watching." Mimi stood up, and hobbled over to the gigantic refrigerator made out of three refrigerators. It had a door held on by a long bungee cord connected to the metal grid at the back of it. She unhooked the cord and let the door fall open. She grabbed two cold cans of XO. "It was probably a squirrel."

Mano laughed, but not because anything was funny. "It wasn't a squirrel. It was a boy."

Mimi cracked open one of beers, and took a slow drag of her cigarette. "Pepe is deader'n dead. Besides, if he *was* alive, he'd be older than you. Remember? Mano, look how old you are. Look at you. You're no boy."

"What am I?" Mano was daring Mimi to call him a monster.

"I don't know what you are. But you're no boy."

For the first time since he chopped down The Reckoner, Mano felt an urge to leave the woods. He wanted to know something other than his festering life there.

Mimi pulled her panties up high on her hip with her one hand. "You fell asleep halfway through eating me out again."

"I did?"

"It's ok though," Mimi said. "I got it done."

"I'm sorry, Mimi. I…"

Mimi interrupted Mano. "I don't need to know nothing else about nothing." She finished the first can of beer, then cracked the second. "I'm on my period."

"I can see that," said Mano. "I have a mop. Don't worry about it."

Mimi wasn't worried about it.

Mano took a few steps outside of the cabin. He intended to walk as fast as he could, so that he'd have enough momentum to not stop, to just keep going further into the woods and closer to the edge, toward The Cure, toward the footbridge near where Pepe died, where his mother had been torn apart by the very woman who was now in his cabin.

Black birds squawked and swooped down in front of him, and circled around his head. Two of them landed on his head and stayed there. They had been waiting for many years to escort Mano back down the hill. But he stopped.

Mano's body was far too big. He was shaped like a pile of trash, and he hunched so far over that his face was out front, only halfway up his body. Mano's face was the only part of his body that could be recognized with any clarity. Needless to say, he was not swift, and the chances that he'd be able to catch up with the boy were nil. Defeated, he returned to his gigantic door, which looked more like the size of a missing wall. The door was still open.

"They like you," Mimi said. She was able to get dressed on her own.

"*Who* likes me?"

"The birds." Mimi gestured to the top of Mano's head with the hand that held her third can of XO.

"Oh, yes. The birds. It's my own fault," said Mano.

"What do you mean?"

"Nothing. It's just that I asked for them, that's all. For my 14th birthday."

"Well, shit. You really get what you want, don't you, Mano? These damned things were all over town for years. After you left. They were trying to land on everyone's fucking heads, squawking, shitting, destroying everybody's shit."

"What happened? Are they still…"

"The Businessman put out a call for bird hunters. No one back then knew what birds were, but everyone learned quick. And bird hunters from other places answered the call, too. They settled in, bought up everything, hunted the birds until they were all gone. It was sad really. I liked 'em. The birds. But the funny thing is, all those hunters all thought that they killed them all. You can't kill them though. That's the thing. You can kill one or two, sure. But you can't kill *birds*. Birds are birds." Mimi cracked open her fourth beer, and had a new thought about the birds. "Everyone thinks they're dead, but they just live up here now is all. A lot like you, I guess."

"Maybe that's why they like me."

Mimi put on her shoes with her one hand, and thanked Mano. She hobbled back into the woods toward XO City where she lived alone in an apartment above XO Donuts.

38.

On Wednesday morning, Inez stood on the front porch of The Good House and knocked. The laughing inside the house paused for a moment, and then the door opened. A little boy wearing a cowboy hat stood in the door and pointed his gun at her.

"Do you know who I am, lady?" he asked.

"Is Zuzu here?"

"I'm a cowboy. You can't come in, lady."

"Look, I need to find Zuzu," asserted Inez. "Is she here?"

The cowboy looked confused, as if he didn't speak the same language.

Inez was unwilling to play his game. "Zuzu. She helps take care..."

"Zuzu is dead, lady. I shot her with my gun."

"No! That can't be true. Vera?! Vera!" Inez yelled into the front room above the cowboy's head. Vera was around the corner in the drawing room where she had been sitting with a table full of other children, and Ernest. They were all drinking coffee and smoking cigarettes.

Vera walked to the front door in June Good's old silk robe, and kneeled down to the cowboy's level. "Igor, what did I tell you about answering the door? And don't point your gun at people's faces. Ok? Look at me." She lifted Igor's hat on top of his brow. She commanded his eye contact before saying anything else. "Ok?"

The cowboy sheepishly put his gun in his own mouth and nodded in apology.

"Now, go finish your smokes with the other kids." Vera ushered the cowboy by the shoulders.

"Vera, is Zuzu here?" asked Inez before Vera could stand up.

"No. I'm sorry. She didn't show up. I figured..."

Inez put her hand over her mouth and her eyes exploded.

"Where is she?"

"I'm so sorry, but I don't know. Did she say where she was going this morning?" asked Inez.

"She wasn't at home this morning. And she didn't come home last night either."

"That's not like her. When's the last time..."

"Maybe she's in here?" Inez pushed her way into the house. "Maybe she's sleeping? She must be so tired. Maybe she's sleeping somewhere inside and none of you noticed."

"Inez, she didn't come to work this morning." Vera reached her hand out to touch Inez on the forearm. "Look, can I get you a coffee? Would you like to sit with us? We're talking about..."

"But Zuzu loves working here. It's all she talks about. She'd never..." Inez rounded the corner into the drawing room. There was a table full of children. She took a deep breath. "Yes, ok, coffee, yes, thank you."

When Inez stepped into The Good House, she stepped into a new world. She felt like a frightened little fish in a new ocean. Everything looked strange yet full of love. The furniture in each room all faced the other furniture so that people could sit just to talk. There were three oil paintings on the wall in the drawing room. The one in the middle was a portrait of a woman wearing a funny pink hat. The other two were of men, one of the men was holding trophies, and the other man was cutting a piece of cake. The ceiling above the paintings seemed higher than the house itself, and where the ceilings met the walls it looked like frosting from that piece of cake. The fireplace was crackling, even though it was sunny everywhere in the house and early in the morning.

Vera led Inez into the room where the children were smoking and drinking their coffees. "Nun Other than a Nun's Hat," Luis, Ernesto and Leda's cheekiest and most gregarious triplet, said to Inez, holding up his mug of Nun's Hat coffee as a greeting when she walked in. Then he took a sip. The mug had a logo of a pyramid of corpses on it. Leda and Ernesto, who were sitting with Luis and a few of the other children, lifted their mugs of coffee and sipped, too.

"Nun's Hats?" asked Inez.

"Nun Other," said Luis again.

"We only drink and smoke Nun's Hat here," Vera explained. After Pie Time got bought out, we just..."

"I see..." said Inez half-listening. She was on to looking at the framed paintings by children on one of the walls in the drawing room. They were paintings of monsters, rockets, families, and sheep.

Igor, the cowboy who was playing like a tour guide for Inez, his gun now in his holster, pointed at a drawing that was his. It was a painting of a family in cages. "My mother said we all used to live in cages. See, this is my mother," Igor kept pointing. "This is my older brother, who was a tiny baby..."

"Who is this little boy?" Inez asked Igor. She pointed to the painting just next to his painting of his family in cages.

"That's Zuzu."

Inez snapped back into recognition of why she was in this house in the first place. "Zuzu! Are you here?" She walked into the kitchen, which was large and bright and smelled like pancakes, then through a door beyond the kitchen. There was a staircase there, and she walked up it.

Vera Good spent her time equally with all of the children in her care. They would sit with her, one at a time, usually on the porch, and she would tell them about June Good, about the caged days, and about when their city was once a town called Pie Time. The children loved to ask her questions about June, about good beer and cigarettes, and about love and death.

Leda and Ernesto spent their time watching the youngest children. They talked to them about their families, about love and death, and they made paintings.

Ernest watched the older children. He read books about love and death with them, and together they worked on mathematics. He taught the children about animals, and the children helped take care of all of his cats, of which there were eight.

Ernesto and Ernest's step-mother, Hera Horn, spent most of her time upstairs singing opera to the old and the very sick. The old and the very sick were most often the same people. Hera liked to feed them, bathe them, read to them, and sing to them. Her favorite old and very sick person was Irene Mire, who was perhaps older than anyone had ever been before. Irene was held together by dust.

Every morning, the first thing Irene would tell Hera was, "I'm ready to die now."

The Shoveler, despite having not dug a grave in over 16 years, still had a face seared with soil and a shiny layer of sweat. He spent his days outside mostly, teaching the children about dirt, flowers, trees, fire, and insects. The children learned with their hands. They sat in a circle, often in the sunlight in the woods, and they talked about what love was, and what death was. All of the older children felt as though they knew something of love, but none of them knew anything of death. The Shoveler knew something about it. In the same way that he would describe what happens to a body once love happens to it, he would describe what happens to a body once death happens to it. He would talk about how it would stiffen, swell, and rot, and how the insects would feed on it. "Life comes from where death goes," he'd say, with the same cadence that Mano used to use while teaching The Death Lessons years ago.

The Shoveler no longer had anything to shovel because no one at all had died in XO City since the exact day that Mano disappeared.

In the earliest days after Mano's disappearance, the people had so many reasons to celebrate. No one was dying, and the fear of God's Finger, that unusual, imminent, and cruel death that had terrorized the people of Pie Time, dissipated into nothing like Sisi's black cloud. Naturally, The Businessman became Pie Time's heroes. They had cured God's Finger. Pie Time built three golden life-sized statues of The Businessman out of the same iron-like material that they used to make XO Life Cages.

XO's success was considered a feat of science and humanitarianism for the rest of the valley to behold. Many more people settled in Pie Time where jobs were plentiful, and where the problem of death had been solved. Soon all of Pie Time's houses and businesses were owned by XO. Pie Time's newest settlers, naturally, mistakenly called the town XO. Eventually, it became easier for everyone to just call the town XO, and Pie Time was officially renamed XO City.

Mano and Sisi's old house was now the XO History Museum, which housed a permanent God's Finger exhibit in what was once Sisi's bathroom. In that old bathroom, the history of God's Finger was on display in the form of Pie Time newspaper clippings, photographs, and interviews, which were given primarily by The Businessman. According to the God's Finger exhibit in the XO History Museum, there were two reasons why God's Finger was no longer plaguing XO City.

The first was the introduction of the XO Life Pill. Once it became clear that there was no longer any market for new life cages, the life pill was introduced. Its only ingredient was refined sugar, but the exhibit doesn't mention this. Many people who were still leery of the possibility of death, but were willing enough to take the risk to free themselves of the discomforts of living in an iron cage, trusted in the life pill. Obviously, this argument didn't account for all the people who were not taking the pill and who wanted death badly.

The second was Father Felipe. He was credited for the eradication of God's Finger because of his legendary pilgrimage to the pyramid of dead bodies in Nun's Hat. He was given credit not only for discovering Nun's Hat, but for feeding its pyramid with the final bodies it needed. Because this pyramid was complete, God no longer needed any other bodies to flow downstream to the monument. And it was Father Felipe's ever expanding and financially successful church, The XO House of Love Everlasting, or better known as The Hole, which continued his legacy, and kept sinners free from their final punishment.

To a few others, the absence of death became XO City's newest plague. No one could die even if they wanted to. Eradicating God's Finger, to some, meant eradicating God. To those people, God no longer paid any mind to the people of XO City. One at a time, the bravest people in the city left their cages. They tasted freedom. When it became clear that no one who had left their cage was being struck by the finger of God, more and more people started leaving their cages. And when it became clear that no one was dying from anything at all, those bravest of people began risking their lives for the thrill of it. People in love did back flips off the roof of the newly constructed XO Factory into each other's arms. Some people swam in the strong, cold, and rocky currents of The Cure. Even those who were very old and in pain, their skeletons turning into dust inside of them, couldn't die. Some people, like Mothers, who were tired, sore, and sad, tried to drink themselves to death. They tried to drown their sad brains in a nectar of painlessness, but could only drink themselves into a living oblivion.

"Zuzu! Where are you? Zuzu! Baby, I'm sorry." Inez was upstairs, looking inside the closets of each of the five thoughtfully furnished bedrooms and five tastefully wallpapered bathrooms that made up the upstairs of The

Good House for Children and the Very Sick and Old. She opened up each closet door and pulled back each bathroom curtain. "You can visit The Butcher down at XO Meats all you want. Ok? You can do whatever you want. You're a woman now. I can see that. You're a woman now, Bebé!"

Vera walked up the stairs behind Inez, just to be sure she would be alright. "Inez, come back downstairs. Your coffee is ready."

Inez ignored her and kept searching. When she reached the last bathroom, the door was unlocked, and the shower was loud and steaming. The wallpaper had a pattern of summer fruits and vegetables, and the red and white checkered shower curtains were drawn. Inez thought Zuzu was taking a shower and couldn't hear her calling her name. So, Inez pulled back the curtains fast with a strength born from panic. As she did, at the top of her lungs she repeated the phrase that had been looping in her mind, "You're a woman now!"

Hera, who was three times the size of Zuzu, and clearly a woman now in every way, continued to move the suds around between the folds of her hairy armpits and long yellowish squash-like breasts while holding Inez's gaze. Hera made up a song on the spot. It was her best talent. "I am a woman now, it's true. I am a woman, like me and you."

Inez screamed and ran at a full sprint, in a straight line, out of the bathroom.

"Inez, please..."

Inez passed in front of Vera like she was on fire, from the bathroom into the bedroom across the hallway, then jumped with both feet onto a chaise lounge, which launched her body through the open window.

Outside, in the back yard, just off of the back porch where the younger children were watching from lounge chairs, The Shoveler was teaching the older children about death, about how the dead used to be buried in Pie Time. "This is how it was done," he said. The children shoveled the last scoops of soil into a pile next to the fresh plot. "Then we just put the dead body in," The Shoveler continued, "and we filled it back up."

"But where do we get a dead body *from?*" asked one of the children.

"We just have to wait. It's never up to us."

Just then, Inez's body fell from the sky above them, landed hard on the edge of the fresh grave and bounced awkwardly into it.

The children began scooping the dirt onto Inez's wet face and into her crying mouth. The children cheered.

39.

Enid stood alone in her strawberry field like a scarecrow.
She wasn't moving at all, but inside of her own mind, she was
moving very slowly. Inside of her own mind, she was picking
a strawberry from its stem. A strawberry has its seeds on the
outside, like a coat, she thought. Or like eyes. Her dress was
white with little strawberries on it. The sun was going down,
orange and pink, just above a few new high-rises, and over
the woods to the west, on the other side of The Cure. In her
mind, she dropped the strawberry into the basket. In her
mind, she picked another strawberry from its stem.

A young man was now standing in front of her.

"Have you seen my lost love?" he asked.

In Enid's mind, she said, "Who are you?"

His beard was full and his eyes were blue. Bees swarmed
around his head. His mouth moved inside his beard. She
couldn't hear his voice in the swarming.

In her mind, she said, "Are you my son?"

The young man's hands pressed against his heart. His
mouth kept moving, and his eyes welled with love and fear.

In her mind, she said, "I'm right here."

The man's mouth stopped and hung open so slightly. The
sound of bees slipped out of it. He looked at Enid's body.
She could feel his eyes on her. He got down on his knee and
looked even closer.

In her mind, she said, "Touch me, son."

After he left, she just kept looking at the high-rises, the
woods, and what little was left of the sun.

40.

"Zuzu!"

"Zuzu, come out, come out!"

"Zuuu zuuuuuu!"

A buzzing swarm of searchers walked from XO Meats into the center of the city, chanting Zuzu's name, and asking everyone that they saw if they knew of Zuzu's whereabouts. The Butcher was at the front of the swarm with Inez, calling Zuzu's name, leaving the swarm every now and then to ask people who were working in their fields. The Butcher asked Enid, who was standing still in her strawberry field, if she knew of the whereabouts of Zuzu. Enid, however, was catatonic as always and was of no help to him.

Inez's new husband, The Barber, was in the back of the swarm of searchers, looking into the windows and open doorways of all the new houses. Inside the swarm was everyone else, some of the bird hunters who remained in town after all the birds were gone, and many of the children from The Good House of Children and the Very Sick and Old. Leda, Hera, The Shoveler, Ernest, Ernesto, Luis, Luis, Lois, and, of course, Vera, were among the searchers, too. They all loved Zuzu very deeply. But they also all knew Zuzu well enough to trust that wherever Zuzu was, *that* was where she likely wanted to be.

In the afternoon before the swarm had formed, Inez carried her own half-broken, half-dead body from the fresh grave behind The Good House to XO Meats to ask The Butcher to help her search for Zuzu. She looked like she had just crawled out of her own grave which, of course, she had.

"I may not know where Zuzu is right now, but I know that she was here yesterday," said Inez.

"You do?" asked The Butcher.

"I do. And so do you."

"I do?" The Butcher's question was genuine. He thought

about the previous day, which was full only of pulling the hearts out of the chests of pigs, things like that. He thought hard about whether or not Zuzu had been a part of it.

"Yes, you do. It's ok. Now is not the time for secrets. Zuzu is in love. I can see it in her body. In the way she talks to me. In the first days of being a woman, you learn how big the world is. And she got lost somewhere in it. But where could she be?"

The Butcher was as intrigued by Inez's revelation as he was confused. He pushed his fingers through his beard. He let Inez keep speaking.

"She's no boy. She's a woman now. It's ok. I know you know all this already. I don't need to tell you."

The Butcher just made a knowing sound, even though he knew nothing. He now pushed his fingers from both hands through his beard. He only knew Zuzu from coming into the shop, picking up pork chops for Inez and The Barber. The only other way he remembered her was as the baby who won the first ever pretty baby contest. The Butcher was just a caged boy then who had lost the smile contest. No one, as far as he knew, had ever been in love with him before. But now that he knew this love for him existed, that it was his heart that Zuzu wanted all those times she had come into XO Meats, and not just the hearts of pigs, he felt love for her in return. His love swelled in a matter of seconds and overcame him, possessed him like a magical spell. Now, for the first time, The Butcher thought about Zuzu as a woman, too, and he wanted to find her just as much as Inez wanted to find her.

Inez asked him direct questions. "Where could she be? If she isn't with you, then where? Tell me you know. Tell me anything you know." Fresh soil was falling from Inez's hair as she shook her head. "I won't be angry at you."

The Butcher wanted more than anything to have answers for these questions. "I think she sometimes confesses down at Lady Bods." Put on the spot, Lady Bods was the only place he could think of in all of Pie Time.

Lady Bods was the old confession booth designed to look a little like a submarine, still run by Mothers, with portal windows to peek through at its naked confessors and a neon sign above the door that once, in its earliest years, read LADY BLOOD'S SUB. In time, Mothers fell behind on his electricity bills, and his energy for maintaining the neon of his sign waned. The neon letters L and O blew out, and then the entire word, SUB, blew out, too, leaving only LADY B-O-D'S. Lady Bods was now in the center of an empty, weedy lot where Mothers' grandfather first found the bear with no legs.

"Lady Bods? No. Zuzu may be a woman now, but I know she's never once been to Lady Bods."

The Butcher had no idea if this was true or not, but he was so newly in love, he needed everything to be true. "Zuzu loves Lady Bods. She is one of its best confessors."

Lady Bods was the first place Inez and her swarm of searchers searched.

They chanted Zuzu's name outside of the booth.

Inez's husband, The Barber, was as concerned about the weather as he was about finding Zuzu. "It's supposed to get cold tonight. I hope this doesn't take too long," he said to the people nearest him.

"Quiet down, quiet down." The Butcher had taken charge of the search for Inez's benefit. He was young and had the energy of new love, and Inez had exhausted herself. The Butcher raised his arms to indicate that the chanting should stop. He continued. "I know Zuzu well enough that if she doesn't want to be found, she won't come out for your chants. We must give it a look."

The Butcher put coins into the mechanical coin slot as if he knew very well how it operated. He pulled aside a sliding door and peeked inside. Even though the night was young and the sun was just going down, Mothers had already passed out face down on the floor of Lady Bods in a bed of empty cans of Nun's Hat beer. His passing out each night was typical, but he rarely passed out so early. There were no confessors in the booth, and no obvious sign of Zuzu.

The Butcher knocked on the portal window with his middle knuckle.

"What do you see?" asked Inez.

"It's just Mothers. He's passed out again."

Inez asked her husband if he'd climb up to the portal on Lady Bods' roof to look inside.

"Inez, my back hurts. I can't..." he complained.

"Here, never mind." Inez politely pushed The Butcher from the side window and stepped up on the stool to peer inside. "Mothers! Wake up!"

"Maybe he's dead." The Butcher said to Inez's back.

"*Is* he? Is he dead?" The question buzzed around in the swarm of searchers with excitement. Death was their prodigal son. The news of death's possible return was like a spark in a dry field of hay.

The Butcher traded places with Inez and looked through the window again. Then he quelled the swarm's excitement. "No, he's not dead, of course. He's stirring though. He's coming over now." The Butcher felt a certain pressure to detail everything that he was seeing for the dozen people standing behind him. "Oh, no, wait..."

"What? Is it Zuzu?"

"No, Mothers is throwing up. He just threw up into a beer can."

The crowd went *ahhhh*.

"But do you see Zuzu?" asked Inez, again.

"Now he's washing his face with the holy water."

"Zuzu?!" yelled Inez.

"What is it?" yelled Mothers from inside Lady Bods. "What do you people want from me?" Mothers' face was big in the circular window now. It looked incredibly old, creased with deep lines, pocked with age. His nose looked like one of Enid's strawberries, beyond ripe. His eyes were fogged with glaucoma. "There's no one here to confess. Come back another day."

"Mothers, it's *your* turn to confess," yelled Inez, who took her place at the window again. Where is Zuzu? Is she in there? Bebé?! Bebé?!"

"Pepe? No. That boy died a long..." started Mothers.

"No, no, not Pepe. Zuzu! You know, Zuzu. Have you seen her?"

"I know you know· where she is, old man," yelled The Butcher from behind Inez.

"Do you want to come in and confess, Inez," said Mothers sarcastically. "It's been a very long time, a long long time." From inside, Mothers hit a switch, and the neon sign crackled and zapped. Just the B-O-D came on at first. Then LADY B-O-D'S.

"She's not in there." Inez knew, deep down, exactly where they should be looking for Zuzu. But Inez wasn't willing to find her there. "She'll come home. She'll come home," she said just to The Barber and The Butcher.

"Thank you, everyone! You can go home now." The Butcher declared.

The Barber tried doing his best to be helpful. "It's going to be cold tonight. And it might rain."

"We'll just have to wait." Inez held the young wanting hand of The Butcher. "Can you wait? When she comes back, everything will be perfect."

The Butcher stood there like a flower that bloomed only when you looked at it.

41.

Zuzu had to stand on her tippy toes to see smears of blood and the four crushed cans of Nun's Hat on the gigantic table. Despite that, and despite everything in the cabin being salvaged and remade into a larger version of itself, the cabin had been kept clean. Or, it seemed clean for a cabin that housed a big monster. It seemed whatever lived here cared about something. It smelled like sweat, bodies, toil, and struggle, but it did not smell like death. There were black birds everywhere, sitting on the windowsill, on top of the refrigerator, and perched on the faucet above the double sink, but they were calm. She couldn't see their shit anywhere. The frame of the cabin's front door was more like the wide mouth of a cave. The door, which earlier hung on only one hinge, and was more like the size of a barn door, now hung correctly on both hinges. All of the doors to all the rooms were also especially wide like barn doors. The cabin itself was one large square, and was made up of four large and equally square rooms, with doors leading from one room to the other: the living room, then the bathroom, then the bedroom, and then the kitchen. Zuzu felt tiny inside it.

"Hello?"

Zuzu wasn't sure why she had returned. She tried to convince herself that she returned to see her first dead body, but the truth lay somewhere deeper inside of her than that. She stood in the center of the kitchen, and reached up to brush her fingers along the top of the table where hours earlier she had witnessed a scene of indescribable bloodshed. Wherever the woman was now, Zuzu thought, she was either wishing for death—a mercy from the mangling, which wasn't a possibility in these deathless days—or she was wishing for more.

Zuzu thought that this cabin either belonged to the monster, who captured the woman inside of it, or it belonged to the mangled woman, who was attacked by the monster inside her own home. Or it belonged to neither of them. Perhaps the most likely possibility, in Zuzu's mind, was that it was the abandoned cabin of one of the professional bird hunters, within which, earlier, a tragically unfortunate meeting occurred between a monster and a woman. That is what Zuzu convinced herself of after she climbed up to sit on the corner of the gigantic bed, and thought about sleeping there that night. Everything was made of wood. The tall walls, the endless floor, the big chair in the corner. She felt like she was on the inside of a giant tree. She felt like a tiny forest animal sitting there on the corner of that big bed. She couldn't bear the thought of sleeping another night on the couch outside of the bedroom her mother shared with The Barber, near the rug that smelled like cat pee.

The bed springs screeched with rust when she bounced. The sheets were tucked and the quilt was pulled back perfectly beneath the two pillows. It was far too big for one girl, she thought, and also, perhaps, too bouncy. And, most importantly, it awaited someone who was not her. She imagined herself being wakened by that someone, maybe the woman, who would surely need the reparative promise of her whole bed to tend to her terrible wounds, like a cat. Or maybe the monster, to whom she'd surely look like another meal, raw and warm and fresh, who'd eat her alive from the inside. Or maybe a bird hunter, who'd be just as capable, perhaps, of terrible things, who'd be surprised to find a girl in his bed when all he really wanted was sleep. Or worse. Or even her mother, who'd likely have tracked her down by scent by morning, and who'd drag her by her ear back down the hill, through the tall trees, over the footbridge over The Cure, and into town. Either way, if she slept in the giant bed, she'd likely learn something of death or, at least, of pain.

"Is this your bed?" she said through the giant door in front of her into the empty kitchen. She turned her head to the right and asked a question into the empty bathroom. "Can I sleep here? Will you be mad?"

Of course no one spoke back to her, because no one was there. "I shouldn't sleep here," she said to herself. The bed squeaked back into place as she stood up and walked into the kitchen. There, she looked around for a place to sleep. The table looked very heavy, as if it had been carved from a single tree, with two placemats ready to be eaten upon. Between them was an empty glass vase. The table seemed like maybe it was just the right size for Zuzu's body. Her body would easily fit there, and she would sleep well there. But it was also where the woman had been eaten earlier. Zuzu worried that sleeping there she'd look like dinner to anyone who'd walk in.

Zuzu found a pack of Nun's Hats on the kitchen counter and stood on her tippy toes to get it. She pulled out a cigarette and lit it. Then she walked outside to stare toward the city. She could only see the very tops of the highest new buildings from this deep in the woods. She could hear the birds above her head in the blackness. They sounded busy. They sounded like they knew where to go, and that they knew where they'd sleep that night. They were just making their beds ready for their bird children before they settled into their own. She remembered the manic sounds of birds in town for a brief time when she was a young girl. She missed those sounds. Without them, the town sounded forgotten about.

She picked white daisies from the foot of one of the nearby trees, and then walked back inside the cabin. She put them in the vase and arranged them with care. She filled the vase up with water from the giant sink, and ashed what was left of her Nun's Hat into the water. The sink was a better place to sleep than the table, she thought. She set down the vase on the table, took off her shoes, and folded her body up into the sink. But, even though it was a good size, it was just too cold. And the faucet was in the way. She hit her head on it every time she tried to move her body into a more comfortable position.

The bathtub in the bathroom, finally, is what Zuzu settled on. It was very large for a bathtub. It looked a little like a small pool. She borrowed a pillow from the bed, which she figured was a reasonable thing to do, then lowered herself into the tub, and back onto the pillow. She brought with her a cold Nun's Hat beer from the refrigerator, and she lit another Nun's Hat cigarette. She cracked open the can, and rested her head back on the porcelain, then blew smoke toward the ceiling, which was so high above her. The smoke formed a little black cloud there. The bathtub was just right, she thought.

"Fill this tub up," she said to the black cloud. "Float me out to sea." She blew more smoke into the black cloud. "Go on. Go on."

42

"Thank you for the flowers."

"Huh?"

The morning sun poured in through the window.

"This is going to be cold at first."

Mano turned the cold handle of the bathtub faucet counter clockwise halfway, and then turned the hot handle of the bathtub faucet counter clockwise all the way.

Zuzu screamed. In that first half-second of opening her eyes, she thought she was being eaten alive, the monster's cold tongue on her feet, swallowing her feet whole. She didn't recognize the room she was in, or what time it was, or what day it was. She knew nothing. She was a newborn baby in that half-second, and nothing of this new world was known. She had to learn everything again. She tucked her legs up into her chest. The monster was sitting on the toilet.

"Hold on. Hold on. It's about to get warm."

Zuzu quickly remembered where she was, and why and how. "Don't eat me!" she pleaded. "Oh god! Please, please!" Zuzu started to cry, and she suddenly regretted not returning home the night before. She wasn't ready to die, not like this.

"I promise I won't eat you." Mano smiled and cracked open two Nun's Hats.

Zuzu felt stuck between two feelings mixing into one, like the hot and cold faucets at her feet. "I'm not ready to be eaten."

"Good. Because I'm not ready to eat anyone," said Mano.

Zuzu was still speaking with a voice that sounded like crying. She rubbed her eyes to let some of the light in. She wasn't looking at Mano, but over the top of her knees at her feet, as the water approached. "But you are. I saw you. You were eating a woman."

Mano thought for a second before responding. He took the first sip from his can. "Oh, yes, that woman. Yes, I was eating her. You're right." Mano laughed. It was then that he realized that this girl he found sleeping in his bathtub was the boy he thought had been Pepe, touching himself with his hand down his pants outside the window while he went down on Mimi. Mano looked carefully at the part in her hair, and her corduroys. He sucked in air through his teeth, and held the can between his knees as he leaned over on the toilet. "But you know what? She deserved it," he said.

"She did? What did she do?" asked Zuzu.

"She tore apart my mother."

"That's terrible. Why did she do that?"

"I can't say. It was just a thing. She was like a wolf. She didn't know what she was doing. But I watched it. Maybe it was a full moon that night. I watched her run off like a wolf, too, with my mother's arm in her mouth."

"Is she dead?"

"Who?"

"The woman you ate."

"No. I didn't eat her all the way. Just a little bit. To punish her, you know? Death is no punishment." Mano was starting to enjoy the worried faces Zuzu was making.

"How about your mother then?" Zuzu asked.

"What about her?"

"What's her name?"

"Sisi."

"That's a beautiful name," said Zuzu. "Is she dead?"

"Yeah."

"What's that like?"

"What's what like?"

"To have a dead mother?"

"Don't you know any dead people?" asked Mano.

"No."

This news surprised Mano, but he answered her question regardless. "It's a lot like having an alive mother. Sometimes its easier to talk though when they're alive." Mano pushed the Nun's Hat along the lip of the bathtub until it was close to Zuzu's hand. "Here, have another beer. I see you already found the refrigerator."

"Thanks." Zuzu tapped the top of the can with her fingernail.

Mano showed her how she could adjust the temperature of the water. Zuzu let the water, which was warm now, lift her heels, and touch the bottoms of her thighs. She took a sip of beer and sucked air through her teeth just like Mano did. The warm water felt good inside of her corduroys.

"My clothes are getting wet," she said as she swallowed her mouthful of beer.

"Your clothes are so dirty. We can hang them up on the line in the sun."

"Then what will I wear?"

"You can wear my clothes. I can't fit into them anymore anyway." He slapped his body, and it made a clanging sound. They both smiled. "I don't need them at all. You know what? You can *have* them."

Zuzu noticed for the first time that the monster wasn't wearing any clothes. But he wasn't really naked either. His body was much more like an animal's than a person's.

She took another sip of beer and thought of the question she really wanted to ask him. "You said my nickname."

"I said your nickname?" Mano was confused. "I don't even know your *name* name."

Zuzu was small enough to turn her body all the way to the side inside the tub so that she faced Mano. He thought about how his mother always faced forward when she was in the bathtub. They had never really faced each other quite like this. "Yeah, you said my nickname after you were done eating the woman who tore apart your mother."

For a magical moment, Mano thought that maybe the girl in his bathtub *was* Pepe somehow, returned from the dead to play a joke on him, or to check on him. The girl looked a little like Pepe, and her clothes were the kind of clothes that Pepe always wore, and she had his haircut. Mano leaned over very close to Zuzu's face and squinted. The world had been blurry for so long.

"Pepe?" he whispered, as if he was trying to speak past the girl to Pepe's ghost, which may have been trapped inside her body. "Pepe, are you in there?"

"I don't know Pepe. You called me Bebé, or at least that's what I thought. It's a name my mom sometimes calls me. But my *name* name is Zuzu." Zuzu said both syllables of her name separately.

Hearing Zuzu's name pulled something up through Mano's throat, something that had been pushed down for a very long time. He swallowed something heavy and studied her. Zuzu had eyes like Inez's. He could see it now so clearly, how they blinked, and how they looked at him.

Zuzu returned Mano's examination with her own. It was her first good look at him. He was so mammoth to her, even in that mammoth room, sitting on the toilet. She could barely see past him to anything else in the room. His hair was long, growing over his shapeless body like a waterfall over stones. His eyes were kind and familiar.

"I'm sorry, Zuzu. I hope I didn't frighten you. I was calling for someone named Pepe. I thought you were Pepe. Maybe you heard me wrong."

"You thought I was a boy?"

"Yeah, I did. Is that ok?"

"Yeah. It's ok." Zuzu smiled. She had a sudden urge to stand up and look into his bathroom mirror. She wanted to see if she still looked like a boy, even this morning. But there was no mirror there.

"What's *your* name?"

"Mano."

Zuzu's eyes opened in surprise, then they squinted for a closer look. Her mother told her to run away if she ever met anyone named Mano. Inez never explained why. Zuzu only knew that Mano hurt her mother in some way. Zuzu remembered Inez once said that Mano was the second of the three barbers she ever loved, but Zuzu got the feeling that her mother only really loved the first two.

Zuzu looked past the bathroom door and out the front door of the cabin, and she could see a clear path from the bathtub to XO City. One option was to dart. But her relentless curiosity far outweighed her disdain-by-proxy for Mano. Whatever had hurt her mother had not yet hurt *her*. At that moment she wanted to be nowhere else in the world other than in that large cabin with that big monster.

Mano saw Zuzu looking for her escape. "The door is open if you want to make a run for it."

Zuzu just settled back down into the water slowly, keeping her eyes on Mano and lowering her shoulders. She thought about all the questions she could ask, about her mother, and about what might have happened, or didn't happen, between the two of them.

"You don't look like I thought you would."

"What did you think I'd look like?"

"More like a barber, maybe. My father was a barber, too, you know. So maybe more like pictures of my father."

"Yeah, I know."

"Or maybe I thought you'd look more like The Barber now."

"There is still a barber down there?" Mano asked. He hadn't really felt any spark of curiosity for what became of Pie Time until now.

"Yeah, he's my mom's new husband. He cuts hair for XO Haircuts. It's all pretty boring." Zuzu ashed her cigarette in the water like Mano's mother used to do, and then took another drag. "He gives everyone the same short haircut."

"A table-top?"

Zuzu laughed. "Yeah, something like that."

"You have to have short hair if you're going to be a barber."

Zuzu nodded. "Yeah, you're right." She followed up her nod with a sip of beer.

"I had real short hair, too. Parted to the side. Just like you have it."

"I can't even imagine it," Zuzu laughed. "Look at you now!"

"It's true. But before I was ever The Barber, when I was real young, everyone thought I was a girl. I had long girl hair, and I liked to wear dresses."

"Gross." Zuzu's laugh sounded like a horse. Her laugh made Mano laugh. "Well, one thing I can say about The Barber is he cuts my hair how I want it. Short, parted to the side. And I wear trousers and boy shirts," she said. "Most people think I'm a boy."

"I like that about you."

"Did anyone know you were a boy, Mano? I mean, when you were a kid?"

"Just Pepe. Well, and my mom, of course. And this one girl named Enid. It's really not..."

Zuzu interrupted. "Who's Pepe?"

"He's just someone I miss."

"Is he dead, too?"

"Yeah."

"Did you love him?"

"Yes. I love him."

Mano wondered if that was the first time he ever said that out loud. He felt the thing in his throat come all the way out. He repeated himself. "Yes, I love Pepe very very much. And I miss him." Confessing his love twice made it feel more real. Mano needed it to be real. "I love my mother, too. I miss her, too."

Zuzu smiled. She took the pack of Nun's Hats out of her breast pocket, which was still dry and above the surface of the water.

Mano wanted to say that he loved Enid out loud, too, but he let the thought pass.

Zuzu set them down on the lip of the tub. "Go ahead." She leaned back into the bathtub, which was full of warm water now, until her empty breast pocket was submerged. Her corduroys and shirt floated her to the surface. They both lit up a cigarette.

Mano turned off the faucet. They both had forgotten what silence sounded like.

"Pepe left me an accordion."

Zuzu looked impressed. "Will you play it for me?"

"I wish I could. It's back there somewhere. I haven't played it for so many years." Mano pointed his hand over the top of his head at his back. "I can't reach it. And it's just a part of my body now."

"No, it's not. I bet I can find it." Zuzu stood up and stepped out of the bathtub. Her clothes were soaked, and she made a puddle of water at their feet in front of the toilet.

"No, please. It's in there good. Besides, I don't even know if..."

Zuzu hushed Mano. She leaned him all the way forward, and climbed up on his shins and knees until she was able to straddle the back of his head. From there, she scoured through the hairy mess of his back. She found the corners and tops, bits and pieces, of many things back there.

"Here it is! I found it."

"It's ok. Just leave it be. It's probably broken by now..."

"No, no, it's beautiful. Look!" She tugged on the top edge of what looked like an accordion on his back. It felt to Mano like the undoing of a crooked vertebrae. He felt his back straighten. The accordion made a sighing sound, and then a sound as if it was clearing its throat. Mano barely recognized it when she set it in his hands. "Ok, now play it," she said.

"Play it? I don't know if I..."

"Just play it. Play it for Pepe."

"I only know dirges."

"What are dirges?"

"They're songs for the dead."

"Perfect!" exclaimed Zuzu.

The sound of Mano's accordion was the most beautiful thing both of their ears had heard in a long time. The music of funerals had been unknown in XO City for many years. The sound of that deep sadness and despair made their hearts beat twice as fast. It made them want to march. So they did. They marched from the bathroom through the kitchen, and out through the large barn doors in the front of the cabin, straight into the forest. Zuzu was in her wet clothes, and Mano was of course underneath all of these things, his hair, and behind his accordion, which after all of the years on his body, seemed to know exactly what to do in that moment.

Mano and Zuzu marched around the cabin in circles, and then they decided they were a part of a funeral procession. They were marching in a line toward the pretend graveyard. Pretend Funeral was the game that Zuzu wanted to play most.

"In order to have a funeral, someone will have to be dead," said Zuzu.

"Who should our funeral be for?" asked Mano.

"How about your mother? She was torn apart, right? So, she didn't get to have a funeral, did she?"

Mano still wasn't so sure that Pepe wasn't haunting him lovingly from the inside of Zuzu's body. He smiled at her, thankfully. "That's a very good idea," he said. And so they did. Together they dug a hole with Mano's shovel. They threw some rocks into the hole, and Mano said all of the nice things he could think of to say about his mother.

"Sisi Let, lover of polka and chain smoking. Lover of warm water and cold beer. She loved the radio and her window, from where she looked at the sky. But most of all, she loved me. She loved me so much. And I loved her so much." Mano let the feeling in his throat take over and he started to cry. "I love you, ma'am, mother." Mano wanted to keep adding on to his eulogy. "Oh, and thank you for the birds. Thank you for playing dress up with me. Thank you for all of the stories about when I was a kid, and about when you were a kid, too."

"Is that all?" Zuzu was starting to cry, too. She wanted to hear a little more.

Mano thought about what else he could add. "Mom, I'm sorry the world got so big for you." At that, the two of them shoveled the dirt back in, over the stones, and Mano played a dirge on the accordion. It was the exact kind of funeral that he had originally wanted for his mother.

Zuzu shushed Mano before his last dirge had ended. "I think I hear something."

"What is it?"

"I hear her talking. She's trying to say something."

"Who?"

"Your mother! Hold on." Zuzu pushed her index finger against her lips, and then walked over to a dead tree to break off a stick. Mano was scared. Whoever the voice belonged to, he wasn't so sure he wanted to hear what it had to say. Zuzu poked the stick deep down into the dirt and wiggled it around. She put her ear up to the hole.

"Shhhh. Sisi's trying to speak."

"It's not smart to listen to what the dead have to say. There's no way to trust them," Mano said, panicked. "I think we should just go. This funeral is over."

"Hold on, Mano! Don't be so scared. You're so scared. Why are you so scared?" With her ear down against the hole in the dirt on the grave, Zuzu slowly repeated what she heard the voice say. "*I...want...*"

"What does she want?" asked Mano, ready to run.

"*...another...*yes, yes, another what? What is it, Sisi? ... *another...beer...*" Zuzu rolled over on her back on top of the grave and laughed uncontrollably.

Mano pretended to throw one of the stones right at her, but threw it far behind her. "Very funny," he said. "Tell her the dead can't drink any more."

"Let's go drink one for her," said Zuzu.

"Good idea."

Together, Zuzu and Mano spent the rest of the day chopping wood for the fire and picking mushrooms in the woods. Zuzu was on her second full day of vegetarianism and Mano had been a vegetarian since leaving Pie Time, so he made something like a steak out of these mushrooms. After dinner, they sat on the floor in the living room and drank more beers, and listened to polka on the radio.

"How do you know when you love someone?" asked Zuzu.

Mano thought about Zuzu's question. "I don't know. It feels like an endless dull pain. Like a deep ache, even when you're with them. Like you miss them even when you're with them. Have you ever felt that?"

"No, I don't think so. I don't think I've ever loved anyone."

"You're young."

"But I think I could."

"I bet you could, too. Do you think you know *who* you could love, you know, in the future?"

"Yes, I do," answered Zuzu. "But she's a woman. And she's much older than me."

"What are you worried about?"

"My mother."

"Oh no, is she your mother?"

Both of them laughed so hard. "No!" shouted Zuzu.

Once they caught their breath, Mano said, "It doesn't matter who she is, or how old she is. But make sure that once you do love her, to let her know."

"Ok."

Mano and Zuzu each drank two more cold Nun's Hats, which completely depleted Mano's supply. When it came time to sleep, Zuzu kissed Mano on the cheek, and promised to bring him more Nun's Hats when she returned. Then she took her place for the second night in the giant bathtub, while Mano slept in his giant bed in the next room.

The next morning, Mano awoke to the sounds of the water draining in the bathtub, the door quietly shutting, and more fresh daisies in the vase.

43.

Friday morning, Zuzu arrived a few minutes early to work at The Good House for Children and the Very Sick and Old. She braced herself for an unavoidable welcoming home, or an interrogation. Maybe her mother and The Barber would be waiting for her on the porch, or maybe the entire neighborhood would be hovering over a map of XO City on Vera's banquet table in the dining room.

But when Zuzu walked through the door, none of that was true. No one was waiting for her in any unusual way. Vera was standing in the kitchen when Zuzu rounded the corner. She was wearing June Good's silk robe, like she did every morning, and her greying hair was in braids. "Coffee's on. You want a cup?"

Zuzu nodded. She wondered if she had even been searched for at all, or if she was even missed. Vera poured her a cup.

"I like your new trousers," said Luis. He hugged Zuzu's leg and petted her pants. He played with the seam down the side of her leg like it was a string on a harp.

Zuzu moved her fingers through his hair like a comb.

"Yeah, they're nice," added Igor, who had traded his cowboy hat for a viking helmet, and who had just started a drawing of Zuzu. "You look good."

"Thanks, you two. You're so sweet. These trousers are..." Zuzu stopped herself. She decided against telling the children about Mano, and where her new trousers were from.

"Are what?" asked Luis.

"Are new." Zuzu smiled at them, asking them to accept her half-answer. "I missed you guys."

"Where did you go?" asked Igor.

Vera cleared her throat. The children looked back at her, and then they lost interest in an answer to their question. Vera handed Zuzu a mug with a pyramid of dead bodies logo on the side, opened the bottom half of her robe, and sat down at the table next to Igor. Vera pointed to a curvy brown line at the top of his page. She crossed her bare legs, and took a sip from her mug.

"That's Zuzu's head," said Igor.

"Ahh, ok, yes, I see it now," said Vera. "It's a beautiful head."

Igor giggled with embarrassment and peeked through his fingers at Zuzu.

Zuzu sat down next to Lois, who was writing a love letter to Ernesto, her father.

"Do you want to read it?" asked Lois.

Zuzu began, quietly, in a voice sized for only the both of them to hear. "*I love you so much. I love how you are strong and can lift me above your head. I love how you teach me about bugs. I am happy that you are not dead.* Lois, did you mean to make a rhyme there?"

Lois shrugged her shoulders to say she wasn't sure.

"Ok, now *you* read the rest to *me*," said Zuzu.

Lois started in, reading one word at a time. "I like it when you let us dig holes in the ground. And we get to bury our fears inside the holes and cover them up." Lois put her fingers in her mouth from the embarrassment of hearing her own sentiment aloud in the world, going into other people's ears. Zuzu pulled Lois' fingers out of her mouth, and Lois kept reading. "And also, I'm sorry how I touch your calf when you tell me not to because it gives you cramps there."

"This is so beautiful, Lois. I'm sure he will love it. What do you mean, *calf*?"

Lois pointed to her leg.

"Oh, *calf,* yes, ok."

Lois finished reading the rest of her letter to Zuzu while the other children came in and sat down. Ernesto, Hera, Ernest, and Leda were all in the kitchen now, pouring coffee, saying hello. Strangely, no one asked Zuzu where she had been, only how she was doing. The house was so full and so loud, and this made Zuzu happier than anything. She thought that maybe she could just continue life as it had been, without ever dealing with the repercussions of going unaccounted for. Zuzu settled into her chair, and watched Vera's bare legs uncross and cross again between the opening in her robe. Vera watched Zuzu watch her.

"I have a job for you this morning," said Vera.

"What is it?" Zuzu wanted a job. She wanted more than anything to be told exactly what to do by Vera.

"We're spending the morning outside, you and me. We have to do some of The Shoveler's outdoor work today. We'll leave the children to the others."

"Where is The Shoveler?"

"He is spending the day down at the train. He is needed to help shovel a new path."

"You mean, the train?" asked Zuzu.

"Yes, I guess XO wants a new wider path for a bigger faster train to the other XO Cities," said Vera. "It'll take more things, and bring more things back. Who the hell knows? I told him he doesn't need to make any more money. I can take care of..."

"This one is going to carry people on it, too," added Ernest.

"So you won't have to walk?" asked Zuzu.

"Soon, we'll never have to walk again," said Vera.

Once outside, in the shade of a large umbrella, Vera sat carefully on a lounge chair so that her body wouldn't spill completely out of June's robe. Before she walked outside, she exchanged her mug of coffee for a can of cold Nun's Hat. She held an unlit cigarette between her fingers in the same hand that she held her beer.

"We're filling in this hole. Well, I should say, *you're* filling in this hole." She lit her cigarette, and handed one to Zuzu. Zuzu lit hers and sat down on the edge of a rectangular hole to smoke it. The dirt of the hole, and the pile next to it was fresh. Zuzu dangled her legs into it.

"Is this a grave?"

"Yes. Have you ever seen one before?" Vera moved her robe off of her legs so they could be in the sun.

"No. At least not the inside of one." Zuzu looked up at Vera for a kind of permission, and Vera granted it with her eyes. Zuzu lowered herself into the grave, and lay on her back in the bottom. A grave was just a bed, she thought. She looked up at the rectangle of sky above her.

"What's it doing here?" Zuzu asked into the sky.

"It's your mother's."

Zuzu almost coughed on her own cigarette. She sat back up in the grave, confused about how graves work—or, for that matter, how death works. She wondered if her mother had turned invisible upon death, or was buried even further down, her corpse below her. Zuzu stood up in the grave, her head poking out of the ground like a soldier in a bunker.

"My mother's dead? How, I mean, what...?" The news that Zuzu had always thought would fascinate her, devastated her instead. "Where is she?"

Irene Mire, who was so old that everyone around her had stopped counting her birthdays, and so sick that her eyeballs looked like they were made of rust, crawled through the back door of The Good House on her hands and knees like a pack mule with a broken back toward Zuzu and the grave. Irene had spent most of the morning quietly sliding her body down the stairs from her room, which was upstairs in the infirmary.

Zuzu wanted an answer to her question, but Vera ignored it.

"You look like a lost sheep that's accidentally escaped from her pen, Irene," said Vera, kindly, like saying good morning.

"I'm ready to die," said Irene, pushing her face through the grass.

"Ok, Irene, go to your grave," said Vera like a dog owner.

"Ok."

Zuzu lifted herself out of the grave and sat on its lip to

make room for Irene.

"Your mother's not dead," Vera finally said. "She only spent a few minutes in it, knocked out. The children thought she was dead, so it was a good lesson. They threw a little dirt on her legs, and then again when she woke up. She woke up like a new woman. Her madness died, but not her. She woke up in that grave with a new fear though. She woke up with the knowledge that you, Zuzu, are *different* from her. She once feared that you'll go away. But now she just fears that when you go away, you won't come back. Or if you do, that you won't come back the same." Vera took a drag of her cigarette. "She's scared, Zuzu, that's all. She's scared you're turning into something she doesn't understand."

Irene Mire was close enough now to the grave that she reached her arm out for its edge.

Vera continued. "Your mother is waiting for you to come home. I promised her that if you showed up to work today, that I'd send you straight home. She's waiting for you at home."

"What do you think I'm becoming?" Zuzu asked.

"A woman. It's all very normal, you know, for a girl," said Vera.

Irene gurgled a deep and strange gurgle.

"I don't feel like a woman. I feel like a different thing," Zuzu said. "I feel like something nobody has ever felt like. Is that possible? I feel like something that has lost something. But I haven't lost anything at all. I'm not even sure I've ever loved anything." Zuzu wanted to tell Vera everything she'd been feeling about her, but didn't know how, not with her mother's grave between them. Zuzu could see right between Vera's legs inside her robe. She looked away, at Irene, who was now leaning her body over the edge of the grave, as if she were about to tip her body into it, and dive head first. "What's it like, loving June?" Zuzu finally asked. "What's it like loving the dead?"

Vera thought about Zuzu's question for a few seconds.

"There's something about knowing right where she is, in that ground in the graveyard. That feels good. Sometimes it feels like love, to know right where someone is. But it's not."

"I'm ready!" shouted Irene. Then she balled up her body and rolled into the grave. She ended up on her back at the bottom, one leg propped up on the side. She made a terrible sound, like the wind was knocked out of her.

Zuzu shoveled dirt onto Irene's leg that was still flat on the ground.

"Goodnight, Zuzu," wheezed Irene. It felt good to Irene to have the weight of cold dirt on her leg.

Zuzu shoveled some dirt on her face. Only a little. Just enough so Irene could feel it. Some of it got into her mouth. Irene closed her eyes very hard, but couldn't die.

44.

The old abandoned Pie Time Factory still sat on the far western edge of town like a dead moon. Unlike the newly constructed XO Factory, which was clean and bright and triple the size, the old Pie Time Factory was always dark, even during the middle of the day with the sun high above it. It looked like a factory that manufactured nothing but darkness and sadness. Even though the XO City streetlights within a block of the old factory came on when the sun went down, the darkness that flooded from the windows of the factory swallowed their light.

Other than the woods, the roof of the factory was the only place in or near XO City where the black birds still lived. No matter how many birds the bird hunters killed from the factory's roof in the years after it closed, there were always more. In fact, the more they killed, the more birds there would be on its roof the following day. Birds seemed to be born from the darkness manufactured there.

Little remained inside the Pie Time Factory—mostly broken chairs, a scattering of janitorial supplies, a few outdated work uniforms with the Pie Time logo still stitched on them, a family of rabbits hiding from the birds, mirrors and sinks. The smell of barley and tobacco was still cooked into the walls, but that smell was about the only thing now that remained. For a few years, a few different families of squatters lived in it. When they left, they took the toilets with them.

The door through which Mano used to walk into work was always locked, but Mano wouldn't have been able to fit his body through that door anyway. On Friday afternoons, he walked through the large opening on the side of the building, which had been cut years earlier to remove some of the factory's largest equipment to transfer it to the new XO Factory. Being inside the building always made Mano feel like a little girl again, sitting alongside the other girls, and working with his hands to make something good for his mother to smoke, and something good for her to drink.

This rainy Friday afternoon was no different. Mano felt lighter on his feet in that dank darkness, and even tried skipping—unsuccessfully. It was all he could do to try to insert some joy into an otherwise overwhelmingly joyless place. Still, he tripped even on such a simple attempt. He was wearing a tie that he had stitched together from ten ties that looked a lot like the tie that The Foreman used to wear to work. He dragged his gigantic body to the stairs that were just off the main room, and he lumbered down the stairs holding the walls for balance. The hallway at the bottom of the stairs was somehow even darker, danker, and more silent than the main floor of the factory, as if it was the epicenter of all that sadness.

"Mano? Is that you?"

"Yes. It's me."

"I've done bad things."

"I know you have. You need to pay for them." Rain water dripped from the rusted basement pipes. "Light the candle," Mano ordered.

The candle lit the basement. There stood The Foreman in the center of it, hands on top of his head, wearing an old Pie Time uniform skirt. At his feet was the old wooden spoon that was once used to scoop tobacco from the steaming machines, a six pack of cold Nun's Hats beers, a pack of Nun's Hat cigarettes, and a sack full of groceries. Mano cracked open the first of his six beers, and lit a cigarette for himself on the candle. Then he said, "Drop your skirt. This is going to hurt."

While The Foreman was dropping his skirt to his ankles, Mano looked into the bag of groceries. He saw more Nun's Hat beer and cigarettes, which pleased him. The Landlord used to only bring him XO beer and cigarettes, until Mano threatened to stop meeting him on Fridays. He was also happy to see some toothpaste, toilet paper, window cleaner, and other essentials. "And I don't want any crying until I get to 50."

"Yes, sir," promised The Foreman.

"Drop your panties, too. To your knees."

The Foreman slid his old pair of June Good's panties down to his knees.

"Now, put your hands back on top of your head."

The Foreman folded his hands onto the top of his head. Mano didn't hesitate. He picked up the wooden spoon and started in fiercely with the first spank, harder than last week, right on top of all The Foreman's old bruises. The heft of the spoon surprised Mano every time he picked it up. It was weighted at the end, and packed a tremendous wallop on The Foreman's bare ass when he swung it. He hardly needed to swing it with any force at all.

"I'm going to need you to do the counting," said Mano after the first spank. He tipped back his Nun's Hat, nearly finishing the entire can on his first drink.

"One," said The Foreman.

"That's right. One. That's the best place to start."

The Foreman counted along as Mano went to work. "2, 3, 4, 5, 6, 7, 8, 9, 10." The Foreman's voice got a little higher with each number. And then he exhaled like he had just come up for air.

"Gather around, girls. I need all of you to see this little girl's penis," Mano called into the blackness. He spanked The Foreman so hard, it made The Foreman's penis flop around until it couldn't flop anymore. It got too hard. Then a black bird landed on its tip, and perched there.

The Foreman moved his hand in order to swat the bird away.

"Hands on your head!" ordered Mano angrily. "I'll take care of it." Mano walked around to the front of The Foreman, and reared the spoon to his side, as if he was about to take a big swing at the bird where it perched.

"No, please, dear God" pleaded The Foreman.

"You're right. Let's see what it does." Mano cracked opened another beer, and they both watched the bird as it pecked at the tip of The Foreman's penis. Mano laughed. He laughed so hard he couldn't take another drink. He laughed as he thought about all the years between his fear of The Foreman and now. The Foreman was just a frightened old man wearing a skirt at his ankles with a bird on his penis. Somewhere beneath this laughter was a whole basement of grief.

"Is everyone laughing at me, Mano?"

"Yes, everyone is laughing at you."

Spanking The Foreman on Friday afternoons was not an easy job for Mano. It wasn't fun for him, or redemptive in any way. It wasn't about vengeance or reparations. It was only work, and it was some of the most difficult work Mano ever had to do. What made it so difficult for Mano wasn't his memories of being spanked as a child in the factory by The Foreman. Like the wounds those spankings left, the cruelty and humiliation of those memories healed quickly in the short days and weeks after they were made. But spanking The Foreman in return in the darkness of the shell of what remained of the factory reminded him of something far more painful. It reminded Mano of the *light* in his childhood, his days with Pepe, how they together, as a team, had a thing to rail against, to hate together. And also of his mother, to whom he ran after those brief insignificant moments of cruelty and humiliation.

Eventually, Mano had no more energy to keep spanking, and no more beers to drink. He finished all six rather quickly, though for someone so large, it was not much of a feat. After The Foreman counted to 200, he collapsed onto the floor, and Mano allowed it. The Foreman crawled into a corner with June's panties still around his knees, and his skirt around his ankles. His bare ass was like an apple. He balled up and wept deeply.

Mano picked up the pack of cigarettes and his sack of groceries.

"Thank you," said The Foreman, once he caught his breath. "I'll see you next week."

"You're welcome," said Mano. He blew out the candle, and walked out of the side of the old factory, toward The Cure, over the footbridge, and back home into the woods.

45

"Are these Zuzu's trousers?"

"Inez?" Mano approached his cabin with groceries in his arms.

Mano had become very used to visitors to his cabin. Two distinct paths had been created to his front door like long loop hikes, although no one could be sure whose feet were wearing down the path besides their own. No one asked this question. To ask it would be to admit that their feet were doing some of the wearing down of the path.

The people who visited Mano with regularity had become his family of a sort, and could be relied upon. The Florist visited on Sundays. He mostly wanted to tell Mano stories about his lost love, Roberto, and then afterward they'd kiss, they'd make love, and they'd hold each other while they slept through the night in Mano's bed. They'd make french toast together in the mornings. French toast had been Roberto's favorite.

On Mondays, Beulah Minx just wanted someone to speak to, out loud, without signing with her hands. Mano didn't strain his face when she spoke. That's what Beulah liked about Mano's face the most. When she told Mano stories of her childhood, and about her love for her first husband, The Postman, Mano's face didn't strain and twist and laugh as he listened to the sound of her voice. On Mondays, Beulah got to feel as though her words weren't any less important than anyone else's just because of how the sound of her voice muddied them.

On Tuesday mornings, Mano was visited by Father Felipe, who wanted to know what it was like to be touched, and to touch someone else somewhere on their bodies other than just their foreheads to bless them. On his days with Mano, Father Felipe's kind of touching had nothing at all to do with blessings.

Tuesday afternoons were for Mary who, as an adult, pined for the weight of her sister Mimi on her back. Mary and Mimi each lived alone, separate from each other, in two different apartments on opposite ends of XO City. Mary thought living separately would be best for them, but now she wasn't so sure why she once thought that. Mary lay in Mano's bed on Tuesday afternoons because she missed that other heartbeat back there, a hot breath on the back of her ear, and how the smell of her sister's body was different than her own smell, even though they were once the same body.

On Wednesdays, even though neither was aware that the other had ever been there, Mimi lay in Mano's bed because she missed being that weight for her sister. She missed being that breath, that heartbeat, that smell. She also liked to sit on top of Mano's kitchen table and drink while he ate.

On Thursdays, Mano was visited by both The Lawyer and The Landlord, who needed to play different kinds of games with each other that had *something* to do with ownership and power, toil and trickery, but *nothing* to do with the exchange of money.

On Friday afternoons, Mano picked up his groceries from The Foreman inside the shell of the old abandoned Pie Time Factory.

On none of those days was Mano ever visited by Enid, nor did he ever visit her. He hadn't seen Enid in 16 years. Enid had been standing in her strawberry patch most of that entire time.

Mano had stopped collecting the things that came out of everyone's death holes, but this did not mean that he had stopped being a receptacle for everyone's grief.

Mano was never visited by Inez before either. But she had always had some sort of spell over him, and that spell never dissipated. When Mano saw her in his gigantic doorway, he immediately felt the need to pour himself into her strong arms, but he also became overly aware of his size, of himself as a spectacle. He hadn't seen Inez in 16 years either, and he realized only then, when he saw her again, that he missed her.

Inez, though, showed no obvious signs of missing Mano.

"Are they? They were hanging on the line behind your cabin. It's funny. My daughter has a pair of brown corduroy trousers just like these."

"Inez, would you like to come inside?" Mano walked past Inez and began unlocking the front door.

"They're still wet, Mano."

"It's starting to rain, Inez."

"I know you used to wear trousers just like these. I doubt they'd fit you anymore though." Inez strained her neck backward so she could see all of Mano at once when she said that. "Maybe she got her fashion sense from you, watching you when she was just a baby."

"Inez."

"Are these her underwear?!" Inez folded the trousers over her forearm and held Zuzu's underwear in front of her own face. "She has a pair of skivvies just like these."

"If you're looking for your daughter, she's not here." Mano pushed open the front door to his cabin with his foot. It made a low long creak as it swung. He set the groceries on the large table. He put some of the things into the refrigerator first, adjusting the cord that held the door there. Then he put away some of the things onto the shelves in the cabinet.

"Is she in there?"

"No. Would you please come in?"

"No."

"Ok." Mano kept the door open, even though the rain was getting his floor wet. He was afraid of saying something that would bring any punishment upon Zuzu. Inez stayed outside in the rain. Mano decided he would wait for her next question. He would truthfully answer whatever she asked. While he waited, he cracked open a warm can of Nun's Hat.

He started chopping the carrots for his soup. The question never came. He could hear Inez crying outside his door, and then he couldn't hear her at all.

As he started to heat the soup, he asked Inez if she'd like a warm beer. She didn't respond.

Mano felt so much weight in the silence outside his door. He thought maybe any information he could put into that silence would lighten it. "She was here yesterday. And the day before."

Still, Inez said nothing.

Mano continued from inside his cabin. "She was just walking in the woods. She wanted to see something else, Inez, that's all. She feels like she's missing something, and she just wanted to find something, anything, as long as it wasn't the same thing she's been looking at her whole life. She saw me, and I saw her. She was tired. She slept here. We talked about things. She's growing up. Don't you remember what that's like? She's scared, just like anyone else." Mano looked out at Inez, who wasn't moving. He kept going. "Anyway, she went back into town this morning. She's back down there somewhere. She'll be fine. She'll be home when you get home. I'm sure of it." Mano stirred the carrots around in the water. "Inez, do you remember when she was just a baby, how she would…"

Inez walked in through the door, but didn't attempt to shut it behind her. Her hair and clothes were wet, and she was still holding Zuzu's wet clothes in her hand. She was looking at Mano differently than before. She was looking at Mano how she looked at him when he was just a boy. "How she would what?"

"How she would…" Mano couldn't remember what he was going to say.

"What do you think you remember? You don't know much. You don't know what you think you know."

"No, I suppose…"

"What do you think you know about Zuzu? What do you

think you know about *me*?"

"I don't know anything. I don't..." Mano stammered.

"I'm married now. Did you know that?"

"No. I didn't." Mano didn't see the point of explaining the things he recently learned about her. "Congratulations."

"Stop, Mano. I'm married to The Barber." Inez looked at Mano for a reaction. "Do you think that's funny?"

Mano shook his head to say no, it wasn't that funny.

"Well, I think it's funny," she said, but she wasn't laughing. "Zuzu thinks it's funny, that's for sure."

"Well, I don't," Mano confirmed.

Inez put her face in her hands and spoke into them. "What do you want with my daughter? Whatever it is, you can't have it."

"I don't want anything."

"Does she love you?"

Mano let out a little laugh to say no, then shook his head.

"Was that funny?"

"No."

"Well, she doesn't love you, Mano. She loves The Butcher. Did she tell you that?"

Mano stayed quiet. He was quickly beginning to realize how little Inez knew about her own daughter.

Inez took a brave breath and continued. "Don't you love me anymore?"

"Inez, look, would you like some soup? It will be ready soon enough. Have a seat. We can eat together."

"I don't want any soup." Inez climbed up into one of Mano's chairs around his kitchen table. Her feet couldn't quite reach the floor. She had a blank stare as she reached into a little pocket in her skirt. Inez pulled out her first husband's old glasses and set them on the table. "I thought I'd return these."

"It's been so long, Inez."

"I thought you'd need them."

"I don't. It's ok. Thank you, but it's ok." Mano taught himself, over the years, how to squint just right. He knew how to squint strongly enough. He learned to see the world as he saw it. "They're too small for me now."

Inez looked disappointed. They were silent for a moment.

"I don't love him," Inez said. "The Barber, I mean."

"Maybe you shouldn't be with him."

"Is that what you would want?"

Mano didn't answer her. The answer would have been, of course, no.

Inez repeated her question.

"The soup is going to boil over," Mano said.

"Let it boil."

"I can't," said Mano. "I'll make you a bowl, ok?"

Inez stood up by the kitchen table, her shoulders slumped. Her body didn't know exactly where or how to be in Mano's cabin. She didn't want to leave, exactly, she only wanted to not be seen.

Mano used the ladle to scoop two bowls of soup, and he set them both on the table.

Inez began to disappear. Only a little at first.

Mano squinted at her. She could still, just barely, be seen. Then she could be seen through. He pulled out his own chair on the opposite side of the kitchen table and scooted himself in, and started to eat his soup.

"Inez, you're disappearing," Mano said.

They sat there at the table silently. It was raining harder now. The black birds were squawking in the tops of the trees. Soon, Inez had completely disappeared, and Mano had no way of knowing whether or not he was alone in the room. That night, as he tucked himself into bed, after everything was very dark and very quiet, he could just barely hear her long slurps.

46.

Zuzu walked directly home from The Good House just as she had promised Vera she would. She was ready to be a woman, and part of being a woman, she decided, was taking responsibility for her own decisions. A part of her—maybe it was the new woman part, or maybe it was the girl part—missed her mother. No part of her missed The Barber, who created a vacuum of joy in every room he graced, even though he hardly ever said a word. Zuzu wasn't even sure he was capable of saying more than one sentence at a time. She couldn't breathe in his house. She thought, maybe if she could just keep the windows open, that would be enough. When she got home, she'd open the windows immediately, she thought. She'd take her punishment unflinchingly, like a new woman, if punishment was indeed in order.

But punishment was indeed *not* in order. Nothing was in order. No one was even at home when Zuzu arrived. No one was waiting for her. There was no evidence, it seemed to her, that anyone at all had even been looking for her. Once inside, she opened the windows anyway, just in case The Barber would ooze from the bedroom and swallow any joy with a few infinite moments of cracking his back in front of her, a dusting of other people's hair floating off of his sleeves after each crack. He didn't though. The bedroom door was open. Their bed was made. No one was inside it.

Unlike being inside Mano's empty cabin in the woods, Zuzu had no interest in waiting around to see what would happen, or to see who would come home, or if anyone would ever come home again. Zuzu got the feeling she was being trapped, as if someone had set her up. She thought if she waited any longer to leave, the possibility of being ambushed right there became greater. Still, an ambush would be *something*. How could no one be home after she had been missing for three days, she thought.

For Zuzu, any future of being inside The Barber's home could not exist without the undying urge to escape it. If she was going to return to anywhere, from anywhere, she wanted to return into someone's arms, not a dead house where there was no bed of her own to lie upon, only a couch that smelled like The Barber, talcum powder, and cat pee. Zuzu struggled to think of any place she wanted to go other than back to The Good House.

She thought of Mano's cabin, of course. There was more than enough space for her there. She would hardly be in the way there. She'd live there if she could. Maybe she'd go back there, build her own room off the back of it, raise vegetables in the garden, pick mushrooms, drink beer, smoke cigarettes, play music with him. Maybe they could start a band that played at people's funerals, if people were to ever have funerals again. She'd need to learn to play an instrument. But first, Zuzu decided, she'd need to grab some peanuts from the cabinet in the kitchen, and her backpack with her overnight things.

Zuzu left for Mano's cabin, but needed to make three stops along the way. Her first stop was the strawberry patch. About twice a week, Zuzu liked to spend a half hour or so with Enid Pine in the strawberry patch. Enid just stood there like a scarecrow, not moving or talking to Zuzu, but it felt good to share that space with her. Zuzu knew nothing about Enid, except for her name. And she only knew her name because her mother told her, not because Enid was ever able to introduce herself. Still, each time, Zuzu would introduce herself to Enid. She'd say her name, and explain that she'd like to help her pick some strawberries. Most of the year, there would be no strawberries at all to pick, so Zuzu would pretend to pick them for a few minutes from the bare bushes, and drop a few handfuls of invisible strawberries into Enid's basket. Enid had stood still in her strawberry patch in the same clothes—a white gunnysack dress with a little red strawberry pattern—for the past 16 years. In the colder season, when the patches were bare, Zuzu draped Enid in one of her heaviest coats, and in the heat of the summer, Zuzu rubbed sunblock onto Enid's face, and poured water directly into her mouth.

This was the season for strawberries, and the patch was bright red and ripe. Zuzu had real work to do. Zuzu decided she'd gather enough strawberries to bring to Mano. They could make a pie in his cabin. Later, she'd bring the pie to Vera, and any strawberries that were left over, she'd give to everyone who lived in The Good House. And if there were any left over after that, any pie or any strawberries, she'd bring that home, to her mother, and even to The Barber. Of course, she'd pick some actual strawberries for Enid's basket, too, not just pretend ones. She wasn't sure if Enid would notice, or ever know, but still, it felt very important to Zuzu to fill Enid's basket with her own strawberries.

"How have you been, Enid?"

Enid, like always, stared straight ahead at the woods to the west, as the sun set over the trees. Her mouth was slightly agape. Zuzu picked a strawberry, and used both hands to put it in Enid's mouth. With one hand she lowered Enid's chin, and with the other she pushed the strawberry in, right above her bottom row of teeth.

"I'm here to pick some strawberries for you. Do you need help?" Even though Zuzu didn't expect a reply, she still looked Enid right in the eyes. She picked about a half basket worth of strawberries, right from the row where Enid always stood, and began to fill Enid's basket with them.

"Would you like some peanuts?" Zuzu unscrewed the lid of the tin of peanuts and pushed a few of them, one at a time, into Enid's mouth. She thought, for just a moment, that she could see Enid's face twitch when her tongue first touched the salt, or maybe it was her jaw closing, so slowly, but Zuzu couldn't be sure. "I'm going to put the rest in your basket. Is that ok, Enid?"

Enid said nothing.

Zuzu set the tin of peanuts in Enid's basket. She could see its weight cause the basket to lower a few inches. She wondered if Enid could feel its weight, if it would be too heavy to hold over time, or if she'd eat them.

"Do you want to know where I'm going now, Enid?" Zuzu waited for an answer, to be polite. "I have to go to XO Meats to get some ingredients so I can make a pie crust to make a pie with your strawberries. I'm going to bake it in the oven in the big kitchen in Mano's enormous cabin. Do you know who Mano is?" Zuzu paused for a moment so Enid could answer. "Yeah, I didn't really know him either until a few days ago. Well, I *did* know him, I'm told. When I was a baby. My mom used to love him, I guess, but he was just a boy then. It was so long ago. He kept getting bigger and bigger. Now he is kind of a giant monster. Or at least I thought he was a monster when I first saw him. But he's no monster. He's just giant. He just seems pretty lonely, that's all." Zuzu thought she saw Enid's eyes look at her, but she couldn't be sure. "Do you know him?" Zuzu thought she saw Enid's bottom lip bend upward, but again, it was impossible to tell. Zuzu moved in much closer, and put her face into Enid's face to study its smallest slowest movements. "I can tell him that you said hello, Enid. Would you like me to do that, Enid?"

Zuzu studied Enid's face, but nothing moved. "Ok, well, I have to get going. If my mother comes by, will you tell her where I am?" Zuzu laughed to herself. "Goodbye, Enid. Eat your peanuts."

Enid bit down. A peanut squeaked between her molars.

47

Enid had been picking strawberries all day. It was the season. They were ripe. There was so much to do. It was difficult to pick so many strawberries alone. She picked and picked, all day, and when she looked around, the sun going down over the woods to the west, her patch looked as if it hadn't been picked at all. She wanted to pick more before it got too dark to see the stems on the bushes.

Thankfully, her regular help, the young boy with his hair parted like Pepe Let's who came by a few times a week, arrived just in time. He had a backpack on his back, and a tin of peanuts in his hand.

"How have you been, Enid?" He slipped his fingers into her mouth, which felt good to her. She licked them. There was a strawberry between them.

"I've been good," said Enid.

"I'm here to pick some strawberries for you. Do you need help?" The boy didn't wait for Enid to answer. He just started filling Enid's basket with strawberries. He picked without taking off his backpack.

"Yes, I can't pick all of these strawberries by myself anymore," said Enid. She felt her basket get heavier in her hands.

"Would you like some peanuts?" he asked.

"Yes. I like peanuts," she said.

The young man unscrewed the lid of the tin of peanuts, and pushed a few of them, one at a time, into her mouth. Enid licked the salt from his fingers. She wanted him to hook her bottom teeth with his finger tip and pull her closer to him.

"I'm going to put the rest in your basket. Is that ok, Enid?"

"Yes, that's ok."

The boy set the tin of peanuts in her basket. The weight of the basket felt good pulling on her arm. She wanted to hold something with real weight.

The boy looked around along the horizon as if he wondered if anyone was coming to look for him. "Do you want to know where I'm going now, Enid?"

"Yes."

"I have to go to XO Meats to get some ingredients so I can make a pie crust to make a pie with your strawberries," the boy said. Enid knew that XO Meats had been grown into a full market, but she didn't know that they now even sold pie crusts. "I'm going to bake it in the oven in the big kitchen in Mano's enormous cabin. Do you know who Mano is?"

Something busted open in Enid's heart. It got so big in her chest that it hurt. It beat too quickly. She hadn't heard Mano's name in many years. She had been able to convince herself that after he had gathered all of his things on his body and left the barbershop that morning so many years ago, that he must have walked slowly and largely to The Cure. She hadn't heard from Mano at all after that morning, so she imagined he sent himself downstream. Sometimes she imagined he hit his head on a giant rock where The Cure meets the sea, and that his big body fell apart, like trash in the tides, and floated down to the deep dark bottom. Some nights, she'd have dreams of him sitting by a pond, growing and growing, and just growing too big for his tiny heart. But until now, Enid hadn't even considered that Mano was still alive, and nearby.

The boy continued talking about Mano, about how he knew him when he was just a baby, and how now he is a giant but not a monster. "Do you know him?" the boy asked Enid. He got real close to her, as if he wanted to kiss her.

"Yes, Mano is the only family I have left," Enid said.

"I can tell him that you said hello. Would you like me to do that, Enid?"

"No," answered Enid immediately. "Please, don't."

The boy put one last salty peanut into Enid's mouth as she spoke. "If my mother comes by, will you tell her where I am?"

"No, I don't want to talk to your mother."

"Goodbye, Enid. Eat your peanuts."

Enid didn't want to eat her peanuts anymore. She didn't want to tell the boy's mother where he was going. She looked around at all the ripe strawberries, and she didn't want to pick strawberries anymore either. They were all unpicked and she could see there was no way for her to pick them all. She could see them, for the first time, as they were—maybe as that boy who looked like Pepe had always seen them—that none of them had ever really been picked.

Enid didn't feel like standing there anymore, herself ripening. She felt like walking toward the woods. And so she did. She followed the boy's path to Mano's cabin, but very, very slowly.

48.

There was already enough flour, sugar, and eggs to make a half dozen pie crusts in Zuzu's shopping cart, next to some bananas and a loaf of bread, when she accidentally wandered into the bright lights of XO Meats' meat department.

The Butcher was cutting off the head of a pig with his back to Zuzu when she asked him where the birthday candles were. She didn't know when Mano's birthday was, but she thought it would be fun to put the candles in the pie.

"Excuse me," started Zuzu.

"Zuzu?" The Butcher said her name before he even turned around. The way he said her name was very peculiar to Zuzu. It was entirely possible he would have known she had been missing for three days, but it seemed very odd to her that he, of all people, would care. Other than her conversation with Vera earlier that day, the way The Butcher's voice said her name was her first real indication that anyone knew she had been missing at all.

"Oh, thank god, you're ok!" The Butcher dropped his butcher knife, and nearly skipped around the side of the counter to give Zuzu a long hard hug. He was still wearing his apron, which was wet with fresh blood and bits of raw flesh from around the dead pig's head.

In his arms, Zuzu felt the overwhelming sense of his relief. It was in the way that his hands pulled her shoulders and the back of her neck into his chest, and the way his chest pushed into the top of her head. She felt his hot breath quicken in her hair. "Yes, I'm ok. I've been just fine. Can you tell me where the birthday candles are?"

The Butcher let go, but not to return behind the counter. He wanted to look at her. He wanted to see if any part of her was still missing. Zuzu looked down at herself, too, to validate The Butcher's examination of her, but all she could see were the smears of blood that he left behind from his apron, and a pig eyelash, on the white button-up shirt of Mano's that she was wearing.

"You know, your mother and I have been so worried while you were gone. I was worried that you were hurt, or that you wouldn't ever come back."

"My mother and *you?*"

"Yes, you didn't tell anyone where you were going. And Inez came here and told me everything. Then together we looked all around the city for you."

It then occurred to Zuzu why her mother had enlisted the help of The Butcher in her search. Zuzu now regretted her little lies, and she just wanted to run away again, out of XO Meats without getting candles for Mano.

"Well, I suppose. I certainly didn't tell *you* where I was going. Look, forget about the candles. I'm just going to leave..."

"Where were you?"

"I was dead and then I came back to life," said Zuzu sarcastically.

The Butcher laughed. "You've always been so funny, Zuzu."

"I have?"

"Look." The Butcher got a serious look on his face. "Your mother told me all about how you feel about me. I want to tell you something very important. I feel the same way about you, too. Every time you've ever come in here, even when you were a young girl, asking for a cut of meat, or this or that, I've always been able to tell that you really wanted something else, something more. I want something more, too. And now you're a woman, Zuzu."

Zuzu was disturbed by The Butcher's sudden sentiment, but she was intrigued by his perception of her. "You think so? You think I'm a woman."

"Yes." He looked at her again, at her whole body. Then he squinted his eyes. "These lights, the lights of this store.

They give me headaches. I chop and chop, weigh things on the scale, clean things, but the lights get to me. They're bright and white, and they hum like an insect. When you walk in, Zuzu, it's like the lights, they dim, you know? They dim and I can see, and the pain in my head floats away."

No one had ever said anything quite so loving to Zuzu before. She could be sure that she didn't love The Butcher. She knew nothing about him. And he was a man, and men, in general, were the kind of people that she had no way of falling in that kind of love with. She knew at least that about herself. But still, she didn't walk away from him right away either. She wanted to hear a few more of his words. Maybe *he* loved *her*. Maybe this is what love felt like when it was returned. Maybe he felt that dull pain of love that Mano had described for her. Even though it wasn't her love, something inside of Zuzu wanted to be near it, even if just for another minute.

The Butcher hiked up his trousers.

"Yeah?" Zuzu encouraged him to say just one more thing before she left.

"Yes. I've been thinking about this a lot the past few days. Your mother and I think it would make a lot of sense if you and me, you know, gave it a shot." The Butcher stood there waiting for Zuzu to say something. But she didn't say anything. She was trying to swallow her laughter.

Another customer did say something though. Irene Mire's younger sister, who was wearing a white silk handkerchief on her head, said, "Do you have any duck livers?"

Zuzu recognized the woman from her visits to Irene at The Good House.

"No, we don't have any duck livers today," said The Butcher without ever breaking his gaze into Zuzu's eyes.

"I'm going to go," said Zuzu.

"No, I'll walk you home."

"I'm not going to go home. I'm just going to go."

"Hold on, then. Don't go anywhere."

"Why?"

"I'm going to go get Inez. She needs to know you're ok." The Butcher started to walk out of XO Meats.

Zuzu thought that she should tell him that her mother wasn't at home, but she didn't.

As he left, he yelled back to her, "I missed you, Zuzu!"

"You don't know me, fool," she said to herself.

Now, in XO Meats alone, briefly, with Irene Mire's younger sister, Zuzu walked back behind the meat counter. "He doesn't have duck livers, but he has cow livers. Do you want one?"

Irene Mire's sister nodded yes, and Zuzu wrapped a liver from a cow in paper and handed it to her. "Thank you."

"Don't mention it." Zuzu smiled at her, and loaded a little more meat into her own backpack. "You know, I saw your sister today." Zuzu decided not to tell Irene's sister that she pretended to bury Irene in a grave.

"You did?" Irene's sister's face lit up with pride.

"I did."

"Isn't she lovely? She's doing well, no?"

"Yeah, real well," said Zuzu. "You know, I can ring you up from back here." There was no cash register behind the meat counter, but Zuzu wasn't planning to charge Irene's sister for any of her groceries.

"Oh, thanks."

"Of course. Did you find everything ok?"

"No. I didn't find duck livers."

"Oh, I'm sorry," said Zuzu. "You know what, those cow livers are on us."

"That's so nice of you."

"Would you like some strawberries, too?"

"Yes. Thank you." Irene's sister began putting her groceries onto the meat counter to be rung up. "How much are they?"

"They're free," said Zuzu. "In fact, everything is free today."

"Excuse me?"

"Yes, it's our customer appreciation day. Thank you for being such a loyal customer."

"But this is only my first time here. I've just been visiting my sister at The Good House. Her name's Irene. Do you know her?"

Zuzu knew that this wasn't Irene sister's first visit to the grocery store, but there was no reason to correct her. "That's even more reason to thank you. What's your name?"

"Mira. Mira Mire."

"Mira Mire, would you want to go to a grave with me and eat some strawberries?"

"Don't you have to work?"

"No. Not really." Zuzu put the contents of her shopping cart into her backpack, and walked with Mira through the aisle with the birthday candles. She put some birthday candles into her own backpack, too, then together they walked out of XO Meats without paying.

"It's customer appreciation day," said Mira to the XO Meats cashier as they past. The cashier looked confused, then kept filing his nails.

Zuzu helped Mira carry her bag a few city blocks behind XO Meats to The Shoveler's Graveyard.

Outside XO Meats, the sky had gone dark. The street lights had come on. There was no sign of The Butcher on the streets, returning from The Barber's house. There was no sign of The Butcher looking for Inez. The streets were dark and quiet.

Together, Zuzu and Mira walked into the gate of the graveyard. In the years since the graveyard had begun with June Good's grave, The Shoveler had installed paved and lighted pathways so that people could visit their dead at any time. It was all he could do to compete with the megaplex that had become XO Graves. The Shoveler let the trees grow back, so that his graveyard looked more like the woods down by The Cure. Wherever a tree stump remained, there was a grave.

As they approached June Good's grave, Zuzu noticed that there was another tree stump right next to it, and a plot, covered with a heavy green carpet, just waiting to be filled. The stump read: "Vera Good is Dead / In Here." But Vera's *not* dead, Zuzu thought. She's *not* in there. Zuzu thought this gesture seemed a strange foregone conclusion for Vera to make. And something about seeing this stump hurt Zuzu. It made her miss Vera, even though she just saw Vera a few hours ago. Zuzu felt the kind of ache Mano told her about, and that meant everything.

Zuzu lifted the green carpet and set it on the grass next to the grave. The carpet was designed to resemble the color of the grass around it, but it was a different shade entirely. Zuzu and Mira then sat on the edge of Vera's empty grave. It was the second time Zuzu sat in a grave with a Mire sister that day. They shared strawberries, and talked about death.

"Has your sister ever been in love?" Zuzu asked.

Strawberry juice drooled down Mira's sticky chin. "I used to have a lot of sisters. Which one do you mean?"

"You did?"

"Yes. We did," said Mira. "They all died in God's Finger though. You wouldn't remember God's Finger. You're too young."

"No, I remember. My father died in God's Finger when I was just a baby. He used to be The Barber."

Mira touched Zuzu on her leg. "I'm sorry to hear about that."

"Are any of your sisters buried here?"

"Who?" asked Mira.

"Your sisters."

"Oh, my sisters are all dead now."

Zuzu watched Mira try to eat another strawberry. She couldn't be sure that she was actually swallowing them because so much of them were spilling out of her mouth and down her chin. Zuzu untied Mira's white handkerchief from her head, and tied it around her neck to catch all the red sticky juices spilling there.

"Have *you* ever been in love?" asked Mira. The clarity of her question surprised Zuzu.

"I don't know. I would like to someday. I think maybe I love Vera Good."

"If you think *maybe* you do, then I think maybe you do, too," said Mira. She slobbered on another strawberry.

Zuzu was focused on adjusting Mira's handkerchief just right.

"Your father is coming," said Mira with the strawberry filling up her mouth.

"Excuse me?" Zuzu figured she was just hearing things. "My father's dead, remember? I just told you that."

"Well, then who is that?" Mira pointed to the edge of the graveyard, where The Barber and The Butcher were opening the gate. "You said your father is The Barber. Isn't that The Barber?"

Zuzu looked around for a place to hide. "Yes, that's The Barber," said Zuzu. "But..." Zuzu didn't feel like explaining. All the trees were too young and too narrow for Zuzu to hide behind. As she looked, she saw her mother walking toward The Barber and The Butcher from the other direction, from the woods. Zuzu had no idea why her mother would have been walking from the west. "Oh, fuck. Mira, I'm going to die now."

Mira nodded. "Ok, it was so nice to meet you."

Zuzu lowered herself into Vera's future grave. "Will you move your legs for me?"

"Of course. It's the least I can do for the dead," said Mira. "I haven't been to a funeral for a very long time. Can I say a few words?" Mira moved her legs, and then struggled to stand up.

"I would appreciate that. Thank you." Zuzu pulled the green carpet over her head.

"I'll start by saying your name. But what is your name, dear?"

"My name is June Good."

"Ok, June." Mira cleared her throat and began saying a few words. "June Good gave me free strawberries," she said.

Zuzu listened to Mira from inside Vera's future grave. She was crouched beneath the fake grass carpet in the pitch cold black of the grave. It felt good in there, quiet and safe. She thought about her mother pulling back the carpet and finding her there, and about what she'd say. Zuzu would tell her that she'd been hiding there for the past three days. That felt like a good plan.

"Her father died in God's Finger," continued Mira.

Zuzu pushed up the carpet just an inch and she could see her mother approaching. Inez was still walking from the woods in the west toward The Butcher and The Barber. In the distance, she could hear just enough of what they were saying: The Barber asked Inez where she'd been, and Inez asked The Barber where he'd been. Then The Butcher told Inez that Zuzu had returned to him, and that she had run away again because she couldn't bear to go home, that she only wanted to be with him, that she wanted to be with him so badly that she could barely speak. Then The Butcher asked Inez where she had been, and Inez asked The Butcher where Zuzu was now. It was a long dumb parade of questions.

Zuzu listened to Mira's beautiful eulogy get interrupted by The Butcher. "Excuse me, we're looking for a girl. She was in the store with you earlier."

As she listened from the grave, Zuzu was very upset that The Butcher referred to her as a girl, when just an hour earlier, he had referred to her as a woman. Being lost to him made Zuzu lose years in his eyes.

"Oh yes, the young woman, you mean? She was very sweet. She gave me free strawberries! She's dead now though."

"No, she's not dead!" shouted Inez. "She's my daughter.

She was just in the store. You must be thinking of someone else."

"No. I'm thinking of the young woman. Her name is June Good. I miss her already."

The Butcher, The Barber, and Inez all looked down at June Good's grave. "June Good is dead in here." The Barber read the worn carving on the tree stump as if he was just learning to read.

"You know, she really loved Vera Good very much. She told me so," said Mira.

"Yes, we all know about June and Vera. They loved each other very much. It's not much of a secret anymore," said Inez.

Into the blackness of the grave, Zuzu stretched her legs. She rested her hands behind her head. She quietly pulled a banana out of her bag and peeled it back. In just a few minutes, her little funeral procession that included her mother, her step-father, her fool of a suitor, and Mira Mire was gone, back into the blacknesses of their own lives.

About an hour later, when it was safe and quiet, Zuzu crawled out of the grave and walked west.

49

Enid's journey along Zuzu's path to Mano's cabin took three months. She walked so slowly that when people saw Enid on her journey, they thought that she was standing still. In the first month and a half of her journey, while she was still in town, she was like a statue, a municipal landmark. To some, she was a statue of a woman with a dress and a basket, memorializing historical Pie Time's rich strawberry picking industry. To others, Enid was a statue honoring the survivors of God's Finger. As she walked, some people set flowers at her feet, or ate sandwiches and smoked XO cigarettes while looking upon her from a spot in the grass or from the sidewalks next to her. Others brought their children to see her. "We used to be known for our strawberries. This is what a typical strawberry picker used to look like," they'd say to their children. Or they'd say something like, "This is one of the survivors of God's Finger. Isn't she strong?" Their children would ask what happened to her and the parents would make something up, or just say something general about bravery.

"There's no such thing as survivors," Enid always said, but no one ever heard her, because she only said it in her mind.

Sometimes the children would crawl on Enid, step up on her slowly bending knees. They'd pull themselves up onto her shoulders. The parents would pull their children off of her, or just yell at them to jump down.

Enid knew no straight path to Mano's, no other path but the one that Zuzu took the night after she left Enid's strawberry patch for the last time, and that path was winding, doubled back, and first went through XO Meats, The Shoveler's Graveyard, and June and Vera Good's graves.

In terms of distance, it was a relatively unimpressive journey. But it was the most remarkable and most ambitious journey anyone in the history of XO City had ever embarked upon. For Enid, it was like taking the first steps on an epic hunt out over a frozen ocean.

In the weeks that Enid slowly approached the XO Meats part of her journey, Zuzu visited Mano with regularity without her mother knowing, and Inez visited Mano with regularity without her daughter knowing. On the very first of Zuzu's regular visits, Mano cut her hair into the only haircut that he knew how to cut. He gave her the same haircut he had always given Pepe, and everyone else in town, when he was the town's barber. It was the first time Mano had cut any hair at all in 16 years. Zuzu had brought him The Barber's spare tools, and The Barber never seemed to notice that they were missing. It was the first haircut she had ever received by anyone other than The Barber, and although it was, essentially, the same haircut, she liked how it looked much better from Mano.

The first night Zuzu visited Mano, they stayed up late drinking beers, smoking cigarettes, and eating bananas. They baked a pie in the oven.

"I was in Vera Good's grave tonight," Zuzu said.

"How did you get in there?"

"I just pulled back the carpet. It wasn't a real grave. I mean, it was a real grave. But..."

"I thought you said Vera was still alive. You said that everyone was still alive."

"Yeah, she's alive. But she had The Shoveler dig her grave already. Isn't that strange? She's not even dead."

"I don't think it's so strange." Mano held out another cold Pie Time for Zuzu. "In fact, maybe it's a good idea. I should start digging my own grave." Mano thought about how nice that would be, to not leave all that work for someone else. "It'll have to be really big though. I'll need some help." He tried to solicit an offer of help from Zuzu with his tone of voice, but she wasn't catching on. "What do you think? You want to help out with that tomorrow?"

Zuzu was forced to admit that she had stopped listening. "With what?"

"My grave. Eh, never mind." Mano got up to check on the pie in the oven.

"Mano?"

"Yes?"

"I felt that dull ache you were talking about. I felt it when I was in Vera's grave, just lying there with all that time in front of me, by myself. The ache was so strong and throbbing all of a sudden that I didn't need to be in the world anymore. I only needed to be in that grave, *her* grave, with her."

"You're lucky."

"Why?"

"Sometimes you don't really feel the ache until they're dead," Mano explained.

"Maybe it was seeing her grave that did it then."

"Yeah, maybe. You should tell her that." Mano opened the oven door carefully, so he wouldn't catch any of his hair on fire.

"It wouldn't do any good," said Zuzu.

"Doesn't matter. Nothing does anything any good."

Zuzu stood up in the chair. She felt so tall. "Mano, can I live here?"

Mano closed the oven less carefully than he had opened it. He walked over to Zuzu and lowered his body in front of hers, like a kind of mirror, and said, "I'm sorry."

The day that Enid finally entered XO Meats, it was a Sunday. It was busy with people buying this and that for their Sunday dinners and for their meals for the week. It was so busy that no one noticed her for a few hours. One woman thought she was part of the banana display, and she set her bananas in Enid's basket.

It was very bright inside XO Meats during the days, and very dark at night when The Butcher, or one of the other two employees, would lock up for the night. They locked Enid inside, and she'd keep walking slowly, tracing Zuzu's path. Enid liked those nights the most, being in the quiet dark of XO Meats, looking at the pineapples in nothing but the red glow of the exit sign. Everyone got used to Enid's presence there for that week. She was seemingly standing still, and they trusted her to go nowhere, to steal nothing, to do no damage. Besides, they knew of nothing else to do with her, or *for* her, but to leave her be. She was doing no harm. If anything, Enid was a delight to see around during that week, a consistent presence. It was like watching the moon wane.

Following the path Zuzu had made, Enid made her way back to the meat department by mid-week. The Butcher watched her approach for hours. He prepared a ham sandwich for her. He remembered her from the strawberry patch, from the day that he and others searched the city, and the fields around the city for Zuzu. Enid recognized The Butcher from that day, too. She remembered how handsome he was, how she wanted to be touched.

Only in her own head, Enid asked, "Did you ever find your lost love?"

The Butcher said, "Would you like a ham sandwich?" He put the ham sandwich into Enid's basket on top of some old strawberries and brown bananas, but he didn't touch her. He was afraid to touch something that couldn't touch him back. The sandwich was wrapped in white paper with black letters, XO. On the sticker that held the paper together, he wrote, "Free" and his initials, "T.B." Enid thanked The Butcher.

For the next few days, Enid grew very hungry. She was hungriest when there was the possibility of food, when something was in her basket waiting for her to eat it. She thought it was important, a matter of manners, that she leave XO Meats before eating. It was another Sunday, busier than the previous Sunday perhaps, by the time she reached the front register. They were so busy, no one even bothered to ask her about her sandwich, about whether or not she should have to pay for it, even though she could see that it was The Butcher's kind intentions to give it to her free of cost. The Butcher, of all people, seemed to understand that Enid had embarked upon a particularly epic journey, and that she'd need provisions. The electric eye of the front double doors opened and closed on her for about an hour. It looked like an animal with no teeth gnawing on its prey.

Mano was holding Inez's naked body up against his gigantic bedroom wall, her long legs wrapped as far around his enormous waist as they could go, which left her bare heels resting on the top of his hips which were overgrown with hair. He was slamming her sweaty back against the wallpaper until some of it peeled off and folded over on top of them.

"I'll have to put that back up later," Mano said. And then a few more slams until a photograph of his mother—taken when she was young, before she got into the bathtub—fell off the wall. "And that, too," he said.

Other than his nights with Zuzu, he looked forward most to his nights with Inez. His weeks were brighter with both Inez and Zuzu now in them. He felt young and unburdened again, but it was different with each of them. With Inez, he was able to learn so much about her body, how it moved and what it wanted. He wasn't ready to learn those things when he was just a boy. When he was a boy, Inez was a young widow with a newborn baby in the room. But now, to Mano, they both seemed ready to learn something. He worried that he had little to offer her about how a man's body moved and what it wanted. He hardly had a man's body. He weighed eight tons and was covered in hair. Still, he had the body of *something*, if not a man, and there was a lot to learn about it. That was certain.

But Mano couldn't offer Inez his love. He couldn't offer her a place to live. He couldn't be anything she escaped into. So, as they collapsed on the floor, with the wet gluey wallpaper making a kind of fort over their bodies, when she told him she wanted to leave her husband, The Barber, and move in with him, Mano was silent. He stood up. He walked very heavily out to the kitchen, and got a Nun's Hat just for himself. He cracked it open and walked outside and looked at the tops of the trees to the east, and the tops of some of the new buildings. There were hundreds of black birds making nests above him.

Mano remembered standing in those same woods when he was very young, at the foot of The Reckoner wanting to die. There were no birds in the trees then.

"Mano?" Inez was behind him in the doorway now.

"You can't live here," said Mano.

Inez didn't want to walk outside, and she didn't want to stay inside either. She asked a question that she didn't want to hear the answer to. "Why not?"

"Because I'm alone. Someone who is alone can't live with anyone."

"You don't love me," Inez said. She was saying out loud what she already knew to be true.

"I'm sorry. Maybe this was a bad idea. I've always thought..."

Inez interrupted him. She couldn't bear hearing him talk about what they had, what they could have had, what they missed out on. "You know, my daughter found love. Can you believe that?"

"You know that? She told you?" Mano turned around.

"Yeah. She's in love. She's going to have the life I never had. What do I get? I fall in love with two people: a lovely and generous man who dies, and a little boy who becomes a monster and doesn't know how to hold anything but other people's shit. And then I end up marrying a bore with a backache."

Mano laughed. He was very happy, if not surprised, that Zuzu was able to tell Inez about her love for Vera Good. It was a conversation he had been encouraging for weeks, but didn't expect Zuzu was quite ready to pull off.

Inez cut his laughter off. "She's going to have something I never had."

"I hope so. Doesn't that make you happy?"

"It should. But for some reason it doesn't."

"Well, I can assure you it won't likely work out between her and Vera. Vera loves June. But I'm happy that Zuzu has found a way to..."

"Vera? What are you talking about?"

Mano felt as though he had made a major misstep, but he wasn't sure how. He tried to keep Inez talking, so he wouldn't have to. "Oh, I must have misheard what you were saying. Who were you talking about? Who has she fallen in love with?"

"The Butcher." Inez stared at Mano. She was trying to read him. "Vera?"

Mano took the last drink of his beer. "Yeah." He started to walk back inside for another one. "Do you want a beer, Inez?"

Inez was silent. She stepped to the side so that Mano could fit past her in the doorway. "Zuzu doesn't love The Butcher, Inez. Wake up. She loves Vera. It's just something you should know, that's all. And after Vera, she will love another woman. She's full of love. She's very lucky in that way."

"But *he* loves her. And if she would just wear dresses...and, oh no, did you know she cut her hair again? I think everything will be..."

"Inez, leave her alone."

"How would you know anyway?"

Mano opened the refrigerator and got out another Nun's Hat. He grabbed the pack of cigarettes Zuzu brought him from his shelf. "I'm the one who cut her hair," Mano admitted. "Smoke?"

"Fuck you, Mano."

Mano lit up the cigarette, and then went back into the

bedroom. He picked up the photograph of his mother and hung it back on the wall.

"I thought she only came here the *one* time," Inez yelled. "She was curious, you said. You said she was just wandering the woods. You said she thought you were some fucked up animal thing."

"I am."

Those were the last things Inez and Mano said to each other.

Still on her journey, Enid lay in Vera Good's future grave for about a week. It felt good to be dead, Enid thought. A worm was crawling slowly up the inside of her leg. One day during the week, Enid heard Vera above her, talking to the corpse of June Good. She overheard Vera tell June that she was happy to have a home in life and in death, that she hoped people would be able to die soon, and that she was sure it would be just a matter of time. Vera talked about Zuzu, too, how she wished June could have met her. Vera thought June would have liked her. Vera brought flowers. Enid knew that because she overheard Vera describe the flowers to June. Vera said they were red, June's favorite color, and bloomed.

Inside the grave, Enid finally ate the ham sandwich The Butcher had given her. She couldn't remember a time she had ever felt so full. Being full made her very tired, so most of that week she spent in Vera's grave, she slept. She had many dreams. In one of the dreams, she dreamed she was on a vast frozen ocean, with nothing but white in sight—no horizon, no sound, just a relentless wind—hunting for mammoths. Even though there was no one else around in this landscape, she felt like she was not alone. Then, there was a tiny red dot on the horizon. It was a red dot that meant everything. It protected Enid from the wind, and it kept her moving. The red dot kept getting bigger and bigger.

A few weeks after Inez left Mano's cabin to never return, Mano and Zuzu were building a fire in the middle of an opening in the woods behind his cabin. Building fires was the thing they liked to do most with each other. They liked to sit around them, drink beers and smoke cigarettes. Together, they grilled some vegetables on a stick. They liked to tell stories about the people in town, which was fun for Mano. It's how Mano knew that Mothers was pickling his insides, face down in a glass pile of liquor bottles and Nun's Hat cans every night on the floor of Lady Bods. It's how Mano knew about The Shoveler and the new train, and all the other XO Cities popping up in the valley. It's how Mano knew that Fran Rile had found a habitable planet with her telescope and was making plans to travel there. Listening to Zuzu tell stories reminded Mano of his days as The Barber. He liked to listen to stories more than he liked to tell them. But something was different about this fire, about how they sat around it. Zuzu felt heavy with something.

"No one can die," she said. "Irene Mire is turning into dust on the inside. She's crawling into graves. She can only fall asleep."

"Who's Irene Mire?" asked Mano, hoping for a story.

"It's not important. It's just so terrible." Zuzu wasn't in the mood to tell a new story. "No one has died since you left."

Mano offered up a theory. "Maybe they're just too afraid to die. Did your mother ever tell you that I used to do this thing with my sheep? I would have kids ride on them..."

"Everyone older than me still talks about it," said Zuzu. "The Death Lessons, right? They sound like they were a lot of fun. Maybe that's why people aren't dying. They don't know how. They need a lesson."

"That wasn't exactly the point, but..." Mano put his stick into a squash, and held it over the fire. It occurred to Mano that he hadn't tried to die in a long time. "Everyone deserves to die."

"You should see them. Irene's eyes are rusty."

Mano didn't feel like eating anymore. He felt like running. He wanted to run into XO City and kill everyone.

"If we could die down there, I'd probably be dead," said Zuzu.

"Why would you say something like that?"

Zuzu took a big breath, and pushed her stick of vegetables closer in to the center of the flame. "I feel embarrassed."

Mano just waited for her to keep talking.

"They want me to marry The Butcher. They say everything will be just right then, that I'll be happier."

"Who says that? Your mom?"

"Yeah, my mom. And The Barber. And I guess The Butcher, too."

Mano laughed. "What did you tell them?"

"Look, I took a job sacking groceries at XO Meats a few times a week. He's a sweet man. He seems to like me quite a bit."

"Is that what you want?"

"You know what I want."

"I'm pretty sure your mother knows what you want, too."

"No, she doesn't know anything. She knitted me a dress. She bought me a pair of Mary Janes. But you want to know what the worst part is? She doesn't want me working at The Good House anymore."

Mano grumbled and closed his eyes. He took a big drink without opening his eyes.

"She's said that caring for people like that has confused me. She says I'm confused, that's all."

"You're 18 years old."

"She still doesn't even know I come up here. She stopped asking a few weeks ago where I go."

"You should tell them everything."

"It doesn't matter, remember? You told me it doesn't matter, and you're probably right."

Zuzu set her stick of vegetables down on the circle of stones around the fire, and walked into the cabin.

"Where are you going?" asked Mano.

"Getting ketchup for the onions. You want anything?"

"Just a beer."

"Ok."

Mano watched Zuzu disappear through the open doors of the cabin. She walked into it like it was hers. She walked around inside of his large life like it was hers. It was that kind of walking through his life that he had imagined Pepe doing when he was younger. With Pepe, with anyone. But knowing Zuzu made him realize he knew so little about Pepe, that he knew so little about anyone at all. When she came walking back out of the cabin with the ketchup and a beer, Mano thought he would ask her if she'd want to share the cabin with him. Together they could build a room off of the back of the cabin for her. They could host their own visitors. They could have meals together. He'd stop hosting his daily visitors. Zuzu could go to work in the city at XO Meats and bring groceries back. Maybe they could start a polka band together.

Zuzu came out of the cabin with no ketchup for the onions, and no beer. Instead, in her right hand, above her head, she was holding what both of them knew was Inez's black bra. "Fuck you, Mano!"

"What's that?" It was the first thing Mano could think to say. His heart dropped into his stomach. He had no idea where Inez's bra could have been hiding the past couple of weeks, but there it was, in Zuzu's hand.

"Where did this come from?"

Mano's head hurt. He needed what was happening to not be happening. "Your vegetables are done, I think, Zuzu."

"Mano!" Zuzu screamed his name and it echoed off the sky. "I trusted you!" She was crying.

"I'm sorry. I..."

"I'm supposed to learn something from you about opening

up?! About honesty?! You're telling *me* I should tell my mother about who I love?!" She was still holding her mother's bra over her head. "Do you love my mother? Or do you just fuck her like you fuck everyone else."

Mano put his big head into his big hands.

"Do you fuck my mother in the bathtub where I sleep?" She waited for an actual answer from him. "Do you?"

"I have, yes," Mano confessed. "And a lot of other people, too," he added.

"You really are a fucking monster."

Mano looked up and yelled. He wanted to hear how loud his voice could get. It became louder as he spoke, more like a monster's. "You don't know my life! You don't know anything about me." He wanted to tell her right then that he'd build her a room. The ache in his chest was so deep it felt like a hole. He thought maybe the promise of that room would fill up that emptiness. Instead, he just screamed, "You're just a girl! You're just a scared little girl!" It was easier to scream those words.

Zuzu threw her mother's bra onto the roof, and it bounced off and landed on the ground. She walked back to it and picked it up. She slingshotted it up onto the roof this time, and it hung down from the gutter. "You're the one who's scared. You have no fucking idea about love. You think you do, but you don't. You don't know shit. Look at you! You're still holding on to your dead boyfriend's accordion."

Mano tried to open his hands, tried to drop everything he had ever held, the accordion, all of it. But that's not how things worked anymore. Nothing could fall like that.

And just like that, Zuzu was gone, a dot on the horizon, getting smaller and smaller. Mano was now just a monster sitting alone by a fire. He picked up the stick she used for her vegetables. He wanted to run down the hill, down the path through the trees to give her the vegetables she had been cooking. They were done grilling now and perfectly crispy. He didn't want her to go without them. They were hers, not his. Instead, he pulled them off with his hands and threw them into the fire. The petals of onions sizzled and curled up around the edges. He could smell the oils from the peppers. With the stick, he wrote his name in the dirt. He didn't want to do any thinking, so he needed to move something with his hands. He needed to do something to something else so that he wouldn't do something to himself. "You're ok. It's ok. It's ok. Let's just go home," he said out loud to himself. With the stick, he wrote his name in the dirt.

Mano Medium.

Then he circled his name with a heart. It was the first shape he thought of to circle his name with. He looked at his name in the light of the fire, how it looked uncomfortable there, and very alone. He wondered if Zuzu ever came back if she'd see his name written there, with a heart around it, and what she'd think about it, what she'd think about him writing his own name at a time like this. He smeared out the heart, and then he drew a rectangle around his name instead. He liked that better. It made his name look like it was being buried in a coffin. Then, he stepped on his name to smear it out.

The first way Mano tried to die was by falling on the fire. He just fell onto it and after the initial flash, he settled into the pain. He could smell some of his chest hair burning. But that pain lasted only a few seconds. His enormous body didn't leave any room for oxygen for the fire, so it was snuffed out.

Now Mano was alone in the dark night, without a fire, and a terrible pulsing burn on the flesh somewhere deep in the mess of his chest. All of the birds, from the tops of all the trees, flew onto the roof of his house at once. It was a loud sound in the sky, like the sound of an ocean freezing over in a few seconds. His roof looked alive with birds. His entire house looked alive. It looked like it was moving toward him as he stood still. The light in the bathroom came on.

He had made his house out of The Reckoner. He knew that much. He was sure of it now, as his house crawled to him. The time for his reckoning was now.

When Enid finally arrived at Mano's cabin, three months after her journey had begun, she was emaciated, having eaten her entire supply of peanuts a few weeks earlier while starting on the path into the woods. She spent the last week crawling toward the cabin with it in sight. There were black birds everywhere, in the trees around the cabin, on the ground on the path to the cabin, on its roof, in its window, in her hair and on her back, squawking and shitting all over everything. Like a true statue, Enid had white bird shit on top of her head, on the backs of her hands, and on her eyelids. The birds needed a hunter, Enid thought. But she would leave that to the bird hunters. She was no bird hunter. There was no reason to hunt for what she could see already existed.

When Enid finally crawled close enough to Mano's door to open it, there was a river of blood trickling from beneath it. Still, she was scared of nothing. She knew that no matter what she found in his cabin, or didn't find, that she wasn't going to go back to where she had been standing in the strawberry fields. At least she wasn't going to go back the same way she had come. She arrived, for better or for worse, at the end of something.

Once inside, Enid could see that Mano wasn't in the living room, but that the river of blood led to the bathroom. It was a stain on the floor now, absorbed into the grain of the wood. It was a day's journey for Enid, on her hands and knees, up that red river.

Inside the bathroom, the river led to the bathtub, which was overflowing with blood. It was the pond of her dreams. Just as big, and just as still. A dozen empty cans of Nun's Hat were floating on the surface of the blood pond. Enid looked for Mano in the bottom of it, but the blood was so dark that she couldn't be sure he was there. So she plunged her arms down below the surface for him. The blood was cold, and it spilled down her chest, and onto the front of her dress. It looked like the strawberries on her dress were being juiced. She couldn't feel Mano's body. It wasn't in that pond.

Enid felt exhausted. Other than her week in the grave, she hadn't really slept in three months. She rested her forehead on the edge of the tub, with her arms still plunged into the blood, and she called Mano's name as she started to drift off to sleep.

"Mano, Mano, Mano. Mano, Mano. You are such a coward."

50

Mano thought he heard his mother calling his name from the bathtub behind the door of his bathroom. He was dead, he thought, but he wasn't sure for how long. He'd been on the floor for a few weeks maybe. The sun kept going up past the hole left in the center of his roof, lighting up what was left of the ceiling, then it kept going down and darkening what was left of the ceiling. People kept coming by, and people kept leaving. The rope was still around his neck. The stool was on its side in the rubble.

Of his post-mortem visitors, he remembered The Lawyer, who just kicked him in his knee to see if he was still alive, then left. Mimi screamed when she saw him, and waddled off immediately, while Mary said a few kind words, and gently combed his dead hair for him. He remembered The Florist lying with him for a few hours, kissing him, and trying to wake him up. Beulah stayed the longest. She made a dinner while he was dead, and told him a few stories as best as she could, in a voice that she herself couldn't hear. She cried over the top of him, he remembered that, and then she said goodbye. Inez never came back to visit him. Neither did Zuzu. That's what made his death the most unbearable. Other than that, death was what he expected.

"Mother? Are you taking a bath?" Mano heard his mother getting out of the bathtub, which was a sound he had never heard before.

"Mano?"

"Mother?"

The door opened. It wasn't Mano's mother who walked through it. It was Enid. She was still on her hands and knees when she opened the door of the bedroom. Her dress was soaked in blood. When she first saw him, she lost her breath. She covered her face with her blood-stained hands. Her forearms were covered in blood. She didn't say anything. She just stared at him.

Enid looked much older, but she was still wearing the same dress, except the dress had blood all over it now. Mano could see in the horrified way that she was looking at him that he must be alive. "Hi, Enid," Mano said.

Her horrified look softened. "Hi, Mano."

"I think maybe I'm dead. Am I dead?"

"No, you're not dead, Mano." She started crawling over to him. Now that she had found Mano at the end of her epic journey, she could move at the same pace as the world around her. "Am I dead?"

"No, you're not dead either."

They both smiled at that.

"You can hear me?" asked Enid.

"Of course."

Enid stood up next to Mano on the floor so she could reach the giant noose around his giant neck. She pulled it over his face, and he ducked down to make it easier for her. "You're too heavy to hang yourself. Do you see what happened?" She pointed up at what was left of the bedroom roof.

"Yeah." Mano sighed, ashamed. "I tried a lot of other ways first though."

"I can see that."

He remembered filling the bathtub with blood. "It must be true," he said.

"What?"

"About how people can't die anymore."

"No, it's not true," Enid said.

"But, no one has died since I left. Isn't that true?"

"That's not true, Mano." Enid pushed some wooden planks of the roof over on the bed, and she stood up on the corner of it.

Mano looked up at her, confused.

Enid wanted to be at eye level with him when she told him

what she came there to tell him. "Our baby died."

Mano couldn't understand. His head still hurt. He never had a baby. "Our *baby?*"

"Yeah, after you left. It died inside of me."

He didn't want to ask any more questions. He wanted to think. He picked up a beer can, but it was empty. His neck was sore. "When?"

"After you left. I came here to tell you those two things. We made a baby, and it's dead. I think it got too big inside of me."

"It got too big? Why didn't it come out?"

"It was in there for over a year."

"That's too long. It was in there too long. Enid, it was supposed to come out before that."

"It just didn't want to come out. And no one knew I was pregnant." She put her face in her bloody hands. "This whole time, after you left, I've had a hole on the inside. It's still in there. This hole is still inside."

"You should have told someone. You should have told me. Enid, we should have...we could have..."

"I read in one of our father's hunting books that baby mammoths stay inside their mothers for almost two years. It wasn't even halfway done growing," said Enid.

"Mammoths don't exist." Mano was still trying to figure out the possibility of what Enid was explaining. "It didn't come out because it wasn't meant for this world. It wasn't supposed to exist."

"Mano, look at you. *You're* a mammoth."

Mano looked down at himself. "No. I'm nothing," he said.

For a brief moment, after hearing that he had been a father, Mano turned into nothing. And as nothing, he drifted up through the hole in his roof, and through the tree tops. The birds were building nests. They looked at him, but they didn't make a sound. He thought this is what a bird must feel like, sitting in nests near other birds, looking down at the world. He could see all of XO City from above the trees. From that height, he could see it and hear it growing. Mano drifted up even higher above the trees, and could see a few more cities growing in the valley to the east and the north. He was a father now, he thought. But what good was knowing that?

From high above the trees, Mano could hear Enid crying inside his cabin. It wasn't the crying sounds of sorrow; it was the crying sounds of pain. Enid was on her back on his bed, red-faced and sweating. Mano was no longer nothing. He was a father. That was something. As something, Mano drifted back down from above the trees, and onto what was left of his roof above Enid. He pushed the remainder of the roof off of the bed so she would have enough space. She pulled her bloody dress up around her waist. He put a pillow behind her head, and she bent her knees.

"What's happening?" Mano asked.

"I don't know. Something's coming out."

"Is it our baby?"

"Of course not." She gritted her teeth. "Our baby came out years ago." She tried to breathe deep breaths through her nose. "I buried her at my feet in the strawberry patch."

Mano put his big hand on her forehead. "It was a girl?"

"Yeah."

"What did she look like?"

"Us," said Enid.

Mano held Enid's hand and touched her hair for hours as she pushed and cried. He was the father of a girl. That was something he could feel proud of, somehow. He had so many questions, but now was not the time to ask them. "So what's coming out now?"

"I don't know," Enid cried.

What was coming out of Enid wasn't their daughter, of course, but what their daughter had left behind. Their daughter was the very last person to die during the plague of

God's Finger, and she died no differently.

The sharp point of the tusk poked out of Enid's vagina just enough for Mano to grip it with his fingers. It was yellow with plaque, and smooth, but he had to pull hard, and very slowly, to get the tusk all the way out. With every tug on the tusk, Mano was causing Enid an indescribable pain. Still, there was nowhere for the tusk to go but outward, through Enid's vagina. She would nod to Mano when she was ready for him to tug, and then he would tug. A few more inches of it came out into the world, streaked with her blood.

Enid's knees were as far apart as they could possibly go, and she made a pool of sweat in the center of the very large bed. Mano pulled for a few minutes at a time, and then walked back around her to wipe the sweat off her forehead. After hours of agony, hours of tugging and resting, the tusk finally came out. They both looked at the tusk with astonishment, like gawkers in a natural history museum, like what had just come out of her didn't belong to her, or to this world. It was a spectacle unlike anything. The tusk was over 15 feet long, and curved down and around. When Mano stood it up on its wider end, it was taller than his roof. The fatter end, which came out of Enid last, was the most yellow with plaque, and it was stained with blood.

Mano retreated for a few minutes to the kitchen, and he came back with two buckets of warm water. With one, he wiped Enid's forehead clean, and her chest, and the back of her neck. That felt very good to Enid. And with the other, he washed the tusk. Both of them agreed how beautiful it was, how it shined.

After everything was cleaned, there was the problem of the second tusk. It needed to come out, too. Enid tried to ignore the pain at first, but the pain became the clearest indicator that their daughter had left behind more than a single tusk. Just like before, Mano tugged, while Enid nodded and breathed. There were a few more hours of screaming and indescribable pain. Then just like the first tusk, the second was born, bloody and shiny and yellow. Enid's body felt emptied and broken.

While Enid rested for hours after the second tusk came out of her body, Mano drained the blood from his bathtub, and cleaned up his house. When she woke up, he helped lower her into the bathtub where she could soak and begin to heal. She slept in the bathtub, too. Mano let her sleep. He set a pack of Nun's Hats on the toilet, so she could smoke one when she woke up. He cleaned the second tusk with soap and water.

Once Enid awoke, she called to him, weakly, from the bathroom. "Can I see them?"

"Yes, you can see them." Mano picked up one tusk at a time in the bedroom. He pointed the first one forward, holding it like a spear, so it would fit through the bathroom door. It was much heavier than he imagined. Both tusks were too tall to fit in the bathroom, but he stood them up anyway. They each tore their own hole through the roof of the bathroom as he stood them up, but he no longer cared about the shape of his cabin.

As Mano and Enid looked at the tusks together, Mano felt a tremendous sense of pride. It was not the kind of pride that a father would have, although these tusks were left behind by his daughter. They were *of* her, of his daughter, so when he touched them, it was like he could touch her. But his pride was a more general kind of pride. He had something to show for himself. And the tusks were both so big, and heavy, just like him.

"Do you think they're beautiful?" asked Enid.

Mano lit Enid's cigarette for her. It was the first one she had smoked since she was just a teenager. "I do," he said. "Don't you?"

"Yes. Very much." Enid coughed on her first drag. "How are you going to hold them?"

"What do you mean?" He lit up his own cigarette without taking his eyes off of the tusks.

"Don't you still hold the things the dead leave behind? Where are you going to put these tusks?"

It had been a long time since Mano had thought about holding the things the dead left behind. "Hmm...I don't know. It's been so long since anyone has died." He looked down at his body, and could see the remnants of some of the things he had held for many years.

"Do you even have any room?" she asked.

Mano didn't think he had any room left, or any strength to hold anything else, especially two incredibly heavy tusks. But these tusks were his daughter's tusks. These tusks were his. They were Enid's, too. He had a family now, he thought. "Of course, yes. I have room," he said.

With her cigarette between her wet fingers, Enid pointed from the bathtub at Mano's face. "There," she said.

"Where?" he asked.

"Right there." She closed one eye, and looked down the barrel of her arm, as if she was going to shoot right into the mouth of the wild beast.

51.

Enid Pine rode her mammoth into town. No one knew how long she had been in the woods, but it was long enough that they had forgotten she had left XO City in the first place. The people of XO City had quickly forgotten her epic journey into the woods, and replaced it with their memories of her return, more than 12 feet high above the ground on the back of the mammoth's neck, riding perilously with full trust for the wild beast. She rode the mammoth fast, at a gallop, and held on, at times, with only her knees. She waved as she passed people, as if she was in a parade. The people remembered that it was past strawberry season because they remembered that when Enid took her mammoth up and down every row of her strawberry patch, as if she was giving it a private tour, that the bushes were brown, and the strawberries were rotting in the dirt. She took it past what was left of the old abandoned barbershop, too. The entire front wall had crumbled, so Enid and her mammoth could easily fit inside. They stayed in there for a long time, her mammoth sitting on top of what was left of the old chair. By the time Enid led her mammoth out through the front of what was left of the barbershop, a few people from XO City started to gather around them. Some people trailed behind Enid and her mammoth like a tiny parade, at first.

"What is that?"
"It's a giant bird."
"No, not all strange animals are birds."
"It's a mammoth."
"What's a mammoth?"
"It's something that doesn't exist."
"Who is on it?"
"That's Enid Pine!"
"The statue of the girl in the patch?"
There was nothing left of the butcher shop for Enid and

her mammoth to visit. Where the butcher shop used to be was now a pet shop called XO Pets. Behind XO Pets was a yard for the pets to play in. The yard is where the sheep pen used to be. And as Enid and her mammoth visited the yard around back, the people of XO City watched Enid water down the yard to make it muddy for her mammoth. They watched the mammoth root in the mud, and they watched Enid pet the muddy hair on her mammoth's side. The mammoth dug in the mud with its tusks. It stood still. Then it flattened the fence with its tusks.

What happened after Enid and her mammoth left the yard behind XO Pets would be disputed by many of the people along the parade route. Some people remembered seeing a low dense fog over the entire city, as if Enid and her mammoth were walking on the inside of a cloud. But other people remembered the sun was bright that day. To those people, they remembered the day Enid came down from the woods on her mammoth was a day so clear that they could nearly see all the way to the pinnacle of the pyramid of the dead in Nun's Hat. They could remember that even the lone apple tree at the pinnacle of the pyramid, which grew from the apple seed left in the stomach of Mitzi Let, could be seen from that distance.

The Landlord remembered Enid and her mammoth planting a few flowers around the garden of the house where Mano grew up, which was now the XO History Museum. And The Foreman remembered Enid using her mammoth to demolish what remained of the brick walls of the old abandoned Pie Time Factory. The Lawyer remembered Enid squeezing her mammoth through the electric double doors of XO Meats, to frighten the few customers inside. He remembered that after Enid fed her mammoth from the produce department, those customers also joined the gathering crowd, and followed her out to Lady Bods for a photograph.

Those who had coins to put into the coin slots of Lady Bods so they could look through the windows, remembered only the mammoth's head and tusks inside the door. Some people say it was Enid who took off her clothes, confessed to the priest, and had her photograph taken by him with the part of her mammoth that could fit inside the booth. Other people who were looking in the windows remembered Enid, with her bloody dress still on, helped Mothers take off his own clothes, and propped him up by the armpits on the mammoth's two tusks. Those people said she asked the priest if he was afraid, and when he didn't answer, she took his photograph.

Mothers remembered none of this however. He remembered talking to Lil' Jorge, asking Lil' Jorge if he heard the parade of people outside their booth. He spoke through the wood slats in the floor. "No one can get in without unlocking the door." He told Lil' Jorge not to be afraid, that there was nothing to fear. Mothers knew nothing of how he died, except for feeling a sudden push through the center of his chest.

Cheers of "Death is back!" and "Godspeed, Mothers!" came from the people watching through the circular window. When Father Felipe, who was watching the parade from the steps of The Hole, heard the news of Mothers' death, he said, "Mercy has come as a mammoth."

By many accounts, the parade stopped at The Good House for Children and the Very Sick and Old. The word of the parade had arrived at The Good House ahead of Enid and her mammoth. Ernesto and Leda saw the children line up on Vera's front porch in anticipation of its arrival. To them, the word was that the mammoth was a kind of beast, with kind eyes, and long smooth beautiful tusks strong enough for the children to play on. Hera helped Luis up on to one of the mammoth's tusks first, and then once up there, Luis helped pull Lois up on top of the tusk. The people at The Good House all remembered Enid ordered her mammoth to lower itself all the way down on its elbows and knees so that Igor, who was on his back on the lawn giggling uncontrollably with a violent joy, could wrap his knees around the other tusk and hang upside down while the mammoth lifted him. Enid's mammoth lifted all three children, and swung them slowly back and forth, up and down, in giant circles, like a ride.

Mary and Mimi, who joined the parade as it was stopped on the front lawn of The Good House, both remembered a very different scene, a terrifying one. They remembered seeing young Igor crying uncontrollably while the mammoth tossed him carelessly and violently in the air. Lois and Luis were doing their best to save Igor, trying to use their bodies to lower the tusks to the ground so his helpless, nearly lifeless, body could slide off of the mammoth's tusk back to the ground. Enid and her mammoth, however, were relentless in their wicked fun, waving the orphan around to the delight of the other strange residents of The Good House, who were clapping and cheering. The people at The Good House had always been a mystery to Mary and Mimi.

Vera's favorite part of the parade was its path from The Good House to The Shoveler's Graveyard. With the help of Ernest, Vera helped three of the most sick of her very sick onto the back of Enid's mammoth. All three of the very sick were also very light. Enid was behind them all, on top of the mammoth's rump, holding them all steady. To Vera, the arrival of Enid and her mammoth was a very rare and special visit, an opportunity to invite death back into the lives of the very sick, who had to be kept in their rooms for the past few years so that the gentle breeze wouldn't blow their body into twos, or so that a few minutes of sun wouldn't burn them alive. Irene Mire, who was the oldest of the three very sick and old that Vera had chosen for the mammoth ride, was first to crawl out of the front door of The Good House. She, too, was happy to see Enid's mammoth. When Irene arrived at the mammoth's feet, she reached up to rub its long tusks like it was a glass bottle with a genie inside coming to grant her final wish. "I'm ready," Irene said.

"I know you are, dear," said Vera. "I know how ready you are."

Vera sent the children out ahead of the parade, along with The Shoveler, to the Shoveler's Graveyard. The Shoveler, who was now done with his part to make way for the new train, would lead the children in a real opportunity—the digging of *actual* graves. "This is not practice," he reminded them over and over again, as they each stepped on their own shovel, piercing the hard dirt of the nearly abandoned graveyard. Some of the children whistled dirges in anticipation. Some of them cried quiet tears of joy and relief.

Enid led her mammoth with the three very sick and old on its back, the few blocks across town to The Shoveler's Graveyard. They slid from side to side, not holding on. Earlier, Vera had given them each a portrait that one of the children from The Good House had drawn for them—a portrait of the loved ones they had each left behind. They raised their portraits above their heads, in the air, and waved them like flags. Two of them hadn't felt real air in a year. They all, more or less, knew it was their final ride into the grave, and even though each of them was in extreme pain, their vertebrae snapping in different places with each of the mammoth's mammoth steps, they smiled. They were too sick and old even to laugh, but if there was one living cell inside their bodies that was capable of smiling, it was smiling.

When the parade arrived at The Shoveler's graveyard, the graves that the children had dug for them were already ready, and nearly everyone in XO City was surrounding them. The names of the very sick and old had already been carved into the stumps by the children. Irene Mire, her portrait in her clutches, was barely able to crawl into her own grave. The other two were carried and lowered.

Almost everyone in the parade lit either an XO or a Nun's

Hat cigarette while they stood to watch what had quickly become a kind of somber and serious ceremony. Each of the very sick and old had their own chance to say a few words at their own funerals.

One of them kept it very simple. He said, "Thank you. That was fun."

The youngest, but sickest of the three, just gurgled, but it was a very sweet gurgle.

When it came time for Irene to say a few words, she asked that her sister Mira speak for her instead. Mira, upon hearing this request, stepped into the center of the crowd. As Irene lay on her back, finally in her very own grave, Mira, with all the love left in her heart, opened her bible, raised her head to the sky, and said, "God, damn you for taking her so soon." But other people remembered that Mira, with all the love left in her heart, opened her bible, raised her head to the sky, and said, "God damn, she should have died a long time ago."

And with that, one at a time, Enid led her mammoth to three graves. The mammoth, with Enid still on its neck, stood tall above each one. In the name of her mammoth, Enid asked each of the very sick and old for forgiveness. Then right after each of them took a big breath, and granted her their forgiveness with their eyes or with a slight nod of their head, Enid pushed down on the back of her mammoth's head, so that it lined up one of its tusks over their chests. It pushed down hard with all eight tons of its giant mammoth body, piercing its long tusk straight through their chests, and into the soft soil beneath them.

"It's God's Finger!" said Inez. "It's so beautiful."

Inez was standing next to her husband, The Barber. When he put his arm around her, she felt the arm of her first husband, The Barber, and wept. What she was watching was his death, once invisible, made visible in the shape of Enid and her mammoth. Inez was watching the beginning of her loss on the ends of the mammoth's tusks. She felt like a young woman beneath his arm for a moment. But then The Barber spoke, and she remembered it was the wrong barber.

"It's so foggy," he said. "We should have brought our raincoats. It might rain." He lowered his arm from her shoulders, and rubbed his own neck.

Many of the children, who were especially curious about death, leaned down into the graves to see what had just happened. Some people remembered that out of the holes the newly dead left behind, the children pulled out a birdcage, a snow globe, and a pair of ballerina slippers. They raised them above their heads, and the crowd clapped, as if they were satisfied with a well-executed sleight of hand magic trick. The children passed the things to the people in the crowd, who then passed them around amongst each other.

The Florist, along with a few other people in the crowd, didn't remember the children lifting things out of the bodies. He instead remembered the children lowering flowers onto their chests, like a final gift from the living, before filling their graves back up with shovels of fresh dirt.

Zuzu, who hadn't spoken to her mother since her last trip to the woods, arrived just in time to see the end of the ceremony. She had been building a little boat out of sticks down by The Cure when she heard news of the parade, where it had been, and where it was going. The crowd that gathered was so large that she could hardly see a thing over the tops of anyone's shoulders, or through the crooks of their elbows. But she could see enough to know that she was watching Irene Mire's funeral. This made her very happy. Zuzu pushed her way through the crowd to say goodbye to Irene in her own way, quietly, only saying her farewells to herself. Zuzu could finally see her life, the shape of it, somehow, now that she knew death was at the very end of it. With death at the end of it, she could see her life would be long. Like The Florist, Zuzu didn't remember any of the things coming out of the bodies, and she didn't remember any of the things being passed around amongst the crowd. Also, unlike everyone else who was a part of the parade that day, Zuzu had no memory of seeing a mammoth.

One person who remembered nothing of the parade was Beulah Minx, who heard none of the city's commotion as Enid Pine rode her mammoth through the streets. Beulah was alone in the apartment that she shared with her husband in one of XO City's high-rises. Their only window faced east. Beulah watched Enid and her mammoth through her window walking along the path that The Shoveler had cleared for the new train. They walked through the valley toward the mountains in the distance. She watched them for hours, until they were too small to see. When there was nothing left of Enid and her mammoth to watch, Beulah lay down on her back in her bed. She picked up the stuffed black poodle that her first husband, The Postman, had left behind for her, and let it rest on her chest. She closed her eyes to imagine what was next for the pair.

Enid and her mammoth left XO City that day without knowing where they were going. They were two hunters, but they didn't know what it was they were hunting. They walked for a couple of days, until they reached the mountains on the other side of the valley. Just as they were too tired to go any further, they came upon a brightly lit clearing in the trees. There they found a pond. Enid climbed down from her perch on the mammoth's neck, and slowly walked in. Then the mammoth slowly lowered itself into the pond, too, one leg at a time.

When they were both all the way in, Enid helped her mammoth let go of everything it held. A rusty microwave oven was the first thing to float off of its body and immediately sink. Then a set of golf clubs, a water bottle, a metronome, and a few encyclopedias. Then a flattened birthday cake, and a saw. A bicycle, a bicycle pump, and many other things, some of which were unrecognizable, floated off, too. Some of the things floated, and some of the things began piling up on the bottom of the pond. Enid and her mammoth were laughing as they pulled more things off. A step ladder, a pitchfork, and a thermos. An empty picture frame. A chair. A toolbox. A set of forks. Sinking, and piling up. Or clanging together on the surface. Then an old accordion floated off the mammoth's back and played a few notes as it knocked into some of the other floating things.

The very last things that the mammoth let go of were its two tusks. Enid gave each of the tusks a gentle tug. Enid and her mammoth each cradled one of the tusks in their arms for a few moments, and then dropped them into the water. The tusks sank to the bottom of the pond, where they settled together in the cold mud. Once the mammoth let go of the tusks, there was no mammoth left at all. Just two people, treading water in the center of the pond, splashing and laughing between the things that remained.

In the distance, on the mountain ridge above the pond, through the trees, they saw a red dot. The red dot grew bigger as it approached. When it got close enough to the edge of the pond, they could see that the red dot was a hunter. Black birds were flying in tiny circles around his red plaid hunter's cap.

ACKNOWLEDGMENTS

Mammother was written during the spring of 2015 in France. Thank you Jacques Rebotier for the use of your mill house outside of Fécamp in Normandy. Thank you everyone at the Château de Monthelon outside of Montréal in Burgundy where I was on an artist's residency. Thank you Allison Cardon. The initial idea for *Mammother* began with the word "Mammother," which was invented collaboratively from a one-letter-at-a-time poem we wrote together while waiting for a Red Fang show at the Wonder Ballroom in Portland in 2011. Thank you Gregor Holtz. Before writing *Mammother* as a novel, we collaborated on making it into a graphic novel. While ultimately we failed to finish the book, many of the ideas for the novel were born from our collaboration. Thank you to all of *Mammother*'s very first readers for your encouragement and for helping me make it more readable. Thank you Alexis Smith. Thank you Edie Rylander. Thank you Emily Chenoweth. Thank you Jesse Lichtenstein. Thank you Joseph Mains. Thank you Joshua Marie Wilkinson. Thank you Mathias Svalina. Thank you to my mother, Nancy Schomburg. Thank you Patrick DeWitt. Thank you Sara Guest. Thank you Kyle Morton. Thank you Tony Tost. Thank you Wong May. Thank you Zachary Hardy. Also, thank you Craig Florence. Your bookshop, Mother Foucault's, is where the first paragraph of *Mammother* was written on one of your typewriters. Thank you Zach Dodson for making this book look beautiful. Thank you Tim Wojcik for representing me and this novel. Thank you Tim Kinsella for your editorial eye, your energy, and for taking the time to get to know *Mammother* as well as I do. Thank you to Featherproof for taking this novel seriously.

And most significantly, thank you Brandi Katherine Herrera, my partner. Because you believed when I didn't. Because you let me read it to you every night at Château de Monthelon as I wrote it. You are its co-writer, and you are the reason this thing isn't ashes in a Norman fireplace. This book owes its life to you.

Publishing strange and beautiful fiction and nonfiction and post-, trans-, and inter-genre tragicomedy.

Available at bookstores everywhere, and direct from Chicago, Illinois at

www.featherproof.com

Keep Up With The BESTSELLERS!

*fp*23 FROM THE INSIDE *by John Henry Timmis IV* $14.95

An autobiographical account of an adolescent's run-ins with—and attempted escapes from—the law, an abusive and uninterested family, and the Menninger Clinic sanitarium. Much like the narrators of *The Outsiders* and *Over the Edge* before him, Timmis recounts these experiences with an adolescent braggadocio, blurring intensely personal confessions and exaggerated fantasies, in hopes of mythologizing himself and claiming a spot in the canon of rebellious youth.

*fp*21 I'M FINE, BUT YOU APPEAR TO BE SINKING *by Leyna Krow* $15.95

In this short story collection, the strange collides with the mundane: close to home and far from it, in suburban neighborhoods and rural communities, with cycling apocalypses and backyard tigers. Each story stands alone, but they are connected through reoccurring imagery and a shared theme of protagonists in emotional peril. At its core, this collection is imbued with mystery, oddity, humor, and empathy, but what it really wants to show us is that we're never really alone—most especially when we're certain that we are.

*fp*20 THE INBORN ABSOLUTE *by Robert Ryan* $60

This book collects the artist's past five years of Eastern deity paintings, mandala studies, and even an unfettered glimpse into his sketchbook. It also includes interviews with iconic performer and artist Genesis P. Orridge and legendary tattoo artist Freddy Corbin, which serve to contextualize Ryan's work and his progression as an artist.

*fp*18 THE TENNESSEE HIGHWAY DEATH CHANT *by Keegan Jennings Goodman* $13.95

Two teenagers are stranded in purgatory: Jenny wakes each morning, the same morning, and chronicles the events of her final day, her mind reaching back into the recesses of time, collecting a mythical past that bleeds into the details of her violent end. John drinks beer, philosophizes about the nature of reality and consciousness, and hurtles his Firebird Trans Am into the darkness beyond the headlights.

JNR170.3 ALL OVER AND OVER *by Tim Kinsella* $14.95

In 2003, living on constant tour through the dark days of the dawn of The War on Terror, Joan of Arc decided to regroup as a political hardcore band: Make Believe. For the next few years they maintained a grueling schedule. These are Kinsella's journals of their final, full U.S. tour—when he had to admit that the cost-benefit ratio of this lifestyle had toppled and he needed to stop.

fp16 ERRATIC FIRE, ERRATIC PASSION *by Jeff Parker & Pasha Malla* $14.95

The content of postgame interviews and sports chatter is often meaningless, if not insufferable. But some athletes transcend lame clichés and rote patter, using language in surprising, funny, and insightful ways. This book of "found" poems uses athletes' own words to celebrate those rare moments, with an introduction by award-winning sports writer Bethlehem Shoals.

fp15 SEE YOU IN THE MORNING *by Mairead Case* $13.95

Set one summer in a small Midwestern town, this book is about three 17-year-olds who take care of each other: Rosie, John, and the book's unnamed narrator, who works at a bookstore and sometimes focuses so hard on reading they see polka dots take over the room. This debut novel entangles the fraught intimacy, painful growth, and utter strangeness of youth in beautiful and lightning-bright prose.

fp14 THE FIRST COLLECTION OF CRITICISM BY A LIVING FEMALE ROCK CRITIC *by Jessica Hopper* $17.95

Jessica Hopper's music criticism has earned her a reputation as one of the firebrands of the form—a keen observer and fearless critic not just of music, but the culture around it, revealing new truths that often challenge us to consider what it is to be a fan. This book is a thoughtful document of the last 20 years of American music making and the shifting landscape of music consumption.

*fp*13 THE MINUS TIMES COLLECTED: TWENTY YEARS / THIRTY ISSUES (1992–2012) *edited by Hunter Kennedy* $16.95

Banged out on a 1922 Underwood typewriter, this 'zine began as an open letter to strangers and fellow misfits then grew into a breeding ground for the next generation of American fiction. Featuring Sam Lipsyte, Wells Tower, David Eggers, Dan Clowes, Barry Hannah, a yet-to-be-famous Stephen Colbert, and many more, with an introduction by Patrick DeWitt.

*fp*12 THE KARAOKE SINGER'S GUIDE TO SELF-DEFENSE *by Tim Kinsella* $14.95

Reunited for a funeral, a family finds dissonance in the fragments of their shared memories: a thoughtful dancer back at her bar, a bitter father working in a toothpaste factory, and a fist-fight addict struggling to keep his nose clean. Across town, a boy is locked up in a delusional man's home, and a teenage runaway looks for a new life in a strip club. Cruelty is a given. Karaoke is every Thursday.

*fp*11 THE UNIVERSE IN MINIATURE IN MINIATURE *by Patrick Somerville* $14.95

In this genre-busting book of short stories we find a Chicago man who is bequeathed a supernatural helmet that allows him to experience the inner worlds of those around him; we peer into the mind of an art student grappling with ennui; we telescope out to the story of idiot extraterrestrials struggling to pilot a complicated spaceship; and we follow a retired mercenary as he tries to save his marriage and questions his life abroad.

*fp*10 DADDY'S *by Lindsay Hunter* $14.95

You ever fed yourself something bad? Like a candied rattlesnake, or a couple fingers of antifreeze? Nope? You seen what it done to other people? Like while they're flopping around on the floor, you're thinking about how they're fighting to live. Like while they're dying, they never looked so alive. That's what *Daddy's* is like.

*fp*09 THE AWFUL POSSIBILITIES *by Christian TeBordo* $14.95

A girl among kidney thieves masters the art of forgetting. A motivational speaker skins his best friend to impress his wife. A man outlines the rules and regulations for sadistic child-rearing. You've heard these people whispering in hallways, mumbling in diners, shouting in the apartment next door. In these stories, Christian TeBordo locates the awe in the awful possibilities we could never have imagined.

*fp*08 SCORCH ATLAS *by Blake Butler* $14.95

A post-apocalyptic novel of 14 interlocking stories, set in ruined locales where birds speak gibberish, the sky rains gravel, and millions starve, disappear, or grow coats of mold. Rendered in beautiful language and in a variety of narrative forms, from a psychedelic fable to a skewed insurance claim questionnaire, Blake Butler's full-length fiction debut paints a gorgeously grotesque version of America.

*fp*07 AM/PM *by Amelia Gray* $12.95

If anything's going to save these characters from their troubled romances, their social improprieties, or their hands turning into claws, it's a John Mayer concert tee. This flash-fiction collection tours the lives of 23 characters across 120 stories full of lizard tails, Schrödinger boxes, and volcano love. It's an intermittent love story as seen through a darkly comic lens, mixing poetry and prose, humor and hubris.

*fp*05 BORING BORING BORING BORING BORING BORING BORING *by Zach Plague* $14.95

When the mysterious gray book that drives their twisted relationship goes missing, Ollister and Adelaide lose their post-modern marbles. He plots revenge against art patriarch The Platypus, while she obsesses over their anti-love affair. Meanwhile, the art school set experiments with bad drugs, bad sex, and bad ideas. This is a hybrid typo/graphic novel which skewers the art world, and those boring enough to fall into its traps.

*fp*04 THIS WILL GO DOWN ON YOUR PERMANENT RECORD *by Susannah Felts* $9.95

At the beginning of a lonely summer, 16-year-old Vaughn Vance meets Sophie Birch, and the two forge an instant and volatile alliance. When Vaughn takes up photography, she trains her lens on Sophie, and their bond dissolves as quickly as it came into focus. This YA novel illuminates the pitfalls of coming of age as an artist, the slippery nature of identity, and the clash of class in the New South.

*fp*03 HIDING OUT *by Jonathan Messinger* $13.95

This collection is filled with playful and empathic tales of misguided lonely hearts: A jilted lover dons robot armor to win back the heart of an ex-girlfriend; an angel loots the home of a single father; a teenager finds the key to everlasting life in a video game. Sparkling with humor and showcasing an array of styles, these characters dodge consequences while trying desperately to connect.

*fp*01 SONS OF THE RAPTURE *by Todd Dills* $12.95

Billy Jones and his dad have a score to settle. Up in Chicago, Billy drowns his past in booze. In South Carolina, his father saddles up for a drive to reclaim him. Caught in this perfect storm is a ragged assortment of savants: shape-shifting doctor, despairingly bisexual bombshell, tiara-crowned trumpeter, zombie senator.

*fp*00 THE ENCHANTERS VS. SPRAWLBURG SPRINGS *by Brian Costello* $12.95

This novel is a satirical, riotous story of a band trapped in suburbia and bent on changing the world. A frenzied "scene" whips up around them as they gain popularity, and the band members begin thinking big. It's a hilarious, crazy send-up of self-destructive musicians, written in a prose filled with more music than anything on the radio today.